BROKEN SLEEP

ALSO BY THE AUTHOR

And the Word Was

BROKEN SLEEP

An American Dream

Bruce Bauman

OTHER PRESS

NEW YORK

Production Editor: Yvonne E. Cárdenas
Text Designer: Julie Fry
This book was set in Scala & Interstate by
Alpha Design & Composition of Pittsfield, NH

1 3 5 7 9 10 8 6 4 2

Library of Congress Cataloging-in-Publication Data

Bauman, Bruce.
Broken Sleep : an American dream / Bruce Bauman.
pages cm
ISBN 978-1-59051-448-1 (paperback) — ISBN 978-1-59051-449-8 (e-book)
1. Families—United States—Fiction.   2. Rock music—Fiction.   I. Title.
PS3602.A955B76 2015
813'.6—dc23
2015006100

To my Mom, Dad & Suzan

In the dark times
Will there also be singing?
Yes, there will also be singing.
About the dark times.

—Berthold Brecht

INTRODUCTION

granmama salome, i am here...
Persephone? At last.
why didn't you come for me?
I sang for you nightly.
i heard only silence.
What do you know of me? Of your father, Alchemy?
  Of your family?
auntie jay gave me a gift, the Book of J...
What? What is it?
the dreams of the savants.

BOOK ONE

I said to myself: You are mad!
What's the meaning of these waves,
these floods, these outbursts?

—Hélène Cixous

1
THE SONGS OF SALOME
For Art's Sake

"I am large, I *consume* multitudes."

So sang my son. For so many of the multitudes, my son's voice lingers and stirs a longing for a time that never was. He sang not only of himself but also of our family, because after him came my granddaughter, and before him there was me. In the beginning, there was my mother.

I spoke with my mother only once. She gave me a hat. A silly red hat. I'd seen her every year on my birthday. That stopped the day I recognized her, and long before we met. I will tell you more about that day later. I live outside the concept of linear time, but many desire a tangible guideline, so I will do my best and start from my newly bornday: September 21, 1966, when I was chronologically twenty-three, and the day of my first happening. I titled it *Art Is Dead*. The idea sprang from me while visiting Art Lemczek, whom I'd friended as a young girl growing up in Orient Point on the northeastern tip of Long Island. Art was a loner who used to do odd jobs on my father's farm and sweep up in Boyle's Diner in Greenport. His complications from diabetes had grown so debilitating after they amputated his left leg, he attempted suicide. Twice.

After I heard about Art's second attempt, I went home to visit my parents. I drove over to his mouse hole of a rented room to comfort him. I found him balled up on his cot, wrapped in moth-eaten blankets, surrounded by paperback books and *Playboys*. I fixed some tea and lemon with a dash of rum. His morning favorite. He squirmed in pain as I helped him sit up to sip the tea. He began to reminisce, speaking slowly, often wincing when forming the words. "You remember the first time you helped me?"

"I sure do." I steadied the shaking cup by placing my hands over his so Art could sip the salving concoction without spilling it.

During a predawn bike ride, when I was about ten years old, I found Art passed out drunk in the middle of Platt Road. I stopped and gave him some water from my canteen and sat beside him. Soon my dad, on his way to the farm, came by in his truck. After Dad finished giving me "heck" for sitting where I could get run over, he drove Art back to Greenport.

"Salome, you've always been kind to me. Never acted 'afraid' of me."

"Afraid? Why? Because you growled at the kids who taunted you? I thought you were funny."

"Me, too. Sometimes. Back then I hated myself when I was sober. Now I hate being alive. There's no relief from the pain."

I had a vision. You might call it coincidence—if you believe in another of those too-human constructs. I don't. I explained my idea to him.

"Salome"—his voice, so soft and resigned, smelled like lukewarm oatmeal served with chopped bits of wet string—"I'd be grateful."

Back in Manhattan, I approached Myron Horrwich, my mentor and lover. He was sexually skillful and taught me about the pleasures of face time—licking below the belt. Horrwich dubbed himself "a world-famous conceptual artist." He had a concept about money, too—he conceptualized that he deserved piles of it. He was fifty-plus years old and still acted like a coddled prodigy. Entranced by his swirling, dilated pupils—unaware at the time that he laced his nose with droplets of belladonna—I explained my idea. Waving his elongated fingers through the air like a maestro, he pronounced ecstatically, "Brilliant. Let's do it."

We spread the word about an "outrageous extravaganza" in the underground grapevine using the *Voice* and *Rat*. Horrwich's lawyers drew up papers that Art willingly signed.

On a late September afternoon, as our unofficial finale to the Avant-Garde Festival, we gathered in Central Park by Bethesda Fountain, soon to be made famous by the *Hair* crowd. The Fugs played. Psychic infusions abounded. Horrwich persuaded Xtine Black, a former assistant of his and not yet renowned, to photograph the event. We distributed handmade ART IS DEAD buttons to the two hundred or so people, including the innovators of the happening scene. I was introduced to Leslie Tallent, my first champion, who also aggrandized himself as one of the "five most prominent art critics in America." Art sat innocuously by himself sipping a bourbon, his favorite afternoon libation. I'd bought him a gabardine suit from Korvettes. He kept smiling at me through his rotting teeth and giving me a thumbs-up that didn't fully dismiss my doubts.

As the autumn sun began descending, I escorted Art around our little group, pushing him in his wheelchair. Just before he entered the prepared Plexiglas booth, he reached up and draped his arms around me and whispered weepily, "Salome, thank you."

Horrwich and I helped Art climb into the booth. Art locked the door. Situated himself in his chair beside "the Art contraption" Horrwich and I had assembled. Without hesitation, Art pressed down on the igniter button. It took five seconds...

...And then—*boom!*—he blew himself into a shower of human confetti. That's right... Killed himself. Assisted suicide before its time.

A few screams penetrated the otherwise boggle-eyed silence that overwhelmed most of the crowd. Then—whoosh—pandemonium! Some people thought it was a joke. Or a trick. Others applauded. More than a few cursed and left. At least one person vomited. Another of Horrwich's assistants set off fireworks. We had a permit for everything—even got the okay from Mayor Lindsay's culture czar, Henry Geldzahler (we'd fudged our proposal—a lot). Horrwich had calculated every possibility. Except he'd never truly contemplated, not even for a minute, the consequences of blasting Art's body into pieces onto the Plexiglas walls. When I'd begun to have reservations about the whole spectacle, he belittled me for even thinking of betraying my own fidelity to art. I fell for Horrwich's BS when he flattered me by saying that I possessed an "original and sensation-filled mind."

Murray Gibbon, who would be my gallery representative for thirty-five years, with his blubbery muffin body, his toadlike head, and his extremities spasming in every direction, began mumbling both curses and novenas.

Horrwich buzzed around on some massive adrenaline rush while I had the urge to flee to Orient and hide. I picked up a chipped bottle, awash in remorse and elation, trying to console myself with what Art said when I first suggested the idea. "There are ways to help someone live and ways to help him die. And you have helped me live, and now—I want this."

Marcel Duchamp, an unabashed *dragueur*, sidled up beside me. "Aha, a perfect ready-made." He calmly took the bottle from my hand and placed it down beside his left leg.

I steadied myself. "For pain or pleasure? The garbage heap or art?"

"For all. For all of them are what makes great art. Art is cruel, and beautiful, and a premeditated accident." His voice was surprisingly timid, with a touch of insouciance. "Don't look sad. Don't you recognize what you have done today? And the *jeu de mots*, the pun—superb. *This* is the new art. Or do you believe all art is truly dead?"

"You tell me. I really don't know."

"I can tell you later. I can show you much. Today you have achieved the extraordinary."

Somehow this parch-skinned, beak-nosed rooster face, thinking he was still some *beau gosse*, undarkened my mood. Maybe what I'd done *was* worthwhile and had meaning and wasn't some modernist Circus Maximus stunt. I regained my composure. I donned the infinitesimal fuck-me smile that was my attitudinal dress code back then. "And just who are *you* to show me?"

"You know who I am."

"Sure, you're Mona Lisa with a five o'clock shadow."

"*Très intelligente.*" He delicately rubbed the light blond hair on my right forearm.

"Look, you're old enough to be my grandfather—"

"But I am not your grandfather..."

Suddenly, there she stood. Off to the west side of the fountain where the cement met the grass. Under the still dusky sky, the lamps flickered around the fountain area, and the fireworks' black smoke disseminated above the Plexiglas booth like a papal signal, a distant goddess in a long leopard skin coat and a big tan hat and oversize round sunglasses. Greta. I had sent an invitation to her apartment on 52nd Street. It came back "Return to Sender. Addressee Unknown." It'd been almost a decade since I'd first noticed her staring at me in the restaurant. The hurts reverberating from that day of discovery, of being found and tossed away again, leeched up my insides like parasitical bloodsuckers, and I wished I'd been inside the booth instead of Art, now freed from the pains of life. I started crying. Just a little.

Duchamp caressed my back. I noticed Duchamp and Greta, quickly, almost surreptitiously, gazing at each other. Both of their faces unreadable. I lasered in on her and tried to will her to look at me, but she never did. She hunched over—she was not as lissome and grand as she seemed on the big screen—and slinked away, up the stairs to the bridge and vanished into a waiting limo. I stood up, wanting to chase her and take the bottle and fling it at the windshield and swan-dive in front of the out-of-control car. Duchamp clasped my left shoulder, grumbled something in French under his breath, and whispered, "Wait." He stood and moved his arm around to my right shoulder. His fingers edged toward my left breast. I eyed him with a sneer that taunted, "That your best move, old man?" He tilted his head slightly to the left. A crooked, thin-lipped smirk on his face. It gave me the chills—the sex chills. In that pause where something is going to happen one way or the other and I wasn't sure which, dozens of cops charged down the staircase and from around the Boathouse. A few people furiously snapped photos. I heard Horrwich screeching, "Salome! Oh, ah Sal-o-me!" as if he were having a damned orgasm. The cops arrested us and accused us of being accessories to manslaughter. Horrwich expected it. He *wanted* it. A well-prepared lawyer who knew the corruptions of the courthouse accompanied us to the precinct. We didn't spend a single night in jail.

When I shook myself awake the following morning, Horrwich, wearing only his boxer shorts, his already tumescent ego expanding to the unbearable, was skip-dancing around the loft in a combination hora and Irish jig waving the newspapers in celebration. "Salome, get up! Articles galore. We did it!" I sifted through them. On page three of the *Daily News* I stared at a black-and-white photo of "the reclusive Greta Garbo" sans sunglasses, her arctic eyes gazing directly at me as I watched Art's exploding body. I saved it. I still have it.

2

THE CANTICLES OF HANNAH, I (1958)

Mixing Memory and Desire

The twenty-two-year-old receptionist, who already possessed a worldview that dismissed the foolhardy hopes and illogical bromides of her family, who believed "everything happens for a reason," stared blankly into space waiting for the next phone call. Into this blank space, through the wooden office doors of Bickley & Schuster, Attorneys at Law, stiffly stepped a perfectly coiffed man wearing a dark blue suit, white shirt, no tie, and holding a fedora in his left hand. He smiled almost brashly. He spoke with a slight accent that made his question, though formed politely, sound like a command. "Excuse me, can you please tell William Bickley Sr., Esquire, that Malcolm Teumer is here to see him?"

"Mr. Bickley left instructions for you to go right in. He and Mr. Lively are in the conference room." Before she could direct him, he winked and disappeared down the corridor. Like almost all receptionists in mid-Manhattan offices, this demure and attractive young woman learned fast how to slough off the flirtations of the male clients. This one, though, handsome as he was, reminded her of the cultured Paul Henreid in *Casablanca*.

Many phone calls and three client arrivals later, William Bickley Sr., the essence of a Central Park West Manhattanite, appeared. "Hannah, may I ask you an awkward question?"

Hannah nodded, fearing if she gave the wrong answer, she'd be out of a job.

"Malcolm Teumer, you saw him before...he would like to take you to dinner this Friday." She bowed her head diffidently. "I ask because he preferred not to put you in a compromising position. Your personal life isn't my business, but I can attest that he is a fine gentleman and of your religion."

Bickley did not know that in the one year since her never-discussed divorce, she'd accepted exactly no offers for a date. "Mr. Bickley, he's twenty years older than me."

"Not quite, but yes, he's older. If I didn't think it was a good idea, I wouldn't be standing here."

Malcolm picked up Hannah at her parents' home in the Bush-wick section of Brooklyn and drove her to the Blue Mill Tavern in the Village. She sheepishly admitted Astor Place and West 4th Street were only subway stops to her, a cloistered Brooklyn girl who scurried home directly after work every night. "My dear Hannah, we must change that," Malcolm told her.

On their second date, at Minetta Tavern, Hannah's swoon deepened. After dessert, Malcolm abruptly pushed up the sleeves of his jacket and shirt and revealed the numbers. She gasped. She should have guessed. He quickly slipped his sleeves back down. "I dislike speaking of my past. Only...Hannah, I fancy you and I wish to see you again, so I must make you aware that I have suffered unspeakable degradations." He crossed his arms over his chest and gripped his powerful biceps with his hands, holding his jaw tightly closed. "Stop shaking. There's no reason."

Her eyes began to well. "I must tell *you* something."

Malcolm dropped his arms by his sides and his tone softened. "Hannah, please don't be scared. You will soon understand very little can shock me."

"I was married when I was eighteen. And my husband divorced me by the time I was twenty. Because I can't have children."

"What a horrible man he must have been not to see the beautiful treasure you are."

Seven months later, they were married and settled in a small apartment in the Yorkville section of Manhattan. Malcolm ran an import-export business, which he had started by using funds his family had smuggled out of Europe. Hannah often thought, better they should have smuggled themselves. Soon, the evenings spent in swell restaurants dwindled. Hannah, who continued working at Bickley & Schuster, hurried home to have supper ready when Malcolm got home from the office.

One evening, after Malcolm finished a meeting with Bickley, he suggested they stop for dinner on the way home. Before they ordered, Malcolm declared, "I think you should stop working."

"Why? Are you sure? Do we have the money?"

"Yes, I am sure. It's time we start a family."

Hannah blanched.

"Ach, my dear"—he clasped her hand—"you misunderstand. I'm sorry to have scared you. We will adopt. During my meeting today with William, he confirmed that he has found us a boy. He can arrange everything."

"Oh, Malcolm," Hannah exclaimed, "how lucky I was to find you!" And in that moment, Hannah blindly accepted her parents' worldview—things do happen for a reason, and there is always hope.

3

THE MOSES CHRONICLES (2001)

Make Room for Daddy

"Your ghost is alive."

Through the phone, Moses could practically feel Sidonna Cherry's self-congratulatory pat on the back as she breathlessly relayed her discovery. He sighed. She continued, "Old and in failing health, but alive. Not only is your father still kicking, he owns a condo exactly three point six miles from your door." *Forty years of intractable angst and three thousand therapeutic miles later, and he ends up in spyglass distance from* my *home,* Moses thought. What a cosmic joke. "West on Venice, north on Ocean. All the way to—"

"Hey, Ms. Cherry, stop." Damn, how he wished his father had been dead. Until he again remembered that he needed him alive.

"Professor, there's more."

Professor? He hadn't told Cherry that he was a professor of American history in the irrelevant department in the Southern California College of Art and Music (aka SCCAM) in Pasadena.

"Okay. Slowly, though."

"He also has a place in Rio, not sure of that address, where it seems he spends most of his time. As of last night, he was *here*, in L.A. According to all official records, Hannah is your birth mother. Are you positive she is not your mother?"

Nothing about Moses's past made sense anymore. Malcolm Teumer had slept with his mom. Hell, they were married. Moses was born on December 8, 1958, and for forty years he had believed Hannah had given birth to him.

"Unfortunately, I'm sure."

"If she doesn't know who your actual mother is, I don't think there's anyone left alive who can help, except your father."

This "father" had stuck around for two years after Moses's birth before (according to Hannah) evaporating into the suburban air. Except for a failed search at the age of seventeen, where certain scents before going dead had hinted toward South America as his ultimate landing place, Moses remained unknowing of where Malcolm lived. Or if he was even still alive.

Cherry waited on the other end of the phone for an answer as he began to imagine for the umpteenth time, in another of what he termed his "daymares," a new version of his father's journey, this time from New York to Destination Do-Over Land.

He gazes up at the gray clouds of the October sky, unmoved by his sister's goodbye wave from the open window of her olive green Pontiac, and before her eyes he vaporizes into the futuristic Pan Am terminal and emerges a new man, wading in the Pacific tides of Avalon among breathless sea maidens, his exhalations emptying the toxic fumes of the Nazis' total war, a survivor reborn with no past . . . and with no son.

"Yo, Hamlet, you faint or something? You want your father's address?"

"Yes. Fax it to me now. Thanks. I'll call you." Almost too cautiously, Moses returned the phone to its bright yellow cradle.

His insides clenched; instead of relieved, he was livid. Now that his father was alive and so damn close, there would be, he hoped, no more forays into scores of imaginary pasts. He slumped in his swivel chair in the room that he kept dimly lit and New York winter dark. Despite two decades in L.A., Moses had subconsciously re-created New York in his room: a groggy Decemberish gray filled with the aura of dread and the resounding roar of an onrushing subway at midnight, even when it was silent. Right then, the sound in his room couldn't have been more quiet and the bursting cacophony of confusion in his head any louder.

Eleven months before, Moses had been diagnosed with acute myelogenous leukemia. Immediately upon hearing the news, Hannah flew from New York, and after a hail of apologies, diversions, and self-recriminations, unveiled the preposterous notion that she and he did not share DNA. Believing them both to be adoptive parents, it was only after Teumer disappeared that she uncovered the truth that Malcolm was Moses's biological father. She bemoaned her inability to help save him, for whom she had sacrificed so much. Moses and his mom fell farther into their abyss of sighs, adding yet another step to their dance of indecipherable silences.

While Moses suffered with his body's cancerous disintegration, trying various treatments that counted as a holding-the-line action of staving off death (not a bad thing unless you had a more sanguine worldview than Moses), they attempted, without success, to find Teumer's whereabouts. Finally, he and his doctor had engaged in a blunt and necessary conversation.

"Moses," Dr. Hank Fielding, a white-haired, square-headed oncologist in his early sixties, spoke in a matter-of-fact tone, "after the last round of chemo, you're in what I like to call 'qualified remission.' The strong probability is that it won't last. Your platelets are still too low."

"Which means?"

"The bone marrow registry still has no match for you. You *need* a donor." Jay, Moses's wife of five years, clenched his wrist in panic. Afraid to look at Jay, trying to control his emotions, Moses stared at the wall behind Fielding while he continued in his avuncular tone, "I'm so sorry, Moses. You must find him."

In Moses's presence, Jay obeyed her father Al Bernes's (né Bernstein) credo, voiced in his art-dealer jargon: "equipoise and stoicism in the face of crisis." Her twitching and bouncing legs, outbreaks of canker sores, and forced reassurances that "It'll be all right" (along with a more frequent late night dipping into the alcohol cabinet) belied the truth. Beneath her varnished exterior brewed a cauldron of fear.

After Fielding's unspoken *or else*, Moses and Jay agreed, although a bit appalled at becoming a California cliché, to hire a private detective to track down his father. Moses told him, "The family name was Temesvar, taken from a city in Hungary where they lived before moving to Germany. I guess it was an assimilated name even then. I think it got rearranged when he came here. Maybe he went back to using it." With so little to go on, the first and then a second detective came up empty.

With her worry outweighing her hesitancy, Jay contacted Randy Sheik, least offensive of the Sheik brothers who owned the successful indie Kasbah Records. After leaving Miami in 1985, where her father owned a world-class art gallery, Jay had attended UCLA, and after graduation she and Geri Allen opened a chicly influential art consulting firm. The Sheiks and Kasbah became a major client. Randy, always happy to hear from Jay, suggested a woman with the Baskin-Robbins 31-Flavors name of Sidonna Cherry. "She's unorthodox. She don't ever let you meet her in person. But she watches you. And she sure the fuck gets results."

Unorthodox suited Moses. Unlike the other PIs, after he explained his situation, Cherry didn't try to snow him about the benefits of a joyous, fairy tale father-son reunion.

Cherry's call delivered the first of many messages from the suddenly undead, which like a siren's unholy song could not be silenced or ignored, unshrouding decades-old secrets and lies repeated so often that they had become truths.

Sitting at the desk waiting for Cherry's fax, he tried to conjure his father's face from the one and only picture he'd ever seen, when he was five, his parents' wedding picture. He remembered that afternoon clearly: His grandmother, who lived with them, had gone to the A&P grocery store so he sneaked into his mother's bedroom closet, her haven against chaos with dresses, shoes, blouses, skirts, coats, umbrellas, and pocketbooks all in their assigned places. If he moved any object one inch, she'd *know*. He turned on the light and on an upper shelf he spotted stacks of papers and boxes, one labeled PHOTOS. With his little hands he tugged the black step-chair from the back left corner. He climbed up and reached as far as he could and pulled down a beat-up sky-blue metal safety box. A few days before, he'd spotted his mother crying while looking at the photos in the box. He sat cross-legged on the floor of the closet. He found pictures of himself as a baby and of his mother with her naturally auburn hair bleached blond. Then he found it—their picture. His father with a solemn demeanor and furnace-hot glare. Dark hair combed in a pompadour with a yarmulke atop his skull. The picture was black and white, but Moses also knew that his father had blue eyes; he, Moses, had small blue-gray eyes, unlike Hannah's hazel eyes. Despite the perfection of her hair, the shine of her gown, the delicacy of her makeup, his mom looked sad in that photo. Beautiful, but irredeemably sad.

He put the box away, hurriedly trying to reproduce the order of the closet; his grandmother would be back from the store any minute. A few days later he again sought the photo, and only one half remained. His father was, once again, gone.

No sound. No smell. No taste. No touch. No image. No words. His father's physical legacy: empty space and a name. He was Moses, son of Hannah and Malcolm, the father who had died in his heart in 1961. His struggle, before he consciously knew it, was to find expression for the inexpressible, the pain of a mother's tears, and the blunted scream of loss that an abandoned child with no words *feels* when grasping for answers.

Over time, Moses compiled these few facts from vague memories and overheard conversations: Hannah was forced to leave the Yorkville apartment and they caravanned with relatives for over a year until settling into a serviceable, boxlike, and minimally furnished apartment in Stuyvesant Town on 20th Street. Moses's widowed grandmother came to live with them. Soon after Teumer's abandonment, Bickley & Schuster rehired Hannah. Suddenly, or so it seemed, this small-statured woman, who moved with the cautious gait of a shtetl Jew, acted with a fierceness and determination contradictory to all previous behavior. She began her career ascent, an obsession that excluded all except caring for her son.

William Bickley Sr. acted as a cross between guardian angel and parental watchdog while she worked part time and attended City College, where she excelled. She went on to Fordham Law School. After graduating, B&S hired her full time and she became a top-notch estate attorney. Moses was given love and whatever material offerings she could afford.

Yet there hovered, like the unseen particles of nuclear fallout, one unspoken condition: The name of Malcolm and the years they were together became unmentionable. Hannah directly informed her young son of only this one fact: "Your father's experiences in the death camps made him unstable." And with that, the young (and even now the older) Moses had asked no more questions. The language of silences and pauses and wordless expressions became Moses's idea of hell.

Sitting at his desk, Moses's upper back burned with stress; his head throbbed with the surging thunderclaps of a migraine, as a single thought pummeled: I have this schmuck's genes and now I need him to save my life.

Drawing on the commanding component of his voice, which was as assuring as the crackling embers of a Christmas fireplace yet tinged with a Wellesian eminence (a formidable tool in the classroom), Moses yelled out from "his" room into the backyard where Jay had her office. "Hey, Jay, come on in." He watched as she walked from her office and came down the hallway, admiring how she moved with the same fluidity and focus as she had in water, a former high school swim team captain. Her midback-length auburn hair swayed behind her. Their connection so strong, she felt his distress before he uttered a word. He recited Cherry's news. She rubbed his back and cradled his head against her body. "What're you going to do?"

Jay and Moses had met six years before at a fund-raiser for SCCAM at the Santa Monica Museum of Art. Jay, then twenty-nine, after a decade of unfulfilling sexual serenades gone off-key, was simultaneously wary and hopeful that she could meet someone who could offer her the security she craved and stimulation she desired. Moses, at thirty-seven, was a scarred veteran of two failed long-term relationships, separated by years of aloneness, questioning whether he possessed the emotional wherewithal to make the final leap to lifelong commitment. They were equally astonished by the compatibility of their desires and lifestyle choices and how quickly they developed a synchronous nonverbal understanding of each other's deeper emotional needs. As nonpracticing

Jews (Jay's father was Jewish, her mother Episcopalian) but proud of their Jewish cultural heritage, they were married by a reformed rabbi in a very small ceremony. Both believed their marriage would be forever. It had been a half decade forever which, with a stunning suddenness, was razed by the wrecking ball of Moses's illness.

Jay, who possessed what her father termed "gravitas" and what others might call "attitude," wanted him to go over to Teumer's and, at least emotionally, decapitate the deadbeat.

"First, I need to call my mom." Moses sat in the desk chair in his room, paralyzed. Jay picked up the phone and held it out to him. He did not reach for it. The phone had become a scepter that would unleash unwanted plagues.

Moses repeated, "I need to call my mom."

"Are you sure now's the time?" Jay asked.

"Yes, she needs to know."

"She'll be out here tomorrow."

He shook his head. He took the phone and dialed her office.

"Hi, Mom." Moses hesitated. This woman who had loved him, vowed to never let anyone ever hurt him, made him the sun in her solar system, would shudder at the idea that the soulless apparition, Malcolm Teumer, could be walking the streets of Los Angeles at that very moment.

"What's wrong?" Hannah heard the tremors in Moses's voice.

"Ma...I found him."

He heard the breakdown on the other end of the line, the crack in the voice, the sigh expelling decades of encapsulated dread of hearing that singular phrase. "Did you see him? Talk to him?" Her tone almost pleaded for him to say no.

"Not yet. I have to."

She sighed. "I know. I'm still trying to find out the name of your, you know...Do you want to wait for me and I'll go meet him with you? The red-eye will get me in very early."

"Jay is going with me."

"Okay. I'll do whatever you want. I'll see you in the morning."

"Can't wait. Love you."

"Love you, too."

Moses hung up. He exhaled air that smelled as if it'd been hiding in the dark caverns of his body for forty years, leaving an emptiness behind. He didn't know why, but he needed to have sex. He tugged Jay close to him and she felt his hardness. "You sure it's safe?" The cancer caused his body to bruise from the merest bump; she touched him always with such delicacy. "Yes, I'll be fine." Jay's eyes, which had the hue of a powdery sulfurous brown, closed slightly. She unzipped her jeans and lay down on the gold-and-red Turkish rug they'd purchased three years before on a glorious vacation. They began to make love. Slowly. He did not surrender to her lovely breath and verbal caresses; his body made the motions of love while he lived another daymare:

Nazi jackboots rain down from the sweltering Berlin summer sky, the troopers' stomp trembles the halls and stairwells and young Malcolm glances to the window. A helmeted SS officer sprays piss from his uncircumcised dick over Jewish graves, saving the last drops for his father, cowering on the ground. His sister Magda holds her dog Toffee close to her chest. A baby-faced soldier lances Toffee with his bayonet. He bleeds, squirms, squeals, and dies slowly as Magda sobs, thrust down the staircase. The slaughter cars rumble to Theresienstadt, and Magda is raped repeatedly. He swears he will never die like Kafka's K., like Magda's dog. Licking snow as manna, he questions the god who allows the human incinerator filled with melted flesh, aging women beaten for uttering a wrong syllable, babies tossed in the air like clay pigeons and shot for fun. Some who survive grow larger. More human. More generous.

He is not one of them.

Hate consumes him. All other emotions have been exterminated...

"I...can't...Ugh."

He knows it is cruel,

"Hold...Jay..."

yet it is less cruel

than if he had come...

Jay, feeling him slip away, hurriedly finished alone.

...home.

They lay silently side by side, holding hands. "Let's drive over there now," Jay said. "Let's surprise him."

While Jay dressed, Moses stood in the shower thinking, *I'm finally going to confront him.* His excitement was tinged with trepidation. The anguish he'd carried for so long like an empty sarcophagus, which he'd believed he'd discarded, returned.

What would he tell Malcolm Teumer? How, because of him, in his late teens he'd become obsessed with the literature

and films of the Holocaust: Levi, Wiesel, Appelfeld, Furstenblum, *Shoah*, *The Sorrow and the Pity*, and countless others?
That he'd moved to Israel after graduating from Columbia and
played Abbie Hoffman with a yarmulke on a radical kibbutz?
That sojourn ended after two years when he attended a debate
between two spittle-tongued kibbutzniks whose only disagree-
ment was whether to nuke all of Israel if they knew the Arabs
would win a war or just the Arab capitals and oil fields. For
him, too many Israelis remained hopelessly embedded in a
mind-set circa Masada A.D. 72. He moved from Israel to L.A.
in 1982 to attend USC grad school, where he wrote his dis-
sertation on "Divorce Rates Among Children of Holocaust
Survivors." He would relate to his father how he had begun
researching a book before the onset of his illness, *Children of
Holocaust Survivors and Their Relations to God*, studying the
problems of survivors, their family problems, their marriages
and divorces, their suicides, their depressions and guilts. How
this immersion had served up unending sources of excuses for
his father's behavior.

Instead of falling into emotional paralysis—Moses's cus-
tomary reaction to any mention of his father—he excitedly
grabbed his L.A. Dodgers baseball cap. Moses didn't like baseball, in fact he considered sports an opiate of the masses, but
he had started wearing hats all the time after the chemother-
apy. His pate was still patchy.

With Jay driving their Honda, they headed from their cozy
home on Marco Place in Venice to Santa Monica, Ocean Avenue and Alta. They parked across the street by Palisades Park
in front of a high-rise condo overlooking the Pacific. Moses

and Jay had strolled past this building scores of times gazing at sunsets. As they sat in the car, Moses remembered how, when he first moved to L.A., as he had in Israel, he'd scoured his surroundings for men he imagined were about his father's age: in bookstores; along Venice Beach; in delis like Canter's or Nate 'n Al; in movie theaters like the old Fox, Nuart, or the Egyptian that showed foreign films; at the Melrose galleries; and more often than any other place, in the supermarkets, fantasizing that any of them—one of them—could be him. Now he knew that in this very park, as he and Jay had lolled hand in hand, his father could have been standing right beside him. This knowledge calmed Moses's roiling emotions. No sweaty palms, no heart palpitations. No waves of desire to melt into easeful death. Nothing like he'd expected.

Jay got out and looked up at the terraces. She came around to Moses's side of the car and knocked on the window. "C'mon. Let's get this over with." They walked across the street, where a well-dressed doorman opened the glass doors and stopped them.

"We're here to see Malcolm Teumer, 10C," Moses said in a monotone.

"Who should I say is calling?" asked the doorman from behind a four-foot-high glass vestibule and in front of a second-rate Sam Francis imitation canvas.

"His son, Moses."

He raised his eyebrows ever so slightly. "I'm not sure if Mr. Teumer is in."

"I saw someone on the terrace," Jay said spontaneously.

"It must've been his friend Mr. Lively."

"Just buzz, please," Moses said politely, but with as much authority as his voice could muster.

The doorman turned his back so they didn't hear the few words that were exchanged over the intercom. An elevator man escorted them to the tenth floor.

When they exited, a man at the end of the hall leaned against a half-open door. He stood a few inches over six feet tall, with a body frame better suited to a creaky wicker chair than human flesh. Under his wide shoulders, he hunched over as if stones in his jacket pockets weighed him down. His big hands cupped the handle of a wooden cane. His thinning brown hair, with touches of gray, was combed back and high and held in place by a gusher of hair cream. On his large feet were scuffed cowboy boots. This, Moses assumed, was not his father.

At the doorway, the man reached out to shake Moses's hand. A huge high-school championship ring glistened on his finger. Moses introduced Jay. The man did not introduce himself.

In a Texas drawl, he politely invited them inside. "Please sit yourselfs down in the living room." Up close, the man's face was withered like a worn-out overcoat, with too many and too large yellowed teeth. Wolfish eyebrows with no visible skin between and big triangular sideburns, leftover from the Elvis era, framed a face as inviolable as an icon atop a pharaoh's tomb. His bland brown eyes added softness to his otherwise harsh expression. "Your father is not here, but we can talk."

They followed him deeper into the living room. Cabinets filled with Hummel statuettes of boys and girls drumming and marching, and sets of multicolored Fiestaware lined the hallway and much of the living room. Two shelves in a credenza were stocked with books that had the look of the unread. Movie posters dating from the 1920s to the present hung on the walls. From the largest poster, framed in gaudy gold leaf and reading *Gösta Berling's Saga*, loomed an imposing photograph of the unsullied yet sullen Greta Garbo. No photos of any real people were visible anywhere.

Off-white drapes covered windows and a door that opened to the eighteen-foot-long terrace. Beige pole lamps stood in the corners of the room. Moses and Jay sat on a beige sofa. Moses noticed half-filled shelves of cassette tapes, DVDs, and CDs but saw no sign of a TV or audio system.

The man positioned himself in the chair with his back to the drapes. The chair was four inches higher off the ground than the sofa so that he always seemed to peer down at them.

"My name is Laban Lively, and I've been a friend and business partner of your father's for decades."

"Are you his *special* friend?"

"Boy," Lively said, his voice dripping with an even-toned I'll-drop-you-dead-right-here brusqueness, "let's be straight. Your father is many things, but he is not a sodomite." Moses couldn't help thinking, *Who the hell is this Bible-thumping cowboy?*

"Does that mean you know who my mother was?"

Lively crossed his long legs and wet his cracked lips with his tongue. "What do you mean? Hannah is your mother."

"No, she only raised me as my mother." Moses straightened his spine and leaned forward, his posture strict. "I'm here because I am sick and I need a donor. All other treatments have failed. I need to know if he can help me or if he has any relatives who can. Or if my mother is alive and if she had any other children. I want nothing else from him. Nothing."

"Who told you Hannah isn't your mother?"

"She did. For over forty years I lived that lie."

Lively shook his head. "He left the country this morning. Not sure he'll be back."

Moses, sensing perhaps this was his only chance to gather new information, pressed on. "You must have known his sister, Magda? The detective couldn't locate her with the little information I had."

At seventeen, Moses, with Hannah's reluctant help, located Magda in North Carolina. When he called, she lambasted him sourly, "I have not'ing to say to you. I don't know where he is. I have not seen him in years. I am not his keeper, and thanks God, he is not mine. Do not call me again." With that, she hung up. Moses, defeated, gave up his search for Malcolm.

"After three, maybe four marriages, Mal refused to help her financially anymore. They lost contact until he was notified that she passed six years ago."

"I'll tell the detective. Did he tell you about his time in the camps?"

"I think it is Mal's responsibility to tell you about that."

"Why would he? Because he's acted so responsibly for the last forty-five years?"

Lively crossed his right leg over his left leg and slowly shook his head. "I am sorry."

"Mr. Lively, if you or he won't help me, I am going to die."

Lively's expression went dark, as if the fuse to his emotional box had blown out. He uncrossed his legs and leaned back. "I'm leaving for Houston later tonight. It's my grand-daughter's sweet sixteen tomorrow and I am not missing that. Family means something to me." His slow Texas accent, laden with the air of gentility, unnerved Moses.

"If I can't see him, I at least need to talk to him."

Lively leaned forward. "May I be so bold as to ask you a favor?"

"Sure."

"When you talk to your mother Hannah, say hello for me."

"You knew her?"

"We met when they were still married. Attractive woman."

"So you'll help me?"

"I'll try." Using his cane, Lively pushed himself up. Moses and Jay followed, and all three turned toward the door.

"Can I use the bathroom for a second?" Moses didn't really have to go; he wanted to poke around. Lively nodded and pointed down the hall. Moses saw nothing of any consequence; still no photos of anyone. He checked the medicine cabinet but found nothing exceptional.

When he came back, Jay and Lively had moved to the far corner of the hallway leading to the door. They were examining a sculpture, which he had not noticed upon entering. Jay had seen the strikingly different piece among the banal furnishings of the apartment and stopped to look as she made her way back to the door. She was kneeling beside a miniature guillotine with a life-size head of Richard Nixon cut off from its body. The headless body was made of the faux aged and crinkled yellow paper that you get when you buy a cheap copy of the Declaration of Independence, which upon closer inspection it turned out to be. The words DO NOT DISTURB hung above Nixon's head.

Moses heard Lively answering what he assumed was Jay's question.

"It was a gift from a friend—"

"Who?" Moses interrupted, almost too aggressively.

"A friend."

Jay, noticing Moses's reddening cheeks, stood straight up and interjected, "That's a Salome Savant piece. It's very rare. She destroyed much of her work before she was institutionalized and doesn't like to sell it. When I was working with Kasbah, I tried to get her son, Alchemy Savant—"

"Excuse me." Lively abruptly put his big hand on Jay's shoulder while looking at Moses. "I'm sorry to be ill-mannered, but I have a meeting before my flight. I will call you. I know how to find you."

Jay and Moses rode the elevator in silence, attempting to absorb what they'd just seen and heard. As they stepped gingerly outside and crossed the street, Jay squeezed his hand. She whispered, "You're a good man, no matter who your father is"—she half grinned—"or how distasteful his friends are..."

That night, Moses, listening to Jay's steady breathing, fell in and out of the semialert state where dreams seem real and reality seems dreamlike. At 6 A.M., he pushed himself out of bed, the maxim he often stressed to his students racing through his head: One person's version of history is another person's version of an incomplete truth. He slipped quietly into his room, where he read an e-mail from his mom saying that she'd checked into the Miramar Hotel in Santa Monica, just blocks from his father's apartment.

4
THE SONGS OF SALOME
Ready and Made

The night after the *Art Is Dead* happening, the scenesters gathered in the back room of Max's Kansas City. Andy, who I think always wished his body were a mesh serigraph, tiptoed in with Viva and a new companion I nicknamed Velveeta. I must say, I outshone them all. I wore an all-plastic see-through top over a silk-and-lace bra and a microminiskirt made of flattened Coke cans (which I figured Andy would appreciate) with thigh-high red boots. I draped a black cape over my shoulders and knotted a red bandana around my forehead. When Horrwich saw my outfit, he susurrated lasciviously, "You're one radioactive treat wrapped inside a cellophane coating." Xtine couldn't stop fawning. "You must come over to my place at the Chelsea. I must photograph you."

Everyone kept handing me drinks. Leslie Tallent, wearing red socks, Homburg hat, bow tie, and the beginnings of a goatee, read aloud his essay, which he intended as the ultimate analysis of the work "as a new kind of art that is the offspring of Duchamp. It poses the question: Is art, like God, now dead?"

I kissed him on his cheek. "Perfect, Leslie. I'll leave the analyzing to you."

I bathed myself in the sweet bacchanalian fever until Raphael Urso, a misogynistic beast who happened to be a lovely street urchin poet, cornered me with his two play-mates—some shy guy I didn't recognize and Blind Lemon Socrates. Socrates is all but forgotten now, but back then he was a sardonic old junkie with a cult following of joy boys who wanted a blow job from the author of *Sonic Nudewords* and the underground film *Hooked*. Urso kept calling me his "fuck for the night" and introduced me as "the soupçon du jour who you better fuck now 'cause she'll be opening soup cans in sub-urbia for her babies in no time…" I rabbit-punched Urso in his shoulder. He snarled. Socrates and Urso moved on. I was left standing in front of this shy guy who just lowered his head and turned his swamp-water-brown eyes behind gold-rimmed circular glasses away from me. He had dark, short hair covered by a camouflage baseball cap and a reddish-brown five o'clock shadow, and wore scraggly jeans, a beat-up khaki jacket, with a satchel slung over his shoulder. His fists were clenched, not in anger, I sensed, but in defensiveness. I pictured him as a human hand grenade waiting for someone to pull the pin.

"So, did you like the happening?" I asked him.

"Do you want me to answer that extremely egotistical ques-tion honestly?" His voice edged out with a slightly patrician Southern accent, yet still sounded kind.

"Yes. Absolutely."

"I quite liked your *ARTillery* show." That was my first solo show from a year before.

"Really?" I sounded too excited. "I got the idea from this military museum in Riverhead. When I was a girl, my dad and

I would drop by and I played with the tanks and jeeps and all kinds of phallic equipment on the grounds."

"I liked the way the humor underlined the seriousness. The way you symbolized how the establishment keeps the war game going and how you manipulated toy tanks, guns, and bombs into art objects. I especially liked the 'lamps' and 'dildos.' I came to one of your performances with the cannons."

"Thank you. Only I suppose that means you didn't like yesterday's um...performance."

"I support euthanasia in its place, but this represents nihilistic flimflam. Someone died."

"He wanted to. I loved Art. He was very sick. I would never have done it otherwise."

"Maybe." His fists slowly unclenched as he talked. "Or maybe it's money for you and that vampire Horrwich and Murray Gibbon, and for your mutual fame. The world is undergoing a revolution because it has to, or we are doomed to a virulent extinction. These people here" — his eyes indicted them — "with a few exceptions, are a bunch of monomaniacal bullshit artists." He crunched his lips together. "And that sucks. *That* art should be *dead*."

His abject negativity stunned me. Everyone else had been so enthusiastic. Even the ones who were repulsed had found some merit to it, or so they claimed to my face. Some were jealous. I expected that.

"I want to change the world," he continued. "Irony without empathy is empty and juvenile. Art is not dead. *Real* art is alive." He sounded so sure of himself. I leaned over and inhaled. He backed away. Amid all the pot and cigarette smoke and cooking fish coagulating into a hardened plume of nause-ating odors, I inhaled his essence, his soulsmell.

"You inhale like wet greasewood, it's the best smell in the world."

"What, I'm a clown to you? Well, yeah, I guess I am."

The band had turned up the decibel level to around twelve, and he thought I'd said "greasepaint." I corrected him and said that I could taste his purity in my nose and throat.

He asked, "What do *you* smell like?" He's the only one whoever turned it on me. The only one. Dr. Barnard Ruggles, my favorite shrink here at Collier Layne, tried to do it in the session after I informed him he reeked of little shards of ran-cid, mayonnaisy potatoes marinated in mothballs. Only then, as I told him, it was too late.

"I am half-burned, still smoldering autumn leaves left to wilt in the rain."

"Is that good or not?"

"It's not like the fresh, hopeful smell of leaves just after a cleansing rain but the odor of nature unnurtured and aban-doned. Abandoned."

He squinted and then his eyes widened behind his glasses, unsure of what to make of me. Urso, elbowing his way back between us, started pecking away again. "So Brock-ton, you making time with my fuck, are ya? Eat me or you'll get burned."

"Oh, shit," I muttered. This shy not-so-shy guy was Nathan-iel Brockton, Ivy Leaguer, Vietnam vet–turned–counterculture icon with the publication of his novel *Tag, You're $#it*. His narrator, Bohemian Scofflaw, an aspiring anarchist who got kicked out of college, was drafted and sent to a futuristic land resembling Vietnam, where Scofflaw and his cohorts' battle cry was, "Eat fire and burn, motherfucker," as they savaged village after village. The phrase became a campus rallying cry.

Damn, did I feel stupid—and I didn't feel stupid often.

I tried to recover by being so unnaturally obsequiouass-kissy—"Oh I'm so, so—I love your—" Duchamp and his entourage, making their histrionic entrance, pushed into the room. Nathaniel coughed as if a brackish odor had oozed into Max's, waved bye-bye, shrugged, and receded into the crowd. Suddenly, I felt so lonely. As if my atoms had deflected the atoms of everyone else in the room so we couldn't connect. I found Horrwich in the bathroom getting sucked off underneath the graffiti that read FAME IS THE BLOW JOB OF THE WAR HOLES. I felt so unhinged. Startled, I felt Duchamp standing right beside me. Our eye contact said, "Let's fuck," and the game was on. "Ah, *ma petite artiste*, you are so vivacious looking tonight." I'm not sure what happened next. This is where my memories mishmash. Maybe it's repression. Maybe it was the joy drugs or the Collier Layne psychotropic shakes or their demonic hot wire. Maybe a spell. Probably all of them.

We ended up at his studio on 11th Street. He immediately disappeared into the bathroom and then waltzed out dressed in nothing but a woman's wig, his face a mask of lipstick and rouge. It was laugh-out-loud outrageous—this old man as drag crone. His alter ego was Rrose Sélavy and I'd seen photos of him by Man Ray—pretty sexy, actually—as a woman. He grabbed my hand and tugged me into an enclosed room. He began to undress me and almost forced me onto a tarp on the floor next to a sculpture of a woman and got on top of me. The old farceur left me decidedly unravished.

"Look." He rolled over and flicked on a single overhead lightbulb while I lay there, naked. "You cannot tell anyone you see this, especially Lez-lie. He would be so *jalous*. I am doing interviews with him, but I have not given him the privilege of a viewing." My eyes focused on the nude woman. My body went limp. I started to shiver and sweat, and I said shakily, "She looks like Greta Garbo."

A tiny leer crawled onto his thin lips. "A little this. A little that. A little her."

"Did you know her?"

"But of course. We meet during the war at the apartment of the genial art dealer Betty Parsons. Have you been introduced to Betty?" I shook my head. "Ask Lez-lie. She would just want to eat you."

"What about Garbo?"

"I see her often for the few months she says she is interested in serious art. She is not serious. Almost never after that."

"What else can you tell me about her?"

"Nothing. You should dress and go." An aggrieved scowl erupted and his features became exaggerated, as if to say, I had you, now get the hell out of here, you inconsequential *putain*. Normally, I would've dismissed him with my no,-I-had-you,-you-ancient-fart gaze. I couldn't. I didn't understand why he'd become so mean. I should have smelled it, but my senses were blocked. I asked, almost pleaded, "Why did you want to show me that? Because I look so much like her?"

He answered with an unsuppressed belch. "You must leave this room. I must work." I stared one more time at the body that became his masterpiece *Étant donnés*. He gave me a push and closed the door. I dressed in the main room. I couldn't bear to go to Horrwich's right then, so I fetaled up on the couch and fell asleep. When I awoke, Duchamp and some other geezer sat at a table playing chess. Duchamp never even glanced up from the chessboard. He merely ordered, "Silence, please." I left.

I thought about going to Greta's and standing outside her window and screaming, "Why did you give me up?" Her melancholic Scandinavian heaviness, that forlorn face exhausted me. No. I wouldn't succumb to groveling for my birthright.

I took a taxi to the Port Authority and bought a ticket for the next bus to Greenport. While waiting, I realized I couldn't handle the Orient Point crowd. They might've stoned me. They would blame me for Art's death. Suddenly everything about my childhood in Orient haunted me. It wasn't simply the vision of Art's disembodied corporeal being. I felt my baby churning and gasping and dying again inside my belly. I left the station. I couldn't go back to Orient. I took a cab to Horrwich's loft. He never asked where I'd spent the night.

5
THE CANTICLES OF HANNAH, II (2001, 1958)
Baby, Please Don't Go

Cigarette in hand, Hannah paced in her room at the Miramar Hotel. She'd barely slept on the plane. She mashed out her cigarette, thinking, *Why him? Why not me? I don't want to live one minute more than him. Will he ever understand why I was forbidden to tell him sooner? Has he forgiven me?* She recalled Moses's quivering reaction as she'd emptied herself of the albatross of truth, battened down for so long inside her chamber of shame.

She lit another cigarette and stared out the window, not really noticing dawn's streaks of light hitting the Pacific Ocean. Instead, she was reliving the day the "love of her life" never returned home. She had been frantic—Malcolm had mysteriously come into her world and then disappeared just as mysteriously.

Three days after his disappearance, while she was rocking Moses in her arms, she heard the key in the door. She placed Moses on the couch against the cushion where he couldn't roll off. Dressed in her white flannel bathrobe, she ran to greet her husband. But it was Lively who stood in front of her.

"Is he okay?" Hannah begged.

"Let's sit down." Lively bulled his way past her before she could answer. She turned on some lights. She pointed to Malcolm's favorite big brown leather chair but Lively chose to sit on the couch beside Moses. Hannah picked up her child and backed away.

"Hannah," he pronounced her name as if he were her older brother, "please, sit by me." He patted the couch cushion beside him. She sat down a few feet away. "It is unmanly, unchivalrous, that Mal chose to act in this fashion. I do not approve. But Mal Teumer is a man who makes his own choices."

"Why did he make this choice? What can you tell me? Anything?" She deplored the meekness of her voice.

"Nothing is what it seems to be." His words flowed in that low-pitched, indomitable rabbi's tactic, if the rabbi were a Texan, that intimated he was privy to the will of God and she was not. "It's best for you and the boy if you do not ask questions. Not now. Not ever."

"What do you mean?" She knew very well that his placid manner belied threats he could make real.

"Mal is gone. He is not coming back."

"What about Moses?"

"Mal has been persuaded to surrender his rights. The vixen he seduced, she gave up her rights some time ago. She will be no bother."

Hannah felt a sudden tightness in her chest. Lively, noticing her complexion draining of color, brought her a glass of water from the kitchen. "Just take a sip. You've had a tough few days. It will get better."

She nodded, thinking, *How could I not have guessed? Of course, the child is his. Yes, life can happen for a reason, if not always a reason that is immediately apparent.*

"Now, Hannah, everything will be taken care of just right. Moses will remain with you..." Still standing above her, he clasped his hands together "...as long as you follow my advice." Advice? Orders were more like it. "You understand that if you ever breach our agreement, and there will be a legal agreement, everything will be rescinded. There will be consequences." He stared at Moses and began edging even closer to Hannah. She felt his animalistic lather. It petrified her. She held Moses closer to her breast. Lively cupped his huge hand on Moses's head, and he bared his filmy teeth. Moses opened his eyes and smiled, and whatever sick thoughts were percolating in Lively's head, Moses's cherubic gurgle stopped them, and he left.

A call interrupted Hannah's thoughts. "Hey, Ma, I'm downstairs, you want to come down for coffee?" Moses's voice bounced with its usual amiability, and Hannah was so proud, because no matter the gruesomeness of most people or his inner despair, he acted with kindness to friends and strangers alike.

"Moses, are you..." She couldn't finish her sentence.

"I'm fine. Worried about you."

"I'll be better when I see you. Why don't you come up?"

Moments later, Moses walked apprehensively into the room. They embraced. Even though she'd seen him two months before, as she felt the bones in his rib cage and back, his frailty renewed her agony. She wondered if Moses meant it when he said he had forgiven her. She steeled herself.

"Mom, why are you shaking? Are you all right?"

"I have good news. For you."

"Let's hear it."

Before she started to speak, Hannah breathed deeply, trying to calm her palpitating heart. "William III finally gave me the information on your biological mother. After all these months resisting, I don't know why, but last night Bill Bickley Jr. gave his son permission. Her name is Salome Savant. She was an artist of some sort. You can find her here." She took a typed piece of paper off the dresser top and handed it to him. "It's the Collier Layne Health Facility in western New Jersey. William III said arrangements have been made. The head psychiatrist is expecting you."

Hannah tipped backward, her legs buckling, and collapsed into a luscious green velvet armchair. Panicked, Moses exclaimed, "Ma, should I, are you—?" Both of her parents had died of a heart attack in their sixties.

"No, no. Just anxious." Hannah sighed. "Can you get me a Valium from my purse and a glass of water?" She took the pill and swallowed it. She almost wished she *were* having a heart attack.

Moses sat precariously on the edge of the bed and looked at the name on the paper. "Yesterday, in his apartment Teumer shares with this guy—"

"You didn't see *him*?"

"No, we talked to Laban Lively."

"My God! Lively and Bickley Sr., they introduced me to Malcolm." She'd never had a reason before, in fact went out of her way never to speak of Lively.

"He claimed he's Teumer's business partner. There's a piece of her art in their apartment." Moses stood up, arms crossed over his chest. Hannah shook her head, aghast—Moses could never have known that he'd inherited his father's signature stance when confronted with unpleasantness. "I don't know what any of this means except I have to go see her. Ma, I'm sorry this has been impossibly hard on you. You'll always be my mom, and I love you. I have to, you know. Get some sleep." He sighed.

They hugged. Hannah held him as if she needed him to save her from drowning in her own tears.

"I'll call as soon as I know anything. Call Jay. She'll come over."

6
THE MOSES CHRONICLES (2001)
Happy Mothers' Day

Outside, the early-morning August marine layer gave the air a gluey mist. For a moment Moses imagined himself gumshoeing in a black-and-white movie, with a crater-eyed Peter Lorre tracking him. He winced; he'd often jested that his students lived so solipsistically, it was as if they were starring in their own private film. During the short drive home, he realized that if he had not been ill this never would have happened; that, triteness aside, ignorance can be, if not bliss, then at least a compensatory manner of living.

He kissed Jay, who sat crouched and crossed-legged on her chair. She looked bleary-eyed, hair tied back in a ponytail, coffee mug with a Salvador Dalí design cupped between her hands. She had been staring at the computer, reading her e-mail. "How is she? How'd she react?"

"She reacted by telling me my mother is Salome Savant."

Jay, now wide awake, mouth agape, screamed, "Holy shit! What the fuck?! Oh, my God, Moses. What does this mean? Are you sure? When did she find out?"

"Just yesterday. My life gets wilder and stranger by the hour," he said, rolling his eyes and shaking his head in total befuddlement. "Any moment, I'll find out my true parents were crustaceans from Mars." Still trying to gain perspective, he felt the truth of a historical maxim. "Remember what I've said about the Watergate break-in and other scandals, that the cover-up compounds the crime?" Jay nodded. "I won't say her silence was a crime, but I sure wish she'd told me before."

"I'm sure she does, too. It was a choice made out of love, not malice." She smiled wanly and reached out for his hand, her even keel of calm restored. Moses felt grateful for her affectionate display.

"I want to get going. I'll take the first nonstop. Drive me to the airport?"

"You don't want me to come?" Jay's unblinking eyes beseeched him to say yes. He shook his head. "I need you to stay with my mom. Please take care of her 'til I get back."

"I'll go meet her at the hotel and stay with her if she wants, or invite her here."

"You can go over and use the pool. Maybe get her to swim some laps with you." Moses half smiled. Hannah's idea of exercise was sitting in a lounge by the pool and doing arm lifts with her cigarette. "She'll appreciate you being there and so will I."

Jay called the airlines, spoke to a supervisor, and managed to get a seat using their frequent flyer miles, while Moses gathered a few items and tossed them into a carry-on. He gobbled down a bagel, cream cheese, and lox, and they got in the car. Jay drove toward Lincoln Boulevard, then south to the airport.

"So, do—hey, watch out." The car next to her had swerved too close to the other lane, but she continued, "Do you think Alchemy knows your father? That you two will meet?"

"Why would he know him and why would we meet?"

"Because Salome Savant is your mother, and your father has her artwork in the apartment." She stated this factually and with slight incredulity.

Apparently, his mom *had* informed his behavior because he'd erected a mental block the size of the Great Wall of China. Only now did it fall away as he made the still unimaginable connection: Alchemy Savant, *People* magazine's "Sexiest Man Alive" was his younger brother.

Like any semisentient being of the past decade, Moses had absorbed plenty about Alchemy. There was no way not to have heard of him and his band, the Insatiables, in the 1990s. He'd even seen them perform in late '95 at a rare club concert at the Whisky, in a benefit for the antiglobalization group Ruckus Society, when Jay, then his soon-to-be wife, scored them a pair of VIP passes through her connections at Kasbah Records. He had been entranced, along with everyone else in the club, from the moment the lights went up and Alchemy, like a ballet dancer pirouetting on a snowflake, spun slow motion in space and turned to face them, swilled a half bottle of scotch in a series of fast gulps, and with his eyes and body subtly signaling multiple allusions, he stage-whispered one of his catchphrases: "Ask not what your rock band can do for you, ask what *you* can do for your rock band..." On cue, the band launched into "E Pluribus Unum Wampum."

Moses turned around and rifled through the CD case in the backseat of the car. He pulled out an Insatiables CD, imagining a thought balloon popping over his head and in exaggerated Lichtenstein canvas fashion exclaiming, "Alchemy is maybe the one person out of six billion on earth who can save your life!" The possibility dazzled. He shook his head as if he were drying his hair after a January dip in the Pacific.

"You mind if I play this?" he asked.

"Not at all."

He played his favorite cut, the trancelike anthem, "Blues for the Common Man."

Evil brothers, singing so saintly
Dreams in shatters, smiling faintly
Hoping high, laying low
It's the blues
The blues for the common man

"His voice, I've never thought about it before, but your voices are remarkably similar."

"Really?"

"Maybe it's just the power of suggestion." Jay paused. "He might be hard to find. You know that Absurda Nightingale OD'd earlier this year?"

"Right, it was horrible. Some of the female students at SCCAM played a midnight tribute concert for her."

"Well, I saw on TV that Alchemy went into seclusion."

"I get that." He hesitated. "Jay, you understand why I want to go alone? I need you to take care of my mom."

Jay's "yes" was surrounded by silences exclaiming, *yes and no. I want to go with you, but what can I do?* She didn't see the purpose in pushing him. If he changed his mind, he'd ask her. He read the hurt in her teary-eyed silence yet couldn't muster a cogent answer beyond "Thanks."

Standing on the curb at the airport, they hugged. Jay held him tightly, in a painful silence. Moses couldn't explain his desire to be alone when he met his mother. There arose in him the vague terror that he'd be a far different Moses Teumer upon his return.

7

THE SONGS OF SALOME

The Sound of the Silents

I must digress. Please don't be impatient. Impatience has the mixed aroma of a too-hot baby's bottle and a freshly unwrapped rubber. Listen closely and you'll see that others hurt me much more than I ever hurt myself. Others burned my brain and others promised new drugs and therapies and others always send me back here. No longer can I be rescued by Alchemy. Now my granddaughter Persephone is lost to me.

Now, my prebirth in Orient: a mix of fragrant colors humming of nature and the sinister odors of incessant prattle. Often splendorously unencumbered by trauma, more often than not marked by days of boredom, nights of tedium, except when the kids and their parents ostracized me with taunts of "retard." The joyless cadavers impugned me for my raucous, intrepid, and immodest life. They were the first, but not the last, to despise me for telling untrue truths. Alchemy always claimed there is no Universal Truth, only shadows and permutations of truth. Yes, I teased him, that is true and false, because I have lived between the shadows of the truths and the lies.

It is my fact that I have suffered periods of despair and staggering pain when I wondered if I should have ever left our isolated two-story clapboard house about a quarter mile from the bay, across from the old slave cemetery. I'd sit for hours on the roof, painting watercolors or just inhaling nature.

Except for Hilda and Dad's room, I painted murals on all the walls about every six months, perhaps more often. My own imagined treeflowers and natural hallucinations. My dad shook his head. He endearingly called me "Salo in Wonderland." Hilda, the woman who called herself my mother, possessed not one iota of magical wonder. We spoke different languages. "Salome," she would declare, "there is no such thing as a treeflower!" When I asked, "Why not?" she turned away from me as if I were a miscreant daughter from another planet, denying any culpability for my behavior. Dad was a man who loved order. He had the most compulsively groomed farm in Suffolk County. Too often my "shenanigans" sent him to his twelve-pack and smokes. But he loved me, my creative chaos, more than he loved order.

My dad said, "We're all common as snowflakes and not near as pure." He was only half right. Thinking of them always raises a guilty sorrow. It never made sense until later. They called me their "number-one girl." Like Dad and Greta—not Hilda, who could rattle on and on—I was introverted and, I would say, socially unemancipated. I barely talked to anyone until I was ten. I never spoke in school.

I knew pretty early on I was different. Hilda was round and short and Dad muscular and compact as a frozen haystack. I ended up even taller than Dad. I looked like *her*. That's what *Life* magazine wrote in '69 when they printed Xtine's photos of me as one of the new "faces of the year with a Garboesque profile." And they didn't have a clue.

Each May we'd take a trip to the city for dinner at the "21" Club. The only extravagance I remember. To Dad, New York City represented the citadel of hedonistic heathenry. We took the trip when I turned chronologically thirteen, in 1956, not long after I'd seen *Ninotchka* on the one television station we got clearly, one Saturday afternoon. At the table next to us: Greta. So regally alone. Hat on her head. Eyes dissecting me. I've never stopped imagining what she thought as she watched me. She spoke not one word to us. Her face implacable. That day, while I sipped my tomato bisque, I felt her eyes, smelled her fatigue, her horrid despair. Yes, I did. I could. She didn't acknowledge me. When we exchanged glances, it triggered the same inexplicable hurt I felt whenever I examined myself in the mirror for too long.

The next day, Dad asked me to talk to him in the living room after lunch. He sat on the awful rose-patterned sofa. He almost never sat there but in his wooden rocking chair with its tobacco-stained tan seat cushion, smoking. He loved those Winstons. I thought about sitting in his chair but chose the sofa. He puffed on his cigarette and then ground it out in the ceramic ashtray I'd made in grade school. He clasped his massive, powerful hands. "That woman you saw yesterday, in the hat, you saw her, right?"

"The weirdess who was constantly staring at me? Uh-huh."

"Did you recognize her?"

"Yeah, some old-time movie star."

"Yes, and well, your mother and me, we were never able to bring a healthy child into this world." He just spit that out and I didn't know what the hell he was talking about and he started tearing up. His voice all strangly, like mine is now. "That woman is your mother. Your birth mother."

I felt discarded and unwhole, like one of the hollowed-out shells I collected on the beach. Hilda had been listening in the kitchen. I heard her weeping and I started crying, too. I picked up Dad's sweaty right hand and squeezed it between my two hands. I used to have spectacularly agile, sexy hands that made men mad with desire. I am seventy-eight in human years and now they look as if they are the hands of a thousand-year-old leper.

I wanted my hands to tell him I loved him.

After a minute, he girded himself and began rambling on about how they "got" me through the lawyer William Bickley Sr., who all the kids made fun of because he was such a priss—found out later he was married—who owned this ridiculous Tudor mansion overlooking the Sound. Hilda's sister, my Aunt Clara, worked for Bickley Sr., and he arranged the adoption even before I was born.

"Dad," I asked, not at all intending to hurt him, "who is my father?"

He wiped his lip, his face a mask of impassivity, but I sensated beyond the mask that my question gorged his soul. "I don't know, Salo. Miss Garbo and Bickley got everything fixed. We are your parents." He lit another cigarette. "Salo, sometimes you have to wait a long time before you realize that the pain the truth has caused is for the best in the end."

I never told anyone in Orient except Kyle. My one true friend. Kyle was a year older than me. With her blond-reddish hair and creamy skin like a Botticelli Venus, everyone on the whole North Fork bowed in her presence.

We first met Malcolm Teumer outside Boyle's Diner. He drove up and parked his two-seater Karmann Ghia, which was something special. He slow-strutted like a Euro Marlon Brando and leaned forward, his face inches from Kyle's. Her voice so provocatively flirty, she asked, "How about you let me drive your fabulous car for a while?" She jumped in the driver's seat. "C'mon, man. Let's go."

Off they went, while I stood there. Art, who was sweeping up the sidewalk in front of the diner, frowned. "Salome, stay away from him. I don't like him."

We started hanging out with Teumer in this deserted, decrepit shed in the Huddler cornfields overlooking the Sound, which he wanted to turn into a winery. One night, I watched the meteor showers sing across the moonlit sky while Malcolm and Kyle fucked. A few weeks later, Kyle left Malcolm's one late night and drove off alone in the Karmann Ghia. Maybe she was drunk, or maybe they had a fight. She skidded into the bay at the end of Route 25 and drowned.

The night before her funeral, I walked alone along the Sound. I sank to my knees on the pebbly beach and cut my palm ever so slightly with the sharp edge of a shell. From my blood appeared Kyle. She knelt beside me and held my bleeding hand. "Salome, my sister, before I leave you, I bequeath my enchantress powers to you." She brought her lips to the cut on my hand and kissed it. "I must go." Her voice and translucent body elevated above the gravitational hum of the waves.

She came to me again only one more time. Other ancestors came more often.

I ached for Kyle. I missed her so. I don't regret my many pleasure-burying-pain fucks, unlike lust fucking or angel fucking, which is when you are in love and which I cherish. Malcolm, I regret. We met in his shed. He made a fire. We got drunk. I got pregnant.

That pregnancy caused Dad and Hilda so much pain. I woke up earlier than usual one morning and went into the kitchen. Hilda was crying. Aunt Clara was sitting next to her, stroking her cheek. She told her, "It's not your fault you couldn't have your own kids." When she noticed me in the doorway, Aunt Clara jumped up and asked what I wanted for breakfast. I pretended like I hadn't heard them.

And then I overheard Dad on the phone with Greta. His voice, usually as sturdy as his tractor, shivered with shame. "I'm so sorry we failed you. We failed. I failed. I just don't know how this happened." The belief in his failure as a father began the decay of his physical self that signaled the first signs of Gravity Disease.

Dad had a talk with Teumer. I bet he did more than talk. Teumer left town. I didn't want him to be the father of my child.

Hilda wanted me to hide my pregnancy. I refused. And Dad agreed. I always stood up for my actions. I began making drawings of *Petra Sansluv, Pearl Diver by the Black Sea*, the story of an abandoned boy who formed special bonds with the creatures in the Black Sea.

When the time came, Bickley arranged to send the doctor. He strutted into my room dressed in a navy blue suit, with his square jaw and comic-book-black hair. He looked and sounded like an actor playing a defrocked doctor on a soap opera. He gave me drugs and then I don't remember much at all...The baby...Stillborn...Strangled by his own umbilical cord. I never saw him. That loss was over sixty years ago, but it was also only a second ago...

We buried the baby in the cemetery about a mile from the house. I burned the Sansluv drawings. I sleepwalked around because that week I was dying, too. I can still feel it in my ancient, dried up uterus—like I have this empty hole inside me—a bloody, ulcerous hole still seeping with babydeath. I can see it when I close my eyes.

I kept slapping my tummy, because I just couldn't believe my body betrayed me.

Greta never wrote or called. She knew. I found out later that she knew all.

8
THE MOSES CHRONICLES (2001)
Future Shock

Moses flew to Newark and rented a car. He thought about calling a Stuy Town friend who now lived in Paramus, but he didn't want to try to explain what he didn't yet understand. He spent the night at the airport Marriott and headed out at 7 A.M. He exited Route 80 at Red Gap, New Jersey, where a sign greeted all visitors HOME TO OVER ONE HUNDRED MILLION B&B CHOCOLATE BARS. From there he drove ten miles to the Collier Layne Health Facility.

Dr. Barnard Ruggles, a small, balding, puckish man in his midfifties, with black-framed glasses and overgrown gray eyebrows, greeted Moses with extreme recalcitrance in his cluttered office. Ruggles explained that he had been treating Salome off and on since 1979 and fully grasped the intricacies of her disorder. Ruggles informed Moses that he needed to take a DNA test and that until he received the results, he wouldn't discuss any details with him. "Get a room at the DoubleTree in Red Gap. Take a tour of the B&B factory. Eat some chocolate." He wrinkled up his forehead and rubbed the small mole on the right side of his cheek, which seemed to usher in a complete change of mind. "I may be out of bounds here. I believe you are Salome's son. I can hear it in your voice. Without qualification I can say it bears an unmistakable similarity to Alchemy's. What?" Moses's face must have revealed both his annoyance and surprise. "Did I say something wrong?"

Moses chose to make it easy for Ruggles. "Second time I've heard that in twenty-four hours. Go on, please."

"If, as we presume, this is true, we will need to talk with serious purpose and you will have even more decisions to make." Ruggles sighed through his nose and looked askance at his diploma from Dartmouth on the wall to his left, as if it could supply an answer. "This, I am sure, has come as a shock to you, but you will come as a, a"—he paused—"a potentially world-shattering shift to Salome."

"I expected something like that."

He nodded. "She had been at Alchemy's compound in Topanga in California, but she's back now because she managed to 'escape' and get down to the main road, where the police found her shining her flashlight at oncoming cars, throwing rocks at their windshields. She violently resisted them, saying she had a mission to accomplish. Which now, she does not remember." He shook his head almost imperceptibly.

"I see," Moses said.

"I suggest a man in your condition get some rest."

"One other question. I assumed Alchemy Savant was paying for this, but you said she was here off and on since the '70s."

"I am not at liberty to divulge any particulars. Maybe William Bickley III can. Let me just say a trust was set up by a person of means who must remain anonymous."

Still maneuvering cautiously, Moses kept his many other questions to himself.

After a visit to the lab, where they swabbed his DNA and drew his blood, Moses got the Collier Layne special at the DoubleTree. He called Jay and his mom, and started to read before soon falling asleep. He spent the next morning brooding at the resort and spa, in the midst of a treacly ex-suburb that made stars of the Barry Manilows and Celine Dions of the world, but also felt like the rural breeding ground for trigger-happy sociopaths like Gary Gilmore. He had less than zero desire to tour the candy factory, but he did make a quick trip the B&B gift shop and bought a box of specialty chocolates for Jay.

After lunch, he lay on the huge bed, aching with exhaustion, wondering, *How many blows can my body absorb and comprehend in such a short time?* This was the not the first, or last, of countless days and nights he would spend obsessing about the lies we are told, tell ourselves, and ultimately choose to believe. Moses steeled himself: Never again would he trust *anyone's* truth to be unadulterated and without motive.

After his nap, he called Laban Lively. The machine-recorded voice played, and Moses hung up without leaving a message. He phoned Sidonna Cherry and updated her. He asked if she could find out some background on Lively and what she thought about the prospects of finding his father in Brazil.

"Now that he knows you have located him, if he doesn't want to be found, he won't be," Cherry said with matter-of-fact certainty.

"What if he has any other kids?"

"I can try. If they're in Brazil, I wouldn't bet on it."

Dr. Ruggles called at 4:15. He attempted lightheartedness. "You're unofficially a Savant. It is still considered preliminary, but I feel confident it will be confirmed."

A silence wafted, which Moses deciphered as trouble. "I can sense an 'and' or a 'but' coming. You don't want me to meet her?"

"Why don't you come over and we'll talk."

In the lobby of Collier Layne, an orderly walked Moses to Ruggles's office. Moses waited at the doorway. Standing hunched over his desk, shuffling papers, Ruggles barely lifted his head as he asked Moses to sit across from him. Moses sat while Ruggles remained standing.

Moses stiffened, waiting for the next body slam. "We are of the strong opinion that Salome will not be a match for the transplant. We've done a preliminary HLA tissue test. We will send samples to your doctor in L.A. You are aware that siblings are the preferred donors. You need to ask Alchemy. Although, as your half brother, there is only a fifty percent chance of a match."

Moses nodded.

"No doubt you have questions, and I will answer the ones about seeing Salome and any others, but first..." Ruggles now sat down and stared at the four Dubuffet prints on his wall before speaking again. He turned his head and stared balefully into Moses's eyes from behind his thick glasses. "Salome believes, I have no idea how to put this...that you are not alive...that you were stillborn."

"What?" Moses shook his head, at first very slowly, then faster and faster until he put his hands on each temple like a vise, clamping his head in place. His felt as if his entire body was retracting into itself, receding, collapsing into an embryonic ball. He remained wordless for a moment. Finally, he managed to push out a barely audible plea, "Repeat that and explain. Please."

"Salome, your mother, believes you are dead and buried in a grave in Long Island close to where she was raised."

Ruggles got up and gave him a bottle of water and a glass. "You want something stronger?"

"How about a shot of liquid Valium?" Ruggles raised his forest of eyebrow hair as if to say, "If you need it..." Moses realized he could in fact give it to him. "No, just kidding."

Ruggles struggled to formulate his words. "This situation has placed me in the most tenuous professional and ethical position. I hate to be the bearer of such an inconceivable" — he paused — "revelation. What I can't even presume is if she was told you were stillborn by her adoptive parents or if she was told the truth but doesn't believe it because the process was so traumatic. She is highly, highly sensitive and alternately elastic and brittle."

"Did you believe I was dead?"

"We had no reason not to. The Bickleys never informed me until two days ago, and there was no mention of you in the trust, as there is of Alchemy."

"Is my death part of her delusion?"

"Possibly, yes. With Salome, one never knows. She does not accept 'psychology' as existing in the remotest realm of science."

"Is she sane?"

"That's a definition question. One's psychological state is based on a cluster of disparate symptoms that, no matter what any authority claims, we don't really understand. Thomas Szasz made some good arguments, but mental illness is *no* myth. Salome's received many reductive diagnoses over the years, 'severe dissociative disorder,' 'depersonalization disorder,' 'dissociative fugue,' 'dissociative amnesia,' 'identity disorder,' and simple schizophrenia. At first, she was accused of faking to escape arrest for her violent actions. If so, she is an even better actress than her mother."

Moses's head tilted forward quizzically.

Ruggles shook his head. "I'm sorry. I should not have said that. In Salome's first visit here in 1976, the doctors treated her and others with insulin therapy and a primitive form of electroshock, which repulses me." Ruggles stopped himself, refocused, and continued. "Sorry, I've been both too technical and veering off course. As I say, it is difficult for me to make a reductive classification for her. We have adjusted her drug regimen. She certainly has a keen memory when she wants to. The ECT caused some retrograde amnesia and anterograde memory loss, but it has not been significant. She functioned for many years, broke down, and then functioned again. Her accomplishments as an artist are well documented. I believe she can function again. She's only fifty-seven and physically in excellent health." Moses did a quick calculation and realized Salome must have been fourteen or fifteen when she had given birth to him. "Right now, with Alchemy being away and Nathaniel Brockton's physical constraints, her risk of another traumatic..." Ruggles waved his hand and pointed toward some unknown beyond. "Alchemy, not the Bickleys, is now her guardian and her anchor."

"Where is he?"

"At a Zen monastery in New Mexico. He's in the middle of a three-month retreat. It was communicated to him that she is back here, but he's taken a vow of silence, which I suggest you interrupt immediately."

"I'm inclined to agree. Let me think about it overnight."

"The question arises: Should you meet and be introduced to Salome now? Should I tell her? I am at a loss. In all the years I've been practicing, and I have experience with extreme and rare cases, never before have I encountered such a conundrum. If you want to meet her, I'll need at least a few days to prepare myself. And her." Ruggles rubbed the mole on his cheek with his right index finger and shook his head as if to acknowledge, *You don't have the time.*

"Meet her? Maybe. No. I think I'll find Alchemy, and then, who knows? I need to avoid any more blows until, well, things are clearer. I'm not sure it is best for her. Or me. Can I *see* her and maybe...?"

"Yes, of course." Ruggles looked at his watch and leaned back in his chair, relieved to be able to put this confrontation off. "She's probably taking her before-dinner walk around the grounds. I can casually introduce you as a visitor."

Ruggles led Moses outside. They walked along a tree-lined pebble path until Ruggles pointed. "That's her." Ten yards ahead of them, a woman ambled as if she were strolling freely in a park rather than a walled-in compound, head angled toward the sky. "If we speed up a bit we'll catch her."

"No, let's follow her a minute."

Moses began to sweat profusely; his knees jellied and his body trembled. Fear overwhelmed his curiosity. He grabbed Ruggles by the arm to steady himself. "I can't. I can't now."

Ruggles, grim-faced, nodded. "You can come back anytime."

Moses drove back to the hotel, still feeling emotionally unmoored from the guideposts, internal and external, that had marked and peopled his world.

At the hotel he called Jay. "Guess what? I got two moms. Both are living on worlds they created. One includes me and one doesn't."

"You should call the one that includes you. She is not in good shape. She feels neglected." Jay and Hannah had spent the morning and afternoon together, and Jay went home after a late lunch.

"What? Why? I called last night and you saw her today."

"It's not rational, but she's afraid to lose you."

"Jay, I am so worn out. I feel so beaten down. I feel like giving up."

"NO! You can't." Jay panicked. "You can't. It would destroy your mom. And *me*. Please, Moses."

Jay's fear of losing Moses was colored by the loss of her mother who, when Jay was twenty-three, began to slide into the netherworld of Alzheimer's. Jay had made plans to move back to Miami to be with her mother and to help her father and brother run the art gallery. Jay's belief in the vows of "for better or worse" were shattered when her father put his wife in a home and began dating one of her nurses. Jay gave up her plans to move back to Miami. Her mother remained in the "home," too physically strong to succumb yet unable to recognize Jay when she made one of her now rare visits.

When Moses's illness struck, Jay resisted the notion that the world could be so unjust. Better, she often thought, if he would flee to another woman's arms than lose him to the sheathing arms of illness and death. She swore unswerving devotion no matter how debilitating his illness became.

Moses understood he had to deny his urge to fade away into nothingness. He had battled with those desires before, and he knew this was the one dreadful fantasy he should never raise with Jay. "I'm sorry. Don't worry. Please. I'm tired. I need to sleep and not think. I'll call my mom now, but you have to take care of her until I get back."

Jay seemed calmer. Moses intended to fly to Albuquerque, find Alchemy, and hope that he'd agree to help.

After they hung up, Moses phoned Hannah. He reassured her that he loved her and all was well and nothing had changed between them. He didn't want her to feel suddenly peripheral. "Look, I'll be home in a few days. Please wait."

Perplexed and overwhelmed, the idea of peaceful surrender appealed to Moses. Nothing like the imminence of death to present one with an existential crisis, to raise questions about meanings and philosophies, God's existence and faith. Moses flashed back to the vacant glare of a man who, when Moses was speaking at the Skirball Center on his work about the children of survivors of the Holocaust, confronted him after the talk. He spoke with a slight Yiddish accent. "You are smart with words, like him." He looked at his hands, which held a copy of *Man's Search for Meaning*. "You make up words and theories to justify the emptiness inside you that knows there is no meaning and there is no God." Moses fumbled to respond. The man, with a disdainful shake of his head, turned away.

Moses still had no response. He didn't understand the meaning in his preverbal drive to meet his biological father, and now his mother. Neither endless hours of therapy nor reading an array of august thinkers delivered any eternal truths from the Tree of Knowledge. No—he felt as if he stood beneath some emotional Tower of Babel and would forever struggle for answers. He cursed himself for possessing no language to explain his feelings, or even understand his own questions.

He lay awake that night as old dilemmas, which had lurked in his nightmares and daymares, and new mysteries rushed along the eaves of his consciousness. Why did his urge to see his father become even greater with each new confirmation that his negation was intentional? And now this new ache for the mother whom he did not know existed—how could he miss what he never knew he had, had never had? Especially when his mom Hannah so loved and nurtured him? And what drove the Savants to hide his birth, if indeed they did? What caused Hannah to abide the charade of the unholy alliance of Teumer, Bickley Sr., and Lively for so long? Finally, fatigue took hold, his eyes closed, and his mind went quiet.

9

MEMOIRS OF A USELESS GOOD-FOR-NUTHIN' (2020)

The Great Fire Escape, 1992

I know, I know most of you wanna hear about Alchemy Savant. The facts of his scurvy-pervey sexcapades and what really happened that night he bought the *big one*. I'll get to that, but I been prepping for some time and I got a story to spill that's more than just Alchemy. I loved the bastid *and* I despised him. Like he said, we was honest brothers, and sometimes brothers fight. Yeah, he rescued me from a life of scrounging for dimes in the deep end of the shitpool. Did that for lots of us. That was him, then and always: a lifesaving con-trol freak. After becoming a rock 'n' roll god, he wanted not to be prez but a left-wing *king*.

I also been advised by the people paying me to do this to start when we met in '92, almost thirty years ago now. I ain't writing a word, just dictating. Don't worry, it's all me. They can fix everyone's grammar except mine. I gotta sound like I sound, not some airbrushed version of me. I ain't gonna soft-sell nothing neither. Some shit will make me look like a crude, ignorant crudhead and a world-class a-hole, which I was way back then and maybe still am. Judge for yourself.

I was born Ricky McFinn. Twisted branch in a warped family tree. Part Italian, part Irish, and all lapsed Catholic.

My journey to becoming Ambitious Mindswallow began late summer of '92, I'd been doing zip for a few years since I got my butt tossed out of the highfalutin School of Performing Arts for acting like a plastic surgeon and "repairing" my piano teacher's nose after he opined my mother should've aborted me. Since it was my third offense, I was fresh out of community service and no-jail-time cards, so I was awarded an all-expense-paid trip to Spofford, the juvee jail. Before I could even join a gang, this motherfucker, who had body tatts of his mama, the Mother Mary, and muscle heads, tried to stick his wang up my anal hole. I elbow him in the nuts and tell him to take his queerass Puerto Rican butt back to his cell and leave me the fuck alone. That night, in the showers, in front of his compadres he gets on me for being so skinny (I was about six feet two, 130 pounds back then). So I put this fucker *down*: "Yeah, so what? I'm carryin' weight in the only place it counts."

"What you mean? You got dope?"

"Wha-utt?" I says. "Cocksucker, you so fuckin' stoopit." I grab my nuts. "I seen four-year-olds carryin' bigger logs." I let that one sink into his big, bald skull. Then wham, I snap him, "Hell, I bet yo' mama's clit's bigger than your muscle!" That did it. They gouged out my left eye, which got me out of Spofford fast and gave me my little good-luck charm. Still keep my eye in a glass marble around my neck. My family was s-o-o-o sympathetic. (My dad and some Jew shyster sued the city. They ended up getting something but I didn't get squat.) So then I was living at home, speculating on what to do with my wonderful fucking life. One night I am sound asleep when I hear my sister Bonnie, who has the other half of the bedroom, moaning and popping chewing gum bubbles while balling some lucky future herpes dick she picked up at Paddy Quinn's. I figure I'll hide in the bathroom, only my older brother Lenny, who'd gotten out of the army and was a speed freak, was shivering and shaking right on the bathroom floor. He liked to use me as his punch dummy, so I take about two hundred bucks and some of his pills. He can't do shit. I feel much better after that.

My mom was screwing her new Korean lovewad—the Asian invasion was getting heavy and Main Street looks like a mini-Peking. My dad hadn't found some pathetic divorcée to put up with his act that night, and he's passed out drunk on the pool table in his half of the living room, which is also the office of the two family businesses. The other half is filled with "secondhand" dresses that happened to be all new that my dad "buys" and my mom sells to the neighborhood wifies. I think, *Shit, Spofford'd be better than trying to make a life with this family a ratbrains.*

I toss a few things into my backpack. I open the kitchen window to the fire escape. We lived on the sixth floor. I take this chair, go out the front door, and lock it. Wedge the chair under the door handle so they can't get out. I climb up to the roof, down the fire escape, and slip back in through the window. I dial 911. I turned on AC/DC so loud it could rattle the Chinese super's place six floors below. They all jump up and start screaming. My mom is wailing, "Ricky, yeh bastid, I'm gonna kill ya, I swearh!"

I plead to the 911 lady, over all the cursing and commotion, to get someone over here 'cause they is dying. If only. I scoot out the window and down the fire escape with only my

Strat and backpack, wearing my leather jacket, though it's late-August shitbowl Flushin' Bay hot. I hear the sirens as I head toward Main Street to catch the Seven, thinking, *They can kiss my bony ass if they ever see it again.*

I start hustling—not, as rumored, letting old queens suck me off, but I do rip off tourists and hang out on 2nd and B at the Gas Station club that is this burnt-out building with only half a roof. For free booze and crash rights, I clean up the broken bottles, crack vials, and vomit. Me being only eighteen was a misdemeanor next to the other shit going down.

One night about 3 A.M., from my seat inside I see this snazzy guy wearing a black sports coat, black porkpie hat, a purple T-shirt, and black stud earring, and puffing hard on an unfiltered smoke, high-step out of a limo. (This was a few years before that hood became a haven for the hundred-dollar-torn-jean crowd.) Beside him is a six-foot blond strung-out model type with albino skin and straw-thin arms clomping onto him. He has the *aura.* Everyone just zooms their eyes on him as he swaggers in and downs like five beers in five minutes. I'm playing my Strat, I plug in whenever I got the urge. After he buys a packet of powder for his babe, who snorts up right there, they split. As he walks out, he says, "I like your playing." I'm thinking, *Fuck you, who cares what you think?* The crazy thing is, already I do care.

To make some extra smash, I was buying junk and toot from this Super Fly knockoff who hung out on the southeast corner, we call him Duckman though he calls himself "Mr. Sam Spade," wearing his big-brimmed hat and brown leather jacket and polished white shoes. He patrols around his corner like Chuck Berry doing the duckwalk and quacking "crack, crack." I buy some stuff from Duckman and cut that shit down so detergent'd get you higher. I sold some shit to a coupla prepsters in the Gas Station, who is acting like they was dirty boulevard homeys. This one guy, showing off for his babe, tries to scam me by shorting me, giving me seventy bucks instead of a hundred. We engage in a minor conflagration. He tries to play tough. "Fuck you, man, that shit isn't worth a hundred."

"You right, it *ain't*." I says to his chick, "Why you sucking off this prick? You should try this white trash missile." I stare real tight in his face: "G'head. Try something, yeh pisshead." As I'm doing this, I spot the snazzy dude from the other night without his hat, sitting with *my* guitar on his lap. He's sidewaysed himself into the corner and is lazy-eyeing us, and then, again, he smiles at me, while strumming the Velvets' "Oh! Sweet Nuthin'."

I say to the prepster, "You think I won't mess your pretty face, you are way mis-tak-en." With my left hand, I pull off my shades. "Look close at my left eye...Yeah, it's *glass*. Gift from my cell mates. Now gimme me the dope and the cash. All of it." I took it. "Now go!"

The guy keeps strumming. No one really listened to the music or poetryslammin' there. The Nuyorican was down the block if you was into that mumbo-jumbo. I grab an acoustic guitar from behind the bar and hand it to him. I take mine back and we start jamming. He drops me a dime worth of lickass. "You handled that real sweet."

"Yum, just swallowed that pussy whole." He nods and starts playing "Police and Thieves," achingly slow and reggae cool. Not at all like the Clash. I says I never hear it like that, and he says, "I always preferred Junior Murvin's original." I say nuthin'. Don't want to show my ignorance. Then he starts messing with more music I never heard. Turns out it's his shit and he sings his lyrics:

I do it for the chicks and money
don't care 'bout no salvations
or gold-plated salutations
all I want is chicks and money . . .

We're jamming when Mr. Suburbia drives up with his boys in a Mercedes with CT plates. I stop playing and step outside. He and his three buddies come at me. I pull my metal before they get close, and I grab the main sucker. I go right at his ear. "Bitch, I tolt ya. I don't care. I'll cut you good and we'll be one pretty pair a misfits."

Mr. Suavola glides out to us like he's Mahatma Luther Kingmaker. "Let's maintain a level of intelligence and decorum . . ." He gently takes my arm and pulls the knife away from the guy's ear. He calls out to the Duckman, who saunters over.

"My man, Alchemy Savant, ain't seen you since I hear your soulman's heart and chocolate vodka voice charmin' us at the Paradise," Duckman declares, and quacks. "So what can I do you for?" These clowns are morgue-meat white. The neighborhood cops drive by and Duckman throws a big Howdy-dee-damn-do kiss at 'em while Alchemy is explaining everything, only he adds this, "My friend and I, we need a car, and I think these gentlemen are going to lend us theirs as compensation for our troubles. What do you think?"

Duckman muses for a sec. "That be fair."

Mr. CT starts howling, "No way. Wait. Please. No!"

Duckman says, like he's sucking the last juice from his whore's hot spot, *"Boy,"* and he's lov-ing using that word, "boy, did you see that black-'n'-white that drive by? You don' do what I suggest, you take your ride, and I call my associates and they stop you before you hit First Avenue. You know what the Tombs is, *boy*? The Tombs is the nastiest cell in America." These tools are piss pants yellow now. "Shee-it, you'll see it for yo'self."

I'm just wishing, wishing this cat had been my lawyer in juvee court. "Okay, boys, past your bed-wettin' time." The CT guys start slinking away and Alchemy surprises me when he yells after them, "Give me your number." They stop and do that, and the screw job, he thanks them.

I think it's finally done 'til Duckman grabs my arm. "How much you get?"

"Hundred."

"That and the shit be mine for services rendered." No way I'm hosing Duckman. "And, one mo' thing, as I am sure you remember, anything you sell to the white boys in here, I gets seventy-five percent. And them other three corners, I *owns* 'em." He and Alchemy shake hands. I hand over the cash and the dope to the Duckman, and he quacks on back to his corner. Alchemy yells out to me, "You up for a ride?"

"Where to?"

"L.A. Going to start a band there."

Never been to L.A. and I ain't got sweet nuthin' to lose and no future in New York. "Let's jam."

Alchemy drove like red lights, slow-moving cars, potholes is just hazards to be avoided. Or not. In minutes, we're over the GW Bridge and jetting away from dumps like Bayonne, the "American Dream Developments," and them putrid gas tanks of the "Garden State." Yeah, a garden doused in weed kill. I'm thinking to myself, *So Looong Flushin'*, when he swivels his head so he's looking backward and stares at the city, and I'm getting a tick nervous here about his driving skills, and he says, "Look at that skyline, and the acolyte cities, the lights, they're like God's dissonant drips merging across the sky on a Jackson Pollock canvas." Uh, yeah, sure. I don't know Jackson Pollock from Jack-in-the-fuckin'-Box, and if God created Hoboken in his image, then book me a ticket to Satanville.

A coupla minutes later he turns and asks, "So, besides taking advantage of foolish college kids, what do you want to do?"

"Pile up chicks and money," I croon. We laugh and start riffing about L.A. and the music we want to play and all the movies we dig and all the shit we have in common. 'Cause I don't know yet, but sense there's plenty we don't.

We drive for a coupla hours and it's like 4 A.M. when he pulls off the 80. Even at that hour it's not like any Jersey that I seen. No gas and garbage smells.

He announces, "I need to see my mom. There's a motel where we can get some rest first." In the room, in like one minute, the guy's asleep. About two hours later, I hear him howling. I am freak-*ing* out, and I don't freak easy, but I ain't never heard such scarifying noises exiting out from no one except when Tommy Huston shot Davy Rathbone in the nuts. I'm thinking the guy is a psycho or he's gonna die on me and that's all the bullshit I need, stuck with a "borrowed" car and a dead body in Nofuckingwhere, New Jersey. I leap out of bed, turn on the lights, and shake his ass awake. He sits up, he's all sweaty, and his eyes—whew! They are a kaleidoscope of light and dark browns with dots of tans and whites, gonzo wild and like he has just seen God *and* Satan—only his voice and body are totally cool.

"It's part of my birthright," he finally says. "You'll see in the morning. Now go back to bed."

I'm more than a bit jittery, so I put on the cable TV, watch some porn, and jack off in the shower while Alchemy is once again fast asleep.

10
THE SONGS OF SALOME
Civil Wars

After the babydeath I struggled to keep my equilibrium, waiting for recovery and regeneration. I finished high school and Dad built me a light-filled studio. Against Mom's "better judgment," they even got me a used Thunderbird convertible. I painted the front yellow and red and flaming orange and called her Kyle. Years later, Alchemy took it. He and Mindswallow drove it off a cliff in Malibu, which appeals to my sense of rightness. Sometimes, but not too often, I'd go to the cemetery and wonder how my life would've changed had the baby lived. Dad found me there once and I bawled my eyes out and he just held me. I remember his cough echoing throughout the house. We had a huge blowout when I burned his carton of Winstons and he grabbed them out of the BBQ pit on the back lawn. He said calmly, "You are still my child and not the other way 'round."

I worked the farm stand, but Dad got frustrated with me because I gave away free food to some and charged others too much. Donnie Boyle gave me a job at his diner as a waitress. I kept telling the customers what they should eat instead of what they wanted. I dropped dishes. Mostly by accident. Dear

Art did his best to cover for me or take the blame. Donnie'd had the hots for me forever and he never would have fired me, so I fired myself.

I decided to do volunteer work as a kind of aide, going to the houses of the old and the sickly in the North Fork. I also painted, read, wrote in my notebooks, and discovered physics. That's when I started to formulate my theories on emotions and gravity.

Entranced by the tide and inhaling the smells of the Sound, hoping to find Kyle, her atom self, but no ... I'll tell you about that soon enough. That night I first understood the secrets of gravity, and the moon, and embraced the power of my acute sense of smell. My first shrink here, Samuel Sontag, who I nicknamed Count Shockula, thought I just made up these smells. I challenged him, "You don't deny gravity, do you? Or its effects on the tides? Or on objects as small as atoms? What are smells but molecules floating in the air? And moon tides — gravity determines their motion. And people are seventy percent water, and have smells inside them that are affected by gravity. I call them soulsmells." He just kept looking down and taking his notes.

After incubating in Orient, I realized I had to leave or become an erased soul inside a physical shape pantomiming the motions of life. Or a lonely oddball wasting away like Art. Dad had told me about the trust Greta and Bickley Sr. set up for me. I decided to attend Parsons in New York. I thought life would be different. It wasn't. I sport-fucked. Made very few friends. Parsons had a soulsmell of dried blood, moldy cork, and self-absorption.

I went to see all of Greta's films. I found books about her in the NYU library, which I later learned got so many things wrong. Yes, she left Hollywood after the perfectly titled *Two-Faced Woman* flopped both artistically and financially, which allowed her studio bosses to use it as a pretext to dump her lovely derriere, and her (to them) inequitable salary. The greed-gods leaked the vilifying "truth" that she'd suffered a nervous and physical breakdown, felt abused by those so magnanimous Hollywood employers. She planned to take one or two years off in New York City and return triumphantly to Hollywood. It wasn't the war, her desire to be alone, even the movie mongrels that stopped her. It was an affair. Like all of Greta's affairs, with both men and women, it was clandestine and doomed. Unlike all the others, this time, in 1943, she gave birth to a child. Me. She chose my name: Salome. And then she chose to give me away.

I would go to her apartment and wait outside, and sometimes I saw her come out and get into a car. Or go for a walk. Few people recognized her. I never talked to her.

For almost two years, I floated though my classes and explored the city. Through the recommendation of one of my professors, I found this small gallery. The gay owner loved my "look," so he gave me my first show, *ARTillery*. After one of my weekly performances straddling one of the cannons, I met the Great and Powerful Horrwich and he invited me to his opening, and so I flitted into the Murray Gibbon Gallery up on 57th and Fifth. (He soon moved to SoHo and later Chelsea.) We consummated our lust-power attraction that night in the closet of the gallery. Soon after, I moved into his loft on Prince

Street. He owned the whole damn building. The industrial plants still reigned like the dying kings of SoHo, unaware of their impending extinction, mighty buildings with soul and the energetic odor of toil and beer-injected muscles.

Horrwich and I became a pair. I all but quit going to Parsons when we got to setting up the *Art Is Dead* happening. Dad found out what we were planning from Art. When I went to Orient to bring Art into the city, Dad picked me up at the bus. "Salo, I know in your heart you want to help Art. But please, this is wrong. I'm asking you to think about it." We went to Art's and I told him what Dad had asked. Art pleaded with him. "Gus, I want this. I need this." Dad gave up.

A few months after the happening, some of the few friends I made at Parsons threw a nongraduation party for me because I officially quit the school. It happily surprised me when Hilda and Dad arrived. They couldn't stay angry at me. But damn, did they stand out: Auntie Em and Uncle Henry venturing to the Emerald City. They seemed to be having fun until Horrwich got drunk. He oozed over to me while I was talking to some guy who was hitting on me. Horrwich tugged me away and asked, prosecutor style, "How many other people here have you slept with?"

"None of your business."

His lips coiled and he smelled jealous. Jealousy has the odor of a steaming iron. He got even drunker and was high on his extract of belladonna, and then, in front of everyone, he picked up a copy of Bertrand Russell's *Selected Letters* and in his pedant's voice yelled, "It is such a shame Russell gave up philosophy. Does anyone know why he gave it up?" No one uttered a word. Dad and Hilda looked bewildered. I cringed. Horrwich's talons were out. I didn't know how to stop him. "I'll tell you. Russell said it was because he discovered fucking. Tonight we are celebrating the lovely Salome, who skipped the philosophy and went straight to fucking, and she is damn good at it!" I wanted to laugh. This so-called progressive artist was just another recondite chauvinist.

Dad marched over to Horrwich and punched him in the gut. Without even talking to me, he and Hilda started to leave. I ran up to them and begged them to stay. His eyes told me he despised my slatternly lifestyle. "We are going and you can come with us," he said. But I couldn't. I couldn't go back to that life. I hugged them and whispered, "I love you both, but..."

I went with Horrwich to his loft. After he fucked me, he nodded off. I couldn't sleep, so I walked over to the window and stared out. Below was a bum leaning against a lamppost—I inhaled his cheap alcohol breath and stale body odor. The streetlight was barely visible through the mist. I watched as he, so carefree, pissed in the gutter. Then I smashed my hand through the glass. Horrwich jumped up. "Salome? What?" I picked up a shard and cut my right cheek. Instead of rushing me to the hospital, Horrwich, still naked, snapped pictures. He said my face looked prismatic with the blood mixing with my tears and circling my jade eyes. He thought it was some kind of art statement. He ended up showing the photos in a gallery and selling them. He didn't give me a dime.

I finally kicked the camera out of his hand, he got dressed, and we taxied to St. Vincent's. The ER doctor didn't call a plastic surgeon and he butchered me. I have this Frankenstein's monsterish scar under my right eye that stretches for a little more than an inch. It's fading after all these decades, as I have faded. Still, you must see that I possess powers worth more than youth, beauty, or natural memory. And those deep scars on my hands have not fully faded. They too are memory and memento.

Each morning I exhale the decomposing cells of my face and my body. And time, the human definition of time, that hobgoblin of impending bodydeath, is my earthly enemy. Disintegration has spoiled my external eyesight, and the new surgeries have failed. Everything outside of me appears foggy. My eyes were always so light sensitive. I have always seen, and still do see, the past and the future. Not seeing is humbling and mortifying, but seeing was often more humbling and mortifying. Others have defined me as a visual artist, but really I am a sensation artist, a sensate morphologist—all of my senses, especially smell, are hyperacute. Even now, I can inhale the pulse of the moon.

11

MEMOIRS OF A USELESS GOOD-FOR-NUTHIN'

Step to the Music (Which He Hears), 1992

I finally catch some z's, and when I get up I see it's all green grassy. You know, in Queens, Jack, 'til I was about twelve I thought all parks had blacktop and cement. A park meant basketball and handball courts. I ain't hip to the notion that most of the world thinks of trees and grass and hills when they hear the word "park."

We stop at the Dunkin' Donuts. This cute virginal-looking Jersey babe behind the counter is salivating over Alchemy. The first of a million times I see this. He's talking in this voice that one of his babes later says "oozes out like delicious, hot cum." I'm watching this in disbelief as he spews his BS. "Are those sugar-covered doughnuts . . . are they as sweet as you look?" She smiles red faced as she hands him the bag. He goes, "I'd just like one little lick." I wanna fucking puke. I mean, she's ready to get down on her knees. While they're mindfucking away, I look at him hard. It's the first time I examine him in daylight and, whoa, he looks sort of different than the night before. Very weird 'cause now he looks *part* something. He's brownish skinned. His eyes look a much darker brown. Maybe part black. Maybe Arab, or who knows what?

He hands me the bag of doughnuts, two coffees, and the keys to the car. "Have to use the facilities. Be out in a minute."

Waiting in the car, I'm steaming. I go back inside. I don't see him or the cutie.

He comes back fifteen minutes later and he pauses outside the car and gives me that smile of his that says, "If you're cool, I'll give you the key to babe heaven." Well, right then he ain't givin' me nothing but agita. He announces like someone important is really listening (as if someday he *knew* I'd be doing this), "This is where the American heartland really begins. Where the towns and communities are bound together by winding blacktop roads like the seams on a baseball. Someday, I want to spend more time here."

I'm thinking, *Why? So you can fuck more of 'em?* Only I learn soon enough it's part of his Big Plan, but me, I care not one rat turd about the American heartland, so I yell, "Did you just fuck that cunt? Did that little whoarh give you a blow job in the bathroom?"

"Hey, man, first, it's not cool to screw and tell. Second, if you call women by those misogynistic names, you will pile up *no* chicks and *no* money."

I shake my head, not real pleased at being lectured, not knowing what "misogynistic" means, and I'm feeling the itch like he's a born-too-fucking-late child-of-the-'60s hippie type. We get going and he keeps chewing his doughnuts, drinking his coffee, and flying down this two-lane road through what looks like Robin Hood's hideaway in Sherwood Forest. We come to this gate all connected to twenty-foot-tall cement walls. Alchemy waves to the guard, who lets us in, and we drive about two miles 'til we're outside the main house that looks like some French castle I seen in the movies. The sign reads COLLIER LAYNE HEALTH FACILITY. The place is famous for housing million-dollar nut jobs. Until now, I ain't seen Alchemy as money. He just don't have that feel that rich schmucks have, that no matter what happens, Mommy and Daddy will bail their ass outta trouble. I think maybe this guy is flummoxing my instincts and I need to be more careful.

"So, you are a spoilt fucker after all? I shoulda guessed when you high-stepped outta that limo. Shoulda rolled you then." I'm still pissed at him for getting sex and talking to me like I'm a doofus.

"Man, is *that* wrong. You have no idea why I was in that limo. Let's just say a two-faced woman paid for the limo and that well is nearly dry."

I think, *Sure, whatever you say, bub. You call yourself Alchemy and we're visiting your mom in biddy-bip-bip land.*

We walk into the lobby. He whispers to the guy at the desk and they start laughing. The guy leads us into this large sitting area with all of these fuckin' trees growing out of the roof. He calls it the "arboretum." I'm looking up for birds and squirrel monkeys that'll be dropping their turds on me.

I find a safe spot and plop down in this fluffy sofa by a TV that is on to the Mets game. Alchemy sits down, too. Turns out we're both Mets fans.

Five minutes later, the hottest middle-aged babe la-di-dahs out, dressed in tight-assed pedal pusher pants and a bikini bra and a fishnet shawl, in sandals with her toes painted purple, and holding a flashlight in her left hand. I do a Jackie Gleason–like double take. Really, she is about the sexiest any-thing, any age, I ever seen. I would've done her in a Flushin' flash.

She and Alchemy hug and hold hands. He says, "Mom, please meet Ricky Mindswallow, a car thief from Queens." I look at him thinking, like, *Whoa there, that was your idea.* And that name? I don't say nuthin' before he says to me, "This is my mom, Salome. A shape-shifter from another dimension."

She looks at me, her eyes a popping deep green and unblinking, and her skin is damn pale. She takes the flashlight, turns it on, points it at his feet, and slowly moves the light up his body.

"Mr. Mindswallow, take a close look at my son of the multicolored eyes," she says, kinda snarky, "I am not the only shape-shifter in this family." Then she turns and shines the light in my face and I can't tell if she notices my glass eye. "A car thief, hmmm. What I need to know is this: Are you a homicider or a suicider?"

Alchemy starts chuckling. I try to block the light with my hand until she turns it off.

"You see, my pretty, splenetic young seedling, there are two main species of bipeds in the world—homiciders and suiciders. A few fit into the smaller category of those who would kill their enemy or lover, and also themselves. Most of us lie about what we are." She pauses and almost hisses. "Then there are those, like my son here, who think they are too superior for any one designation. Right, honey?" That don't sound like a question, but a threat.

"No, Mom, I'm an apple cider."

"As long as you're not a matricider." She points the flashlight at him but don't turn it on. "Doing much fucking lately?"

I think, *yeah, like half an hour ago*, but he slides right beside her and he takes her outstretched hand in his, and like Fred and Ginger they do a pretend tap dance while singing to the tune of that awful Three Dog Night song, "Sub-li-mate, Sub-li-mate, dance to the mew...zak..." and chortle like they're both nuts. They had what Alchemy calls their "undercover language." Then she turns to me.

"Now, I'll ask you again. What are *you*?"

"You bes' believe I'm a killah."

"Yes, I bes' believe you are. Oh, that Queens accent, it's such an aphrodisiac." She sidles up to me, and she rubs this tiny kind of sexy scar on her right cheek. Then she scratches my right cheek with her long fingers and pulls almost too hard on my skull earring. With the nail on her pointer finger, she circles the tatt on my right forearm. Then she kisses me on the lips in the sexiest way. This daffy bitch gave me a fucking hard-on! Then she grabs my cock, my balls, really, and squeezes them so I'm doubling over in pain.

"Mr. Ricky Mindswallow, you are rotten. I smell that. You smell like a pestilential rat encased in fossilized peanut butter with rusted nails for claws." She shrugs and lets go. I kind of want to slug her and I feel like she sees that. I don't hit no women. So she just giggles again, and in a real motherly way—well, not *my* fuckin' mother—she takes my hand between her hands, and I don't know what the hell she is gonna do next. She says, "My son needs a Sancho Panza of evil by his side." I'm wondering who the hell is Sancho Panzer?

I say, "Okay." I mean, Christ, what do you say to that?

"Mom, let him be. Let's go talk to Ruggles of Red Gap."

"Just a piece of advice, Ricky. You also smell ambitious, like bathrooms on the stock exchange." I got no freaking idea what she's talking about, but she's so intense, like some funky TV goddess, so I'm listening close. "If you want to be friends with my son, who is, in ways you cannot fathom, more dangerous than anyone you have *ever* met, you better grow some extremely resilient testicles to go with your ambition."

Alchemy gives me the eyebrow signal to wait for him, and they disappear into the back rooms of Collier Layne to "commiserate" with the doctor. I'm twiddling my thumbs, half watching the game, thinking this duo is too loony toons for me, and maybe I should beat it back to New York.

They come back, almost an hour later, silently holding hands like they're doing a slow step to the gallows. Salome stops, eyes half closed, says, "My teenage killah, I was, I am a good mother. I love my son more than my own life. Because I can't now, please take care of him." She rests her head against Alchemy's chest for a minute, before he gently tugs himself away. I'm not into any woe-woe-pity-me shit, but I never seen two people look more beat than Alchemy and Salome that day.

We walk back to the car through the parking lot and he ain't saying squat, just spitting on the ground every few feet. We get to the Benz. He asks, "You coming?" like he senses my hesitation. "I'll take you back if you want."

"Nah, California, here we come."

He flashes that Alchemy combo sheepish-wolfish smile that says, "I know what you want even better than you know what you want." Guy could read people's faces, voices, body language like no one I've ever met.

I suggest, "Since I'm a car thief, why don't we sell this jalopy and get some bucks and buy a cheap piece a shit?"

"It's a loan."

"What?"

"That was the deal. I'll call that guy when we're ready to dump this car and they can come get it. Mr. Mindswallow, a man got to have a code."

At first I'm thinking, *What the fuck?* Actually, way too often he had me thinking What the fuck? But one thing I got to give him, Alchemy always had *his* code.

12

THE MOSES CHRONICLES (2001)

The Sun, the Moon, and Eleven Stars

Moses flew to Albuquerque, rented a car, and spent the night at the airport Best Western. The next morning he drove north, past Santa Fe and Los Alamos, the womb of the nuclear dream. As he got higher and higher, seven thousand feet above sea level, out of the clouds appeared the Anok Monastery, glorious and ominous, like a castle in the sky from an Italo Calvino parable in a Douglas Sirk film.

After parking the Ford Focus in a small, unpaved area, he walked fifty yards to where cement walls closed upon a rusting wrought-iron gate seven feet high and circling the monastery grounds. His chest tightened from the altitude. He peeked inside the gate at a haphazardly maintained Japanese garden. No one was visible. A sign on the gate with words written in Magic Marker read PLEASE LEAVE ALL MESSAGES ON THE BULLETIN BOARD. Moses wrote "Urgent—Life and Death—for Alchemy. Please Call." He wrote his cell phone number. Outside the gate, half buried among the grass and weeds, under the shady native aspen and pine and a few imported eucalyptus trees, was a corroded cement bench. Moses lay down. With stress taking its toll on his already battered immune system, and amid the hum of the soporific surroundings, he fell immediately asleep. When he opened his eyes, a rail-thin, angular-faced middle-aged woman dressed in white pajamas hovered over him. "I am Desiree. I dared not awaken you. I hoped you were resting peacefully."

Moses pushed himself up to a sitting position. Desiree remained standing while Moses explained his dilemma. Looking confidently knowing, Desiree nodded, grinned, revealing tiny teeth. "I will seek him out. It is his choice." Desiree spoke in a wispy, soft voice. "From the cocoon comes the butterfly when the winter rains turn from tears to laughter." Moses barely nodded, thinking, *Sure thing, whatever you say.* "Wait here. Meditate if you can. Listen to the songs around you." Desiree strode barefoot to the gate, and Moses fell back into a semiconscious semisleep state. His head filled with gauzy visions of breathing tubes extending from his nose and IV tubes from arms as he lounged poolside beside hospital beds holding both of his mothers while prehistoric birds soared above in a smoldering sky.

After some time had passed, he couldn't say how much, the monastery gate clanked open and shut. He jumped up to a sitting position too fast, leaving him feeling as if his head was aloft in space and detached from his still supine body. Not entirely clear of his somnolent visions, Moses watched an almost translucent, shadowy puppetlike form floating out from a liquid mist of yellow-whiteness. This waking reverie solidified into a human form dressed in white pajama pants and a white T-shirt, a shaved head, with a face perfect in its symmetry. Walking barefoot, a duffel bag slung over his right shoulder and a guitar case in his left hand, this apparition was, unmistakably, Alchemy.

Moses slumped in his spot, feeling like an unraveling ball of crumpled clothes masquerading as a body.

"I see that my reputation *exceeds* me," Alchemy said laconically. His voice did sound remarkably familiar to Moses.

"No, yes, um, I was asleep and you startled me," Moses answered, a bit embarrassed by his dishevelment.

"The sleeper is the proprietor of an unknown land." Alchemy smiled enigmatically, dropped the duffel bag and guitar on the wild-haired grass. "I am so glad you came. Not because of why, but I discovered I am just not that Zen-ish. I need to get laid. And have a smoke." He spoke with a self-assured intimacy, as if they were old friends. He bent over and pulled a pack of Camels from his duffel bag. He tossed the pack in the air and caught it nimbly in his right hand. "Had these for the entire time and didn't touch them. You'd think now I'd want to quit for real." Alchemy lit up, puffed, sat down, and relaxed his lean body against the back of the bench. "Desiree said you might be my brother. You'll be the first." Alchemy's luminous eyes, one blazing blue and one quiescent green, further unnerved Moses. Alchemy narrowed his gaze with the slightest condemnation. "So far I've had three brothers, two sisters, a dozen kids that weren't mine, and about fifty guys who claim to be my father."

Moses knew nothing of Alchemy's paternal parentage, and although he was more than a little curious, for the moment he decided to forgo any prying. Alchemy tapped his chin with his hand that held the cigarette and sneaked a peek at Moses's bald head. "The chemo?"

"Yep. Though it was eking back even before..."

Alchemy pursed his lips but only nodded in sympathy. He took one more drag on the cigarette and put it out. "So, if we are related, looks to me like you must be a scion of Salome."

"I guess. Yes."

"You got the family feline mouth and lips." Moses hadn't had time to process any resemblances, physical or psychological. He hadn't yet been face-to-face with her. "I guess you spend too much time in a classroom to be an L.A. sun worshipper." Moses glanced down at the slightly pinkish–off-white, freckled skin tone of his wrist and hand and then glanced at Alchemy's unblemished, lacquerlike copper complexion.

"So you don't need anything but a dose of my marrow?"

"That's plenty, because if I can't tolerate your marrow..."

"It's time we get going, then. Now fill me in."

Moses detailed what Ruggles told him about Salome believing he was stillborn and his now urgent medical situation as succinctly as possible. While he did, Alchemy stared intently at Moses, slowly transforming from meditating monk into the quintessence of rock star cool, changing into black jeans, retro suede Beatle boots, turquoise T-shirt, and an unbuttoned red denim jacket. When Moses finished, Alchemy edged closer and bent over so they were at eye level. Moses pressed himself harder against the bench. Alchemy announced in a cryptically serene voice, "I've been to your grave with my mom." Moses shivered. He imagined himself compressed inside the small coffin. Still alive. Was he implying that he thought Moses was an imposter? Lying? Moses was afraid to ask. Alchemy stood tall and backed away. "Someday, I'll take you there. Maybe we'll have an unburial ceremony." Alchemy reached down into the duffel bag again, and this time he pulled out a pair of sunglasses and a .22 caliber pistol. He put on the sunglasses and inserted the clip into the gun and then returned it to the bag. "When I don't have Falstaffa or Marty, or my bodyguards, Mr. Beretta is my companion."

"Have you ever used it?" Moses decided this was not the moment to bring up his opposition to all guns; he believed the Second Amendment had been parsed in such a twisted way to misinterpret its meaning.

"Used...as in useful. Never shot anyone. I've had dozens of spurious threats and a few serious ones. People come up to me all the time. Most are cool, but some are belligerent. They want to fight because they think I've fucked their wife. Or because I won't fuck them. Or they caught their girlfriend getting off to a photo of me. Or I've stolen their songs. One guy stalked me because he said he was the true Son of God and I was the Antichrist. You wouldn't believe this shit. You just wouldn't." Alchemy's accent struck Moses as that rare mix of American everywhere and nowhereness that sounded as if it were created for someone speaking Esperanto. No matter the angst or impatience of his words, and here Moses felt they differed, the melody of his voice possessed the tranquil quality of a Bach sonata.

"Or they want your bone marrow."

"That I can give. Desiree sensed you have good juju. Me, too." With those two words Alchemy assured Moses that he believed him.

"Thanks."

Alchemy's tone lightened. "Can I drive?"

Moses hesitated. "It's rented and—"

"I got insurance policies and lawyers you wouldn't believe exist. I've been sued by someone who claimed I copped his wallet at an Insatiables concert. I testified at a trial 'cause two brothers swore I recorded secret messages in 'Papa's Gun' for them to kill their father. You know the song?"

"Sorry, no. Not that one."

"Good. I like that. Anyway, fucking two-legged leeches make them all go away but they bleed me. Me driving someone else's car? Popsicle money."

Moses, overwrought and achy, didn't want to drive anyway, so he gave him the keys. "I thought we'd stop in Santa Fe for the night and then fly to L.A. My doctor's there."

"Have you told anyone?" Alchemy tossed his bag and guitar in the trunk, took out the pistol, placed it under the front seat, and got in the car. He adjusted the seat. He was about six one, long-legged, and lean to Moses's five nine and, before the onset of his illness, stocky build.

"Just my wife. And my mom. Geez, well, the woman I call my mom, not my biological mother. This is going to get confusing." He laughed nervously. "She's the one who told me about your—our—mother."

"Make sure, for your sake, they keep it to themselves," Alchemy warned. "I prefer we drive. We can stop in Jerome, in Arizona, for the night. Best for you to remain unknown for now or your life will be hell."

"How so?" Moses asked, naïvely curious.

"The princes of the paparazzi."

"I'm beginning to see."

Alchemy replied, "You. Have. No. Fucking. Idea."

As soon as they got close to Santa Fe, Alchemy asked to use Moses's cell. His own was in New York or L.A. or any of a number bedrooms. Moses dialed for Alchemy, who talked as he drove.

"Trudy, I'm coming through in about six, seven hours. Staying one night." He hung up and talked to Moses. "She's an old friend. Did some of the first pics of the Insatiables. They paid for the down payment on her place. Now she teaches yoga and does nature photography."

"You mind if I ask how it went up there? I always wondered about that much isolation, if I could do it. I think so. Maybe ten percent of the time, because I want to keep that hope, I believe in God or an afterlife. I want to believe but..."

In the previous decade Alchemy generously shared his controversial opinions on politics, sex, drugs, and scores of arcane subjects in hundreds of interviews. When the Insatiables released *The Multiple Coming*, he didn't dodge provocative discussions about God or religion. He was careful never to reveal his personal beliefs (or lack thereof) and explained that the entire album consisted of different characters' relationships to faith.

Moses continued, "I'm thinking, if I survive this, I might try something like that."

"Maybe you should. Meditation is pretty addictive when you get into it. I got going on both dysphoric and euphoric hallucinations. I thought I had weird sleep patterns before, but this place messes you up on purpose, three hours here, three hours there. My brain got so disoriented that my nightmares were happening when I was awake and screwing with my daytime reality..."

Moses wanted to interrupt and ask about his nightmares. He thought about his own daymares. But Alchemy seemed to be on a talking jag.

"Desiree advised me to lower my adrenaline levels. I'm an action junkie. Have this need to get off on crowds and attention. It was hard to withdraw from phones and e-mails. Ended up cathartic. I'd do it all again, except..." He shook his head and exhaled a loud breath. "No sex. You're not supposed to, um, pleasure yourself. I was walking around with a permanent stiffy. I gave up. Haven't jacked off that much since I lost my cherry when I was a kid in Berlin." Alchemy paused and took both hands off the wheel, held them aloft and strummed an air guitar, gave a childlike "Woo—woo." He sang the Country Joe song, "And it's five, six, seven, open up the pearly gates...Whoopee! we're all gonna die...," as the car lurched perilously close to the edge of the road. Moses glanced down at what would be a thousand-foot drop, clamped his hand on the door handle, and clenched his jaw. Alchemy finished singing, retook the steering wheel, and jammed his foot against the accelerator. "Nathaniel, my mom's guy, used to sing me that song when I was a pup-star. Had no idea what it was about but it stuck in my head. Mose, it's going to be okay. I promise." Moses was only half listening, thinking that if Alchemy kept driving like a drunken Evel Knievel, any marrow transfusion would become moot. "I'm jet-streaming nonstop. I don't like it. I prefer to think before I talk. Not like Salome, who, you'll see, you never know if she's just channeling her DNA or is in one of her 'Blue Savant' periods, that's what she calls it. Ruggles got other names for it. You meet Ruggles?" Moses nodded. "You have to beware, sometimes you think she's out of it but she's just playing you. Now, Ambitious, you'll have to meet Ambitious, there's one cantankerous moth-erfucker who talks or punches before he thinks. If you call what he does thinking. He's PO'd at me now.

"Shit, though, almost six weeks of being a mute. Of nodding or shaking my head. I've have my silent periods but—phew. Mind?" Alchemy pointed with his right elbow to some bottles of water in the backseat of the car. Moses handed him one. "Thanks." Alchemy finished an entire bottle, then another. "So, am I what you were expecting?"

"Don't know yet. Hadn't thought about that."

"Ever?"

"No." For so many years Moses had imagined meeting his father, but he'd never imagined life with siblings. For some-one as introspective as he considered himself to be (and he had considered the possibility his father ran off with another woman), Moses was confounded by this omission. "Four days ago I had no siblings and a different mother."

"That is one mindfuck. Maybe it was too painful? You didn't want to miss what you could never have? Hey, Mose...You got a brother now." As was his habit, Alchemy renamed him. No one had ever called him Mose or Mo or Moe. "Mose" sounded romantic and sin-street tough, misleading perhaps, but so what, he liked it.

Alchemy was deified by the luck of the genetic evolution-ary hierarchy. It wasn't that he talked different, was smarter, more graceful, or even more beautiful than so many others, but he radiated an energy that no hype machine could manufacture. Moses had run across plenty of "stars" in New York and L.A., and instantly you could spot the ones whose eyes yearned, like a starving discarded dog, to be noticed and coddled, and yet would shoo you away if you approached them. Only a rare few possessed presence that commanded you to gawk at them. Alchemy had that specialness, charisma, magnetism, those overworked and abused adjectives that cannot capture or quantify the inimitable and illuminative qualities that transcend logic and language.

As Alchemy continued his monologue, Moses thought about the night he'd seen the Insatiables at the Whisky. As one of their encores, they jammed on a harder-edged version of the Lovin' Spoonful's "Do You Believe in Magic." Alchemy sang, almost beatifically, "The magic's in the music and the music's in me..." It was true, Moses thought to himself. He was *magic*.

As the Focus descended the mountain, Moses now hoped this magic man would not only transfuse him with his bone marrow; he longed to be blessed with a few sprinkles of Alchemy's miracle dust.

13

THE SONGS OF SALOME

It's a Small World After All

When we left the hospital, it was early morning. I could taste and smell Horrwich's soulsmell of overcooked hair dye. I told him to go home, that I wanted to be alone. I traipsed toward the Chelsea Hotel, where I knew lots of people. Just as I was crossing 23rd Street, I was in such a tizzy, I stooped over and an oncoming ambulance almost decapitated me. I didn't even hear the siren! Three, maybe four people grabbed me. One of them was Horrwich's photographer friend, Xtine. Aha—you could claim coincidence that at precisely this moment she would be crossing the street—she lived at the Chelsea. It wasn't. The second she told the bystanders we were friends, I knew she was *there* to help me. She seemed quite unflappable. I looked repulsive with my eye already black and blue and bandages covering the stitches on my face and left hand. "What happened? Are you all right? You were so radiant the last time I saw you. I'm sorry. I shouldn't have said that." She held my unbandaged hand as we walked. You could have knocked me over with one of Andy's wigs. "Please come upstairs to my place and rest."

People have this notion of the Chelsea as a roachy rat hole. (The wanton acts only took place in some of those rooms—such sweet decadence.) Xtine had this grand apartment with high ceilings and spectacular windows. Although they were cracked and it was damn drafty. She had installed a darkroom. I lay down on a futon in the main room while she boiled water for herb tea. I remember watching her as she sashayed across the wooden floor. Not dyke-ish at all. She had an alluring angular face with high cheekbones. Deep brown, small, almond-shaped eyes. Lithe but short. Her soulsmell was a pungent mix of cerulean blue and baking bread. Of course pure colors have smell, and sound, and taste. You've heard of the blues, as in the music? Alchemy wrote the song "Salome's Sensation Bluz" for me. It sounds like how I feel when I'm low.

I used to urge everyone, especially my shrinks, to get in touch with their inner sexual music. To get laid by loins that sing. All of my shrinks—men and women—needed to unbutton their crotches and screw more. Even my latest "caretaker" here, Dr. Zooey Bellows, with her soulsmell of fresh pineapple and steamy ice right out of the freezer that lingers for hours after she has gone, reeks of repression.

Xtine was the first woman to make my sex sing. Yes, we were lovers. Her photos of me were the ones that ended up in *Life*. Unlike any male photographer I've ever known, she could bring out my sexuality and vulnerability without it seeming porny or kittenish. Maybe it was the delicate manner of her touch.

I broke up with Horrwich and I began enjoying life. Sportfucking was fun. The only sport at which I excelled. Art was fun. Serious was fun. I put up one of my favorite shows at Gibbon's new gallery on West Broadway in '69. There were only a few galleries then. Paula Cooper, OK Harris, Cunningham Ward, Hundred Acres. I collected Do Not Disturb signs from dozens of hotels in dozens of languages, and I made paintings, collages, photos, all centered around Vietnam, Biafra, and the riots in Selma, Nixon and an American public complacently snoozing away.

I followed that up the next year with *This Is Not a Pipedream*. You know, playing off Magritte. I slept in the gallery and people watched me. Behind a curtain I did some pipedreamlike acts. Xtine filmed it. Andy had made a film called *Sleep*. His twin obsessions were ennui and celebrity. Me, I wanted to explore what happens in the worlds outside you and inside you when you're asleep, that in-between dimension of insomnia and slumberland when you think you are awake but you're asleep, and when you wish you were asleep but are awake. I wanted to record the act of sleeping in the gallery and how people reacted.

We filmed for the entire month. I wouldn't sell it. Same with the sketches I'd made from my dreams and of the people in the gallery. I told Gibbon that I'd hold on to the original video and all but a few of my sketches. I gave him some so he could pay his alimony and maintain his potbellied plumpery. I gave a few to Xtine and some other friends. I burned or hid the rest with the original films.

Then the good times came to a stop. Dad's emphysema got serious. He'd never quit smoking. I spent a lot of time at home. I needed to be there for him. Hilda wanted my help, although she didn't understand me. She believed that I'd grown into some kind of whore, though she kind of absolved me because

I was the spawn of a fallen woman. She wanted to love me unconditionally. She couldn't. Her eyes always scolded me.

Dad died fast and slow. Each day he withered just a little more until he looked like a shrunken bag of water and bones with two bulging eyes as his internal organs began to fail. He died of a squashed spirit as much as from the disease. We talked a little then. It was cleansing. In his luggy way, he told me how much he loved me.

"Salo, it made me so happy to watch you drawing up on the roof or just staring at birds and the sky. Or watching you ride off on your bicycle as free and determined as an osprey." At night, alone, I cried and cried, seeing this once powerful man reduced to where the simple act of breathing became unendurable. We buried him next to the baby.

I had to fend off Dad's Gravity Disease from seeping into me. Gravity, as everyone knows, affects water and the tides and our balance. Besides aging cells, there is emotional aging. An unseen force, an invisible weight that arises in the direst of moments and is the destroyer of so many strong spirits—my dad, and then Nathaniel, and even my Alchemy.

Alchemy. I *was* successful, in one wonderful way. Despite having me for a mother, or maybe because he had me for his mother, he was blessedly impervious in his young life to any major symptoms of Gravity Disease. He bled with the fluid of despair when Absurda, who suffered with a lifelong vicious case, died. But the intrusions of the Pretender and Laluna, Alchemy's traitoress entrancer, and all those stupid political demands, that's what did it. He couldn't run away like me. I survived because I flew off, went astray. He couldn't allow himself to do that.

Emotions have weight and force and mass. They are made of quantum-size, blood-dappled molecules existing in multidimensions. There are those who feel this weight more than others, and it shows on their faces. Some balance it out. Others get dragged down and become bitter and small people. Some become more generous in spirit. Some even go slowly mad. Gravity Disease is the death of cells exhausted by sadness and disappointment over a lifetime. The doctors have discovered genetic causes for so many diseases. No matter what they find they'll be stymied—they'll never cure them all, and new ones will arise. The raw pain of life is the true cause of Gravity Disease, and there is no cure for that except bodydeath. Those who suffer from chronic disease of the mind or the body or the heart carry tremendous emotional gravity. My disease began to weigh when my first son was stillborn and I blamed myself for his death. The heavier your gravity, the greater your wound. If the gravity becomes too great, your life force is crushed too soon.

It happened to Nathaniel. I miss him so.

When we met for the second time, in 1970, I was pregnant with Alchemy. I'd been hibernating in Orient. After what happened with the first baby, I'd suspended all drugs, drinking, screwing. I didn't want anyone's dick inside me, getting in the way of me bonding with my child.

Hilda was lighthearted for the first time since Dad got sick. For her, life was returning to the house. Xtine came out off and on, and Hilda was mostly cool with that, except when we played "Guess who's the father?" although I had a good idea who it was. We read aloud from our favorite books. I played music for Alchemy, everything from Lizst to Stockhausen, Holiday to Hendrix.

I visited Xtine in the city for a few days to nourish the unborn Alchemy with art. I was drifting through the old, old Modern when I got a little tired. I headed to a room where I could relax on a bench and began dreaming in the *Water Lilies*.

"Sniffing Monet?" I looked to my left, and there stood Nathaniel. He hadn't changed at all. I mean literally. It looked like he hadn't changed his clothes in four years. Still slightly motley, with short hair, a reddish-brown goatee, and gold-rimmed glasses. Scraggly jeans, beat-up khaki jacket, and a satchel slung over his shoulder. Just no camouflage cap.

"Inhaling the colors and letting him or her feel art." My eyes veered toward my mildly expanded belly and his gaze followed.

"Just as Urso predicted."

It took me a minute to remember Urso's insult about the "soupçon du jour," suburbia, and babies. Instead of teasing him about his need for a wardrobe consultant, I stuck out my tongue and tasted the air around Nathaniel. "Alchemy—that will be my child's name, boy or girl. Next to me is a man who has one of the purest soulsmells, but he just spit out a comment that is unworthy of him because it is not genuine. In typical male fashion, he does not understand that raising a child is an art at which most people fail."

He laughed and put up his hands. "Okay, I stand repri-
manded. I saw you in the Matisse *Swimming Pool* and you were
humming 'row, row your boat, gently down the stream...' not
noticing a soul."

"Communing with my child. Levitating out of my body,
exactly the way Matisse wanted us to do. It felt glorious. So, how
are you?" I'd kept tabs on his career the best I could. I'd seen
him on TV when that porcine-faced Mayor Daley had his cops
arrest him at the '68 Democratic convention in Chicago. I'd also
read a few newspaper and magazine articles by or about him.

"It's going better than *Time* magazine would have you
believe, but not so well if you're an American grunt or Viet-
namese peasant getting a napalm skin tan." Nathaniel had
been on the front lines of the Movement for seven or eight
years by then, but he still managed a well-balanced mix of rage
and optimism.

"I meant you personally."

"The life of a full-time revolutionary is a big gig."

"Unless you want me to go back to my dreamworld, you
have to *talk* to me."

"What do you want to know? I spoke at over a hundred col-
leges the last two years. Not as much fun as a rock star. Sure
as shit doesn't pay like an arms contractor for the Pentagon.
Still, I dig it. I guess I'm part of the new class of rev celebs.
Warhol's a bloodsucker, but I'm afraid he's right about fame
and its currency. I'd give up whatever minor recognition I have
in a second if the war ended. That's my life."

He shrugged and moved his satchel from his left shoulder to the right. "I saw your *Do Not Disturb* exhibition. Damn

good. I wanted to send you a note or something. You working on a new show?"

"Not seriously. Mucking about." I followed what came naturally in these situations, to say exactly what I was thinking. "Can you take some time off from bringing down the American Empire and spend a few days with me in Orient?"

Without answering, he stood up and then bent down to tie the shoelace on his combat boot. With his head tucked into his chest, he said in a muffled voice, "I'm sorry. Please don't say another word." He stood back up, about-faced, and scurried away.

Fuck, that startled me. And hurt. My reflexive action would be to follow him and give him hell. Just because he had all these political ideals didn't mean he could act like a dickhead. I tried to lose myself again in the painting. I couldn't concentrate. I canceled my plans and took the bus back to Orient.

Two days later, as I was painting the porch a vibrant gold, a taxi pulled up. Out bounded Nathaniel with a bouquet of sunflowers and a copy of *Catch-22*.

"Hey, so sorry, but a Clouseau showed up." That's what he called the Feds. "I didn't want him to catch me talking to you. It took me two days to lose them."

Nathaniel later discovered he'd made Nixon's Enemies List. He got hold of his FBI and COINTELPRO files during the brief time when the Freedom of Information Act was being enforced. I found out later they still didn't divulge everything.

We spent the first three enchanted days together—without having sex. He was totally understanding after I explained why I was so scared of losing the baby.

Also, I didn't want to rile Hilda. We'd been getting along. Nathaniel behaved with the cordiality of a 1940s gentleman caller despite his appearance, which resembled a *Mad* magazine version of an anarchist. He gave her the flowers and asked her to show him to the extra bedroom. Later, he treated us to dinner at the Yacht Club. His natural sweetness won her over. Me, too.

The day before he left, we went for a bike ride out to the fields by the Sound and I took him to my and Kyle's beach. Because the brush was so high, over six or seven feet, and thick, almost no one bothered to trudge through to the clearing. (The developers tract-housed my mini-Eden years ago.) Nathaniel chilled as if I'd slipped him a quaalude. He lay on his back. I took off his eyeglasses and put them by his side. He closed his eyes and, for the first time, remained still with none of his bouncing or body shrieks. Although we'd had some good talks, he hadn't revealed the deeper Nathaniel, the pure soulsmell that made him, and I yearned to hear it.

"Nathaniel, why do you do what you do? No Vietnam horror stories or superanalytical lecture on protest movements in America allowed!"

He pushed himself up with his palms and patted about for his glasses. I put them on for him and he straightened them out. He began to speak, almost apologetically.

"I told you my parents were blue-blood Americans, right?"

"That's all you said."

"I'm a descendant of Mawbridge Brockton on my father's side. He was a Virginia signer of the Constitution. My mother was old line Dutch, of the Van Buskdraats of New Amsterdam, who were entrenched long before the English docked their boats on Wall Street. They made a fortune in the "shipping trade," which meant slave trade. Down the line they became abolitionists. By the time we got to my parents, the money was gone and their main occupation was drinking and behaving like unappealing Southern gentry.

"My father could either be imperious or charming. Mr. Political Science Professor preened around the U.Va. campus like he was carved from one of its stone pillars, looking for boys to verbally emasculate and coeds to copulate with. My mom, when sober, was a petite, timid woman of leisure, who knew how to hold a teacup, precisely like so." He held up his right hand as if he were holding a cup with his knobby pinky sticking out.

"When drunk, which took up too many of her waking hours, she turned into a violent shrew. She once slung a shot glass and knocked out my sister's tooth for purposely using her maiden name when singing 'Who's Afraid of Audra Van Buskdraat?'"

I rubbed his back, and his posture, which had sunk, straightened up. "I know talking about yourself is not your style, but Nathaniel, that was about them—not about you."

"What is this, the Salome Rorschach?"

"If you like to think that, then yes. Tell me something that made you *you*."

He leaned back and gazed at the clouds breathing by, and sat back up. "When I was six years old, Adele, who worked as a cook for my parents and was very cute and very black, and my uncle George Turnbull Brockton—that's how he referred to himself and made us do the same—they had a terrible row. It was a summer morning and I was zipping around in my red fire truck in the backyard. I heard this scream and looked up and saw Adele and Uncle George entangled on the second-floor veranda. The next moment she came flailing to the ground. She broke her arm and a leg but survived. I never saw her again. I guess 'row' is Orwellian family-speak. Families perfected it before governments—"

"No politics. What happened next?"

"We were told that Adele was 'slow' and Uncle George had been attempting to persuade her not to jump. That was life among 'colored' and white in Virginia in the '40s.

"When I was fourteen, I had an argument with my father about the South's peculiar racism. I brought up Uncle George Turnbull Brockton and Adele, and said I thought they were having an affair. He shook his head condescendingly and told me I had a creative imagination and my notions of race and American history were silly and clichéd. I answered that he lived a life of privilege based on maintaining the racist status quo. Boom. He went to slap me across the face. My reflexes were quicker than his and I caught his hand in midair, and I just held it there. I'd never defied him before. I let go and he stormed out of the room. That fall it was, 'Pack your bags, Nathaniel. You're on the next train to Exeter.'

"The day I left, I went to say goodbye. Robert, one of the 'workers' in our family for years, was driving me to the station. I looked in on my mother in her 'studio,' already soused, some Charlie Parker coming off the record player while she gadded about in her free-form modern dance. I didn't even bother to interrupt her.

"I knocked on the door of my father's study and peeked in. He tilted his head up—I'll never forget the book he was reading, *The Lonely Crowd*—and said, 'Remember, you are a Brockton. Do not disgrace us. We'll see you at Thanksgiving.'"

Nathaniel's eyes were so bleak, I cupped his cheeks between my hands and placed my forehead against his and held it there for a moment. "It's because you are you and the way you were born—honest and good—that you do what you *do*." I kissed him. He tensed. An egret flew over and cawed—it was Kyle. I clutched Nathaniel's arm. "You won't hurt me. You're no homicider. I told Alchemy about you last night." The way I talked to and about Alchemy made Nathaniel a tad nervous. "Jesus, Nathaniel, people talk to God all the time, do you think they're all crazy?"

He laughed. "Yeah, I do."

"My baby is real and he can hear my voice." I kissed him again. I envisioned we'd end up together, at least for a while, when the time was right. I never would've guessed it'd take another five years! I wanted him then. The sex didn't make the highlight reel. I didn't care. Although he wasn't the father, I treasured the idea that Nathaniel's seed swam within me and the unborn Alchemy.

He left the next day for a college speaking gig. He promised to be in touch very soon. When I didn't hear from him, I told myself the untruth that I didn't care. Then I heard the news on the radio: The Feds busted him for dealing drugs and he jumped bail. I knew they'd set him up. I followed his

exploits the best I could from the mainstream and underground papers. I read a piece he wrote in the *Voice* and heard a
couple of taped interviews on WBAI. After almost a year I got a
call from a guy who didn't give his name. "Nathaniel says he is
sorry, but he can't contact you and he hopes you understand."
He hung up before I could get more information or say, "Send
him my love."

14

MEMOIRS OF A USELESS GOOD-FOR-NUTHIN'

Don't Know Much About History, 1992

After we left Collier Layne, I postulated we'd beeline it to the California surf 'n' sunbathing society. I mispostulated. I could get around the subway blindfolded, and my compass said Northern Boulevard runs east-west across Long Island, and if I head north I end up drowning in the Sound and that the East River is *west* of Flushin', but Iowa, Idaho, all them is the same. So I got no clue we'd sort of detoured in the wrong direction as Part II of the Alchemy Experimental Family Tour. When we stop for taking leaks and gassing up, I see a sign that says D.C. 30 MILES, and I think we're halfway to L.A.

"We gonna go have a cocktail with the prez? Got some advice for him from my brother and my dad. My brother got back from Iraq last year, and my dad, who was in Nam in '69, they love Bush and they think nukin' Hussein and taking the damn oil fields is the right fucking move." I think he's surprised I know who's the president and even more surprised that I'm clued in to Hussein and oil.

"We're skirting D.C. and heading to the Shenandoah Mountains. We need to swap cars. I need some clothes and cash or we'll be hitching to L.A."

He ignored my family's input on solving the Iraq situation.

"I still say we hit up the prez for some dough. His family's loaded."

"I don't take gifts from an Ivy League warmonger who once was Chief Spook."

"That's exactly the cheese balls whose palms I wanna tickle. Makes 'em feel superior and gets me on their good side. Besides, he's still the prez. Even you," I razz him, "must respect that." He just nods like he's keeping score of my answers. He had this way with everyone, almost never saying out loud that he is judging you so *you* couldn't call him on it, but I damn well sensed it.

He announces we're seeing Nathaniel Brockton, like he's the pope or maybe Ozzie Osbourne. I inquire, "Who the fuck is that?"

"Nathaniel's been my mom's main man off and on for years." I'm guessing they'd met at a biddy-bip-bippers convention. "He's been a leader in antiwar movements from Vietnam to Iraq. He just came back from Yugoslavia. It's unconscionable that we're letting that happen." I got no inkling of what we're letting happen. "He's a great patriot and the most *just* man I know."

"My dad and brother hate antiwar wimps. Me, too."

"Re-ally?" he says, all sarcastic. "Do us both a favor, don't argue politics with Nathaniel." Alchemy takes a sec, then mutters, "Or maybe I should tell you to *start* an argument, since I'm beginning to see a pattern of contrary behavior that is all too familiar."

"I'll take that as a compliment. So, why the fuck not?"

"If you want to spend the night listening to me and Nathaniel debate the intricacies of the failure of American democracy, be my guest."

"Nooo thank you. Where's the next stop?"

"Magnolia College. We lived here for a few years when I was a teenager. We, no, my mom was good here. For a while. Nathaniel took a position here because he thought it'd be a tranquil place for my mom."

We turn down this tree-lined road, and he tells me about the school and the campus and how it was founded by some lady named Sylvia Lancaster in honor of her daughter who died when she fell off her horse and whose nickname was Magnolia. The girl, not the horse. We turn down a road, and I see these gigundo three-story houses. Brockton's was painted with orange, red, and yellow boxes. Even then I could surmise that was a Salome job.

Brockton ain't there. The door is unlocked, so we slip in and take a few beers and some slices of roast beef from the fridge. The place is like some minimuseum with paintings and photos covering the walls. I was staring at a black-'n'-white with Brockton and a real young Dylan.

"He hung out with *him*?"

"Way back. A little."

"Ya meet him?"

"No."

"Who're all these others?"

He names the faces as we move down the living room wall. "Allen Ginsberg. Angela Davis. Abbie Hoffman in Chicago during '68. Joan Baez. That's a cover of *Osawatomie*, an underground magazine from the '60s."

I heard of Baez, she being Dylan's babe in her prime. I had a vague idea about Abbie Hoffman 'cause Pete Townshend clocked him with a guitar at Woodstock, but that's it. "Who's the dogfaced old fart with the funny eyes and big glasses who looks so cum-fucking happy nestling with all them young titties?"

"Jean-Paul Sartre. In Paris. Not sure when. The girls? His groupies, I guess."

I remember thinking, *If a guy that butt-crack ugly could get chicks, so could I.* Or maybe I should move to Paree. Alchemy was always giving me books, and he gave me some by that guy. Most of them are boring as a bologna sandwich except the one where the people get locked together for all time—sometimes I think that was us in the band.

Right next to the picture of the Frog was a black-an'-white of Salome in come-on-over pose. Her backside facing out. Man, she had a killer ass. Her face was turned profile with a beret tilted over her forehead. Alchemy nudged me. "Xtine took that. She took hundreds of photos of my mom. Some were for *Life*. She helped raise me, too. She did some great shots of the Dictators and Television at CB's way back. You want the rest of the magical history photo tour?"

We start inching down the hall, and I catch sight of some major spiders crawling on the ceiling corners, creeps me out. Alchemy stops and raises both his hands and touches the wall with his palms and fingertips, slowly like he's searching for an invisible portal. The wood is burnt and charred. "This is why my mom is now back in Collier Layne. She locked Nathaniel in his office"—he pointed down the hall with his chin—"and started a fire." He shook his head, half laughing in disbelief.

"Alchemy!" Brockton blustered in an accent that was a mix of Foghorn Leghorn Southern and Manhattan clothespin-on-the-nose hoity-toity. He seemed like a pretty old dude by then even if he was only fifty or so. In them early photos he was real skinny, but now he was lumpy with a potbelly. His face was full of lines like a scruffy old basketball, and his hair going thin and gray. He reminded me a bit of this nerd in grade school, Ronnie Nadler, who never sat still. Drove the teachers nuts. We call anyone whose body parts were out of control "Nadling." Brockton was a Nadling champ.

They shook hands, stopped, and then bear-hugged. In all the time I know Alchemy, there are only two guys I ever seen Alchemy bow down to—Brockton and Buddy Sheik. And, well, Laluna. I got plenty to opinionate about her later.

Brockton drummed his fingers against the wall. "I didn't repair it because every time I start missing Salome and want to go get her, I look at this and accept I can't take care of her anymore." Alchemy looped his arm over Brockton's shoulder.

"Nathaniel, my mom can make anyone feel horrible when she doesn't get what she wants, but you're the best thing that ever happened to her." They both shrug in a kind of holy communion of helplessness.

"So, who is your uncivilized-looking friend with the jaundiced mien?" He smiles like he done paid me a compliment. He reaches to shake my hand. I wanna show him uncivilized by rearranging his damn crooked teeth. I'm ignorant of what he means by "jaundiced mien" 'cause I ain't yellow eyed, so I don't shake his hand. I only says, "Hey." Alchy introduces me as "Ambitious Mindswallow, member of the Insatiables." First time I hear my full moniker de rock 'n' roll. I gotta admit, I took to it right away.

We move single file back into the kitchen, and Alchemy turns and tosses me a take-a-hike glance. I get the message. Magnolia is like some massive male fantasy camp. Seven hundred chicks.

This was my first up-close and personal view of the split between the truly rich and the rest of us. In the city you felt it 'cause of Park Avenue bullshit, but they don't flaunt it in the same way. Even after we made it and I become one of *them*, I feel like the snotass from Queens. Only in America could a farting, cursing juvee degenerate like me crawl from the sewer and into a penthouse.

I pass by the tennis courts filled with blondes and bouncing boobs. I keep going, sticking to the path. I hear the girls squealing and splashing down by the lake. I sense this is snakeville. Snakes is my kryptonite, so I make a U-turn to see this goddess babe on her horse galloping down a dirt road. A sign points BARN. I head to the stalls, which is fuckin' bigger than my folks' apartment. The babe who was riding and two others are brushing their horses. I'm trying to think of something clever, but all I can think of is the time when I was about eight years old. I had a crush on Suzy Balboa, who was having a birthday party at the North Shore Country Club. What a joke! Place stank like a bowling alley bathroom. My dad, Mr.

"Ricky, you ain't nuthin' but a useless good-for-nuthin' and will always be a useless fuckin' good-for-nuthin' loser," gives me his fatherly drunken advice. "Ya watch it when ya go inta the pool, 'cause they got a special dye that mixes with pee and chlorine, makes your bathing suit burn off and the lifeguard blows his whistle and everyone nyahs-nyahs at the dumb fuck with the tiny dick who peed in the pool." I never go swimming the whole afternoon.

Alchemy comes swooshing down the road in this '60s T-bird. It's gonna be our new ride. Was once Salome's. "How'd you find me?"

"A lone guy with shades, biker boots, and tattoos all up his arms is not blending into the local mountain foliage."

"I was just gonna make my move." I see he's already scoped the babes.

He ambles out of the car. "Go for it."

"Hey, these yours?" I ask suavishly.

They keep brushing, hardly looking at me, so I step closer. "I had a dog once, a German shepherd named Uzi." The girls don't react. Not sure they get Israeli firearms. "He do not live too long." (I'm trying to talk with no accent.) "My brother took him up to the roof of our apartment building and he threw his bone as far as he could off the roof, and Uzi chased after it, and *phfft.*" I wave my hands like I was reaching for him.

The girls look like they're gonna barf. Alchemy laughs and says, "He's kidding." He slouches up to the superbabe's horse and starts to pet it. "Big guy. How many hands?" I'm thinking, *hands?* Since when do horses have fuckin' hands? They start talking horse poop. He asks, "Will you be at the Magnolia

Patch later?" The girls giggle and glance at each other. He says, "We will. Around ten. See you."

When we get in the car, he is amused. "That was one classy bit of seductive reasoning. Uzi for a German shepherd? Why not Lugar?"

"Like it. Maybe next time. Truth, man, that's what happened to Uzi, though I left out that my brother spiked Uzi's food with PCP."

"And you listen to his advice on foreign affairs?"

"Hey, he been to war. Have you?"

"Yes and no."

"What the fuck's that mean?"

He don't answer right away. Then deep from one of those moments I come to call "Alchemy in Collidascope Land," he says, "Depends on how you define 'war.' Some people need to leave home to escape war. Some need to leave to see war. In the end, no one ever really leaves home and you're always at war. You're only rearranging the furniture. "

At the house, Brockton cooks about the best BBQ I ever ate. We're getting drunk and riffing on cars, movies, sports, only it keeps swerving to the serious-politico, and Brockton and Alchemy rant about the L.A. riots and President Bush being a WASPy sub rosa racist. Brockton's face is sliding from easy rolling to mean-motor-scooter drunk, and his eyes and lips go school-nun stern and his body stops bouncing except for him clicking his teeth and he finally asks me, "What do you think? You a Republican?"

"I'm a nuthin'."

"You're apathetic?"

"Let's say I'm noncommittin'." Alchemy, he forgets zilch and hears everything, 'cause years later he comes up with *The Non-committal Nihilists for Nuthin'* record. It's sharp mouthed, none of Alchy's hookie-dookie or political stuff, just us as a band.

Brockton looks like he's ready to explode on me. Alchemy sees it, too. "Nathaniel, cut it. He's only—"

"Nah, man, I can handle myself." Brockton's too old to smack, so I take an empty beer can and crush it in my hand. Brocton snorts at me. "Look, pals, I don't know all this crap like youse two, what I learnt in that shit hole where I come from is if you ain't committed to saving your own piddly ass, zero else means squat. Most of the people ain't got the dough to be committed to nuthin' but making their rent, and no one is sending them to 'horse-grooming college.' The way I see it, it's on such highly educated ass wipes like youse to make the world a better place for us dumb-as-nails lowlifes."

"Good rap, kid. You're no fool. In fact, you're pretty savvy. How much TV do you watch? How much tobacco and dope do you smoke? And your folks? Do they vote?"

"My dad says he's gonna vote for that Pro guy if he stays in the race."

"You mean Perot?" Nathaniel asks kinda snotty. "Why him?"

"'Cause he's different. He ain't one a them."

Nathaniel don't talk to me but to Alchemy. "See? Third parties, it almost doesn't matter what you stand for. Perot is a weasel with the money to promote himself. He's funny look-ing with a squeaky voice and announced his candidacy on CNN. He has no serious policy but, like the kid says, he 'ain't one a them,' and he's neck and neck with Bush and Clinton."

Alchemy nods and Nathaniel turns to me again. "So, Ambitious, will you vote for him?"

"I tolt ya, I'm noncommittin'."

"Nathaniel, he's not even old enough to vote."

"Am so. Am eighteen now."

"Hang on, guys." Alchemy decides to change the course of the conversation and disappears from the kitchen. He reappears with a book and starts reading:

> "Let's get the stones a throwing and the bombs a bursting and punch some holes in the souls of the monsters running the Military Industrial Oedipus Complex. It's no time to lay back, because if you do, you're going to GET FUCKED instead of getting laid. It's time to turn off the tube, turn on your heart, and change the world. Let them eat fire and burn!"

"Alchemy, stop."

He closed the book and laid it on the kitchen counter. "I'm still waiting for the return of Bohemian Scofflaw. Or, at least, your memoir."

"You'll have to keep waiting. The powers that bemoan the death of literacy do not care one whit what a dinosaur like me has to say." Brockton hangs his head and reminds me of Larry Bird when he was washed up and couldn't play no more. "I sent out the memoir to some agents at Distinguished Writers International who once represented me. The top agent of DWI called me all excited. They wanted salacious gossip. Not my thing. The self-indulgence trip leads to degradation and gracelessness." (In that regard nothing's changed in the thirty years since '92, 'cause they ask for plenty of gossip in this particular masterpiece. Only I got less scruples than Brockton.)

"Nathaniel, you think that's true of Rousseau, Nabokov, or even Fitzgerald in *The Crack-Up*? They wrote great memoirs."

"It was a different time and I am not them. I can't read *The Crack-Up*—it's both pathetic and bathetic." He runs his hands through his hair and ties it up into a ratty ponytail with a rubber band. "I'm a guy who, almost by mistake, wrote a book that caught the zeitgeist. Guys like James Simon Kunen or George Jackson, we're not true writers. I'll keep working the front lines. I'm going back to Sarajevo during the Christmas break, but as a writer, I'm done."

Alchemy gulps his drink and sits down next to him. "I can't believe I'm hearing this defeatist line from you. You always insisted that the personal is political."

"I said that all *politics* is personal. But all that is personal is not political. Your personal life can make you political, but that doesn't mean it has any meaning to anyone. It has meaning in our life choices: How we spend our money, who we vote for, or who we work for. It does not mean squawking about your mother's drinking problems, the finicky sexual diversions of your father, or your mate's emotional crises. My personal life is not for public consumption."

"I agree on that principle. What about a follow-up to *Tag*? Everyone loves Scofflaw."

"I can't get the voice right. Besides, I was full of hope back then. Now I'm a fifty-three-year-old earnest secular preacher who believes the bad guys are winning."

That self-analysis sounded perfecto to me. Alchemy cups his right hand into a loose fist and then rubs his nose with his knuckles, a sign I come to recognize meaning he is displeased. He takes another hit of scotch. Brockton ain't finished yet.

"Alchemy, you have it all: musical genius, business sense, beauty, and integrity, a true American mutt heritage. Use it wisely."

"I hope you're right. And I will. My word."

They stare at each other. I see that Brockton idolizes Alchemy, and Alchemy, well, he worships Brockton and becomes all smush-brained when he's within five miles of this good-for-good's-sake bullshit, like Brockton's his damn dad or the dad he wished he had.

"For now, keep in mind what Shelley wrote about poets being the unacknowledged legislators of the world. Your way will be the hardest challenge, but you can do it, the third-party way. Too many American artists have surrendered their ideals in favor of fame or esteem. All art *is* political, whether they want it to be or not, and by accepting these rules of the game, their art will suffer." He stood up, pretty whomped. "Anyone who says there is no relationship between art and politics is selfish. Or cowardly."

All of that bull, that's what led to Alchy getting involved with the Nightingale Foundation, which led to the Nightingale Party and him dressing up in his save-the-freakin'-world costume. It all goes back to Sir Brockton. Nah, that's not fair. It was Mose. And Salome. And Laluna. And me, too. And the masses. Truth is, he loved talking politics to anyone. Used to drive me up the fuckin' wall when we was on the road. Still, that don't matter either, 'cause in the end, it came down to all of us, what we wanted and what we put on him.

Alchemy glides into the living room, which is cluttered with magazines and books and record covers, and sits at this Steinway. He swings into Porter and Gershwin, which my grandparents loved, before he slides into this strange riff I don't know.

He catches my eye. "What's *that*?" I ask.

"It's 'Blue Monk.' Man, we're gonna have to teach you about music."

Brockton growls, meaning "good fucking luck." I was blown away by Alchy's playing and how he was like some music encyclopedia. I learnt a whole fuck of a lot from him and later Absurda and Lux—no bull, they was the bestest teachers anyone could've had.

Alchemy then slides into a smoother but complex set of chords. I see Brockton don't know it either and asks, "What's that?"

"Just something I'm working on." Years later, we record it as "No Master, No Messiah" for the *Multiple Coming* sessions.

Brockton tilts his head back, and I swear he looks like he's ready to bawl his fuckin' eyes out. When he recovers, he says to me, "Hey, kid, I'm sorry I went at you. Bad form. No class."

"No sweat. That was nuthin'. My dad would've popped me one for mouthing off to him." He shook his head at me like some holy-guru-y guy, but I still wasn't buying his Papa Bear act.

"Ambitious, you ready?" I nod. "Nathaniel, we're going to the Magnolia Patch."

Brockton, shaking his head, just blows air from his cheeks, "Alchemy, please make sure they're legal..."

All three babes showed at the Patch, and them girls, they wouldn't go all out, but they sure liked to gobble the rod. Alchy wakes me at like 6 A.M. and we light out for L.A. without bidding Brockton goodbye.

15

THE SONGS OF SALOME

Let's Do Naked Lunch

Last night I drifted back in time through my DNA; the power comes with being a sensate morphologist. I am descended from Greta, but we possess the mitochondrial genomes of our personal mystagogue, Salome. Not the Salome who served Herod and danced with the head of John the Baptist. The Salome who witnessed the Crucifixion, the beloved disciple who, according to Mark, sought out Jesus at the tomb to anoint him with spices. I engaged first with Big Mama Salome just after I gave birth to Alchemy, during an evening walk on the beach at Gardiners Bay under the half-moon. I stepped on a cracked shell. My heel began to bleed. From my blood flowed the stigma of my ancestor Salome. Not in bodily form but in the infinitesimal sparks of energy that forever live inside and outside of us. She communicated with me in words that were not spoken but heard. She introduced herself, before asking if I knew the Bible.

"Dad and Hilda read it to me as a child."

"Good. Young disciple Mark purposely misinformed the masses. Those male disciples are the most unreliable narrators in all history." She laughed. "Jesus was alive then, as he had been when they helped him off the cross. The Romans did crucify him. We announced his death at the time not because we wanted to start a religion but to fool the Romans so we could slip him out of Jerusalem to a safe haven. I helped him escape to Galilee. He hadn't arisen anywhere."

She didn't tell me that night, but later, that she slept with Jesus. There are intimations to all that in the Apocrypha and the Gnostic texts. Jesus was one carnal man. And he was a man—just closer to perfection than most.

Memory is planted in our genes for those who have the ability to commune with themselves. It will be proved that we can transcend our corporeal bodies and through our DNA traverse what you call time. I might or might not be "alive" when genetic historians prove that I am right, but I can and I have transcended "time."

When Alchemy was about seven months old, I decided he needed to be exposed to the only other living link to our lineage. He, his grandmother, and I needed to have a nice little group hug.

Greta had become more of a legend in some circles, and those who realized she wasn't yet dead proclaimed her the world's most famous recluse. I'd been splitting my time between Orient and Xtine's. When in the city I rewatched as many movies of hers as I could find, and I saw that the camera understood that she could never love or be loved, that her heart was broken—truly broken. All of those doomed soap-opera screen romances fit her so perfectly. Her eyes, her voice, her leaden walk belied by the erect posture that refused to fall under the burden of so much emptiness. I went on reconnaissance missions, tracking Greta's walking regimen. She often walked alone. Sometimes with a friend. If she saw me, she never let on. She would drift into the upscale antiques and thrift shops and then lunch at Aquavit, a Scandinavian restaurant, or Raul's, an unimposing bistro on Madison and 66th.

On an overcast late October morning, I said to myself, "Okay, today." I dressed casually in a longish black skirt, boots, a turtleneck sweater, and green poncho, and tucked Alchemy into his papoose. I followed her from her apartment to Raul's. I tried three phone booths—someone had stuck chewing gum in the first two coin slots—before I found one that worked. I wanted Bicks Sr. to accompany me, so I called his office on Park and 56th. I begged him to scurry touty sweety to 59th and Lex. I'd never done that before, so he felt compelled to come. I loved/hated New York in the late autumn. Still do. That's why I wanted to meet her then. More than winter, the dim fall light shrivels my insides.

I stood in front of Bloomingdale's window with the mannequins in perfect winter wear. The acrid perfumes from the lobby mixed with the Sabrett hot dog stand. The steamy smut wafting up from the subway station, the sobbing rubber from the gnashing wheels of the buses and taxis, the masses of jockeying bodies whizzing by all sounded like a thirty-three record playing at forty-five speed, which is how everyone walks in New York when it feels like rain but it hasn't yet come. The swirling cacophony made me want to strip and do an antimodern noise dance while balancing Alchemy on my shoulders.

I spotted Bicks Sr.—the man in the Brooks Brothers suit up the street.

"What is so urgent? Is something wrong with the child?"

"He is perfect." I took his hand and pulled him down the block. "C'mon, Bicks, earn your money."

The second we turned onto Madison, he slowed down and clasped my shoulder. "Salome, stop. I think I see. Why now? Why this way? This is a serious breach of protocol."

"Since when do I fucking care about protocol? If I asked, I doubt she'd deign to meet me. And if she did, she'd pick the time and place on her terms. If you catch someone off guard you get to their essence. If you accompany me, it'll be less awkward for all of us."

He sighed and his face turned pinkish. "Please, Salome, no scenes. No funny business."

"I just want her to see Alchemy. I assume she knows about him."

"If she'd wanted to meet him she would have told me."

"Since before I was born she's tried to manipulate me like I'm a cloying extra in one of her movies. I'm her daughter. I'm an adult. We're equals."

He looked into my eyes and understood that no lawyer's chicanery could dissuade me.

We arrived at the front of the restaurant. He halted under a rust-red awning. His cheeks puckered. "Bicks, if she turns you into such a coward, you can leave."

"Let's go," he said firmly. He took my left hand, led me down three brick steps and, ever the gentleman, opened the door to the restaurant. Immediately, we were hit by chalky air. Cigarette smoke hung below the dimmed lights of the low wooden ceiling with exposed pipes. Odors of garlic and pâté breathed from the walls. I thought about my dad and how he would've joked, "The food here sure must be lousy, otherwise they'd turn up the darn lights."

I spotted Greta sitting by herself. Her posture erect, cigarette in hand. She wore a tan double-breasted jacket, dark glasses, and a red scarf draped around her neck. Only years later have I come to appreciate the uses of neck scarves. The glasses were a bit of overkill for someone who wanted to be inconspicuous.

Raul, the restaurant owner, a squat middle-aged Frenchman, cut me off before I got within five feet of her table.

"Pardon me, do you have a reservation?" He pressed his hand against my shoulder. I figure the only way to deal with obnoxious people was to be obnoxious back. I blew at his hand as if were a fleck of dust and flicked it with my finger.

"*Ne touche pas, mon petit steak frites,* can't you see the baby is asleep?" I pressed Alchemy against my chest as his head rested on my shoulder. "We are here to see Lady Garbo."

Bicks tried to interrupt. I'd never seen the old bat so ruffled, sweating and *phumpfering.* "This, this is, Salome and her son who and she—"

"William, stop. We do not need you." Greta stood beside us sans sunglasses. "I think we can do whatever it is she has in mind by ourselves." She glanced at me, but her gaze ran no lower than my head and did not move toward Alchemy. I looked intently at her. Even she couldn't defy time or gravity. But despite the mudslide of flesh covered by too much powder and rouge, the face that millions had worshipped remained. Her voice, almost unchanged in pitch and timbre, carrying the freight of an aged soul with only the slightest vibration of the wounded, the perfect emanation of her silent screen presence. Only now, that distinct vibrato's ache had been replaced by a dull throatiness.

"Raul, we will be moving to a back table." The owner nodded and set out to move her handbag and prepare the table. She turned to Bicks. "William, you can go."

"Are you sure?"

"I will call you. Do not worry. Now, please." He bowed to her like an English butler. She turned to me. "I assume you prefer if it is just the two of us."

"Three." I dipped my head and my eyes focused on Alchemy. "He's not a year yet, but he is here and I will make sure he remembers this."

"Three, then. Please." She pointed to the table for four. She followed behind me. I offered, "Do you want to hold your grandson while I take off my poncho?" She shook her head. Raul held him. I sat with my back to a brick wall underneath posters of the French countryside. She sat to my left, facing the front of the restaurant. She asked if I wanted a glass of wine. "Yes," I said, "red." I caressed the still sleeping Alchemy's back while we talked.

"Do you want to eat?"

"Not yet."

She ordered the wine. The candle at our table lessened the graininess of the restaurant's light. I could see the broadness of her shoulders under her jacket hiding delicate bones. I shifted my spine and I felt my bones as hers.

The waiter brought my wine. Greta raised her glass but did not touch it to mine. "Chin." She sipped her wine but did not speak. I could not read her thoughts. Not for one second. I closed my eyes and inhaled her soulsmell. She had none! Nothing repugnant like a man's sweaty socks. Or remorseful like a European railway station. Nothing entrancing like an old jazz club. Nothing. Either my smell sense was experiencing some Electra complex block or she had no smell. I couldn't believe it.

I'd tragically miscalculated. She was right to have given me away, to stay away from me, and now, from Alchemy. Hilda and Dad had wanted me, raised me, and yes, we infuriated each other, but we always loved each other. And Hilda adored Alchemy. I don't think Greta loved anyone, not even herself.

Sitting there, I understood that Greta was not a narcissist. It wasn't that she was too big for real life, but much too small. And it scared me that my mother's machinelike detachment could become me, was the *her* in me. I hate that about myself, but it's never changed. I still can't control the on/off switch to my emotions. Even now, I prefer pain to numbness, to be too emotional than to be inert.

As Greta took an interminably long sip, swoosh, and gulp of her wine, my On switch snapped.

"Fuck this. If you won't, talk I will. This sleeping little child is your grandson. Do you care to meet him? To know him?"

At last her lips parted into that exquisitely doomed smile that hid, well, nothing. "Yes, but I cannot."

"Okay, I'm going. You're not human. You're not..." Instead of answering, she bent down, and out of her bag she pulled a hat. A red beret. She reached over and tugged it onto my head. "Perfect." Her face brightened; the gesture pleased her.

Suddenly, I pitied her. "You don't have to worry. You'll never see the headline, 'Garbo's Daughter Speaks' in the tabloids."

"I never thought that I would."

"I need to ask you one question and then I'm leaving. Who was my father?"

She lowered her eyes, sipped her wine again, and then stared directly at me. I'd hoped to see tears of reflection, the regret of a lost love, or even the flippancy of a one-night stand that ended with me. She sat there, unmoved.

"A man, a woman, a child... He once said I was like a glass rose and he was like a fossilized rose. You think you know the lovers in your life, but truly not." A slight sense of whimsy had slipped into her voice, but it quickly disappeared. "He's dead now. So it is impossible for a meeting, you see? There is no reason you need to be preoccupied with him or who he was."

I could think of a few reasons, more than reasons—my *right*. But I knew—never was she going to violate her personal philosophy of ultimate restraint.

I stood up and took off the beret and tried to hand it to her. She rebuffed me. "No, no, it is a gift."

I didn't want it. Yet I felt impelled by some outside force to take it. I struggled to put on my poncho as Raul rushed over to help. Alchemy, at last, opened his eyes and I kissed him on his head. I bent down so she could see him. Her eyes veered away. I moved closer. I tried to feel an odor beyond the faux essences of her makeup and perfume, to find her soulsmell. Again, nothing.

I placed my lips on hers. She neither kissed me nor pulled back. I whispered in her ear, "We could've loved you and made you less alone." I stood up, strode toward the door, and didn't look back. I regret now that I didn't turn around to see her face.

She was about seventy. She lived another twenty years. I could've gone to see her, but I never did. To me, she was already dead.

I was incarcerated here and heavily sedated at the time that she physically died. One day, perhaps a year or more after she passed, Ruggles squirreled his way toward my little *chambre d'enfer*, gnawing at his knuckles outside my door.

"Good Morning, Doctor," I greeted him. He had weaned me off the worst of the drugs by then. "Hmmm. You smell like you have a question. My olfactory senses are especially keen this morning. Your unpleasant question has the textured odor of the burned plastic of cheap shoes."

"Salome, you are right. I wondered, after our session yesterday, if you remember the time we discussed your mother's passing."

I didn't recall that session. But I had read about Greta's death later, in the papers.

Ruggles's face said he was appalled by my lack of reaction.

"Am I supposed to care? I don't." Unlike when Dad or Hilda or Nathaniel passed away and the weight felt like it was severing my heart from my body, I felt nothing.

16

THE MOSES CHRONICLES (2001)

Maybe We Ain't Us

It is no profound revelation to posit that we experience days or weeks or months in our lives that we remember as if they took place five minutes before. There are years that meld and dissolve as the memories race over us in seconds. Perhaps they stay fresh because we continually relive and reinterpret them. What is bewildering, often frightening, are the moments that we relive like cancerous lesions on the unconscious that turn a dream to a nightmare, or strike capriciously while lolling down the street. One would think that it was Alchemy's selfless act that Moses would remember most fondly or most distressingly from those first few months of their initial meeting. But no, it was not that at all.

Moses immediately got swept up as another passenger on the juggernaut that was Alchemy's life from the moment the Insatiables became an essential phrase in the cultural grammar in 1994. A ride that Moses would jump off and on for many years hence.

The fiery speed at which Alchemy lived his life was antithetical to Moses's contemplative nature and slow dialectic of reason, where he could spend hours deliberating whether to give a student an A or A–. Even though he had long accepted chaos and uncontrollability as the determining forces thwarting one's will and intentions, he always did his best to foresee the vicissitudes of life. The cloistered safety of a tenured job perfectly fit his self-image. Unlike too many denizens of the academy, he accepted that he was, at best, a concubine to the central culture. Even with the looming imminence of death, Moses speculated his worldview might change under the optimistic sway of Alchemy, of Alchemy's lightning-fast processes of both calculation and instinct. Could he rediscover the momentary, youthful adventurousness that had once led him to Israel?

As the Focus passed through Albuquerque and sped west along I40, Alchemy began assessing and planning the days ahead. "I have to call my managers." Moses dialed the number and handed Alchemy the phone. "Hey, Sue, I'm out... No, it wasn't exactly jail... Listen, I'm coming to L.A. tomorrow... No, to my brother's... Yes, *brother*... No, he doesn't want money."

They glanced at each other, smiling, while Alchemy held the phone in one hand and the wheel in the other.

"Not a cent," Moses said.

"Just my blood... Yes, I am sure. He's a professor. Sue, any change on Nathaniel?... Tell him to stop worrying and I'll either take him or go to the WTO protests for him... Sue, fuck my image... Yes, time meditating made me want to be more active... I'll see Nathaniel as soon as I can, but he can't tell my mom I'm out... I don't care about anyone else's e-mails or calls. Tell no one else for now." Moses flinched as the car swerved to the right. Alchemy didn't stop talking. "Right, not Ambitious or Lux. I can't deal until we fix up my bro here. Later." He hung up. "I assume it's okay to stay at your place in L.A. One night. If I go anywhere near my home, a snapping finger of stalkertude will be nearby."

"Of course. Um, I'm a little tired."

"No problem. Take a nap."

Moses tilted the seat back and gazed out the window. He regretted having spent so little time excavating the history of this part of the country. He envisioned a scene directed by John Ford, written by John Steinbeck, scored to Woody Guthrie, and photographed by Walker Evans—his mix of western myths conjoined into a false majesty. The true director of the early twentieth-century West was not John but Henry Ford, and the real producers were Harry Chandler and William Randolph Hearst. Maybe one day he'd even write an essay about this mix of myth and history, Moses thought.

Soon, he dozed off. He didn't awaken until they entered Gallup, a sun-scorched and desolate, mainly Native American town, whose streets and storefronts of liquor, pawn-, and gun shops were interspersed alongside the ubiquitous McDonald's, Pizza Hut, and Burger King.

Alchemy flicked on the radio and bypassed the harangues of Rush Limbaugh and Louise Urban Vulter. He settled on a station with Native American music, which the deejay interrupted to speak words neither of them understood except for the hyperenunciated English "Big Sale at Gallup Ford" and "NO Money Down" repeated about seven times. At the same second, they both cracked up. It was one of those seemingly insignificant moments that made them feel like brothers who had shared a childhood of birthdays and Christmases or Passovers, silly games and arcane TV shows, lost toys and cracked bones, angry fights with sorrowful partings, first loves and ruptured hearts, and alliances with and against their parents.

"We need gas. Way, way back we played two high schools around here, and there was a great Mex restaurant we ended up finding at three A.M. after doing peyote. No time to look, I guess." They pulled into the station. Alchemy ambled inside to get supplies and Moses pumped the gas. Then he called Jay. "Hey, I found him!" His voice burst out with a rare effervescence.

"Good, no, great. How are you feeling? Where are you?"

"New Mexico. We're driving. And I'm fine. Better than fine."

"Oh, Moses, I miss you."

"In less than twenty-four hours I'll be home."

"I'm so scared."

"I don't know why, but I'm less scared now. You'll see. He wants to stay at our place. Can you call Dr. Fielding? Tell my mom, too. I'll call her later. The phone service goes in and out."

"Alchemy's staying with us?"

"Yep. Tidy up my room, okay? He can sleep on the futon in there." He was talking too fast and out of character; he didn't absorb the meaning of the beats between her silences or the tremulous cadences.

"Moses, it's such a—"

"Look, it'll be fine. Jay, I'll... Shit, there's a small mob gathering inside the gas station. Love you, and see you soon."

Someone had a digital camera, and then everyone in the minimart wanted a picture with Alchemy. Moses stepped inside and Alchemy mouthed to him, "Wait in the car."

A few minutes later Alchemy came jogging out. He hopped in the car and tossed two plastic bags filled with water, Cokes, Gatorades, chocolate bars, doughnuts, potato chips, and pretzels into the backseat. He placed a copy of the *Star* on Moses's lap. It was open to two gruesome pictures of Absurda, one of her gaunt body, half naked with a needle by her side, dead on her bedroom floor and another photo of the obviously grieving Alchemy slumped beside her casket. The headline read, "The Tragic Last Days of the Nightingale."

"This is exactly what I wanted to get away from. Guy handed that to me so I could autograph it for him. I do autographs, and most of the people in there were respectful, but that is too much. *Too much.*"

"It's ghoulish."

Alchemy lifted his hands off the steering wheel and then grasped it hard with his long, agile fingers, his voice pleaded to no one but himself. "What the fuck do they want me to say? I couldn't save her. I tried. I fucking tried."

"I'm sorry," Moses said. He closed the magazine and put it under his seat. Alchemy pressed his foot down on the gas pedal as they sped back onto the 40. "Is this kind of crowd reaction typical?"

"Goes up and down. Depends where I am and if we've been in the news. It's part of the bargain and I accept it. I despise mewling celebs, but sometimes you just want to buy a few Cokes and potato chips in peace. Or be allowed to die in peace."

Or grieve in peace, thought Moses.

Alchemy lapsed into a turgid silence.

Moses didn't know the extent of Alchemy's tangled relationship with Absurda. He assumed that they'd had some kind of affair. They sped along for a long while with no radio, no talking, just the sound of the Focus's hissing engine and the roars of eighteen-wheelers.

Alchemy broke the silence by asking Moses to grab him another water. He drained the bottle and asked Moses pointedly, "So, what did you think of your new mom?"

"I didn't really meet her. I saw her. What I know comes from Dr. Ruggles. I wasn't prepared to confront her."

"Understood. If I'm still trying to get my head around the idea that you weren't stillborn, no telling how she would react."

"With what little I know, I can't separate the various dueling mythologies."

"Fabricate, bro. Family tradition."

"I sort of have done that, but now that needs to be refabricated. If I don't, I figure I'll have some kind of nervous breakdown. If I even survive this other shit."

"Mose, nervous breakdowns are also part of the Savant heritage."

"You? You worry about that?"

"Hell, yes. Sometimes I feel like I'm in a state of *perpetual* breakdown." Moses, unprepared for this admission, didn't know if Alchemy meant it or was just trying to make him feel comfortable in his new clan. "It's not just me or the genes. Famous people are the most unstable bunch you can ever meet. You said you're a history prof, right?" Moses nodded.

"How many of the people who had a tangible effect on the world were nuts?"

"Highly neurotic, most. Nuts, too many."

"See? And with a mother like Salome...how can I not worry about a breakdown every now and then?"

"Great, I'll add that to my list."

"Ah, Mose, yours spiked in your body. You're steady upstairs, I can feel it. You still have to meet our mother. After the operation, when you're stronger"—Alchemy's innate confidence that they'd be a match did not derail Moses's pessimism—"we'll both go see her. I need to spring her from Collier Layne again."

"I'd appreciate that. You said before that about fifty guys have claimed to be your father. You don't know him?"

"I guess you don't tread in the gossip troughs much."

"Depends what you call gossip. I read history books that are filled with academic-jargoned polysyllables dissecting Lincoln's possible homosexuality or Hitler's getting off on erotic asphyxiation while having someone defecate on him."

"That's what I mean about famous people being nuts. And politicians are the most craven 'cause they have the most power. Who was more twisted than the Adolf? Him getting dumped on makes sense to me. Was it a guy? Girl?"

"Supposedly it was his niece who did the dumping. I believe it."

"Me, too. And Abe, a lover of *man*kind, that figures. Why he'd have the balls to free the slaves. I bet being a repressed gay guy back then was like being an invisible Negro. Who knew that you history guys were such a lurid bunch? Good thing they didn't have the *Enquirer* or *People* back then, or you'd be out of business."

"It's not exactly a lucrative calling now."

"Back to your original question, I do know who my father is. We met when I was six and then again when I was thirteen. And neither of us had any desire to keep up the relationship. It's the one secret I've been able to keep from the predators."

From Alchemy's hard-edged tone, Moses understood that this subject was off-limits. But then he continued, "Our mom was pretty active and they had a one-night stand and, as she says, his sperm won." His voice was once again relaxed, intimate.

"So you don't know anyone named Malcolm Teumer?" Moses asked, not sure he wanted Alchemy to answer yes.

"Nope. Should I?"

"Guess not. He is my father. His relationship with Salome is a blank slate to me. He married my mom and then split on us when I was two. Never seen him since."

"Mose, you got the double, no, triple whammy. No wonder you got cancer."

"What do you mean?"

"Oh, it's that Salome, she's got these theories about disease. Don't worry, she'll tell you all about it."

Moses didn't respond right away. He wanted to meditate on cancer and his "whammies" and how Alchemy spoke with such equanimity about their crazy mother and his own barely known father.

In the enveloping sunset, the Focus hiccuped up the mountain pass from Sedona, which, in twenty years, had transformed from pristine landscape to a tourist town dotted with signs for the Vortex Inn and the Crystal Rubbing and Convergence Committee, before arriving in Jerome, a former copper-mining town. Jerome remained less New Age commercially corrupted than Sedona. As they neared Trudy's home, Alchemy asked almost offhandedly, "Hey, you want me to see if I can hook you up? Trudy might have some friends."

"Um, I—"

"Sorry, Mose, that's trespassing. Upon a moment's reflection, I sense it's not your gig."

"Nope. Not my gig."

"I respect that. I've partied with musicians, athletes, politicians, and civilians like you, and they all were fucking their brains out before crawling home to wife and kiddies. I'm not into subterfuge." Although he didn't sound like he'd completed his thoughts, Alchemy paused. "I didn't mean 'like you,' Mose."

"No, I understood."

"Okay, good. I've been to shrinks and I've always been exceedingly cautious when it comes to their analysis of me. Most accuse me of being a sexaholic or a hedonist with intimacy issues. Fine. I counter that they have a control problem and most of them are envious and the others are phonies. I'm just doing what most guys, and women, too, would do if they had the chance. I do my best never to hurt anyone. I never coax. You wanna dance? Great. If not, cool. They got to know I don't promise more than one night of dancing before I bounce."

"Bottom line, though, how many women...I mean all those rumors of the legions, they're not an exaggeration?" Moses figured one injudicious question deserved another.

"Well. No. The answer is too many and not enough."

"Come again?"

"Oh, hell. What BS." He mocked himself. "That's my standard response: 'Too many who just wanted a quick fuck and not enough who were about love.' Come on, who buys that? I get more love than anyone deserves. I got all the intimacy I can handle in the band. You get to know the other members better than you could ever know your wife. Being in a band is like being married. My loyalty is to Absurda, well, shit, was, and Ambitious, and Lux. My mom, Nathaniel, Xtine. That's it. And now—maybe you." He paused and let the promise or threat of that remark reverberate. "I'm thirty years old. Maybe someday I'll change and want a wife and kids. Now, no way."

Alchemy slowed the Focus as they neared the two-street town. He stopped in front of Trudy's adobe-style house, which stood atop the mountain overlooking Sedona's red rocks to the north and Prescott's Verde Valley to the south.

Trudy greeted them in her kitchen, where she was cooking dinner. She was in her midforties, much older than Moses had imagined, with a pretty, kittenish face and brown-and-gray-streaked hair. She gave Alchemy a loud smooch. She served them two of Alchemy's favorite entrees: buffalo burgers and veggie lasagna. After dinner, Trudy showed Moses to his room on the first floor, and then she and Alchemy mounted the stairs to Trudy's bedroom.

Moses called Jay and got the machine. He left a message. Then he called his mom.

"So how are you feeling?" She asked in a taut voice.

"I'm good. Very, very tired but good. We should be in late tomorrow afternoon."

"Jay told me. We're all frayed and stressed. She's so distraught that she didn't even come over to swim and have dinner. She made your appointment with Fielding for the day after tomorrow."

"Fine," Moses said perfunctorily, now worried about Jay.

"Moses, are you still angry with me?" He heard her inhale deeply on her cigarette. He wanted to nag her about quitting but held back.

"I told you I wasn't angry at you and I'm not now. But Ma, you need to control your nag genes." Again came that poisonous word, *genes*, which had once bonded them but now divided them. Neither one responded to its new meaning. "I'm not going to let forty-plus years of love and devotion change anything because of this. Got that?"

"Yes," Hannah said, not quite convincingly.

Too enervated, Moses refused to play the cajoling game. If he answered with a hint of uncertainty or impertinence in his voice, the conversation would continue in a circular fashion for hours. "Mom," he said in an even but firm tone, "I need you to be strong for me now, the way you have been all of my life. Okay?"

Hannah, satisfied with Moses's answer, allowed the conversation to end on a note that signaled a truce in this new phase in the war of parental territoriality.

At around eleven, Moses heard a commotion in the front room. He stumbled out to see Alchemy fully dressed and with guitar case in hand, while Trudy talked on the phone. "We're headed over to the CopperPot bar on Main Street," Alchemy said cheerily. "Come by, if you're up to it." Moses took the accompanying pause to the invitation to mean that Alchemy expected him to come.

"You go ahead. I'll meet you down there." Feeling both obliged and curious, Moses got dressed. By the time he strolled outside, half of Jerome's four hundred inhabitants, like characters in a '50s zombie movie, were marching in lockstep toward the CopperPot.

Moses sat next to Trudy, who had saved him a seat. Alchemy, perched on a stool on the tiny stage, Gibson guitar slung over his shoulders, gulped a beer and puffed on a cigarette. No doubt this appearance would hit the still-embryonic Net. Apparently, Alchemy couldn't handle five weeks with no sex and no adulation. As the crowd in the bar swelled, Moses felt, as he had that night at the Whisky, the oceanic presence that was the public Alchemy, and what it promised: *I am your dream, and in me our dreams merge as one.*

He began abruptly, "My homage to Mr. Hemingway." Alchemy started strumming and nodded slyly in Moses's direction.

Irony and pity
Oh so witty
A little Aristotle
in a bottle
The son not only rises
it also surprises…

Was Papa havin' fun
when he wrapped his tongue
'Round his gun, say ... hey,
please blow me ... away ...

He spoke as if talking to an invisible presence. "Because I never thought we could do justice to Roky and Lou Ann, so now..." He effortlessly slid into a song called "Starry Eyes."

When he stopped singing, Alchemy smiled glowingly at the audience. "As some of you know, I'd been in solitude for five weeks and five days until I was rescued. In fact, if anyone asks, I'm still not here. Tell 'em it was an impersonator, goes by the name of Dusky Goldplate."

His fingers meandered on the guitar strings for a while before landing on a Leonard Cohen paean to youthful need and hope. Unlike Cohen's husky Old Testament chastising drone, Alchemy's voice flowed out like a hymnal with sweet and tortured resignation. He let the last notes linger before he addressed the audience again.

"I wrote this during my recent monastic vacation. I've never sung it aloud before so it's a virgin ride for all of us. It's called 'Mystic Fool.'" He stooped, picked up his bottle and finished his beer. "For Absurda."

Hey, careful there, pretty boy,
Let's sturm und drang
Up the good brew
And take on the entire crew.

But don't putsch me too far
'Cause when hugs turn to shoves
I'll be making war and love
With my gun an' guitar

She left without a good night kiss
Staring at the human abyss
I'm searching for the last note
Of god's silent song
To carry me along
Carry me, carry me, carry me, please carry me...

The room pulsated with a man-on-a-high-wire tension. Alchemy closed his eyes and bowed his head, and almost everyone found themselves in their land of private laments and regrets, with the echoes of Alchemy's voice to carry them along. A drunken guy yelled "Chicks and Money!" and another chimed in "I Wanna Be Seen!" breaking the spell. Alchemy unclipped his guitar strap. In seconds, a gaggle of women, young and old, surrounded him. Trudy tapped Moses on the shoulder. "Let's go." He arched his eyebrows quizzically. "I'm tired and he's gone for the night."

"You're cool with that?"

"Have to be. He's Alchemy."

In the morning, more than a little concerned about Jay and why he hadn't heard from her, Moses called and woke her up at 7 A.M.

"Hey, where were you?" Moses heard his voice dart out with a mix of accusation and fear.

"At the gym. A late Pilates class. I didn't want to call you last night in case you were asleep."

"My mom said you are distraught."

"Distraught? What should I be, a happy idiot?" Now Jay's tone was accusatory, petulant.

"No, I'm not saying that. But there's some hope now."

"I'm sorry. I'm just anxious. I'm so glad you're coming home."

"Me, too." To lower the tension, and keep up some pretense of normalcy, Moses asked about Jay's meeting with her latest demanding client. They made more small talk and Moses promised to call her later.

Alchemy strolled by alone while Trudy and Moses were having breakfast at the Flatiron Café. Trudy teased him with lighthearted jests unique to those who have had a long friendship punctuated by casual sex. "Did you play Romper Room teacher with the *leetle* girls?"

"You could say that. Gave them some, um, breathing lessons. I advised them to take your Tantric yoga class so they can learn new positions from the expert."

"Thank you," she said sarcastically, "but *that* class is full. No beginners."

"I wouldn't call them beginners. Not anymore."

Trudy placed her palms together in front of heart and closed her eyes deferentially, "Namaste, my master."

Alchemy placed his palms together in front of his heart and bowed his head slightly. "No mistakes, dear guru."

Their game over, Alchemy asked Trudy to take some photos of him and Moses side by side, which she did. "Unless I call, please don't release them. And then only one mag, *People* would be my first choice. I want Mose here to have his privacy until he decides otherwise."

Moses took the wheel for the first few hours, while Alchemy napped. When they stopped, Alchemy called Sue Warfield; his hunched shoulders and low-toned voice made it clear he didn't want Moses to hear this conversation. Moses bought the supplies this time.

Alchemy drove the last four hours while they listened to the radio and spoke about Moses's illness. The conversation lacked any mention of moms, dads, band members, women friends, or potential nervous breakdowns. At first Alchemy's distant, almost detached manner discomfited Moses. In time, he realized there were many Alchemys, and that trying to comprehend or predict his behavior was probably best left to astrologists or cultural prognosticators.

As the Focus cruised along the I10, the brothers contemplated their own theories regarding the psychic rumblings of what was then the middle ground of American society: a seemingly pleasant world held aloft by the repressive rules of black and white, right and wrong, and where all questions have answers, no matter whether the physical plane was a canvas of sorrowful grays and unending rows of stolid, protective redbrick apartment buildings, developments of dingy doublewides, or shiny new tract homes in brown deserts.

At a fairly young age, Alchemy had determined that those rules and those tired or monumental edifices contained the foul dust of the American dream. Under the surface seethed resentment and paranoia—sentiments that alternately exploded and imploded in a needful catharsis every few generations, often in wars in far-off countries—and at that moment, unbeknownst to either Alchemy or Moses, was about to explode again. But even before a new screaming comes across the sky, both had their own explanations for the complexities of their America. Moses sensed the unseen viruses that contaminated the collective soul. Yes, he had specific ideas on how to remedy the virus, from passing a one hundred percent inheritance tax to doing away with private education and eliminating the electoral college. What he believed America needed most was a constitutional convention.

Moses didn't have faith in himself to change much of anything. And now, with his illness, he yearned only for the cocoon of his home with Jay.

Alchemy, too, felt his country had gone astray, and would, if he had known them, agreed with Moses's propositions. Alchemy didn't think in terms of political policy bullet points. He believed America was destined to plod recklessly into the future before it eventually imploded upon itself, unless someone with grander foresight and vision came along to change the course of history. And he had a pretty keen sense of who that person could be.

17
THE SONGS OF SALOME
Spy vs. Spy

The bicentennial sissy boom-bah God Bless America blitzkrieg and the anti-rah-rah blather of the downtown scene made me almost want to be... French. I ingested some mesc on the 4th and traipsed to the river. With the fireworks exploding inside and outside my body, I envisioned what I'd create for my mid-September show.

All summer I hid in my studio in Orient as if a two-millennia-old and long-searching dybbuk had ascended. I painted bright and dark landscapy abstract visions of the dying bucolic, pristine landscape of farms and marshland of Orient—brilliant greens, autumnal golds, scorching summer whites, and winter Savant Blue. Yes, there is a color bearing my name. Two colors, in fact. The work was more emotionally tactile, sensual, and visually subtle than anything I'd done before. I titled the show *Flowers, Feminism, and Fornication.* Only Xtine had been privy to my studio until Gibbon came by from his Hamptons home. He erupted into a hissy stomp, "This isn't Salome Savant art!" Like I would ever listen to him.

"Taunt piss, Murray," I answered.

Of course, money trumped misgivings, so Gibbon promoted it in the Hamptons over Labor Day weekend. I went to the city to generate noise for the show. New York in the mid-'70s was still fun, in a deranged sort of way.

The city was undergoing one of its periodic skin sheddings. The Fillmore closed and the hippies fled, taking their colors with them. Downtown dissolved from an LSD light show to a heroin-cocaine black-and-white muck, a studied, cool sepia wash. Lost was the mix of hedonism and purpose, and the hipguard became a superficial veneer of seriousness covering too many grabby, frivolous poseurs. My city shrank down to the area below 14th Street, while the rest went from excessive to anorexic before the next "rebirth" in the early '80s, when it became obese and bloated once again. Except for the AIDS ghettos. Those sections of the city smelled emaciated, like dried bones, and looked like the washed-out browns of old leather pants. It happened again after 9/11, when the city's hungry ghost arose from the crater in search of its soul.

Xtine babysat Alchemy. I donned a leopard-skin *Sheena, Queen of the Jungle* top, a sheer rust red skirt with a belly-dancer's belt and bright red hot pants underneath, stilettos, and an orange scarf wrapped around each arm, and went to Blind Lemon Socrates's reading at St. Mark's on 10th and Second Avenue. I doubt old Pegleg Peter Stuyvesant, who is buried under the church, appreciated the moral turpitude of the Poetry Project's congregation.

Socrates was already in midread when I fluttered into the courtyard. I nearly choked on the cigarette and pot fumes.

I'd arranged to meet Alexander Holencraft, a young sharpie who dubbed himself a "writer." I'd been floozying around a bit again. Less spontaneously because of Alchemy, but asceticism was never me. Holencraft scribbled copy for the ad agency of Yorkin & Stunkle. We met briefly during a photo shoot with Xtine, and he'd asked to do my head shots. He had bigger plans for me and for himself; he was in the formative stage that would lead to his becoming a major tastemaker. He later invested in Manhattan real estate and started the celeb magazine *I, Me, Mine*, which he named after the Beatles song, but devoid of any irony. He claimed he'd written the famous poster phrase "The night the underground comes uptown" about Lou's Alice Tully Hall show and coined the term "cool hunter." I'm guessing he was in the room with the guy who really created them.

An SRO crowd jammed into the room, which was hotter than a Chinese laundry and about as well ventilated. I stood at the back. Sitting behind Socrates as he read was Anne Waldman, the poet who ran St. Mark's, and the novelist Ally Sendar, who'd written the foreword to Socrates's new novel, *The Floating Prickhouse*.

Socrates slumped over the podium, almost hidden in his oversize houndstooth jacket. Occasionally, he'd glare and take a puff from one of the three cigarettes he'd strategically placed—one in his right hand, one in an ashtray on the podium in front of him, and one hanging off the edge of a chair. The skin of his oblong face looked like mottled mercury and cooled lava. His thick-lensed glasses made his eyes look bulgy. His voice drizzled out with an Olympian sneer of superiority.

Crazed child Nub pulls his metal casquet over his loopy eyes. He munches on Chilean eyeball apples. Sucks skin-sap through his braced teeth. Comes up from behind and spits in my mouth. Mumbles "Protofacsists' liquid dick sauce. Your favorite." He pulls my harness and rams his Tin-Can-Do into the hard crack of my buttocks. Yvulva announces, "It's the midmorning of mindfuck. The pubescent mind-melders are at the gate."

Socrates didn't acknowledge the applause and whistles. Leaning heavily on his ivory-handled black cane, his body teetered like a rickety wooden-and-barbed-wire fence. He disappeared through a side door and out of sight.

Holencraft shot me a flinty glance from the opposite end of the hall and waved me toward him. I smiled and waited for him to come to me. From behind, a hand tapped me on the shoulder. I swiveled around and was about to give this Mr. Blanding's guy my icy-eye brush-off when— Nathaniel! I wanted to jump up and wrap my arms and legs around him. I knew better. He'd changed his wardrobe. No more outfits designed by Che & Fidel, Inc. Here stood Mr. Suntanned Middle America in navy blue chinos, a lime-green Lacoste polo shirt, and brown loafers. He looked so out of place among all the pallid faces and their ordained black garb. (Is "garb" short for Garbo or garbage?) His hair was shading gray, cut short and neat, his face clean shaven below new, black-framed glasses. He caught me staring at his nose, which stuck out like a half-blind plastic surgeon had pinned a pink rubber eraser on the end of it. "Yeah, I look like Cyrano but without his poetic gifts."

His soulsmell, even after all the hiding and unjust charges, was imbued with the pristine and hopeful odors of a newly gessoed canvas. As I was about to give him a polite hug and verbal pinch, Holencraft clawed the knotted end of my bandana and leaned over to kiss me. I backed away.

"Alexander, this is uh, um..." Nathaniel interrupted me—

"Philip Noland, an old friend of Salome's."

"I need to talk to Philip. Alone."

Holencraft gritted his perfect teeth in displeasure. "I thought we had a rendezvous."

"We agreed on a potential meeting to talk of my modeling for you. Nothing more. Nat...um...Philip is an old friend."

Holencraft eyed Nathaniel as if he were mentally photographing him. He looked perplexed—how could I choose to go with this doughnut-bodied big-nosed guy over a stud as handsome as him? "Okay, but I will hold on to my ticket to Salome's back room."

I lightly grazed his arm with my fingernails. "Alexander, I know exactly what you want. Don't piss me off by acting like a proprietary male beast, or you have no chance of cashing that ticket. Behave like a good boy and you never know..." I grinned voluptuously and turned away.

I tucked my arm around Nathaniel's waist. "I'm so happy, really, truly happy to see you."

He removed my arm and backed away from me. "You must be very careful. Meet me at the Odessa in half an hour. Please, do not tell anyone where you are going or who you are meeting."

I waded through the crowd doing my kissy-kissy come-hither-to-my-show. Then I headed to the Odessa, a favorite of

Nathaniel's but not of mine. The place oozed with the odor of foam rubber, or maybe fossilized blini, bulged from the torn, red plastic seats. In lieu of tablecloths, a thin film of syrup, sour cream, applesauce, french fry grease, and coffee covered each table. The waitresses, graduates of the Joseph Stalin Charm School, took pride in wiping the tables down so that any free crumbs landed on your lap. Flies performed kamikaze missions first on your meal, then on your face.

Nathaniel was seated at a back booth. "So, Mr. Philip Noland, what the hell have you been up to the last five years? Besides running from the outlaws who call themselves the 'protectors of the people' and having some defrocked doctor enhance your nose."

"Mainly that. Being a nine-to-five blender. It's been heavy times for me. I live in the Southwest. So-called enemy territory. It's not. I've realized that Nixon's 'silent majority' is ready for us, if we learn how to talk to them without sounding so snotty."

"Being restrained must give you some major case of heartburn. Like this food."

"Delectable." He rolled a blini around his tongue. "Salome, for your own good, I can't divulge too much. They are still running black bag ops on me. Even though we got rid of the Trickster, and the Congress is investigating the secret government, I don't trust them to end it."

We left the Odessa and strolled around Tompkins Square Park. Nathaniel's once nervous energy now seemed just nervous. His eyes were fidgety and his gait furtive and unassured. The park was still seedy with the homeless living in cardboard boxes. The street kids blasted dump-truck-size boom boxes. Everyone seemed high on something, be it junk, glue, or spray paint fumes.

"Don't worry, Nathaniel, this is a cop-free zone."

"Yes, these are our Untouchables. No one gives a shit about them. Maybe I should move here and they'd get off my case."

"Why'd you risk coming back? Because you needed to see me?"

"If you knew how often..." His eyes watered ever so slightly. "My mother has incurable liver cancer. My sister is taking care of her alone. I need to be with them." He sighed. "My lawyers are close to swinging a deal with the Feds."

"Oh, Nathaniel. I am so sorry."

"Me, too. Only, after decades of imbibing any fluid containing alcohol, it's not a surprise."

At the corner of 9th and B we stopped in front of the Christodora. A miniskyscraper built in the '20s, it had fallen into a shambled shell of itself—like me, now. After a fire, the city had it condemned. It got a makeover later, in the '90s, with the "whitey-fication"—that's what Nathaniel called gentrification. I often snuck around the boards and yellow tape and foraged inside, peeling off the blue-and-white wallpaper with its images of St. Christine and collecting ornaments for ready-mades and collages.

"Let's go in." I stuck a finger through the belt loop of Nathaniel's pants and tugged at him. We stepped over two grizzled fellows with their bottles of Thunderbird couched between their legs, sleeping shoulder-to-shoulder in the doorway. The ground-floor rooms were shooting galleries lit by candles. The higher you climbed, the emptier it got. A few rooms were lit by the sudden flash of hash pipes. Light from streetlamps flickered through the cracked windows. We climbed the staircase to the ninth floor and found an empty room with a view of the East River and Brooklyn to one side and the World Trade Center to the other. We made love, which, this time, was dreamy. He understood the pleasure of my pleasure in being multiorgasmic. After, I climbed onto the sill facing south toward the river and the Statue of Liberty. The sky, a mix of Wolf Man–movie blue-blackness and low, foamy white clouds with a peekaboo moon imbued the city with an eerie tranquility. Nathaniel squeezed me against his chest.

"I want to go with you. I don't want you to disappear on me for another five years. I'll even skip my show." He smiled almost sardonically. "What? Are you living with someone? I don't care."

"No, no one else. It's been impossible for me to keep up a relationship. I've had to move and I can't tell the truth to anyone"

"I already know the truth, and I'm my own movable fiesta."

"Salome." He bowed his head. "If the Feds make a deal, I hope to get some time with my mom and then it's off to prison. If not, it's back into hiding. It's the opposite of your razzmatazz New York life. No readings or openings. If you dress like this," he teased, "*you* might get arrested."

"I can do it. I can. It'd be good for Alchemy, too. You have to meet him. You'll love him." I could tell he was thinking, *You can't and why would you...for me?*

"You'll see. I can do it!" Suddenly, I began to tear up. He thought I believed he didn't want me to come with him, but no, I was overtaken by a moment of clairvoyance. Over the next few days I needed to spend whatever time I could with him.

He wouldn't divulge where he was staying, but we rendez-voused the next day and went to the Met with Alchemy. As we strolled into the Impressionist room, these two teenage girls ran up to Alchemy. One of them ran her fingers over the smooth skin of his perfect face and practically undressed him with her gaze. Nathaniel whispered, "Is it always like this?"

"Yes." I didn't think much of it. Little girls, women, old queens—they all wanted to fuck him. No one ever said it aloud, but I could always smell lust in all its pleasant and nefarious variations. Incidentally, or maybe not so incidentally, the Collier Layne psychvoyeurs have often gone shrink-style ballistic (no yelling allowed) at my blasé attitude toward sex. Though they've tried to conceal it, a few of them almost popped their penis out of their pants when I elaborated on some of my sala-cious anecdotes.

The next day Nathaniel took us to the baseball game at Shea Stadium. Alchemy's first. He was so excited. I drew pic-tures of the field and drank beer that tasted like vinegar. On the subway ride home, Nathaniel gave us—mainly me—his fulmination on why standing up for the national anthem was some form of collective brainwashing. It irked him that he had stood up, against his principles, because he couldn't afford to be singled out. The born explainer needed to explain to someone. He smelled like my dad's old leather-bound encyclopedia when he got on one of his unending explain-the-world ragas.

We got off the subway at 23rd Street. Alchemy and I were going back to the Chelsea and Nathaniel to wherever he was holing up for the night. Alchemy reached up and hugged Nathaniel, and I thought, *Hilda is always telling me Alchemy needs a man around. Maybe she's right.*

We arranged to meet the next day at Fanelli's in SoHo before going to see my new work. The opening was the following Saturday.

Alchemy and I walked blissfully cross-town to the Chelsea. The desk clerk handed me a note in an envelope from the firm of Bickley & Schuster. "Be at my home at 11 A.M. Urgent."

This was a first for Billy Jr. All of my previous interactions, and those of Dad and Hilda, had been with Bicks Sr. I wasn't one bit anxious. It'd been a few years since I'd seen Greta at the bistro, and I thought maybe she'd discovered a dose of grandmotherly devotion and desired to see Alchemy. So I took him with me.

Billy Jr., his wife, Lorraine, and their ten-year-old son, William Bickley III (sweet kid, Billy the Third) all lived in the same building as Bicks Sr., on 64th Street off Central Park West. Right around the corner from the West Side Y, a notorious gay pickup spot, and probably where Bickley Sr. did his queenly business. Billy Jr.'s apartment was, like so many Upper East and West Side digs, *Town & Country* austere, immaculate. Beneath the tasteful furniture and accoutrements, I sensated the encrusted scum of immorality.

"Thank you for coming on such short notice." The lilt in Billy Jr.'s voice betrayed his real sentiment, which was, "Take a cyanide pill, why don't you?" He led me down the hall and we stopped outside two closed doors.

"Lorraine," he called out to his wife, "come fetch the boy and have Marcella prepare some milk and cookies for him." Lorraine was a thin woman ten, fifteen years younger than Jr. She reached for Alchemy's hand. "He's adorable." Alchemy eyed her with some suspicion. I bent over and whispered in his ear, "It's fine. Don't let them take you out of the apartment without me."

Billy Jr. opened the doors. We entered a study with floor-to-ceiling bookshelves on three walls and, on the fourth, a bank of windows and a brick fireplace. He pointed to two peppermint-green-and-white striped divans. I kneeled on the left divan, leaned my arms on the seatback, and took in the expansive view of Central Park. This Philistine, I'm sure, never appreciated its beauty.

He lit a cigarette and asked if I wanted one. I declined. He remained standing.

"*Junior*, where is your father?" He was about fifty then and moved with the audacity of a once healthy frat boy gone soft and paunchy. He was a homicider. His putridity contaminated anyone close to him.

"My father is turning seventy-five soon. He's semiretired to the family compound in Palm Beach. It is out of deference to his wishes that I am speaking to you."

Despite or maybe because of the visceral indecency of his work, I never felt like Bickley Sr. judged me beyond the difficulties my existence caused him and his "client." But Billy Jr. considered himself superior to me.

"Junior, you smell like you have a question." His question had the offensive odor of rotten eggs. "So what is it?"

"Why did you bring the boy?"

"I thought *you* were the boy."

"Don't be snide, Salome. I know all about you."

"You think you know me. All you know is what's in some crackpot file that I'm not even allowed to read." We glared at each other. "And if you mean my son, Alchemy, Greta's grandson, I thought perhaps she wanted to see him."

"She has no desire to see him or you. None."

"That was not your intended question, was it?"

He asked, almost giddily, "Why are you seeing Nathaniel Brockton? Don't try to deny it."

"You little prick. What you really mean is: Will I help you send him to jail? Junior, see this?" I stuck out my fuck finger. "You suck it until it squeezes out of the pinhole in your skinny dick."

"Your insults will not help him. He is being arrested at this very moment." My fury at his arrogance overwhelmed the sword thrust to my heart. I leapt up and moved closer to him. "You know what Diogenes said about a rich man's house?"

"No, no. I don't."

"He said that the only place to spit — is in his face!" I launched a gob that nailed him in his right eye.

"You crazy cunt — "

He lunged at me as the door swung open and this not-so-jolly giant, who must've been listening, lumbered in. Jr.

had got me around the neck and I was clawing his face. The giant tossed Billy Jr. away and grabbed me with his glommy, Cyclops-like hands. His ring dug into my arm. He lifted me as if I were a feather duster and dropped me onto one of the divans. He was too massive for me to kick or bite and do any real damage.

"Miss Savant, please do not move." His voice, stern with me, switched to agitated contempt as he turned to Jr. "Bill, you should go wash up. Come back when you've regained your self-control."

The galoot stood well over six feet, dressed in a green poly-ester suit with a ridiculous handlebar mustache and a '70s crew cut. His soulsmell reeked of larceny and fired gunpow-der. He turned back to me.

"Please excuse Bill, he is not always the most mature of men. Miss Savant, you must understand that your response, despite his tactlessness, was most unwomanly."

"Your definition of unwomanly, not mine."

"Let us agree to disagree about that for now. We asked you here today to consult with you on a vital matter. To help you avoid trouble for yourself."

"Are you threatening me? I haven't done a fucking thing wrong."

"I agree you've probably done nothing illegal. Which is dif-ferent from wrong. Now, our purpose is to inform you that Nathaniel Brockton will be arrested today. I am asking you, for your own good, and for that of your son and your mother"—I sensated when he said "your mother," he hadn't meant Hilda—"to spare them pain and embarrassment, to refrain from seeing Brockton when he is imprisoned. Also during his trial, if there is one." I realized he knew much more than I first suspected.

"Is there a deal? Is he surrendering?"

"I am not at liberty to answer that. There are forces at work, and some of them would deem you unfit to retain custody of your son if you were to cosset a criminal and an enemy of America such as Brockton."

"He's a patriot. If you believe he is an enemy, then you are the enemy."

"Miss Savant, as you said of yourself, do not presume to know me."

"So fill me in, then. You a Fed? CIA?" That face, which looked like a drunken sculptor had pasted it together from used coffee grounds, didn't reveal a damn thing.

"Let's assume I work for the government. Our country is one in which people are free to disagree as long as they do not break the law by distributing illegal substances or acting in a violent manner to destabilize the constitutionally established order."

"Nathaniel never dealt a drug in his life. And he does not advocate violent revolution."

"That will be decided by the justice system."

"Fucking bullshit. You and Billy Jr. with your illegal spy games, threats, and self-righteous attitude. Since you are so concerned with protecting Greta—"

"Miss Savant, we are here to speak about Nathaniel Brockton. I may be able to ask William to work with you regarding other matters, but first you have to work with me." Obviously, Papa Bicks was playing some version of puppet master.

"Depends on what you mean by other matters. You tell me who my father is and then maybe we can 'work' with each other about Nathaniel."

The phone rang. Junior must've picked it up in another room. A minute later the doors burst open and he came charging at us. "The bastard disappeared." Billy Jr. turned to me. "Did you talk to Brockton last night after you got my note?"

"Bill, shut up. Just shut up." The galoot curled his upper lip and sniffed through his large nostrils in absolute disdain. "Goddamn incompetent. Sh-eet. Miss Savant, I must go. For your own sake and for the sake of your child, please stay away from Brockton if he contacts you. We will talk again." The two of them left the apartment.

Lorraine and Marcella the maid brought Alchemy to me. Oblivious (willful or not) of the atrocious machinations of her husband, Lorraine complimented Alchemy. "Your son was playing our piano. He plays splendidly. He's quite precocious."

"Thank you, Lorraine." I wasn't sure if there was another implication beyond his musical ability. "What's the name of Bill's friend?"

"Oh, that's Laban Lively. He's more of a business associate than a friend."

"Of course," is what I said, thinking, *How lucky you are to live in Blissland!* We got the hell out of out there right then and took the bus crosstown. At 68th Street, we took the 6 train down to Spring Street. I checked Fanneli's. Maybe he'd left a note. No. So we walked over to the gallery. I asked one of the gallery assistants to take Alchemy back to the Chelsea before I strutted outside. If they were watching me, I didn't want to appear afraid. I hailed a cab, and some Russian coot picked me up. I told him to keep driving around SoHo.

Nathaniel never showed up.

I'd never felt so lonely or helpless. I'd had plenty of men come and go—a few meant more than others—but they never reached inside *my* soulsmell. Nathaniel certainly wasn't the best looking or even the best lover, though he became more skillful under my tutelage. But he could be silly and smart, and unlike so many others who went on a charm offensive until they got sex and just became offensive, Nathaniel accepted me for me and remained true to himself. Sitting in a room while he read and I sketched, or in an abandoned room in the Christodora— those times with him and only him, I felt safe from myself and the forces of the dark matter. Even as he grew despondent by political defeats and frustrated by his inability to end my "episodes," he was always the kindest man, in all respects to all people. He didn't parade around like some famous do-gooder in public life and become a double-dealing whoremonger in private. In the end it was a stroke that killed him. But Gravity Disease corroded his cells.

Xtine was too smart to offer superficial salves for my oozing sore-of-a-self. She took special care of Alchemy. I spent a lot of time at the gallery hanging and rehanging the show, hoping Nathaniel would reappear. I heard nothing from him or the Bickleys.

The night of my opening, I forced myself to don my party mask, wearing a black cocktail dress and a jacket I pastiched out of an American flag, cut from the bastard cloth of Abbie Hoffman and Jasper Johns. Xtine was Alchemy's "date" for the night, and he'd be sticking by her side at the gallery, so I felt safe in disobeying my usual preopening injunction—no drugs, no drink until the after-party—and snorted a couple of speedballs Holencraft had brought to the gallery. I had no idea what to expect.

"Decorative." "Soft." "A total regression." Those were the rehearsed phrases lip-synched by the pandering class. Myron Horrwich sniggered with his new student appendage by his side. Les Tallent's remarks emasculated me like no one else's: "Retinal painting is dead and you will not be the one to resurrect it."

Andy, who would've been perfectly cast as Tinker Bell, looked mortified and slinked away. It wasn't the real Andy. My theory is that after he was shot in '68, there was no "real" Andy Warhol, just five skinny guys with bad skin wearing silver wigs who showed up everywhere. The real Andy had moved back to Pittsburgh and skulked around, hardly leaving his room with five TVs playing twenty-four hours a day.

After Andy II or III sylphed away, Leslie tapped his foot, until I finally answered. "I thought you were more sophisticated than your average critic!" The art world is as provincial and cliquish and mean-spirited as the corporate world so many artists despise. Which is pretty damn funny.

Ezekiel Panti, a critic and cohort of Leslie's, joined the flogging fray. "Salome, I admit that these are beautiful, but my question is, So what? Beauty without meaning is meaningless, and for art to matter in this age, it must have meaning." He stroked his goatee with his pig-in-a-blanket fingers and positioned his weight forward as if he was about to make some grand pronouncement. "I'm a Duchampian, you know..."

"I was one, once. Now I'm just a simple beautician."

Panti didn't crack a smile. Maybe he'd heard I'd nicknamed him Smarty Panti. He was oh-so-proud of his PhD in philosophy from Brown, and he panted after girls like a neutered dog.

We were in a stare-down when Xtine, without Alchemy, her mouth and eyes wide open, came rushing through the crowd and whispered in my ear, "There's some Southern-baked golem in a brown suit in the office who says he has to talk to you. Now."

I understood immediately. Lively.

I shoved Leslie and Panti out of the way and hurried to the office, Xtine trailing closely behind. Alchemy was playing his harmonica for him. Lively did a rather disgusted double take when he saw my flag jacket but held his tongue on that subject.

"Miss Savant, I won't dilly-dally. We've arrested Brockton in Michigan. He was fleeing toward Canada. I want you to hear this from me because I'd much appreciate your cooperation. It would benefit us both. You know there are some people who believe you aided Brockton's escape."

Alchemy sensed my depleted hope and sudden heartbreak. He got up and bit Lively on the leg. In the midst of my pain, I laughed. Lively, incomprehensibly, seemed paralyzed, almost intimidated by Alchemy. I pulled him away and he clutched the bottom of my dress. "Please don't cry, Mommy. I'll play you a song. Please."

I gripped his hand. "You go now with Xtine back to the Chelsea. I have to do something that may take a while." I hugged him hard. I kissed Xtine on the cheek and whispered that she should take him to Orient Point if I didn't call her in an hour.

"Lively, I'm sorry." He looked pissed. "This is a big night for me, so can you wait here about ten minutes? I need to take care of some business. Then I will cooperate. I won't run. Deal?"

"Deal." He put his massive hands in his jacket pockets and bared his primitive incisors. Almost as an aside, most assuredly as a threat, he said, "We have two men outside."

What happened next? The drugs, the hotwires have all conspired to muddle my memory. From what I remember and heard from others, I ducked into the closet where they kept the supplies and borrowed a pair of box cutters. I snuck up behind Lively and slashed his back through his suit. Almost in slow motion, he buckled and fell to the floor. I ran out of the office and barreled through the crowd, then stopped in front of a canvas. I ripped two long gashes from top to bottom. I did it to another piece, and another.

Because of my previous work, some people (including Tallent, Gibbon, and even Horrwich, for fuck's sake, who should've known me better) thought it was a performance. They thought I was making a "statement." They started applauding. But they stopped when I took the cutters and slashed one thumb, and it began to bleed. I felt no pain yet and took the cutter in that hand and sliced it from cuticle to wrist. I still have five-inch scars on each thumb. People started gasping and yelping at the spurting blood. Finally, Gibbon yelled, "Stop her! STOP her!"

Lively, who was bleeding through his thrashed suit jacket, and his two henchmen came ramrodding through the crowd like football goons, knocking everyone aside. Holencraft claimed he put himself between Lively and me because Lively had a murderous gleam in his eyes.

My last sensates from that horrendous day are of Alchemy screaming "Mommy!"—Lively had not let him and Xtine leave—while one of his agents bear-clawed my five-year-old son as he struggled to save me. Lively's men pinned me to the floor.

Lively (whose wounds were superficial) and Billy Jr. worked out an agreement so I wasn't prosecuted for any crimes. I received a ticket for my first vacation here at the Collier Layne amusement park, with a bonus package of drugs and rides on the electroshock roller coaster. I was never the same after that stay. Never.

18

MEMOIRS OF A USELESS GOOD-FOR-NUTHIN'

On Your Mark, Get Set, Go, 1992–1994

I was one of those New York snots who bought the whole la-la land as a town full of Jell-O heads and faggots, as in wimps, not homosexuals, though there are plenty of those, or Mexies who can't speak English no better than me, which like everything about L.A. is true and not. There was some hard-core shit going down. Parts of the town still smelt like a giant ashtray after the '92 riots, which blew up six months before we got there.

As we drive into L.A. that first night, Alchemy goes all hookie-dookie again. "This city—underneath the spit shine of Hollywood—is a phenomenal metropolis with a cursed soul. At first glance, too much of the architecture is graceless, without symmetry, and they keep tearing down the inspired structures. The homes on the coast should be planned so the mountains and the sea meld with the man-made landscape. No one is a better architect than Mother Nature. Ambitious, whether you look at the surface or below, you'll see that L.A. is America's future."

My mom had two books in the house when I was kid, *The Joy of Sex* and *Jonathan Livingston Seagull*, and I says, "Alchemy, you sound like that gooey-brained Segal guy floating above us all."

He laughed. "Yeah, I guess, sometimes I am gooey."

We'd been driving fifteen hours straight, when we pull up to the Pantera Rosa. Yeah, the song of the same name is about that dump. Was a former "Beaner bar," off the 10 and Olympic Boulevard. A pink wooden shack outside and black and murky inside like a murdered body is hidden in the ceiling. Was a few artists living in the hood, though mostly working class and bangers. They tore down the Pantera around 2000 when the hood got ritzy, but we was long gone.

Falstaffa and Marty live in the apartment above the Rosa, which they used as their office for an, ahem, "car service" delivering "packages" to movie and biz types and the platinum card kids from the private school down the block. Some of them and their parents was our first fans.

Falstaffa, a 350-pound tough Tijuana Santería princess, lumbered out to meet us. With her buzz-cut orange hair and tattooed forearms and thighs, and a switchblade-sharp fuck-you sneer, she gave me the willies. Wrongo. She turned out to be the biggest-hearted no-crock-a-shit person I ever met. We did a shitload a laughing and partying together before the hep C got her.

She picks up Alchemy and twirls him around like he's no heavier than a picked-clean chicken wing. Out preens Marty, a four-foot-eleven Mick midget. He smacks a kiss right on Alchemy's butt. When Alchy introduces us, Marty squeezes my hand so hard it's like he's trying to break the bones. I'm squeezing just as hard back when this loopy boxer comes streaking at me and jumps at my back. Marty lets go and orders the dog, "Get the Fuck Over Here," yep, that's the name to which he answers. I'm thinking, *My life is forever gonna be a three-ring freak show.* Alchy informs everyone that I'm his bass player. I don't protest about nuthin' right then 'cause I am so damn tired.

The next day Lux Deluxe and Absurda drop by. Lux I'd heard of as the drummer in the Hip Replacements, a punk-funk band of black and white guys that had an indie hit with "I'm Your Black Doorman." Turns out Alchy penned them lyrics. Lux's spangled up in a fringe jacket, bling hanging from everywhere, and Frye boots. I want to tell him that Hendrix been dead for twenty years. I find out later he wants to tell me that Sid Vicious been dead for almost twenty years! We got a good laugh out of that one. Lux has a style and swagger like a western hero, only black, old-fashion strong-silent type. He introduces Absurda, with her vacuum-sucking eyes, natural blond hair, and swooshy bangs, Goth makeup and an itchy-bitchy walk that says she *needs to fuck.* She's just my type—lanky and tight and all attitude. I figure if she ain't with Lux, all chicks are Alchemy's or wanna be Alchemy's, so I lay back. While Lux and Alchy are huddling up, I ask Absurda how she met Alchemy.

Her speaking voice sounds like a clarinet with a cigarette in its mouthpiece. She was born and raised Amanda Akin in Fond du Lac, Wisconsin. She left at eighteen and met Alchemy at Juilliard. I don't volunteer that we had a coupla interns from Juilliard when I was at Performing Arts and I hated the bastids.

"Alchemy was only seventeen when he started. Finished at twenty. I left because I couldn't take the hypocrisy, and despite the lip service, it wasn't as progressive as I'd imagined. Guys were still getting the preferential treatment and I was just getting buzzed by Sally Timms and Kim Gordon, and the forevers like Marianne Faithfull and Chrissie Hynde. I transferred to CalArts. Much hipper and less testosterone heavy."

Alchemy never breathed a syllable about the diploma stuffed in his back pocket 'cause he thought it would ruin his rock cred.

"Bet he also never told you he joined the army?"

"Fuck no. He seems like a, pu—ah—"

"Pussy? I got your number Mr. Ricky-Tough-Guy." So she did. "Yes, he enlisted. When Salome freaked again, they had to let him out before his time was up."

That almost explained his crazy "yes and no" answer about being in war. I'm beginning to see this guy is full of surprises. When I ask him later about this army shit, he starts lecturing me that everyone should serve in the army or do some kind of service as their patriotic duty.

We plan to start rehearsing later in the week. The first rehearsal I pick up my Strat 'cause I ain't no second-fiddle bass player to a chick. Absurda hooks up, too, and eyes me like "You wanna go?" so I start playing and she mimics whatever I do. Then she starts leading, and, well, I got to give it to her, she could flat-out scorch that baby. First her Flying V and then the Winged Nightingale that Fender made for her. Falstaffa fronts me the money for a bass. I learn to love it.

Alchemy and me are crashing over the Pantera, though he ain't here that often. He never had no problems bouncing from bed to bed. He told me that growing up with Salome made him feel like no place and every place was home. You know the phrase "any port in a storm"? For Alchy, it was just "any port." He claimed he found something beautiful in every woman and that gave him comfort and hope. It sounds like a load, but it wasn't. And even when he was rich and went loopy over Laluna and moved to Topanga, he didn't feel totally settled.

A coupla weeks later, me and Alchy's drinking down at the Pantera. I been thinking about scoping him on Absurda, only he beats me to it.

"So, are you going to move on Absurda or not? Better do it before long, or it'll be too late."

"Whataya mean?"

"Come on, man, I see the way you're lusting for her."

I despised him when he spoke like he had that superior insight from a voice that told him all. "You or Lux ain't done her?"

"Can't speak for Lux, but they are certainly not together now. As for me, nope, not even a kiss."

"Why? 'Cause she done so many guys?"

"If my mom heard you say something so dim-witted and sexist, she'd squeeze your nuts so hard they'd turn to Silly Putty. The rules of getting laid: Approach sex with some sensitivity. Women have a right to fuck as much as we do without being called whatever epithets flash into your head. And remember this, if done right, they enjoy it as much or even more than we do."

"Scratch the Alchemy doubletalk an' answer my question."

"Okay, I 'ain't done' her. So go for it, but remember, she's like my soul sister. I'll be watching."

A couple weeks later after we been rehearsing all night, she and me head down to Tacos Por Favor and I'm stuffing my face. I notice she hardly eats, and I ask her, "You a puker or just don't like food?"

"Neither. I get ninety percent of my calories from gin and cigarettes..." She licks them cat's lips a hers and meows, "the other ten percent from hot, creamy cum. Now Ricky, can I have a taste?" and she eyes my enchiladas but I don't think that's what she means. She pulls out two hits of X and sticks one right on my tongue. We hook up for the first time. It was hot. I mean *hot*. We done shit I never done before. I'm dissin' myself by admitting this, but hell, I was a kid and not that experienced.

We'd ended up at her room in the house she shares with a bunch of losers in this old three-story firetrap in the Rampart district. I am starting to see L.A. is huge, and there are hoods like Rampart, which feels sorta like Flushin'. The TV makes the whole place out to be either Beverly Hills or Compton. Ain't true at all.

The next morning she is dressing to take off to her waitressing job at Barneys in West Hollywood, I ask, "We an article now?"

She grins and shakes her head, "No, we're a preposition..."

"What?"

"You meant an item, not an article. Never mind. What do you want us to be?"

"A particle... If ya promise not to go all teachy on me 'cause a the way I talk."

She kisses me and holds my hand, Catholic school girlie–like. "I won't do that to you, Ricky." She never got used to calling me Ambitious, and she's the only person, after I get to L.A., who I let call me Ricky.

A few months later, I finished my last drop for Marty at around 5 A.M., that's how I was earning my keep, and I'm gonna crash at the Pantera that night rather than head to Absurda's. Alchy, he wanted zip to do with that shit, and because he's allowed Falstaffa and Marty the privilege of being in his inner circle, he don't have to earn his keep. The Pantera was closed so it was just me and Marty at the bar drinking. Get the Fuck Over Here is snoring on the floor. Falstaffa is upstairs sleeping, and we figure Alchemy has found himself another bed for the night. About three beers in, Marty asks, "How's it hanging between you and Absurda?" His voice punches out like he's six feet, not some putz who comes up to my knees.

"Hangin'."

"You know why Alchemy named her Absurda Nightingale?"

"Yeah, 'cause of the crazy bird squeals she gets from her guitar."

"More like the squeals she makes when she's sucking on some guy's bazooka. And she's sucked plenty."

"Yo, dwarf dick, tell me she done you."

"Meaty enough so I deep-throated her 'til she gagged. Absurda, she's so horny, she fucks like a man."

Suddenly, there's a spitting noise in the doorway that leads up to the apartment. Marty starts trembling, bleating, "Alchemy, please! I was just shittin' him. You knew I was just fuckin' with you, Ambitious, right?"

Alchemy calmly strides over. Marty is shivering. Alchemy lays his hand on top of Marty's head. He holds it there. Marty is bug-eyed. Not breathing. Alchemy coolly says to me, "Pack up. We're leaving." He slides his hand down Marty's forehead and over his eyes and gently closes the lids.

19

THE MOSES CHRONICLES (2001)

Just a Family Affair

Alchemy parked the Focus in the driveway, and Moses felt his body relax. He was glad to be home. He cherished the womb-like solace he found in the sanctuary of his and Jay's olive green stucco house.

From the small front yard Moses called out, but Jay didn't respond. His cell phone rang. Moses answered it. "Andrew Pullham-Large for Alchemy." Moses tossed Alchemy the phone and hurried inside, his panic meter rising. He found Jay asleep in their bedroom. A barely touched bottle of water, a half-filled glass of white wine, and her mother's jeweled pillbox containing a dozen or so of his Xanax sat atop the wooden bedside table. Her body expanded and contracted with her slow, sleeping breaths. Moses sat on the bed beside her and gently rubbed her tanned shoulder.

Her lids opened, glazed over by a film of white plasma. Her tongue sought to dampen her dry lips.

"Jay, what the hell is going on?" He eyed the pillbox.

She placed her hand in his. "Oh, I'm just scared and I love you so much and..."

"It's going to be all right." He gently touched her cheek with his right hand. She inched herself upright and leaned back against the pillows. She reached limply for the bottled water. Moses handed it to her. Jay tilted her head slightly upward, shook her hair so it flung back, and took a very long drink before she spoke.

"It's not that. Well, yes, it is that. Is he here?"

"Yeah, outside, on the phone."

"Moses, I have to tell you something. Did he..." She exhaled, then exhaled again even more deeply. Her hands began to shake. She released her hands and drank more water. Moses took her hands in his and steadied her. Only then did he begin to comprehend this space between sounds and what they intimated—

"You and him?"

"It was nothing. Meaningless. Insignificant."

"A one-night thing?"

"It was *so not serious.*"

"When?"

"It started before I met you."

"And ended?"

"When I met you."

"How soon after we met?"

"Soon. I don't remember exactly. Soon."

Jay, who had remained free from the increasingly mangled sexual web of his "family" was now intractably and unalterably linked to Alchemy in the one way he could never have imagined, and now could never forget.

"Kasbah rented the Dresden for a party and Randy Sheik invited me and introduced me to him because of the art connection."

He stopped hearing her words and descended into the suffocating space of a daymare.

Moving with a graceful locomotion that radiates sex, he approaches her at the Chateau Marmont bar for what she knows will be the last time. Before they finish the second drink, they've tongued their way to an upstairs room, where immediately his mouth sucks her ass. He whispers—I want you here. The head of his "most glorious cock in rock" reaches virgin spaces. Moments later, under the shower's driving water, she takes him inside her mouth. Finally, hungrier than she's ever been to be fucked—she feels him inside her—each thrust a lightning shock of pleasure. She comes and comes again and again. And again. And so does he. No man has come inside her so many times in one night. No one ever will again.

"Hey, Mose, your mom, Hannah, is on the cell phone," Alchemy calls from the front of the house.

In the morning they share champagne. She wants him one more time. She holds him inside her, fingers digging deep into his flesh, wishing the moment would never end.

The landline rang and the answering machine picked up. "It's Sidonna Cherry. If you're there pick up. Okay, call me. I found your father's address in Brazil."

She hustles to her small cottage in Los Feliz, changes her clothes, and readies herself to apologize to this new guy for canceling last night's dinner because she had a sudden meeting with an important client.

"Moses, it was nothing. Nothing. I love you."

She fantasizes about feeling his cock inside her when she is alone, or when she is having sex with me, her husband.

Tears misted in Jay's eyes. Moses crossed his arms against his chest, bowed his head, and shut his eyes tight. A wave of nausea overcame him. He felt as if he needed to expel an internal projectile of irrational jealousy. He tried to quell the impulses of self-annihilation surging in him. He imagined the blackening blood cells expanding at an ever-increasing rate, mocking him.

"Jay"—he reached out and held her hand—"can you get yourself in shape to come down in five minutes?"

"Moses, I love you. Only *you.*" Jay reached over and hugged him. "Make it ten. I need a shower."

"I love you, too. Take your time." He squeezed her hand, bent over, and kissed her gently on the lips. He pushed himself off the bed and slouched down the hall, trying to decode his own roiling emotions, the clashing of jealousy and empathy.

"She okay?" Alchemy flipped the phone back to Moses, who fumbled it but caught it before it hit the ground.

"Got a killer migraine. Lot of tension lately. She'll be out soon."

"I told Hannah, your ma, that'd you'd call her back in ten minutes."

"Thanks."

"Change of plans. Andrew's driver will be here any minute. We have some serious business to untangle. Kasbah is being taken over by Der Saurbrugger Gruppen," he overenunciated the corporation's name in a Chaplinesque German accent, "and we have buyout or bonus clauses in our contract. I'll stay at his place tonight and meet you at Cedars-Sinai tomorrow at eleven."

Moses exhaled. He'd been spared the indignity of the renewed meeting of his brother and his wife until he had a chance to process their relationship.

A black four-door BMW pulled up. "Good trip. Was a good trip. And Mose"—Alchemy touched his shoulder, then hugged him—"you're gonna be fine. Probably outlive me." He disappeared behind the frosted windows of the car's backseat.

Moses stepped onto the small porch, the front door still open, where he stood stupefied. Once again everything had changed, yet truly nothing had changed, and he attempted to escape this irrationality by imposing an almost perverse dialectic: Did Jay love him less? No. Had their years together somehow been nullified and degraded? No. Had she betrayed him? No. But still... History had taught Moses that all nations—and individuals, too—must, in order to survive, obfuscate, deny, and rearrange the exact composition of the smelted logic of lies and silences into "truth." He had formulated a General Principle of Livability: Hope + Need − Denial = your Livability Quotient. Now, his "truth" undone, he wondered if could rebalance the equation. If it even mattered anymore.

20
THE SONGS OF SALOME
The Waves

I had another "episode" last week after suffering three nights of exile from my sleepself. Thankfully, these new burns are not severe. Dr. Bellows did not exactly react with compassionate rectitude as I tried to explain the terror of clarity.

The terror begins when I see my life as one long nocturnal arc of sleeplessness. I become enraptured by visions of such persuasive and vital detail—when the veils that divide the mist of real and dream, past and future, fall—and all the timeless dimensions stretching between Dream and Reality become one. These dimensions, except during the "clarity," are as unseeable as the eighty percent of the universe that is hidden, dark matter. The invisible tentacles of light eviscerate my soul-smell. I feel the light tentacles transforming into laser blades that slice into my synapses, which sets off an uncontrollable panic that I will be separated from my body. The psychic protons that hold me as a consciousness are jettisoned, and I am disseminated into the universe, into nontime, lost in the dark matter. I fear I will never again find myself whole.

This is not at all similar to the transcendent out-of-your-body creative experience that is familiar to every true artist.

Or when I am communing with my DNA. The clarity is no spiritual reverie. No, I am ripped from my essence, my body and soul. I never know if I will come back to myself or if I will forever be torn, trapped in this unforgiving, odorless realm.

It happened again last week, the same way it first happened when I was teenager. After the baby died—and he *did* die to me!—I awoke during the night and ran shrieking into my parents' room. They stayed awake with me all night as my body trembled. Hilda put warm compresses on my head. Dad rubbed my feet. It happened once with Horrwich, too, on the night of my ungraduation party. It happened when Alchemy was murdered.

When I hurt myself or hurt others, it is because this terror is seething and I can feel the waves beginning. My cuttings, my burnings are my declaration: I am real. You are real. I can hurt myself and hurt you and I can bleed. I will remain tethered to this reality, no matter how painful. The doctors think my behavior reflects self-loathing or a desire to escape. It conforms to none of those categories. It is unclassifiable.

Only in those etheresque episodes, sucked into the invisible dark matter, have I felt unvarnished fear. I have no fear of what has been done to me or what will be done, because nothing has power over me except for that one incurable terror. I never want to feel it again. Yet I always know that I will.

Now that Alchemy is gone, I have no one who understands. If only I could see my granddaughter, Persephone.

O Persephone, if you could only sing for me and I for you...

BOOK TWO

*At evening she leads him on to the graves of the longest
lived of the House of Lament, the sibyls and warners*

—Rainer Maria Rilke

21

THE MOSES CHRONICLES (2001)

De-lirious, Di-laudid, De-lusionary

The swirls of the ashen apocalypse at dusk, the eyes of unseen assassins, the ferric pyres, and the incandescent collapse of a great American edifice: eternal images from that inconsolable September day. In that stark moment of communal suffering and rage, Moses hoped that he would be forgiven for his small exaltations. The doctors proclaimed Phase One of the operation a success.

Waking up in his bed in Cedars' Bone Marrow Transplant Unit, his mind bathed in morphine, Moses wondered if the events of the previous weeks—discovering the truth about Hannah and Salome, Alchemy and Jay, and the Trade Center tragedy—were some kind of drug-addled mirage. But when his mom and Jay rushed into the room for the first time after he was released from isolation, his aching heart told him it was no illusion.

He remembered that first morning at Dr. Fielding's office, after he and Alchemy returned from their road trip. Fearing that any memory of Jay had been lost in Alchemy's cascade of conquests, Moses quickly introduced them. "You remember Jay from when she worked for the Sheiks at Kasbah."

Alchemy's eyes opened wide, and for a split second he froze in place. Almost immediately, his expression became unreadable. "Great to see you again. Though not under these circumstances." He turned to Moses. "Your wife tried her best to get the Sheiks to buy real art. They bought posters." Thankfully, the nurse came out and escorted them into Dr. Fielding's office.

In the days before the operation, after the HLA test had confirmed him as a match, Alchemy behaved blithely confident that the transplant would be a formality and its happy result a fait accompli. Moses, Hannah, and Jay blamed the palpable tension on the seemingly interminable wait and the twenty-five percent chance that Moses would not survive the operation.

Hannah often paced, smoking or imitating the motions of smoking without actually lighting up, desperately wanting to ask about Salome but holding her tongue. Like her son, or he like her, she preferred ignominious ignorance to confrontation and finding her fears confirmed. The unspoken social contracts among them, between husband and wife and mom and son, remained in force.

Alchemy's marrow was harvested as an outpatient. Moses underwent three more days of chemo, and four days of cleansing after the surgery was performed. Afterward, Moses spent just over three weeks in complete isolation to protect him from infection, receiving blood transfusions and waiting for the marrow to be accepted and take hold, or be rejected.

Moses languished in his solitude, contemplating his belief in one universal truth: The past, present, and future are fixed and ever recurring, inextricable and singular, and always, always at once, dead and alive. And from this very alive past came two vital questions: Was Jay screwing Alchemy *while* she was seeing me? and Why didn't Hannah push harder and so much sooner to find out about Salome's existence and whereabouts?

In the abstract, he accepted that the answers didn't matter. His wife and mom loved him now. Only, this acceptance was compromised by derision—to hell with abstract notions of fairness and morality! His mind revved into overdrive: Am I a fool? Am I, at my core, just a pseudoliberal, antihedonist with a latent strain of puritanism?

Moses tried and tried to extinguish these negative, soul-depleting thoughts. He wanted to confess his shame. He wished for a pill that could vacate his memories, erase the spiteful thoughts and primitive urges, the guilt that engorged his empathy and compassion.

No mythical memory-erasing pill arrived. Instead, here arose a daymare from the depths of his postoperative miasma. A vision ascended not from his unconscious but from elsewhere, from *outside*:

A plaguelike mix of rain, hail, and vicious winds obscure the last rays of sunset while two hundred cultists glossolate a mocking serenade, countering the braying of drunken Roman guards singing, "99 Jews on the cross / 99 Jews / if one of them we happen to toss / 98 Jews on the cross."

A horde of sadistic voyeurs cheers the luridness of the drip-by-bloody-drip of his slow death. I think, I am a stranger in the strangest land. A ferocious wind scatters his blood and pieces of his torn flesh into the crowd. A woman draped in soaking white robes, bearing spices and carrying a torch, approaches me. She daubs my cheek with a dampened shroud and then speaks.

—Moses.

—*You know me?*

—*I have watched you.*

—*And you are?*

—*Shalom.*

—*Shalom, the shaman and dybbuk?*

—*I prefer "healer."*

—*As he claimed as well.*

—*You have forsaken those who love you.*

—*Forsaken? Who? How?*

—*Moses, you will have another chance.*

—*Chance to do what?*

—*To heal the future . . .*

The aging sibyl sprinkles me with spices and touches my forehead with her torch. I feel no burn. There is no scar.

The daymare ended. Moses felt himself in his hospital bed, bathed in sweat and staring through the window bank toward the San Gabriel Mountains. He closed his eyes and awaited the arrival of his wife, mother, and brother.

22

MEMOIRS OF A USELESS GOOD-FOR-NUTHIN'

Merchants of Venice, 1992–1994

Falstaffa begged Alchemy to give Marty another chance. 'Cause Alchemy loves Falstaffa, he does, and they become our roadies. Sue Warfield, who swooshed her Malibu manse booty, starts unofficially managing us. She cracked me up. She says, "If I am there, I make the scene. And you want to be seen at MY scene so you make the scene." That's why Alchy gives her the nickname Trendy Sue. We showed up at the Viper Room, Tatou, the Sanitarium, 924 Gilman in Berkeley, SOMA in San Diego. My antennae is on high alert 'cause I'm inkling that Alchemy is doing the mystery dance with Sue and not exclusive, which worries me. I am wrong and right. 'Cause Sue's preference is other women. She scored us our first gig at the Troubadour. Soon she partnered with Andrew Pullham-Large, this upper-crusty English wanker who was in love with Alchy, and they started Surface-to-Air with us as their first client.

Alchy set up a rehearsal sked for six to sixteen hours every damn day. He comes off so Yo, Bro nonchalant, Let It Be, baby. What horseshit. Lux got so mad at him once he typed a list of everything he did in the day from brushing his teeth to taking a piss and presented it to "the micromanaging Generalissimo

Alchemyo Savanto." Alchy laughed, but I ain't sure he thinks it as funny as the rest of us. He always had a plan. No, lots of plans. One day he asks for a list from each of us for songs to cover. He's nodding and smiling at Absurda's list, which is all chick shit, and Lux's list, which is a mix of funk and punk. He scans mine, which has lots of heavy metal, and don't say shit. So I says, "Fuck you. What?"

"What? Nothing what."

"Nothing what, says nuthin'. Say somethin'!" I muscle up in his face and give him a little whack on his left shoulder with my open right palm. He don't react. Don't clench up, just puffs on his cigarette and blows the smoke away from me. So I pull back.

He says, "I feel these are a tiny bit *pedestrian.*"

I says, "Okay." Again, I ain't sure what he means. Like pedestrian traffic? I says, "What's yours?"

It's all political, like "There's a Riot Goin' On" or shit I don't know, which I'm guessing is political, so I says, "Are we a rock band or a political group?"

"We're a rock band with a point of view. You get two vetoes like everyone else."

Lux and Absurda are with him on this, so I got two choices—agree or step out. I let it go. Later, at the house, I look up "pedestrian" in Absurda's dictionary and it says "dull or uninspired." Me and Absurda stay up all day and night doing speedballs and fucking, but I am still pissed when we get to rehearsal. Right off, he apologizes in front of Absurda, Lux, and Falstaffa. "I'm sorry. They're some good songs." We choose Deep Purple's "Never Before" and Grand Funk's "We're an

American Band," and they became crowd pleasers. Years later when I do my solo covers, I title it *Songs for Pedestrian Tastes*.

But his apology don't cut it and I'm still sizzling from the coke. Before we split for the night, he corners me alone and this time he gets in my face, inches up to my nose, not his usual style, and says matter-of-fact, "We, the band, need your unpredictable edge. I'm glad you and Absurda are together. Only thing...if you two keep hitting the smack and coke so hard, it's you who's out. Not her—*you*."

Protesting is useless. I could eat shit or I could quit. For once, somewhere, I figured out, truth, he was being selfish, but also truth, he was trying to protect me and Absurda. I still did more than a bit a dabbling after that. I can't understand why I never got hooked. I could quit easier than quitting eating Twinkies.

It's clear Alchy was in such a damn hurry 'cause he was obsessed with springing Salome from the funny farm. He was writing songs like one a day. Before we even had a contract, he wants to start a company to handle publishing rights. Sue hired some clammy-mouthed entertainment lawyer who asked for some scambooger deal. Alchemy didn't buy that shit. He found Kim Dooley, a super-juicy, super-sharp paralegal who saw us early on at a USC frat party. She and Alchy had a quick thing and stayed friends. Kim set up Scofflaw Music for a few hundred bucks. A few years later, we paid for her law school and she got richer than she could've ever dreamed because she became our lifelong lawyer. Alchemy gave us each credit for writing the music even though he wrote ninety percent of it, and that turns out to be mucho millions.

In the summer of '93, Sue and Andrew invite a bunch of A&R guys to the St. James's Club on the Strip. That day we was as nervous as I ever seen us. Even Alchemy, who's usually the picture a confidence. Before we go on, Alchemy tosses me a T-shirt that says CAN I KILL YOU, PLEASE with a drawing of a 357 on it, a riff on the "Please Kill Me" shirt Richard Hell designed with a bull's-eye back in the '70s. Alchy yells, "My mom made it for you."

"Really?"

"You're a killah, right?"

'Course I put it on.

We're standing just offstage and I see two hundred men in suits. Even if they ain't in suits, they're in suits with their shiny STDs — Silicone-Titted Dollfaces — on their arms. I see a few grungy crit types, and some who is old enough to be my father. Not our usual audience. I hear Alchemy muttering and repeating, "Failure equals death. Failure equals death." Which kind of scares me.

When he's ready, he leads us out. The lights is dim and we're so fucking amped we hit the stage and never lose it. This big-shot critic, Zed Cone, who was a friend of Sue Warfield, wrote about the show for *LA Weekly* and really started the buzz.

THIS WEEK'S ZED CONE
What Is the Color of Alchemy
in the Silence?

"Tonight's the dream you've been waiting for all our lives..." With a glint of cheek and irony, the Insatiables singer-songwriter and soon-to-be superstar Alchemy Savant led his band into the spellbinding "Futurific." Never was the future so danceable. Song over, still in his trance, eyes closed, he swilled the last drops from a bottle of whiskey as his band mates, whose musicianship is as precise as a Swiss clock and their stage presence as combustible as a Molotov cocktail, strummed and drummed to a bristling backbeat.

Savant glided into the mesmerized crowd, and in one graceful motion placed the empty bottle of whiskey on the tray of a nearby waitress. A group sitting at a front table leaned forward, nearly propelling their bodies out of their seats toward him. Savant flashed an enigmatic smile, leaned over, made a slow snakelike motion with his right arm, and swiped a beer bottle from a woman at the table. He took two huge gulps.

Savant wet his lips salaciously with his tongue and staccato-stepped backward in time to Compton's own Lux Deluxe's smashmouth drumbeat. Then—*bim bam BOOM!* The lithe, erotic, and dexterous CalArts-trained lead guitarist Absurda Nightingale and the menacing, teenage ex-con bassist Ambitious Mindswallow bashed into the rock noir "Licentious to Kill." The song over, the stage went dark until two spotlights settled upon Mindswallow and Lux Deluxe, face-to-face and clench-fisted. In a harrowing reimagining of Sly Stone's "Don't Call Me Nigger, Whitey," they raised the tension from taunting to warlike—and ended with Lux kissing a stunned-looking Mindswallow on the lips.

For the encore, Savant returned to center stage and led his cohorts in mayhem into "More (Is Never Enough)" their three-chord,

jaw-breaking comic anthem declaring that all
he—his band—each of us—that all *America*
ever wanted was more, more, and more.

Zed Cone answer: The color of the music
in your dreams.

(I read the thing about five hundred times. Sent it to my parents, who had asked for money. I toss in fifty bucks with a note
that says, "Thanks for nuthin'." Signed it, "Your useless son."
My bastid father writes back, "Figures, he don't hardly mention you except when you kissed a nigger. You always was a
nigger lover." I wish I could've beat the fuckin' crap outta him.
I settle for ripping the note into a thousand fuckin' pieces.)

Sue and Andrew had strategerized right. Lotta the big company dudes showed up. During "Face Time Is the Right Time,"
Absurda skanked into the audience and pretended to give head
to half the old fart execs. She spread her legs like she wanted
them to suck her pussy, and poor Randy Sheik, no fuckin' lie,
spurted in his pants!

Man, the Sheiks, they were real beauties. Their rep is as bit
players and hustlers with second-rate acts who had finally hit it
big with the rapper MC Kreep, and Samureye, four nerds from
Brooklyn whose gimmick was dressing up as the heavy metal
band Samurais. They made a star outta Viviana Kerry, this teenage lollipop music slut queen, who was doing Buddy.

You had to love the Sheik's chutzpah. They went from the
Sheicksteins of Bayonne to the Sheiks of Venice, CA. Their
offices was like Leonard's of Great Neck meets an Arab oasis.
Splashed out all blingy lamé and shiny shit and fake palm

trees and stuffed camels. The waiting area was designed in the shape and dirty brown color of a chopped-liver camel.

They was three brothers. Randy, who thinks he is a Jew Luca Brassi but he's only the family water boy. Absurda used to jive him that if he lost fifty pounds and cut his 'stache she'd give him the best blow job in the world. Walter was maybe forty and stooped over like a Jewy bookkeeper with his black-rimmed glasses, short and skinny. I use to peek down and tickle his bald spot and tease him, "Walter, you forgot your pope's cap."

Buddy, though, he was one smooth alligator. All greasy groomed and expensive clothes but could snap your neck and never think twice. His extra-boldfaced gold watch sparkled on his dark, hairy-gazairy wrist. His voice raspy like an overheated seltzer bottle.

In the dressing room, we were kiss-the-sky high. We'd slayed 'em. I was spraying everyone but Alchemy with champagne. Andrew'd ordered plastic glasses that didn't shatter, so I was stomping them with my boot. (Hey, I was young and doing what I thought rock stars should do.)

Alchemy, though, none of us dared enter his space until he gives the signal. He'd find a corner and cover his head under a towel. After a show, it was like he was some giant Thanksgiving Day parade balloon with the air hissed out and shrunk down. The energy he let loose was so atomic, and he needed time to rev up to be *Alchemy*.

He had finally uncovered his head and was gulping a bottle a bubbly when Buddy Sheik rams backstage, flanked by Randy and Walter. Buddy gloms on to Alchemy and Sue. Randy talks to Absurda. Walter is on me, Lux, and Andrew. Then Buddy says real loud, "Deal?" and reaches to shake Alchemy's hand. Alchemy nods and says, "Not yet."

Buddy barked, "What? You don't trust me?" We all turn to watch them.

"Why should I? Besides, all four of us have to agree."

"Man, I could grow to love a boychick like you. You *shouldn't* trust me. Yet. I'll change that."

Buddy paced around the space like a combo strip club pimp and used-car salesman. "Alchemy, *you* are like no one I've ever met—you've been kissed by God. And I'll be blessed to have you as a member of the Kasbah family. The question you should be asking is: Why am I here? The answer: I want *Thee* Insatiables. I can feel how much I want you because it sickens my kishkes to think we won't get you. We will give you 'More' than any other company..." He stops, waits, begins again, his voice calmer. "I know you're thinking, Man, this schlemiel got nothing to say to me. Yeah, I'm a low-life *schmateh* peddler who never had a *class* act like you guys. You'll see, you take risks. Me, too. If I didn't, I'd still be selling rags. You got your dreams. I got mine."

Buddy walks up to me and pinches my cheek. "Even you, you got class. Most of it low." I slap his hand away and Randy inches up to me. Buddy keeps spieling. "Ambitious, here, I bet he thinks, and maybe the rest of you do, too, that we're missing the boat on the 'grunge scene' and we need you. *No!* I want. I never *need*. Me and my brothers, we secretly been to see you twice. And we agree—you are *it!*"

Buddy keeps his focus on Alchemy and Andrew while slipping glances at the rest of us. Alchemy, who could keep a tractor beam stare on anyone, never takes his eyes off Buddy. They're playing mind macho poker.

"Talent is not enough. Dedication is not sufficient." His voice crackled now. "You need vision, need to see the lay of the land. Where the rat traps are and where the gold mines are. You sign with me and we'll disarm the rat traps and find the gold mines.

"Anyone here know what *schvartz gelt* is?" He looks around. "No takers? Andrew, what'd they teach you at Cambridge?"

Andrew mumbles, "It means black and gold."

"That's kaiser-speak. In Yiddish it means..." He pauses ten seconds before whispering, "This never goes beyond this room. *Schvartz gelt* is Yiddish for T&E. The taxmen call it 'Travel and Entertainment.' Bull. It's 'Tits and Ego.' Taste-makers make stars. Some need a massage. Every company will supply you with 'party' favors, but *we* best everyone in this business at giving the *right* people T&E. We'll give you *ten* dollars less than anyone else... *Less*, because I want you to be able to tell every mother-effing person who asks that artistic freedom is what *we* gave you. This comes from my heart and my pocketbook. I will personally write in an extra $50,000 T&E to promote *Thee* Insatiables."

Buddy looks around, pleased with himself.

Alchemy says, "Ten dollars won't do it. We'll take ten thousand less." I wanna scream, What the fuck? Sue and Andrew don't look over the moon either. We all kinda know Alchemy is testing them. "You give five K to the ACLU and five K to Bernie Sanders's campaign in our name and Kasbah matches it."

None of us in the room knows this Sanders dude is some commie congressman until Alchemy explains it later. I ain't thrilled, but after listening to Alchy and Nathaniel, I ain't surprised either.

"We can do that... And remember, you can call me or one of my brothers any time of the day or night. Can you do that with SONY? No damn way. We answer to no one but ourselves. Call me or any of us anytime."

He walks up to me, stares at my shirt. "Don't kill me just yet. Deal?"

"We gotta vote."

He reaches for my neck and pulls out the chain with my eye. "Can I kiss it for luck?"

I nod. He does. "Decide soon."

We sign with Kasbah. In no time, the tagline "When the Buzz Becomes a Scream" with pictures of us four, mouths open wide like we was screaming, is plastered all over L.A. In two years we zip from playing for free at family street fairs, beach parties, scuzzy unlicensed bars, and high schools to basketball arenas, to stadiums. When I think back how fast it happened, it's like the genie granted me three hundred wishes that all came true.

23

THE MOSES CHRONICLES (2001)

What's So Funny About
Peace, Love, and Misunderstanding?

At the same moment Moses was in the throes of his reverie, Alchemy and his driver in his vintage 1963 Jaguar (refitted with an experimental biodiesel engine) rolled down Gracie Allen Drive. Alchemy caught sight of Jay's long-legged, determined gait, with a slight hitch to her swaying shoulders. He asked the driver to pull over and he called to her as he stepped out of the car. Feeling ambushed, Jay took off her sunglasses and placed them in the breast pocket of her jean jacket, which gave her time to regain her bearings. "He's still not ready. Call first." She quickly added "please," but there was no question that she was issuing an order.

Alchemy tapped the hood and signaled the driver to hang on. "Sure, of course. Call me later and let me know how he is doing and when I can come. But um..." He paused.

"Alchemy, what? Moses is waiting."

"We should talk, about you know, I guess." Mr. Savoirfaire sounded uncharacteristically maladroit. She nodded. "In here?" He pointed to the limo and they slid inside.

"So, talk." Jay's tone was brusque.

"When I walked into the doctor's office and I saw you holding Mose's hand. Whoa. Incredible coincidence."

"I'd say incomprehensible karma trumps all other interpretations."

"I'd say coincidence and karma are different words for the same thing."

"I have no time for this." Jay put her hand on the door handle, ready to get out.

"Hold on. It's nothing like the path you have to negotiate, but it's tricky for me, too. Besides, I was never proud of the way things ended with us."

"Ended? With us? There was no 'us.' We had a few dates strung out over a few months until I met someone else."

"Was it Mose?"

"If I cared enough, I would've called you." She paused, allowing Alchemy to reevaluate the idea that he'd had her, rather than she had him.

"Jay, okay." He stared right into her eyes. "It can't be undone. The most important issue now is Moses. We need to protect him."

"Too late."

"You told him? Jay, why?" Vexed, he continued, "How much?"

"Very little but enough. He always says the cover-up is worse than the crime. I won't lie to him. I'm not ashamed. I wasn't a nun. He knows that. He won't ask any more questions. *I* know him." She paused as if to emphasize *and you don't.* Not telling Moses about their affair would be, to her mind, unjust. Unlike Moses, for whom truth was subjective and mercurial, or for Alchemy, for whom truth was situational but potentially knowable and informationally advantageous, Jay held fast to a belief in her objective, knowable, and universal truth. Once she admitted the affair, there was no lie. Jay believed that withholding certain information was never more inflammatory than a blatant lie, and saying little about a meaningless affair was more truthful than trying to explain it as meaningless.

"Alchemy, you and I can never be seen alone together, or he will drive himself mad. He may be forty-three and imagines himself a cynic, but he doesn't really *live* cynically. I can't bear the thought of hurting him anymore. Do you understand?" She drilled her stare into Alchemy's round gold-flecked brown eyes, the same eyes that had entranced her years before but now seemed impenetrable.

"No. Not totally. But mum's the word. He worships you."

Jay's tone and attitude remained arch. "One piece of advice: Watch yourself with Hannah. When it comes to Moses, she may not be his mother, but she is his mom."

"Thanks for the tip." He gave her a subtle yet visible once-over. "I'm sorry you're having a tough time now. You're wearing it well. You look as good as the night we met at the Dresden."

She took pleasure in his remembering the party where they first met, and his compliment, which she refused to acknowledge with even the wisp of a smile. She wanted to believe that Alchemy wasn't being a cad, that he wasn't coming on to her, that he was genuinely concerned and was being open and penitent. With him, she decided, one could never be sure.

She closeted her ego. "Never, never say that or anything like it again. You call the hospital in two hours to talk to him, and he will give you a time to visit. This conversation never happened." With that, Jay stepped out of the Jag.

Ten minutes later, after a quick stop in the cafeteria for coffee, Jay arrived in Moses's room, unusually harried. She tied her hair back in a ponytail and donned the necessary masks over her mouth and nostrils. At his bedside, she explained that his mom was taking the day to rest. Moses nodded, relieved, because in no way could he describe his Visitation in front of his mother. "Jay, I was there. I felt, smelled, tasted the air. The blood. The rain. Heard the screams. And that woman Shalom, freaking eerie."

Normally, when he told her of his daymares, Jay was sympathetic, if overly analytical in her dissection of their meaning. (She called them nightmares and Moses stopped correcting her because, although she denied it, the idea of a waking intrusion on reality unnerved her.) This time her response bordered on the callous. She insisted the nightmare arose from his fear of dying without belief in any salvation. "Maybe you should convert and be saved."

"Jay, don't go snippy on me *now*."

"Come on, Moses, you're still high from the drugs."

Later, as they held hands, he in bed and she sitting in a chair beside him, watching *Idiot's Delight* on AMC, she turned to him. She said, almost apologetically, "I have another interpretation of your dream."

"Shoot."

"You're absorbing the fact you're like me, only half Jewish. Now you sweat *and* you *schvitz*." Jay was needling Moses's belief in this cultural or perhaps glandular difference that means WASPs, if they perspired *at all*, sweat. Jews *schvitz*.

"I'm not sure, but possible," Moses conceded, for the sake of avoiding a debate. He acknowledged the discovery meant he was not a full-fledged Jew, but he paid no heed to that. He didn't suddenly become born again or a believer, or doubt his true religious identity. His father was a Holocaust survivor and Hannah had raised him as a Jew. He'd been bar mitzvahed. He still *felt* Jewish. Besides, he knew well that from the Inquisition to the pogroms to the Nazis, those goyim would have invited him to be a main course at one of their lovely human desecrations.

Perhaps the greatest implication of the vision, to Moses, was his new obsession over losing his grip on his sanity, a paranoia that was heightened by knowledge of Salome's psychosis. He continually questioned the rightness of meeting his father, who had disinherited him in every way, yet from whom (he now worried) he had inherited a perhaps sociopathic ability to emotionally disconnect. These fears propelled him into a world where the pain of the past overwhelms. He sometimes lost perspective, forgetting what history had taught him: Only a fool believes that the future is not at the mercy of the past.

Dr. Fielding recommended resuming psychotherapy as a necessary component of healing after the operation. The therapist Moses had begun seeing after his initial cancer diagnosis visited him at home. Moses did not care to talk about his illness, his mortality, or even Jay's affair. He couldn't repress the unshakable images from his daymare and the implications of his new mother being "crazy."

"Yes, if indeed your biological mother is schizophrenic, that could increase the chances. At your age, it probably would've happened already."

This almost amateur bit of diagnosis didn't serve as the mind-settling sedative answer he wanted to hear. Instead the doctor suggested "the new apple, an antidepressant a day keeps the demons away," which Moses rejected.

Fearful that he could one day he could wake up inside Collier Layne beside his mother, whenever he thought about confiding this Visitation to anyone else, he stopped himself. He recalled a passage he remembered from his college days:

Man is but an ass, if he go about to expound this dream. Methought I was—there is no man can tell what.

24

THE SONGS OF SALOME

When You Wish upon a Star

I'm feeling better today, though somewhat melancholic. I want to get on with my story before my corporeal disintegration renders me voiceless.

My first "vacation" years, from '76 through '79, were fraught with bouts of insulin therapy. I was drawn and quartered while the hotwire singed my synapses and rearranged my molecules. It caused the opposite effect of its intentions, made me heavier and deepened my Gravity Disease. My body was a blizzard of glassy windblown snowflakes scudding aimlessly. I feared I would melt to the ground and dissolve into the universe. The world inside me smelled like a decomposing cat picked clean by the buzzards of the art world and the witch doctors that first "treated" me here.

Good days were rare. Mostly, I was alone. When Anaïs Nin passed, Xtine brought me some copies of Nin's diaries and I made three penis and three vagina papier-mâché sculptures from them. Then we burned one of each in her honor. I gave two to Xtine and two to Gibbon, who claimed that because of me, Lively had sicced the IRS on him.

Shockula was the bastard in chief before Ruggles arrived. With his batlike ears, simian head, corpulent ego, he celebrated like a sadistic vulgarian who got a rush every time he pushed the button on his zapper. I will forever be grateful to Bickley Sr. for halting the treatment. I'm sure Billy Jr. would've gladly ratcheted open my cortex like a coconut. He and Shockula won over Hilda with their Latinate shrink-speak. The first time she visited here, she broke down and pleaded, "Why, Salome, why?" I had no answer that would appease her.

It was many months before I was allowed to see Alchemy. I tried to convince myself he'd thrive living with Hilda, but I didn't believe it. Hilda acted as if she'd received a dispensation and could raise him away from me and my wanton ways. Her voice had frowned at me because I'd serve him dinner at 11 P.M. and cursed in front of him. Now, she gave him "structure." Just another name for control.

I lived for Alchemy's drawings and letters at first written in crayon, then black pen. I started sending him drawings of *Petra Sansluv, Pearl Diver by the Black Sea*, which I'd started again when he was a baby. He would do his own drawings of her and send them back to me.

I waited eagerly for Nathaniel's letters, with his bold script so much more macho than his persona but as sturdy and pure as his soulsmell. I've always distrusted e-mail, IMs, twits, p-mail. Any and all of the always-new cypherworld slango. These nanocommunications arrive without the demure or sexy dress code of an envelope, the personal saliva of a licked stamp, the revelations in words flowing from brain to hand to paper, with their swirls and curves of febrile emotions.

They do not fulfill the beautiful agony of waiting...Waiting. I love getting letters, real letters. I don't get many of them now. I wait for them from Persephone. I know this seems odd coming from me because I can be so impulsive. But these nanomessages—their words never get to simmer and boil through the winding routes of the night. No wonderment and pain in when they'll be read. No imagining the delight or disappointment in shaking hands of the reader.

Even at his bleakest, Nathaniel searched for the possibility in new innovations. He exclaimed how e-mails got millions of people reading and writing again. He had a point. Only not enough of one to persuade me.

Alchemy understood. He always wrote me letters, even when we lived in the same house. Sometimes he slipped them under my door or mailed them.

They didn't bring him to these grounds that first time. Instead we met at the B&B chocolate factory. His hair trim and tidy. His eyes, which had been so agog at the world's sensations, were now dulling, bereft of their dreaminess. He was suffering the first dollops of Gravity Disease.

We both beamed with joy when we kissed. "Mom!" he yelled. "Alchemy!" I shouted back.

As I hugged him, Hilda said, "We call him *Scott* now." Before he was born, to placate her, I told her I might name him Scott. "Not in my presence, you don't." Drug-shocked and feeling impotent, I wanted to reassert my authority. "Alchemy, what do you prefer I call you?"

"Scott, you don't have to answer that," Hilda commanded.

He answered anyway. "Alchemy."

Years later, just as he was being crowned the new Prince of Pop Culture, we were sitting on the deck of the first house he'd bought, in the hills of Los Feliz, sharing a midnight joint, listening to Dietrich peddle her "illusions." I'd played that for him often when he was a child. "Mom, sometimes I wonder if all of this isn't some form of illusion." I heard a kernel of self-doubt, which he rarely expressed to anyone but me.

"Of course it is. We are all living under the spell of illusions. Even you. As artists, we are illusionists. This house, all of this, is transient. But your music is eternal and it is perfection. Alchemy, you are my purest creation."

"You remember that day when I came to visit you outside the B&B factory?"

"Yes…Why?"

"I think Grandma Hilda never forgave you for asking me about my name and never forgave me for answering 'Alchemy.' And you've never forgiven me for using Scott when we lived in Virginia."

"Yes, I did. As soon as you reverted to Alchemy. And Hilda never forgave me for anything, from the moment I got pregnant and lost the baby." I'd started telling Alchemy about the babydeath when he was in my womb. "You're wrong about one thing, Hilda forgave you for everything. She doted on you unconditionally."

He finished the joint, lit a cigarette, blew the smoke into the air, and watched it dissipate. "Where did you come up with my name? And none of that bull about how you were sure I'd be a rock star."

"Why not? You certainly have used that story to your benefit." We laughed.

"True, but your stories *do* change."

"As do yours."

"Stop stalling."

"Years before, someone had given me some books. I found them again in the house in Orient when I was pregnant with you."

"Who gave them to you?"

"Cigarette, please." I didn't smoke much, but I wanted one then. He handed the pack to me. I didn't light up just yet. "I don't remember. It was long time ago. Before the hotwire therapy."

He asked skeptically, "But you remember what those books had to do with my name?"

I lit the cigarette and was frozen in my memories for a minute. "They were a gift from the father of your dead brother."

"Mom, I didn't mean... Sorry."

"No need." I took a puff before continuing. "In the midst of a Savant Blue period, I was terrified of losing you. One late afternoon, a beautiful Orient twilight, I climbed to the roof and I began meditating in tandem with the cicadas, whose vibrations entranced like the entreaties of a thousand mantraing monks, and I was deliriously reading Rimbaud's 'Alchemy of the Word.'" I stopped. I had occasionally intimated our family's ability with DNA travel, but he, having not experienced it, never responded and only listened. "I had scraped my leg climbing up to the roof, and from my blood there appeared Kyle"—he'd heard about her—"who introduced me to Mary the Jewess, the first female alchemist. We communicated. As it darkened, I inhaled the odors of the full moon when it appears translucent and yellow-white-pink-and-blue like shimmering linen, both gorgeous and foreboding, and at that moment you gave a kick in my belly. The cicadas hymned like angels whispering your destiny as 'Alchemy Savant, mystic of music and moon.' From that moment on, I knew you'd live to be born."

He nodded. My son did not need to question my truths. I asked him, "Would you have preferred I named you Scott?"

"No. Well, sometimes, when I was a kid and the jerkoffs in Greenport called me Alcrummy and the bullies in Charlottesville kicked my ass. And your solution was to sing Bowie's 'Kooks.' But you prepared me for life with you and life as I am living it. Would Scott Savant have become leader of the Insatiables?"

He was, like me, an acoustic morphologist. And he understood that his name was filled with music. And we morphologists know that in every language a "rose" is a fragrant mixture of sounds and odors, and that an asp sounds like an asp...even when his name is Lively.

Ever the conniver, Lively paid me a visit maybe eighteen months after Nathaniel had struck a deal to serve two years in Allenwood and two years on probation. They dropped the drug charge and he pled guilty to obstruction of justice. Which is perfect Lewis Carroll logic, because if he wasn't guilty of selling drugs (which they knew he wasn't), he was on the lam, so to speak, for a crime he didn't commit. Nothing was obstructed but the truth.

When Shockula informed me of Lively's impending arrival, I expected some form of retribution. I warned him, "Count Shockula, if Lively's expecting me to apologize for our incident, he's going to be waiting 'til Godot finishes brunch."

On a sweltering late July afternoon, I swooshed outside wearing a salmon-colored sundress and big-brimmed white cotton hat with peacock feathers hung from its back brim. I sat on a white marble seat at a round table. Shockula came over with Lively and then walked off to the side and spoke with another Collier Layne vacationer. Lively coiled himself in the seat across from me. He seemed rather nervous, his body less domineering, hidden under a loose-fitting pin-striped blue suit that looked like he picked it off the spy rack at the CIA mall. His eyes covered by his unintentionally fashionable FBI '6os-style drugstore sunglasses.

"Is Nathaniel okay?" I feared something had happened to him, and that was the reason Lively came to visit.

"I have not seen him."

"Is he still getting out in September?"

"I have no news contradicting that." Lively dabbed at the sweat forming on his temples and forehead with a white handkerchief.

"Are you checking up on me for Hilda?"

"I have neither seen nor spoken to her." He rat-a-tatted the table with his gnarly knuckles and gaudy ring. "What do you know about your biological father?"

"Nothing. Hilda and Gus claimed they were never told who he is. The one time I met Greta, she was more than elliptical. My personal research says that he must have been an artist." I quickly covered myself. Lively would never accept my genetic travels as anything but the hallucinations of a madwoman. "It's fact that Greta was friends with many artists when she arrived in New York."

Lively scratched at his cheek but said nothing.

"You have more than an idea, don't you?"

"Unhmm."

"Lively, I'm listening."

"First, in regard to Hilda, I have my qualms about your abilities to keep a secret."

"I don't ever purposefully hurt her."

"That is exactly my fear. Your lack of purpose." He tilted his head toward the sky, then leaned forward over the marble table and gave a smidge of a nod toward Shockula. "Your father was Gus Savant."

"Oh, please!" I sputtered. "It took you almost two years to come up with that twinkle-twinkle-nursery-rhyme explanation?"

"Accept it or not. It's a fact." He paused, letting the needle he'd slipped into my consciousness evacuate its message. "I'm sorry he was not an artist. From what little contact we had—my meetings with Gus were fleeting—he impressed me as a most decent man."

"He was better than decent. I loved him. I'd be proud to be his offspring." I sat pensively for a moment. Never had I connected Gus's chromosomes to me. "He would never have done that to Hilda."

"Salome, even good men falter. Gus was adamantly, and rightly, opposed to an abortion. No one wanted to risk a public explosion. It would have guaranteed ruining Miss Garbo's image, and your father's marriage. Gus and Hilda got their child."

"Lively, what do you want from me?"

"Nothing. I'm trying to do right." He took off his sunglasses, placed them on the table, and without wiping the sweaty curlicues forming on his cheeks, aimed his Shiva the Obliterator eyes onto me. "I have no reason to lie. I'd have more reason to lie if it weren't true. Hilda was never told of Gus's paternity and he never wanted her to hear about his lapse. That is why you best have the sense not to tell her."

"Who told you? And why should I trust you? Why didn't you tell me that day in Billy Jr.'s apartment?"

"As I said then, William Bickley felt honor bound to keep his word to Gus. At the time, I felt honor bound not to act against his wishes. Still, I am not under his jurisdiction or hogtied by any legal agreements."

"When did they meet? How?"

"That is not relevant."

"To me it is. Give me proof. Were they in love?"

"I haven't the faintest idea. As far as proof, my proof is my word."

The man was so taken with his own benevolent hubris he brought out the violence in me. I wanted to dig my nails into his gorillalike sideburns and scream, "You're fucking with my life!" but I stayed seated and sipped my water before asking my next unanswerable question. "Was Greta a spy?"

Lively's incisors ground into each other to maintain his posture of gentlemanly formality. We sat silently. I had sensated correctly. "Of course she was. She worked for you and Bicks Sr."

"I wouldn't say that. Not exactly."

"What would you say?"

"Let me propose that she was sympathetic to us."

"And Gus, he was a spy, too?"

"No, he was not." Lively stood up, towering over me. "Despite your previous attempt to injure me, I bear you no ill will." As always, he made me feel as if his blandest statements were a lethal threat.

"Since you are in a giving mood, think you have the resources to dig up whether my mother and Marcel Duchamp ever had an affair?"

He tugged at the perspiring chicken skin around his massive Adam's apple, suddenly perplexed. "You mean the French fella who is the mime?"

I started giggling. "Forget it."

He shrugged. He bent over and put on his sunglasses. I should have thanked him. But I couldn't be that phony.

I called Hilda a few nights later. "I was looking at an old picture of Dad from when he was in the navy that I have here in my room. What did he do during the war?"

"You heard these stories when you were a child. Have you forgotten?"

"The doctors told you. Some of my memories are scrambled from the treatment."

She tried to answer jokingly, "Some of them were scrambled before."

"That's your opinion."

"Let's not fight."

"I'm not fighting, I'm asking a question."

"Gus had done two years in the navy when he was nineteen, before we started dating. He reenlisted right after Pearl Harbor. We were married by then. After serving about a year at the Brooklyn Navy Yard, he was reassigned back to Greenport, where he became the liaison between the navy and the Picket Patrol, the group of civilians from the North Fork who sailed out to scout for Nazi submarines. Why do to want to know?"

"Because I miss him."

"I do, too." And she did. She never suspected that Gus betrayed her, if indeed he did. Never did I find Dad within me. I could only commune with Greta's mitochondria and they, like she, never revealed the secret of my father.

25

THE MOSES CHRONICLES (2001)

Toilet Humor

Alchemy came by the hospital three days after he and Jay spoke in the Jag. Jay remained purposely absent. He relaxed in a burnt orange plastic reclining chair beside Moses's bed, both of them half watching the TV talking heads yammering, when Alchemy asked, his voice oddly muffled by the medical mask, "How come you guys decided not to have kids?"

Moses muted the sound on the TV. "At first, selfishness and vacillation. We traveled a lot in my time off. We enjoyed our freedom. I had no grand desire to subject a kid to this world or relive my childhood by proxy through my progeny." Moses did not volunteer that Jay's mother's dolorous descent into a waking coma, then her father's cavalier behavior, kept her ambivalent. At least, at first. "Just before my diagnosis, Jay, well, we reconsidered. We were going to try. Then I got sick..." His voice trailed off.

"Maybe there'll still be time after this. Mose, you'd be a cool dad."

"Good, maybe. Cool, don't think so." They laughed. In that moment, Moses decided to hand Alchemy a piece of near-sacred information. "Can I tell you something? Will you keep it in confidence?"

"My word."

"Before we met, Jay got pregnant by a boyfriend she wasn't serious about and she had an abortion. Sometimes I think she regrets that, only when I ask her, she insists it was the right choice and the discussion ends there."

Moses didn't mind if Alchemy pondered the possibility that it might've been his child. It wasn't. Moses and Jay occasionally ran into the old boyfriend, a businessman, whom she had met at an art auction that she had organized for Doctors Without Borders, and for whom Moses felt barely a trickle of jealousy or resentment.

Feeling a bit nervy, Moses probed deeper. "How about you, are you so sure you never knocked someone up?"

"As sure as the paternity tests I've taken. I fully expect there is a legitimate kid out there as opposed to all the wannabes. Andrew has bullied and paid, and I mean bank account balloons, for abortions for women who were with Ambitious or Lux, and they each got at least one unplanned kid they pay for."

It struck Moses as "normal" that rock stars would be propagating machines. He was surprised that Alchemy had produced no progeny. "So what you said when we were driving, you really don't want to settle down and have kids."

"Highly unlikely. Although I have to say I don't want to end up like Mick or, worse, Hef. Poor guy looks like a brine-embalmed blue mummy. Kids? I don't need that affirmation.

I get what you say. Almost everyone has to fight their way out from some family curse or escape a parental tendril. Lots of people have grown up with what they consider lousy parents. Half the marriages end in divorce. Half the ones that stay together suck. Still, none of them had Salome for a mom."

Moses nodded agreeably. Alchemy leaned forward in the chair; beneath the mask his soft, feminine lips pursed, his nostrils tensed, and his usual pliant posture stiffened. "My father, I told you I met him. You know the song 'Fast Enough'?"

"Sure, was a big hit back in the '70s. The Baddists. British band, right?" Moses sang a few bars, "Why ain't I fast enough for you..."

"The lead singer, Phillip Bent—he's my father. He and Salome had about a twenty-minute wham-bammer during a Central Park Summer Stage concert in the artists' Porta-Potty. That is either the crudest or the most perfect place ever to conceive a rock star. Maybe both."

"She admitted that?"

"Admitted? She boasted that it was the *second*-best time she ever had in a portable bathroom. I never asked what was first. Bent cared as much about me as I do about"—Alchemy scanned the room and pointed—"that water pitcher. So Mose, maybe not finding your old man isn't the worst outcome."

"Was it that horrible when you saw Bent?"

"I saw him twice. The Baddists had a minor hit with *Chain Saw Disco Massacre* and were touring in '77. I was about six and met him with my grandmother during Salome's first time in Collier Layne. I remember zip except that he kept repeating in his Cockney accent, 'So, you're the fuckin' lit'l swine.' Seven or so years later, we were living in Berlin, Salome finally persuaded him to see me." For the first time, Moses heard Alchemy lose control of his perfect-pitch voice. "Nathaniel flew with me to London so I could meet him. Stone-cold junkie. I've known dogs that make more sense." He took out a cigarette and twirled it in his fingers. "I've never told this to anyone but my mom and Nathaniel, not even Ambitious, so if I hear it anywhere..." Moses nodded. "Fucker kept calling me 'Mimi' and 'Chemistry.' After five minutes I realized he was not worth the piss in the toilet. All Salome ever said was, 'He was so gorgeous.'" Alchemy shook his head and flicked the unlit cigarette against the window. "The prick 'sold' me to a squishy lord who had a hard-on for teenage boys. I kicked him in the nuts and got my ass outta there and back to the hotel where Nathaniel was staying. We flew back to Berlin."

"I'm so sorry." Moses, feeling guilty for his little ploy earlier, reached to give him a loving pat on the back, but he couldn't quite make it. Alchemy extended his hand and they slapped five in a jesting, congenial display of brotherhood. "You ever see him after you became famous?"

"Nope. Andrew made arrangements with him so he stayed away and quiet. I look at it this way, the people who raised and loved me, I'd do anything for any of them."

"You sure you don't want kids? For a shiftless rock 'n' roller, you sound pretty damned sensible to me. You wouldn't be like Bent."

"I wouldn't do *that*. I have no idea what I'd be like. None. Uncle seems like the perfect role for me."

Alchemy's cell rang. "It's Bruce. Have to take it for a sec. It's about the concert for 9/11." Moses gave him the thumbs-up and Alchemy stepped out of the room.

By the time Alchemy returned, Moses had flipped on the sound to the blabber-blatherers and was "arguing" with Louise Urban Vulter, radio and TV host, who was bloviating as a self-anointed Middle East expert. "An *expert* would know it's Osama bin Laden and the blind sheik, not Hussein." Moses mumbled and again tapped the Mute button on the remote control.

"Mose, who'd you say did it?"

"I'm betting it's Al Qaeda, the same people who went after the WTC back in '93. Hussein and bin Laden are enemies."

"You sure? I think Hussein wants revenge because Bush Sr. tried to off him."

"I'm not saying he wouldn't like to see either Bush dead. Hussein's a megalomaniac whose prime directive is self-preservation. This kind of attack guarantees that someone will pay. Even if it is the wrong someone, or millions of someones."

Alchemy pulled a paper from the inside of his sports jacket pocket and handed it to Moses. "Take a look. I scratched this out over the last two days."

"It's poetic, but from my perspective, it lacks historical context," he said when finished.

Alchemy appeared taken aback by Moses's frankness. "How so?"

"Before I answer, what's this for?"

"Op-ed piece. I've been in contact with the *New York Times* for a while about penning something. Tragically, this is the right time." Alchemy announced with unmistakable determination, "Someday I'm going to get more involved in politics. Nathaniel wants me to start a *real* third party. He claims all we have now are two different sides of the same coin. Not sure what I'll do. Eventually, when the time is right..."

Moses tilted his head.

"What? Rock stars are excluded from politics when movie stars and athletes are not?"

"No—no."

"Rock 'n' roll has always been not just the soundtrack but the agent of change. Look at the best of it: Cooke, Baez, Lennon, Marley, Fela. I got everything materially I could ever want. Building houses and giving to charities, that's all for the good, only I can do more."

Moses decided that the outrageous events of this last week had taught him it's never wise to underestimate the possibility of the remotest, most far-fetched idea becoming truth.

"Mose, tell me where I've gone off course." There was no air of defensiveness in his voice, only genuine inquisitiveness.

"First off, it's a bit too glib for what you want to achieve. More important, it's historically inaccurate and a woeful American conceit to think that this 'is unique in history.' Great cities—from Rome to Delhi, Moscow to London, Baghdad to Jerusalem—have been plundered, burned, and bombed. Innocent people have been raped, maimed, and killed. It's not even unique in our history. Washington, D.C., was burned to the ground by the British in the War of 1812."

"Right, right. Good. Go on."

"Aside from the fact that we don't know who to fight yet, before you make any war you need a plan to win the peace. Which doesn't mean crushing the enemy. These chicken-hawks are clueless about the inferno that is war and have no idea how to calm the fires that we, literally and figuratively, will create."

"You're damn right about that." Alchemy sat back, impressed. "Thanks, man. You saved me from a potential public pillorying."

"Least I could do." Moses leaned back against his pillow and his eyes gazed upward. "You saved me from dying."

In the next two days, they hashed it out. Alchemy offered to publish it under co-bylines. Moses demurred. The credit would've been good for his career, but it didn't outweigh what the loss of anonymity would do to his private life. A week later the *Times* printed it. The last lines of the article read:

What happens not in the first three weeks, or three months, after the murders but in the years to come will determine if the songs we sing will tell of darkness becoming darker, or darkness becoming light.

26

MEMOIRS OF A USELESS GOOD-FOR-NUTHIN'

The Homecoming, 1995–1996

Alchemy used to joke that Lux's family was more like the Beaver Cleavers than the Eldridge Cleavers. That wasn't exactly right, but his parents stayed married 'til death did them part. His father, Big Lionel Bradshaw, was an East Coast–born NWA. Don't gimme no grief, he called *himself* that. He grew up in Red Hook, Brooklyn, when it was the city's deathliest hood. He enlisted in the army and shipped out to Nam. He survived, and his best army brother was a Compton homeboy who got Big Lionel a job as a roofer in L.A. He meets Lux's mom, who works at the DMV. They are military-strict parents. Like me, Lux goes to a magnet school for the musically gifted, only *he* don't get thrown out. When the Crips or Bloods or whichever gangstas fucks with Lux or his sister, Big Lionel threatens them if they mess with his kids, he'd take out ten of them before they got him. They listened. Lux got a scholarship to some all-black college but ends up back in L.A. and meets Absurda in around '90, when they was working at McCabe's guitar store.

It was rare to come across a real playa worth dick who didn't have a chip on his shoulder. I ain't going deep on you—that was Alchemy's MO, not mine. Me and Absurda never wanted to cozy up with our families. Sure, we were generous with them. But it was more like blackmail: We'll give you cash to stay the fuck away and shaddup. Lux claimed when he was onstage he felt like the invulnerable Lux Deluxe. His face turned rust-red pissed off if someone called him Li'l Lionel. I get that. I hated being Ricky McFinn.

Alchy, his situation was confusing. He never spilt no numbers on his pop. In his stonewalling or stories he'd spin to the media about the guy, you could tell he despised him. When I ask him about why the hell he enlisted in the army, he joked, "To sublimate my hostility toward my father. He was the enemy." Later he'd say he'd planned it 'cause he wanted the army cred when he went into politics. I thought it was to mess with Nathaniel 'cause of his pacifist bullshit. Alchy, no matter his antiwarmongering, was never no pacifist, and he said he regretted never getting to Iraq because Salome cracked. Salome and him, they was like a two-headed monster who had a love-hate thing going that they both needed and resented.

All of this is my backdoor way of sliding up to the first time I met Absurda's family. I don't like rehashing it but I got to.

It was Thanksgiving '95. We was touring between *More* and *Get Large*. Mostly now, those shows merge into one after another after another. It was party time and we loved the audiences. This show in Madison, at the college, was nuthin' special. *After* the gig, that's when things started to get memorable. First, Absurda's sister Heather, who was a college student, came backstage with like five of her bosomy buddies. Heather is an Absurda knockoff with the same tight body, only shorter and tatt free. She don't cover her tiny freckles with makeup. Has a bigger, well, chest area. Longish blond hair, unlike Absurda's, whose is cut asymmetrical sharp at the neckline and in front. Surprise, surprise, one of the girls (not Heather) kept Alchy busy that night. That got Absurda pouty faced as I ever seen her. She never blinked at Alchemy's carousing before.

The next day me, Alchemy, Absurda, and Heather drive to Fond du Lac to celebrate the holiday with the Akin clan. Lux and his babe head to Chicago to be with her relatives. Falstaffa and Marty "decline" the invite to Fond du Lac, which was most definitely motivated by a few words from Alchemy. They drive the bus and we're gonna reconvene in Minneapolis for the next gig.

Before we get going, I see Absurda in a head-to-head with Alchemy. Later, I inquire if all is copacetic, and she snipes, "Why shouldn't it be?"

"No reason." I'm thinking, but don't say, *If all of youse was coming to meet my clan, I'd be scramming out of town.* She persuades me to stay with her in her mom's house by the lake. Mr. Alchemy gets to lounge in the hotel.

I'm itching to hear what she's told them about me. She'd always been slightly cagey when it came to the details of her family. What I picked up over the years is that her dad was a local hockey star. He goes off to college and discovers he's just another middling jock. So he comes back, knocks up Absurda's mom, and settles on being a math teach and football coach. Her dad is the town ladies' man. Her mom, Geez, was Miss Wisconsin Dairy Queen or something. Heather is born after they divorce. Her two older brothers are big blond dudes who look like they were sculpted out of ice.

We drive to the white two-story house by Lake Winnebago. It's like finger-freezing cold. Only had my leather jacket. It's starting to snow, so we hustle inside. Instead of hugs, her brothers greet Absurda by offering her (and us) shots of schnapps, which we take, and they lay out in front of the fireplace playing Styx's "Too Much Time on My Hands," for chrissake. Got that right. We'd be meeting the wives and kids at Thanksgiving dinner.

They act like they last seen Absurda (or Mandy as they insist on calling her) yesterday rather than two years before. Her mom is up in her bedroom. Absurda tucks my hand in hers and pulls me upstairs. Mrs. Akin is sitting up in bed watching CNN, munching American cheese slices and saltines with a glass of red wine by her side. She's wearing a pink sweater with a silver cat face on the front, pink plastic-framed glasses, and pink sweatpants. She don't move. Absurda goes and kisses her. Mrs. Akin acts like she'll get freezer burn if she presses Absurda too close. And Miss Dairy Queen? She must've a won a lifetime supply a milk shakes. Still got a cute face, though her skin is a little blotchy.

Absurda introduces me, and Mrs. Akin nods, a half smile, reaches for my hand, and clasps it way too familiar. "So pleased to meet you, Richard." No one, I mean *no one*, has ever called me Richard.

"Me, too, Mrs. Akin." I feel like a smarmy doofus in a John Hughes movie.

"Come downstairs, Mom."

"Mandy, is your father here?"

"No. Why? Is he coming?"

"He promised to make an appearance. Do you want to call him?"

"No. I can wait to hear his rhapsodizing about how crime free and pristine life is here, and how grotesque and squalid it is in L.A."

The three of us go downstairs, and her brother Jim says to Absurda, "Jody Messerschmitt wants you to call her. Think she's looking for a reunion of Mandy's Men and the Big Gulp Girls?"

Absurda turned, rolling her eyes, toward me. "The Big Gulp Girls was my first band."

"And so aptly named," Jim cracked. I don't appreciate the fucker's snide attitude, but I keep quiet 'cause I know that shit goes down between brothers and sisters. We were always slamming my sister Bonnie.

Her mom turns to Jim and pops him not so gently on the head. "Shut the hell up." Then she goes and *hugs* Alchemy, who obviously she has met before. "Mandy is so lucky to have you as a friend."

"We are lucky to have met each other." Alchemy, who been downstairs getting chummy with her brothers, puts his arm around Mrs. Akin and pulls her close like they're longtime buddies and says, as if he's confiding a special message to only her, "It's great to see you, but I'm eager to get to the hotel. I have some ideas I need to work out." Heather volunteers to drive him. I see Absurda's displeased with that arrangement, so I interrupt before trouble brews. "I'm gonna go, too. We got to do some reconnoitering." Absurda decides she'll join us. The four of us head out.

Absurda sits in the front seat with Heather. Me and Alchy sit in the back. While we're driving, Heather imparts the latest news about Mrs. Akin. "Mandy, I should have told you before that Mom is off the diet pills. On Sunday, she and Jimmy's family went to dinner. She said the waiter insulted her and she started flinging silverware and ashtrays."

"What do you want me to do?" Absurda snapped, and then sighed. "Sorry, Heath. You want me to talk to her?"

"To say what? Just warning you."

"Where's Dad living?"

Heather makes a swift right turn and we head down a few streets. I can't see nuthin'.

"There." She points to a one-story dump, between two much bigger homes with their Christmas decorations already up. The lights are on and the curtains are drawn. "You want to drop in? Never know what or who we might find."

They snickered. Absurda says, "I prefer ignorance." It spooked me out. This whole damn town spooked me out. Makes sense to me why vampires and werewolves always live in places like this.

We drop off Alchemy at the hotel, which was still way better than most of the *Psycho*-like death traps we was crashing in then, and then we head back to the house.

The next morning I hear Absurda up early, thumping her feet and banging drawers, a sure sign she is in one ugly mood. I stick my head between the pillows and go back to sleep.

When I get up later, I take time to explore. Her room is painted pink. Some posters of GG Allin, Poly Styrene, and the Runaways on the wall. A photo on a desk with the Big Gulp Girls with socks taped over their nipples and spread over their twats, goofing on the old guys' trick. Other pics with friends. No guys. I don't go spying in the drawers. Figured that is not cool. Actually, now I wish I'd done it.

I head downstairs, and her mom is in the kitchen dressed in white pants and white blouse with a flower print apron over it. She looks slimmer and is taller in high heels. All perfumed and made up thicker than the snow outside. No glasses. Peeling potatoes and fixing the stuffing. The sisters-in-law are making turkeys they'll bring over later. Mrs. Akin serves me coffee and rolls and scrambles up some eggs and bacon. I don't see Absurda, so I ask where she's at.

"I was out early this morning, and when I got in I found a note saying she went to meet Jody. I invited her for dinner. She was Mandy's partner in crime when they were teenagers."

"She coming? I'd like to meet her."

"Doubt it. Mandy's close friends are afraid she thinks she's too good for them, being such a *star*. You are almost stars. It's *funny*." She shook her head in disbelief. She puts the egg plate down and scopes me out. "You look like maybe you can handle her."

"Whataya mean?" I ask.

"Mandy can be difficult. She's like me that way."

"I never found her difficult. We get along super."

"Lucky you. If she ever gets out of line, you give her a good swat." She tosses that out like she's advising me to buy candies instead of slug her daughter.

Suddenly, appearing at the kitchen door like Scotty beamed her down and all bundled up in a green parka is Absurda. She takes off the jacket and unwraps her scarf. "That's not Ricky's style." She pours herself a cup a coffee. "Mother, I always treasured your advice. You know, since you've done so well with men."

"Mandy, honey, what are you up to now? I thought you'd at least get to fifty, sixty, even seventy before you found someone."

"As usual, you thought wrong."

Mrs. Akin turns to me with a toothy grin. "People always thought we were sisters."

"People are phonies. I found someone who respects me enough not to hit me or cheat."

"How do you know?"

Both sets of eyes now zoom in on me. I was going to defend her (and me). But Absurda needs no defending. "He hasn't and he won't." I realize I'm just a spectator in this sport. "Because you had a child with a man doesn't mean you found a real partner."

"I did the best I could, given the material."

"Mom, you could've left Dad sooner. Left town. It doesn't take long to discover the gene pool here is severely limited."

"You certainly did more than your share of pool sampling before you came to that decision."

"Don't know 'til you try. So, okay, I dated everyone worth dating in this town—and that isn't saying much—since I eliminated anyone whose father you'd dated."

"Dear, don't believe everything you hear."

"It'd be wonderful if you'd do the same for me."

"Oh, Mandy, let's stop. Can we?"

"*I* can."

"Will you help me today? Your sisters-in-law will be here soon. I could use your help. Heather is out with friends. It's her vacation so I gave her a pass."

I move some chairs and tables around in the dining room and then I'm assigned Alchemy pickup duty. I'm thrilled to get the hell out of Bicker Central Station.

The town has one main street. I think there was more people crammed into my block in Flushin' than in that entire county. Everything is closed. Most of the signs are either for wedding and baby shit or For Rent.

Alchemy's room has a bed and dresser from like 1800 an' a new TV, which is tuned to the Lions game. When I take a leak, I see a pair of pink socks on the floor by the bathroom. I kick 'em out with my boot. "What's these?"

"I was uncovered" (even then he registered under aliases, that night he used Marv Throneberry), "so I entertained her."

This time, I got no wish to know more, so I switch topics. "I kind of wish Lux had come. This place is so fucking vanilla."

"What? I'm too bland for you?"

"You? You're whatever people want you to be." Which I heard was one of his superpowers. Salome was as white as Fond du Lac snow. His father, who the fuck knows?

"What I am is Absurda's friend. She needs us. And you haven't met her father yet."

"You met him?"

"Once. The family came to New York to visit Absurda at Juilliard. We should get moving."

There were twenty or twenty-five guests at dinner. Don't ask me no names. I didn't care enough to memorize who was who. Jody ain't showing up. None of Absurda's friends is showing.

Some local gawkers knock on the front door 'cause they found out we was there. *More* had just gone gold. That's not as big as it sounds. Later all our records went multiplatinum. We sign CDs, T-shirts, and stuff. Part of me wished we had played a gig. Given those blandheads some razzle-dazzle and showed them what Absurda could do.

Mr. Akin arrives late. Right away I see this surly mother-fucker owns a pair of ornery eyes and mean lips.

Absurda got up to greet him. They act nervous. They don't sit next to each other at dinner. Most of the blah blah is about sports, the weather, local gossip. Alchemy as usual is talking politics. That might've been the first time I hear the name Louise Urban Vulter, who's gonna be Alchy's political rival in about fifteen, twenty years. She was just starting out doing her talk radio show.

The little demon known as alcohol is getting the crowd louder, and Mr. Akin is slightly riled up. He hollers across the table so everybody is listening in on this exchange.

"Mandy, my princess, what's it like to travel the country and be famous?"

"Better than being here."

"You always thought you were too good for this place."

"No, I was too bad." She laughed and so did most of the guests. "Dad, you should come visit me in L.A. You might change your mind."

"Maybe I will."

"I'd like that."

That seemed to end it. After the main course and before dessert we go into the living room. Mr. Akin comes up beside me and says real low, "I can still eat punks like you for lunch."

"Figures you like to eat dick." I flick him with my fuck finger and turn away. From behind he grabs my wrist and tries to pulverize it. Coaches. Hate 'em. I says, "I promised Absurda I'd behave. It'd take me one second to misbehave. So if you want to go, you keep holding on and we'll see who goes down."

Alchemy slides over and he grabs both our wrists. Mr. Akin releases his grip.

"Ambitious, back off." Which I do.

"I don't want no trouble," I says, not really meaning it. Alchy and Akin step out to the enclosed back porch and have a smoke. Mr. Akin don't look at me again.

After dessert and some folks are leaving, Absurda nudges me. "Hey, all," she lets everyone know, "we're going for a ride by the lake."

Only we don't go by no lake. We drive to her dad's house. Door is unlocked. A bunch of half-busted trophies is laying on the stinky living room rugs. She walks into his bedroom. We do a few quick lines. Then she starts undressing.

"Fuck me on this bed."

Sounds appetizing to me. The asshole has already enemized me.

We are pumping away and just as I'm about to blow my wad, she feels it and she pushes me off her. I come all over his sheets. She takes his pillow between her legs and wipes it with her juice. She gets her lipstick and draws a heart on the pillow and inside writes "mandy & ricky" and tosses it on his bed.

I was impressed by her well-planned vendetta. On the ride back, one thing is rankling me. "Did he ever touch, like sexy, touch you?"

"Never. If he had, I would've done more than come in his bed."

The last few folks is getting ready to leave when we get back. Her father is waiting and asks, "Nice ride?"

No doubt everyone believes we got high.

"*Great* ride." We look away from each other so we don't crack up.

Mellowed by the food and drink, everything seems calm. Even Mr. Gym Teacher, who puts his arm around Absurda. "I was just waiting for you to get back to say a proper goodbye. Mandy, my princess," he says that again, not quite sounding sarcastic, "it's time for me to return to my present, less than palatial home."

There's hugs and fake kisses all around as everybody leaves except brother Jeff (who came in his own car), Alchy, Heather, Absurda, and Mrs. Akin.

I'm curious if Mr. Akin will be sober enough to guess what we done.

Twenty minutes later, while we're cleaning up, we find out. I hear a car door slam, and in flies Akin. Not even wearing a coat, with the pillowcase in his hand, foaming at the mouth. He lunges straight toward Absurda. "You're a sick, perverted bitch."

"I'm sick? What do you call fucking Jenny Heckendorf in *my* bed when we were sixteen?"

Then Mrs. Akin slaps Mr. Akin across the face. "Get out. Get out the hell out of my house." Me and Alchemy are on either side of him. Akin surveys that this is not the appropriate moment to prove his manhood, so he flings the pillowcase at Absurda. It flutters over and she catches it. "Souvenir of my trip home." I see in her eyes she wants to fold up and cry just like a little girl.

We, well, Absurda, decides we should leave the next night instead of Sunday, so we rent a car. As we're standing outside, finishing packing the trunk, it's so freaking frigid I'd've drunk blood to warm me up, Absurda collars Alchemy and me in the driveway. "Keep reminding me of this disaster if I start to go all mawkish about my childhood." She tilts her head toward the sky. She's shivering, so I take off the Green Bay Packers knit cap that her brother Jimmy give me. "Here." I pull it down over her hair and ears. I put my arms around her. She whispers as the wind is whipping off the lake, "The next time I come back here, it will be for their funerals."

27

THE CANTICLES OF HANNAH, III (2001–2002)
Smoke Gets in Your Eyes

No one could miss hearing Hannah's ecstatic cry of "Thank God!" when Dr. Fielding pronounced that her son would live. The doctors refused to speculate for how long, but no oncologist would have bet on Moses's thriving for another twenty years.

Yet beneath Hannah's outward glow, the armor of her perfectly coiffed hair and meticulous outfits, hovered the penumbra cast by the unspoken volumes between her and Moses. She blessed each day that Moses survived, and yet, in the darkest circle of her hell danced the shadow of Salome. Hannah compiled a lawyerly list of reasons why she should not talk to Moses about her: His recovery was taking so long; the doctors had warned them that the process was arduous and that he'd be frail for a year, maybe more. He was weaker than before the operation.

Hannah had lured Jay into playing go-between. Jay did her best to reassure Hannah, who visibly winced at the utterance of the name Salome: Moses had zero intention of coming face-to-face with Salome anytime soon. Moses said he wouldn't make any decision about Teumer until he's, and she quoted him, "'regained a semblance of physical and emotional fortitude.'"

Jay's words only temporarily mollified Hannah. They did nothing to end the odyssey of hushed histories between mother and son.

Hannah and Alchemy began bonding when they agreed America needed to do away with all insurance companies in favor of a single-payer plan. Alchemy joked that it was good to have a lawyer in the family since the insurance company, with its usual audacity, had reduced Fielding's hospital stay request for Moses. They were appealing, but if they lost, Moses would have to pay. This led to private cigarette chats, when Hannah and Alchemy would sneak out to the plaza patio connecting the hospital's two towers. At first, they exchanged insignificant talk of the weather, or the guilty pleasures of smoking; at other times they spoke of the immensity of the calamity that had befallen New York. Eventually, Hannah had ventured into the realm of the personal when she thanked Alchemy for his "sacrifice." His answer: "Never gave it a second thought." Alchemy, deftly if indirectly, then raised the specter of Salome.

"This is unsolicited and presumptuous, but you did a great job raising Moses. There was always the prospect of a headline declaring I had a brother or sister who I'd find intolerable. I'd have no problem returning them to oblivion. Mose and me, we're dissimilar in many ways, but he is a damn good man." Alchemy's grace and empathy disarmed Hannah's psychic tripwire for silver-tongued boys.

"Thank you. I did my best under extremely difficult circumstances."

"Difficult circumstances bring out the worst or best in people. In you, it brought out the best." The look in Alchemy's aquamarine eyes, saturated with the soft fluid of understanding, dissolved Hannah's lingering qualms about his sincere goodwill toward Moses. "No question, he was better off with you than with Salome."

"You think so?"

"Without a doubt."

She felt a compulsion to reach out and embrace him. She saw now that Alchemy's gift was the ability to raise either the maternal, sexual, or fraternal instinct so it precisely suited the needs of his audience, be it one fragile woman or one hundred thousand roaring fans.

"Without a doubt," he repeated.

Never again would they speak of Salome.

After Moses returned home from the hospital, Hannah rented a furnished apartment in Beverlywood on a month-to-month lease. The doctors informed them: Moses must remain at home, and entertain few visitors, for up to six months. None of them were psychically prepared for the lengthy recuperation period. Hannah took quick trips to New York but did most of her work in L.A. This allowed Jay some respite from being the lone caretaker and also allowed her to give Geri Allen relief from carrying so much of their business load.

One morning while Moses dozed in his bed, surrounded by books, Hannah and Jay sat around the white wrought-iron table in the small backyard drinking coffee underneath palm and pomegranate trees. They were looking over an article in the newish issue of *People* magazine with the ridiculous heading, "The Sexy Savior." Worried that he'd be outed by any number of doctors, nurses, and orderlies who could connect him to Moses, Alchemy decided to preempt any sneak attack. He made a deal that *People* would get the first photos of the Insatiables with their new guitarist if they ran this article without any photos of Moses and without mentioning Jay, Hannah, or Malcolm. Alchemy supplied a few quotes about how happy he was to find his brother, who had been given up for adoption at birth, only he wished this wasn't the reason. All of them, including Moses, were satisfied. It looked like Alchemy's gamble worked; although the story was picked up by a few places, no more details or slanderous innuendos came out.

A call from Sidonna Cherry interrupted their perusing. "How's our boy?"

"All in all, he's doing very well," Jay answered while holding up her hand, indicating to Hannah she'd explain in a minute.

"Super. It's taken a while, but Lively got back to me, and he is game to arrange a meeting with Teumer if asked, and if Moses is willing to travel to Brazil. No guarantees, though."

"I'll speak to Moses. I'd say any significant travel is months away."

"You ring me when he's ready. Later."

Jay cautiously explained the conversation, as Hannah's lips curled with indignation. "I've never known that man to say 'good morning' without an ulterior motive."

"I suppose you're right. He probably has an angle."

More than probable, Hannah thought, although that was a lesser worry. "You think Moses will see him?"

Jay recused herself from the role of judge or accomplice in her husband and mother-in-law's game of Tag—You're Guilty. She did her best to alleviate Hannah's insecurities regarding Salome, but frustration edged into her voice. "Why don't you ask him?"

Hannah still couldn't broach that subject. Instead, she delighted in the fantasy of mother and son embarking on a revenge trip. Moses would reject him outright, and Teumer would realize that she hadn't needed him at all. She'd inform Teumer in no uncertain terms that she preferred living alone, being independent, focusing on her career and her son. It was a damn rewarding life. If, in the Book of Fame, her achievements were negligible when compared to Salome, the big-shot artist, at least Hannah was sane and proud: She'd become a prominent attorney. Her son loved her and was thankful for the love and care she gave him. He was kind. He'd faced his illness with courage. Above all, he was a mensch. What more could she want?

Peace of mind.

28

THE SONGS OF SALOME

There's No Place Like Home

Ruggles replaced Shockula, and after almost three years of extended vacation, he freed me on the condition I live under Hilda's supervision. Ruggles believed the healthiest place for my soul was beside Alchemy. I sat uncomfortably buckled into the passenger seat as Hilda drove along Route 25 toward Orient. I felt oneness with the fallow fields streaking by. Before I even entered, I sensated the house vaporized with the same fallow air. Still, I was free to love my son. All summer Alchemy bounded about, almost giddy to have me around, the three of us living a near-ordinary life. I could walk anywhere in Orient whenever and wherever, eat when I got hungry, climb to the roof of the house and commune with the moon. Go to the movies. Have sex! Only, Hilda's wary gaze seemed to follow me everywhere. I was not going to spend my life decaying in Orient, nor ever again would I part from Alchemy.

Nathaniel, "rehabilitated" and released from prison, remained on probation. In his letters, he'd been pressing me to move in with him to his apartment on 3rd Street between First and Second Avenues. Xtine had a steady girlfriend. Even if she hadn't, full-time coparenting didn't suit her, and the

Chelsea would not be Ruggles's idea of an ideal home. Before we could move anywhere, I had to win Ruggles's approval and find out from Bicks Sr. what legal rights Hilda possessed to keep Alchemy from me.

Another condition of my release ordered therapy with a New York mindsucker chosen by Ruggles, which afforded me an excuse to go into the city every week. I would vamp around for the day and take the last bus back. A few months after my release, I spent four days with Nathaniel. On our second night, he dressed up in his "courtroom suit," hair patted down, gray-brown goatee trimmed neat. He planned an evening not exactly in keeping with the revolutionary who believed dinner at the Odessa verged on extravagant. We stopped at the Barclay for a drink and imbibed the waterfall-like playing of an underfed harpsichordist. As we strolled up Fifth Avenue to the Top of the Sixes for dinner, at a corner newsstand Nathaniel eyed a *Post* headline lauding Reagan. I waited for his usual tirade, but instead, he clapped his hands. "No politics tonight. Promise."

Near the end of the evening, both of us tipsy doodle—he even danced with me during "Night and Day"—he placed his hands flat on the table. "Salome, we should think about getting married." I gagged on my champagne. He quickly handed me a napkin and added, "for practical reasons."

"Nathaniel, I'm the paragon of impracticality."

"That's why I love you and why I'm prepared to wait. I agree with you that 'marriage' is often a codified ritual that keeps a woman subordinate to a man. You don't need to answer now." He began twirling his napkin, his legs wriggling like a Saint Vitus' dance sufferer. Marriage would undermine Hilda's claims to Alchemy. (Though, he joked, a convicted felon and a "certifiable" might not make the ideal couple in family court.)

I tried not to cry. I couldn't help myself. I swilled my champagne, thinking, *What response would hurt him least?*

"Oh, Nathaniel" — I hiccupped between sobs — "I love you so."

"As well you should." He deadpanned.

"I can't promise you monogamy." I couldn't admit that I'd been occasionally sexing it up with one of the stud fishermen I'd met in Orient, and two weeks before I'd checked out the scene at Studio 54. Studio's odor smelled of a snooty Philistine profligacy, not democratic Dionysian freedom. I made sport with a coltish South American tennis player there. After three years of celibacy, nothing could put a damper on my libido.

"I'm not asking for it, nor am I promising it to you. We'll practice a polyamorous lifestyle."

"I'll make your life more than a little untidy." That was one massive understatement. "And I'll always be a liability."

"Life is a risk. You think I want safety? Look at my life. Your instability is my stability. Do you think I don't know who and what you are?"

"And who and what do you think I am?"

"A selfish, out-to-lunch artist with a heart as big and soft . . . as a marble."

He made me laugh. I loved him and wanted to be with him — most of the time. He believed he could accept my flighty ways and catch me before I stumbled. He was the right father for Alchemy. Male artists throughout history had wives and mistresses—why not start a new trend?

I took his clammy right hand between mine. "Let's live together first. When I'm ready, I'll propose to you."

What could he do but acquiesce? I redecorated his shabby two-bedroom walk-up. Alchemy helped me paint the walls bright red and blue and hang yellow velvet curtains over the windows. I brought in fresh flowers and began picking up furnishings at thrift stores. Yes, I became nesty. But nests are not built to last forever.

When Bicks Sr. arrived from Florida a few months later, we met for dinner at the Café des Artistes, his favorite eatery just around the corner from his apartment.

"You're looking hardy." His voice strove for effervescence yet limped out ruptured and hoarse.

"I most certainly am." Unlike him. Beneath his usual sartorial uniform of bow tie, vest, pressed suit, and shined shoes, he looked less lifelike than a rotting wax museum mannequin.

"Salome, don't tell me what your expression is saying. I look sickly because I am."

"I'm sorry."

"Don't get sentimental. It's not like you. I've had a good, long run."

"Okay, Bicks. Question, then. If I marry Nathaniel, will that get me out from your son's control when you…"

"Die? Probably not. Which leads me to a serious bit of business. Your time in Collier Layne has drained your trust to a low level. We made some nice deals on the land that was once your father's farm. We have no other source of replenishment."

"Which means?"

"Though small, the monthly stipend you received before is being withheld."

"In case you decide to send me back to the brain-burn unit?"

"It will not be my decision. But yes, if you must return." I appreciated Bicks's honesty—honesty within limits, at least. "Irrespective of your financial situation, you should marry Nathaniel if you love him. Other impediments can be overcome." The old undercover swisher understood my needs better than most.

"Speaking of fathers, you know that Lively came to see me at Collier Layne?"

"No, no, I didn't." He adjusted his hearing aids.

"Don't get your diapers in a knot." I decided to test his limited honesty. "Something in his Bible Belt forthrightness forced him to fess up that Marcel Duchamp and Greta had a quicksilver assignation that produced me."

His cheeks puckered, and I thought he might spit out his foie gras.

"Miss Garbo never revealed that information to me."

"That my father was Duchamp, or someone else?"

"Neither. I never asked and she never volunteered."

"You wouldn't tell me if she had, would you? Don't bother to answer."

"You're not going to try to stalk her again, are you?"

"I wouldn't call wanting to meet my mother 'stalking,' and no, I don't want to see her." I pulled out a brand-new red beret and handed it to him. "This is for her. She'll understand. Promise me that she'll get it." He nodded.

Inside I'd taped a picture of Alchemy and written on the back of it, "Now we're even."

29

MEMOIRS OF A USELESS GOOD-FOR-NUTHIN'

Pee Brain, 1996

The fiasco in Fon du Lac—or "Fun to Fuck," as we called it—brings me and Absurda closer than ever. Life, and I ain't being sarcastic, was great. Even though we played New York a bunch of times, I don't see my family. I took Absurda for a drive 'round Flushin' once. We come back to the city to play a three-night sold-out gig at Irving Plaza. The shows was nutso. We'd only play such small venues when we're doing some Alchy political deal or the KROQ Almost Acoustic Christmas shows 'cause they gave us airplay that helped launch us.

On the third night, I invite some of my guys from Flushin'. Most of them has moved out 'cause the hood is changing. Only Nova and two other guys made it.

Sue and Andrew think they're doing me a favor by inviting my mom, my sister Bonnie, and my brother Lenny. My dad ain't invited but shows anyway. Like I wanna see their grizzly mugs. They never stopped panhandling me and I ain't ready to donate even more to the lavish Lifestyles of the Lowdown and Pusillanimous. Learnt that last word from *The Wizard of Oz*. Don't think I'm some cheapo, 'cause when we signed our mega-mil deal with Kasbah in '98, me and Walter Sheik work out a charity-tax-trust where I lay out over a million large for them to divvy up and then put the closed sign on the Mindswallow ATM. I buy Bonnie a house in Valley Stream and a beauty salon so my mom lives and works with her. Does well, too.

They're all together just to the right of the stage. We're jamming during "Licentious to Kill," where Alchemy usually swoops into a Jack the Ripper act. He slows us down and starts one of his raps and we follow his lead. "Lots of you know Ambitious here, and he and Lux are my brothers. Ambitious's family is in the audience tonight." My guys, they boo my family. Others applaud and whistle. I'm feeling anxious about where he's going with this. "Now, Ambitious, tell me. What'd your father always say about you?"

Catches me totally unprepared. My guys are hollerin' "Asshole," "Moron," "Jailpussy." I'd forgot about that beaut. Still, I spit out instinctively what Alchy's wanting. "That I am forever gonna be a useless good-for-nuthin'."

I stare at my family, who is thinking this is pretty damn funny, except my father, whose eyes are popping, and I hear his ferret hiss like he wants to rip my skin off.

"Yeah, now this might surprise you, Ambitious...because I agree...I think you're a damn useless good-for-nuthin'." I look at him like, "What the fuck side you on?" I hear my guys laughing and I mouth for them to "shut the fuck up, you cocksuckers," and above it all I hear my dad's squeally laugh. Alchy keeps going, "You heard of Oscar Wilde?" I nod, though I'm not fully sure who he is except some gay writer who got tossed in jail for doing what comes natural. "Oscar Wilde said, 'All art is quite useless,' and I agree with that, too.

So to me, that makes you an invaluable piece of *beautiful art that I wouldn't trade for nuthin' in this world.*" I want to go over and hug him, only he wails on the word "Killllll..." and we pounce on the chord.

Years later, he pens "Friendsy for You"' for the *Nihilists* CD, which has my fave lyrics:

With a frenzy like yours, who needs enemies?
With enemies like you, who needs friends?
Your sex life goes in one hand and out the other,
True enough, you wanna do my mother
With a soul brother like you, the fun never ends
Your father says "you a loser wit' no heart"
I say you're a piece a priceless fuckin' art

After the show, I allow Nova and my family backstage. I introduce them to the band, and my mom starts cozying up to Absurda right away. I invite Nova (but not my family) to the private party downtown at Madam Rosa's. My mom's parting words is, "Ricky, ya always was a selfish little shit."

At the party, me and the guys are getting bombed and also doing some excellent blow. Everyone in the club, including Mr. Alchemy, is inebriated on something. The Sheiks and Andrew has arranged for Absolut Vodka to sponsor the minitour and they was gonna sponsor the next big one, too. So the spirits was flowing. The club is filled with all kinds of slurpies wanting a piece of the Insatiables' action. Alchemy is poontang king of the road. Sometimes, I'm sort of jealous because me and Absurda are still a pair. Been about four years at that time. I never before had no girl love me like that.

Around 4 A.M., I need to piss something fierce and the bathroom is fill up 'cause Falstaffa and Marty is using it as their pharmacy. I step outside. Madam Rosa's was on St. John's Lane, this tiny street just below Canal. I stumble past the bouncers, and after about fifty feet, I see Alchy's back, and at first it looks like he's pissing, too. I'm about to yell, "Stop right there, you're under arrest for desecrating the spotless streets a New York." But before I do, I hear Absurda. She's squatting down in front of him, so she can't see me and I can't see her face. "Thank you, oh...Alchemy...thank you...You're the best. Ever." I don't need to see her to get what *that* voice means.

I just feel sick. I feel so burnt. I say screw them, it's too fuckin' perverted. I lam back inside and Nova is rappin' with these two chicks. I join the discussion. Then this guy, looks like to be around my age, steps between us. "Hi, my name is Stevie Stevens and I work for the ad agency of AY&S Worldwide, and I'm dying to talk to you. We'd love to use your song 'American Van' for one of our GM commercials."

I'm more than a tiny bit distracted, and I says, "'American Van'?" Nova and me, we look at each other and roll our eyes at this tool. The girls are giggling.

"Yes. Your song, 'We're an American Van, We're an American Van, we're coming to your town...' The lyrics are perfect for our spot."

"Sure. Sure." I really can't concentrate 'cause I'm discombobulated by Alchemy coming back into the club.

"Can I give you my card?" He sticks out his hand.

"No." I slap his hand away. "You call Andrew Pullham-Large and talk to him first."

Absurda is back and surrounded by her girlie fan club, the Nightingales. (They still exist. Only it's creepy now.)

I feel like I gotta get out of there or I might have to kick some ass. Nova, the chicks we been talking up, and me, without saying goodbye to no one, hop a taxi uptown to party at the Plaza. We go up to my room and are just getting into it when my brother Lenny—fucking Andrew told him where we was staying—starts slamming his fist against the door and screaming, "Ricky, why are you treatin' us like we're some smelly ragheads?"

I open up, and he puts his tattooed mitt on my naked shoulder. I take his hand and snap it away like it's pigeon shit. "Lenny, if I hadn't made some dough, ya bastids woulda thought a me 'round about I dunno…never."

"You think you're so freakin' special. A somebody. You ain't shit. You just got lucky. I coulda been in your band and do the same bomp, bomp, bomp crap you do."

"You coulda been…but you ain't. Now take your fucked 'tude and get the fuck outta my sight."

"Not 'til I let ya know how Ma was a fuckin' wreck after you left. She didn't leave her room for weeks."

"Like that's new? Lenny, Ma was doin' half the dickwads on the block for a bottle a cheap wine. Christ, she even fucked Nova's pop." I look back at Nova and he turns his head away. We never done spoke about it, but I knew. "And Lenny, our dad is a wife-beatin' prick. And you're a loony met' head. Choke on them facts, Mr. Tough Guy."

He smacks me across my cheek. I jump him and we roll around like two retards in the hallway. Nova's pounding

Lenny's head, and one of the chicks is all right and starts kicking him. The other was taking pictures with her little camera. Some guest called security. Lenny and me get arrested. Nova flushes the drugs down the toilet, gets dressed, and scrams 'cause he was on parole. I made the cover of the *Post*. MTV News loved me. Man, Kurt the Lode practically ran the nightly Mindswallow report for a few months.

A lawyer bails me and Lenny out. I don't hear from Alchemy. Turns out no one else has either for like twenty-four hours. We all assume he is off sexing half the city. Nope. He's with Salome at Collier Layne visiting her shrink. They're driving back that night.

My emotions was all confused. I'm still pissed at what I seen and heard and want to pummel him. I'm also, I gotta admit, intimidated, well, fucking terrified, that he's going to toss me out of the band. And I ain't exactly thrilled about having to do time in a nonjuvee jail. Before we confab at the Chelsea, I meet Lux in the lobby of the Plaza and he is majorly PO'd. He noogies my forehead like I'm Curly and he's Moe.

"Ambitious, what the hell were you doing? You shouldn't be dissin' Absurda, picking up other chicks in public. Or private."

"Buck," I says, itching to try to describe the shit goin' down between them, "I expect this jive from Alchemy. Not from you."

"Ambitious, this isn't jive. This is your band. Absurda is your lady. Don't blow it."

Lux, he never come down on me before, and though I'm seething inside, I can't bring myself to explain more fully so I take his abuse. I need to see Absurda and Alchemy first. "I wasn't thinkin'. Let's leave it at that. Me and Absurda, we'll handle our private business privately. And you don't know my family."

"Right. And I don't want to."

We laugh, and that puts a lid on it. We go to Xtine's place at the Chelsea. She's this dyke friend of Salome's who I heard about but never met. Only Alchemy ain't there. Salome and Absurda are buddying up beside each other on a futon.

Salome yells out to Xtine, who is in the kitchen on the other end of the loft. "Meet Mis-ter Lux Deluxe, a fine representation of the human race. And Mr. Ambitious Mindswallow, he's a former teenage killah." Salome grinned kind of loopily at Absurda. Absurda gives me a soft smile but don't defend me or nuthin', like she would've done twenty-four hours before. I'm feeling shitty for her *and* thinking, *Fuck you, I seen what you and him was up to.*

Salome, strutting in tight blue jeans and leotard top, nuthin' fancy but dick-busting sexy, sashays over to the kitchen table and holds up the picture of me in the *Post*. "Cute. Photogenic. Xtine should shoot you sometime. Not as cute as the photo of me when I was accused of *murder*." She holds out that word like it's glistening hot in her mouth. "You think you're the only *killah* in the room?" No doubt in my mind, she's a killah. "Someday I will tell you about how I was called a 'murderer' by some who I thought were my friends." She cranes her neck in my direction. "You must take care. There are those who you think are your friends who aren't real friends. Beware the schadenfreude! You know what that is, my killah bee?"

"Something to do with Singmut Freud and shocking people?"

"Not bad, not bad. In fact, I quite like that definition. It is when others take pleasure in your pain. I am sure you are most familiar with the concept from the side of the envious. The more you succeed, the more others will want you to fail. And when you fail, behind your back there will be an orgy of gloating."

I figure my mother and father is having a damn good gloat right at that moment.

The front door opens and Salome announces, "Here is the man who can resuscitate your image." Alchemy shows up with Andrew, Sue, and this cocky-looking dude in a black suit, shiny leather shoes, and hair that looks like he just left the car wash. Reminds me of some '50s dandy. Or maybe Bryan Ferry. It's Alexander Holencraft, a PR expert. I got to say, against my initial instincts, he ends up being a decent dude. Holencraft got me on *Entertainment Tonight* and angles the whole episode so I look like a stand-up guy who is real generous to his family.

Alchy ordered in about ten pizzas from Lombardi's. After we eat, Alchemy signals we need to huddle up. So me and him head into the bedroom alone. I'm expecting a conflagration. Only he's all Mr. Sunshine and Hippie Love and says that me gettin' in some scrums with the law is more than predictable. He wished it hadn't been with my brother. Then he takes his fist and rubs it against his nostrils, and I think, *Uh-oh, here it fucking comes.*

"Holencraft spoke to his protégé from AY&S, the one who talked to you about the GM commercial and 'American Band.'" I nodded. "I advise against doing it. It's up to you and, I guess, Don Brewer and Grand Funk Railroad. Count me out on that one. It's bad enough I had to give in about Absolut and the tour. I, the band, we won't ever do ads."

I'm so stunned I'm practically choking on my tequila.

"I'll see." I'm still anticipating the death stare or some ultimatum.

"Look, it's up to you and Absurda to work this out. How it plays out for the band." That's the threat I been expecting. He ain't done. "It may not be possible"—he's half smiling—"but try to be a little more cautious. If you and she are over, it upsets me but I get it. Don't do anything rash—think before you punch—to make it worse for her. Or you."

I'm really wondering if he spotted me the night before. I have no freaking idea how to handle what I seen. My compass of not caring was all upside down, and the two people I normally would've asked for advice I can't, 'cause they is Alchemy and Absurda.

Back in the living room, Brockton has arrived and is priestifying on Clinton being a closet Republican. I stop listening. I'm feeling agitated with my own case of Nadling, and I got to talk to Absurda.

I sidle up to her and whisper, "Let's go for a drink."

"I guess we should."

"Yep."

We bid our goodbyes. In the hall I ask, "Where do you want to go?"

"Let's just walk." Which we do. Neither of us saying nuthin'. I let her lead the way. It's about ten or eleven at night and freezing. We head west toward the river. Chelsea ain't fully happened yet and 22nd Street is like "follow the crack vial road," with whores and trannies playing the part of Munchkins. We head south toward the Florent restaurant on Gansevoort. She knows the Froggy owners and we get a table in the back. Finally, she murmurs, "Why'd you do it, Ricky? *Why?*"

I'm sitting there, my fists clenched, knowing I can't hit her, trying to figure out how to say what I seen without screaming, "You lying two-timing fucking cunt," when she just slumps down over the table, looking skinny and wasted instead of raunchy and slinky, and starts to sniff, holding back tears. It rips me up, and suddenly *I* feel like crying. I can't say nuthin'. She says, sounding like a funeral march, "I guess we're not a preposition anymore."

"Guess not. I'm my own front-page article." She don't laugh.

"You don't love me anymore?" She looks up, and for the first time all night she stares right into my eyes and doesn't even blink until I answer.

"Not that way. Ya know." I shook my head. "Four years. Long time, ya know."

She gets up and scampers outside to the corner and I follow her. I grab her and she buries her head on my shoulder and I hold her while she is gasping for air and sobbing and sobbing.

I loved her like nobody I ever loved before. Truth, I love Carlotta, my wife, and I was wacky over Bryn, and then some other women for about ten minutes each, but I never loved no one like Absurda again. I didn't care about all of them other guys she fucked or whatever she done. Only, after what I seen and heard, I couldn't bear to stay with her no more. I just couldn't.

After like fifteen minutes, she says, "You don't know how sorry I am."

What she don't ever know and I wish to this day, to her dying damn day, I wish I had told her how fucking sorry *I* was.

I know you ain't supposed to curse the dead, and the guy made me rich and famous and well fucked. Only sometimes it don't matter one little rat turd 'cause I still think...

Damn that Alchemy.

30

THE CANTICLES OF HANNAH, IV (2002–2004)

The Dead See Scrolls

Hannah had begun spending more and more time in L.A. She fretted that she'd become a nuisance to Moses and Jay's insular life, although Moses continually assured her the opposite was true. Jay welcomed Hannah's company on "mother-daughter" outings she'd missed with her own mom, like shopping and getting their hair and nails done. During these outings they spoke about what being a woman meant in a business world still too dominated by men, and most important, they grew emotionally closer.

One day, while she and Jay shopped at the Venice farmers' market, she caught Jay eyeing a group of mothers close to her age with young kids. "Cute, yes?" Hannah ventured.

"Cute for about an hour and then it's work."

Hannah suspected that Jay's implacable expression and terse tone served as a defense to her desire to be among them. Hannah let it go.

A few days later, when Jay was at a client's, Hannah broached the subject with Moses. "So, I know you two decided long ago not to have kids, but I wonder if you've ever reconsidered making me a grandmother."

Moses answered in a voice tinged with annoyance, "We reconsidered. And came to the same conclusion."

"You or Jay? Or both of you?"

"Ma, with my future so unpredictable, I think it's more responsible not to."

"And Jay?"

"Why? She say something to you?"

"No."

"Mom, I'd love to make you happy. Only sometimes, I can't. Okay?"

Not wanting to upset him further, Hannah changed the subject.

"Moses, you know I'm going to be sixty-seven soon, and this cross-country commute is getting harder and harder."

"Jay and I have talked about that. We hope you'll give up your New York place and move here permanently. You can continue to work from here. Or retire."

"You want that?"

"Why wouldn't we? I just never thought you'd leave New York. We could celebrate holidays together and drop around whenever we feel like, all without it becoming a major ordeal."

"That would be wonderful. I'd like to do some pro bono work. Make my own hours."

"I, we'd love it."

Hannah, almost teary-eyed, decided right then to move to L.A. by the end of December.

A week before Christmas Eve, Hannah sat alone in her New York office. Suddenly feeling a bit light-headed, she took a gulp of water from the cup on her desk and scanned the place where she'd spent the majority of her waking hours for the past thirty years. All the small artifacts, the external architecture of her life, would soon be condensed into a few cardboard boxes.

From the top right drawer of her desk she pulled out a favorite picture, one she knew would have upset her parents: a six-year-old Moses wearing a white shirt and red vest, and sitting on Santa Claus's lap at Gimbel's. For some crazy reason she began to list, in no particular order, all the department stores she'd seen disappear over her lifetime: Loehmann's, May, Stern's, Abraham & Straus, Altman, Ohrbach's, Korvettes, Best, Bonwit Teller, and Gimbel's. Interrupting her memories of a lost New York, William III ambled into the office. "Last chance to change your mind." William III smiled, knowing she was determined to go.

"I appreciate it, but as well as Moses is progressing," she said with a sigh, "I want to spend some good years with them."

"Hannah, you feel all right? You look a little flushed."

"Tired and understandably anxious. I think I've chosen the right time to retire."

"You think it's the right time to 'retire' this?" He placed a manila folder with the name "Malcolm Teumer" typed in the top right-hand corner on her desk. She assumed William didn't know that despite her desperate desire, never once in forty-five years had his father and grandfather allowed her access to the "Malcolm/Moses" dossier.

"Your father wouldn't mind?" Hannah pressed her hands between her chair cushion and thighs so he wouldn't see them shaking.

"He hasn't looked at it in years. When you're done, into the shredder."

She tried to control the quavering in her voice. "Can you leave it? I want to finish packing first."

"I'll be heading home in an hour or so. Bring it by my office before then?"

"Of course. We'll retire it together."

Hannah waited until William was safely down the hall. She stood up, a bit dizzy. She steadied herself, circled her desk, closed the door, and sat back down. She shut her eyes and exhaled. She opened her eyes and put on her reading glasses. Finally, she beheld her holy grail. Her breath and pulse quaked as the ghost ship of the no-longer-obliterated past arose.

She relived that final morning: By the time she woke, Malcolm was already out of bed. His pajamas neatly folded on the chair and bathrobe hanging in his closet. She stepped into her slippers and shuffled down the hall to Moses's bedroom. She smiled at seeing Malcolm leaning over his son's crib. He tilted his head toward her, his now all-too-common gaze glacial, and announced matter-of-factly, "I was just saying goodbye." He walked toward her, barely grazing her cheek with a dry kiss. His shoes rat-a-tatted down the steps and he grabbed his coat. "I will see you at dinner."

She picked up Moses and clutched him to her chest. She yelled after her husband, "Pot roast tonight. Try not to be late."

Back in her present, she cursed aloud. *Late? Maybe better never.* Her anger at allowing herself to become spellbound by such a transparent rainmaker had never subsided.

Her hands shook above the pages, as if they were the flickering candles of the Friday night prayer service that she was about to bless. She took a cigarette from the pack on her desk and reached for the "secret" ashtray that she'd already put in the carton on the floor. She lit the cigarette and inhaled. She blew out the smoke. She coughed and put out the cigarette in the ashtray. Her hands and forehead gushed sweat. "Calm yourself, Hannah, calm yourself," she whispered, and wiped her forehead. From her pocketbook she pulled out a tiny pillbox filled with aspirin and Valium — she swallowed only the tranquilizer. She exhaled and opened the file. Her chest began to tighten. She felt a throbbing in her forearm as she gripped the glass and took another sip of water. She stared down at Laban Lively's notes. "As a member of the OSS advance cadre, I was among the first men to enter Germany and it is then when I first encountered the man we now call Malcolm Teumer..." The enormous pressure in her chest intensifying, she gasped for air, feeling as if a massive fist had punched her in the jaw. She struggled to reopen the pillbox to take the aspirin. Teetering on the edge of her chair, Hannah collapsed to the floor.

Forty-five minutes later, tired of waiting, William swung by Hannah's office and knocked on the closed door. "Hannah, I hate to rush you, but I have to get home." When she didn't answer, he opened the door. "I know it's so hard to lea— Hannah!? Oh, my God. Somebody call nine one one!"

31

THE MOSES CHRONICLES (2001–2005)
Kaddish

Not since he was a brooding teenager had Moses contemplated life without his mother for more than five minutes. Now, five excruciatingly long weeks later, when the thought entered his head, he banished it. The hemorrhage of sadness over her sudden death was suffocating him. One thought, underscored by his daymares, pounded away: That a Faustian bargain had been made and Hannah died so he could live to meet his biological parents. It was irrational, he knew. With whom was this bargain struck? Some god? Some karmic force? A vision of the Virgin Mary on a potato knish? No, we live in the quantum universe, answerable only to the emotionless laws of science. To assign the timing of Hannah's death an ascertainable logic was to find a grand design where none existed. His mother, finishing her last days of work, had suffered a massive heart attack. Simple as that. Years of smoking, no exercise, a simultaneously aggressive yet bound-up personality, and pernicious heart genes finally caught up with her. Her death had nothing to do with his survival.

When his tears stopped, no sermons could dispel his internal sobbing. His actions in the world of objects and people were those of a man drifting in a somnambulistic trance. On a good day, numbness prevailed. Already emotionally trauma-tized by Moses's illness, Jay flailed helplessly to keep their spir-its from succumbing. She begged Moses to go out more often with her. Or have their friends over. He refused.

Moses's social interaction was limited to the Internet. He and Alchemy often e-mailed and IM'd about politics, books, music, and movies, the virtual locker room verbiage common even to nonathletic guys like Moses. Alchemy continually solicited Moses's views on the national and geopolitical events of the day. Sometimes Moses answered. Sometimes he didn't. Alchemy let Moses know he'd been elevated to the role of "chief history and current events adviser" alongside the ailing Nathaniel, who had suffered a series of disabling strokes. More intimate and delicate was the subject of Salome, whom Moses made clear he was still not ready to meet. Not infrequently, her "presence," her madness, rattled through their conversations; they spoke of mood swings, bipolar disease, and the genetic basis of lifelong depression versus the postoperative form, from which both agreed Moses was suffering. One July middle of the night, as Moses surfed sites on psychosis and genetics, he tapped Alchemy's IM moniker.

MThead23: Talk time? Yay, nay, or way dismayed?

Sctfree1: way dismayed, but still, yay i say. how're you feeling?

MThead23: More so-so than yay-yay. You know my motto? What doesn't murder me only makes me more tired.

Sctfree1: astutely mottoed.

MThead23: You just get in from carousing?

Sctfree1: carousing in the nightmare. woke up. sleep deprivation demon now lurking.

MThead23: Lurking here too. What's worse the nightmares or the insomnia?

Sctfree1: i'm easy or uneasy with either.

Sctfree1: one is fear of sleep. the other is fear of life…

Sctfree1: in one you have no control. the other, you have the illusion of control.

MThead23: Both presume a fear of death. I'm afraid of the fear of the fear of death.

Sctfree1: the only thing we got to fear is fear itself? i fear anyone who buys or sells that can of bullshit.

MThead23: Yeah, with food lines stretched from the Hudson to the Mississippi, that was one good sales pitch. That fear was real and so is my fear of death.

Sctfree1: after what you been thru, damn right. my fear – the void is de void and then the big id panic hits and i get undid by my id.

MThead23: You got any ideas how to handle it?

Sctfree1: feed the id…fuck drink play music. do good works. try to avoid acting like a self-righteous nihilistic hypocrite.

Sctfree1: you?

MThead23: I fantasize about doing some of those things.

Sctfree1: i see this shrink, ben butterworth.

Sctfree1: does random associative nocturnal therapy. basic idea in RANT is that insomnia is a form of exile from your subconscious. that dreams and nightmares can help explain and repair the exile.

Sctfree1: he has legit phds from stanford and the psychological institute.

MThead23: Is it helping?

Sctfree1: well, "the void is still the void/and I'm still awake..."

Moses laughed and sang to himself the next lines of the Insatiables' "Sleep of Faith," which he knew well: *and with rocks in my roll / holes in my soul / and gods to forsake / I'm searching for the sleep of faith* before reading farther.

Sctfree1: yeah, some. i figured out a few things. ben helped me accept and embrace both my nightmares and insomnia. other shrinks willied me out as voyeurs with degrees who wanted to mess with or understand my "creativity." ben respects that and wants to leave it alone unless i want to delve into it.

Sctfree1: and i don't.

Sctfree1: he calls you at indiscriminate nighttime hours and if you're awake you have a phone session. if you've been asleep he wants to know what you were dreaming/thinking the second you woke up. his theory is that in scheduled sessions the brain and body prepare beforehand and your defenses rise too high. in trad therapy most people pretend and blab about themselves.

Sctfree1: if you're interested…

Moses did not immediately contact Ben Butterworth. He stuck with his "trad" therapist, and aside from the occasional Xanax, continued to resist the pharmacological antidote. He had started teaching a limited schedule. He still spent much of his time at home, where he often hibernated in his room, feeling stranded, a Robinson Crusoe who feared more than desired finding Friday's footprint. He stared blankly at books he could not concentrate on enough to read, or the computer screen pouring out endless bytes of forgettable minutiae. More than once, twice, ten times, he found himself reaching for the phone to call his mother who, of course, could no longer answer. *How goddamned idiotic,* he berated himself.

One afternoon, a messenger delivered an envelope from Alchemy. Moses read Alchemy's enclosed note: "Three tickets to Rio. Open-ended dates. You alone. You and me. You and Jay. You, me, and Jay. Your call." Jay watched as Moses dropped the envelope on the wood floor and crumpled up the note and threw it against the wall. Jay strode in from the kitchen and uncrumpled the note. She read it while Moses stood motionless.

"Moses, what is wrong? He helped save your life. He wants nothing and is—"

Moses stepped in front of her, picked up the envelope, took out the tickets, and marched down the hallway to his room. His eyes indicted Jay with a clear warning: *Do not pursue this line of questioning.*

On a top bookshelf of his room stood the menorah that once belonged to Hannah's mother. Around it he'd hung Hannah's favorite faux pearl necklace, which she'd also gotten from her mom. He lifted the menorah and placed the tickets underneath its stand. He knew damn well at that moment he was not honoring his mother's wishes: "Moses, do me proud and act like a mensch in a world of putzes." He collapsed on the Turkish rug. And simply lay there.

Jay eased into the room and knelt beside him. Her eyes welling up, she cradled him. "Moses. Cry. Cry. Please."

After many moments, she spoke in a calm yet determined voice. "You can be mad at me, at your illness, at Salome, at your mom, your dickhead father, *whatever* else you want... You have lots of reasons to be angry and sad, so be angry and sad! Let it out! And then, be generous. Be thankful for all you *do* have."

"Jay, I could not have survived without you." Moses searched for the adequate words, but he could only muster, "I'm sorry. So sorry."

Neither one could articulate exactly why or for what he was apologizing.

Over the next month, Moses skirted his glance toward the tickets. He could neither rip them up nor act upon the offer.

Finally, thinking, *Why not?* he decided to get Ben Butterworth's number.

Butterworth, a stocky man in his late sixties, with still-black, neck-length knotted hair and a withered face, looked like a mixture of Gertrude Stein and Geronimo. His brown-eyed stare was as brawny as his heft. A former college wrestler, Butterworth carried himself like someone thrilled by psychically pinning his patients to the mat. "My aim is to excavate and translate the essential messages from the dross embroiled in that lava mass that we label the unconscious," he began. "This instant, tell me three fears. *Don't think.*"

"I have these daymares. I had one in the hospital that haunts me. I don't want you to confuse these with fantasies, sexual or otherwise. They're nothing like that."

"Don't explain. Don't digress. Talk."

"I'm afraid of losing my mind. That my wife really wants my brother, who she slept with before we met, and that I was her second or third or twentieth choice and she settled for me after she'd had her fun because I'm a schlemiel. And meeting either of my biological parents." He surprised himself that he had not mentioned death.

"Tell me your 'daymare.'"

Moses pressed his back against the worn gray couch with equally worn and gray pillows. It was either spill or get the hell out. Butterworth remained inscrutable during Moses's halting equivocations of the "Visitation" daymare. When he finished, Butterworth volunteered his reactions.

"There are many dimensions of 'reality' we don't understand. Odd things occur that can't be explained. That does not make you a candidate for a mental breakdown. I believe in what can be proved and I'm agnostic on what cannot be disproved. I do not subscribe to past life memories, extraterrestrials, time travel, ESP, or any other speculative sci-fi concoctions. This doesn't rule them out for eternity. It rules them out for now. There's more in here" —he pointed to his head and then to the heavens—"than there is out there. We work with your daymares. Your dreams. Your all-too-human insecurity and jealousy probably have more to do with you and your self-image and your parents' desertion than they do with your wife or brother. Still, those are universal emotions that have implications we can examine, and they will become less detrimental if we resolve the issues with your parents. Your daymares intrigue me. They seem to be a form of night terrors, *pavor nocturnus*, accompanied by hallucinatory sleep paralysis. Most so-called professionals are ill equipped to properly diagnose and treat these disorders. I am equipped. I can work with you." He stopped. His eyes projected compassion without sentiment. "Go home. Think about it. No questions asked if you choose not to proceed."

32

THE SONGS OF SALOME
You Talking to Me?

In late August, Alchemy and I moved in with Nathaniel. Hilda didn't put up much of a fuss after Bicks Sr. informed her that I was within my rights. Nathaniel, Gibbon, Ruggles, even my New York therapist blathered on about how I needed to rent a studio and get to work. I lacked inspiration. The opportunity to use it for activities other than making art might be too enticing.

I'd kept my polyamorous diversions to zero until Nathaniel left town to do a series of university lectures deploring Reagan's election and the few flatulent and toothless protests. Alchemy spent the weekend with Hilda. Holencraft finally received his long-awaited reward (he rented us a suite at the Pierre), which was sexually gratifying, but after the fact added a nasty odor of moldy banana bits and rusty nails to my soul-smell. It put me off flings...for a time.

I was still unmotivated to make art or exhibit until one late night while vagabonding across the Brooklyn Bridge. Awash in the East River's aquatic mist and the skyline's iridescent flickers of light and death, a corpselike man wearing a long overcoat bumped into me. I stumbled, snapping the heel of my silver mule, and scraped my right palm on the pavement. I leaned back against the rail and yelled, "Watch out, asshole!" Already far ahead of me, he turned and waved a massive fist and kept walking. I felt droplets of blood oozing from my hand. I dabbed at them with the bottom of my blouse when the psychopomp communes of Lou Andreas-Salomé—DNA ancestor, rapturer of Nietzsche, Rilke, and Freud—vapored through my body. "Do not let men or their desires intimidate you, not by physical strength or the demands of marriage or sex. Never let any man dictate the designs of your life."

She absolved me for my slavish behavior when I was under Horrwich's sway. "Oh, I understand. I lament that the photo of me whipping Nietzsche and Paul Rée has become my legacy. It overshadows my books on female sexuality that predated Master Freud. True child of mine, do not let us down. I expect you to right the wrongs of our history."

Inspired by her visit, I created the *Women of the Scourge* series of representational canvases (which appalled Gibbon), challenging the historically accepted phallocratic histories of my women. My first painting was Juan de Juanes's *Beloved Disciple and Jesus* with Jesus as Salome's disciple. I modeled Salome's face on Greta's. Using the same role reversals, I did Charlotte Corday and Marat (Jacques-Louis David), Salome and John the Baptist (Caravaggio), and of course the photograph of Frau Lou and Nietzsche.

At the opening, Alchemy came running up to me. He had scraped his elbow, which was bleeding. Gibbon fetched a Band-Aid and I bandaged it quickly, but not before Frau Lou ascended to me. "Salome, you must protect him. Explain to him the history of these works. It is essential to his future and ours."

Gibbon and I made a pact about selling the paintings, which were fetching five figures—I could veto a sale to anyone I deemed unworthy. Over Nathaniel's protests, I sold one to Malcolm Forbes, who gave me a ride on his motorcycle.

A few nights after the exhibition came down, Nathaniel and I went to our favorite Chinatown dive. After the salt-and-pepper squid, he sighed and shrugged his shoulders.

"Yes? Speak," I demanded.

"I received a letter from Jean-Marc at Vincennes University in Paris. They offered me a one-year position." Nathaniel had adopted the tactic of unveiling any potentially inflaming situations while we were in public, and with Alchemy present. He thought that might keep me from erupting.

"Are you asking me to join you? Or telling me you don't want us to come?"

"Of course I want you to come. But there are extenuating circumstances."

His desire to escape the U.S. didn't surprise me. He was appalled by Reagan's election, felt thwarted by the apathy of American college kids, and was energized by the promise of the new French Socialist prime minister Mitterrand. He explained that Vincennes was no longer the radical flash point, but it still offered an opportunity he couldn't find in America.

I didn't erupt then—not because we were in public but because his evasiveness wounded me. "Are you sure this isn't a ploy so you can leave me? Or so I'll marry you? What happened to offering us stability?"

He removed his glasses and rubbed his eyes. His bottom and top teeth clicked against each other as if they were tapping an urgent telegraph. I understood that his once vibrant hope for domestic calm was wrecked by me. In dark moments, I feared he saw himself debased by the cunningly crazy dominatrix with whom he had tragically fallen in love.

"Not at all. I won't desert you. I want you two to come."

"And I want you to take it."

Over the following weeks, Nathaniel never mustered the courage to say: I am going to France with or without you. Our relationship became laden with recriminatory jibes and plaintive facial tics. I finally erupted.

"Stop looking at me as if I'm your ball and chain!" I stomped off and locked myself in the bathroom. Facing the door, I shrieked, "I love you, but if I marry you, you'll share power over me with the Bickleys. I can't give you that!"

His bare feet thumped on the wood floor toward the bathroom and he bellowed in his self-righteous/aggressive/injured Nathaniel-Brockton-on-the-podium tone that he rarely used with me, "Is that so terrible? You can't possibly trust them more than me!"

I tempered my voice. "You love me and they don't. You'll act with your heart. You'll feel guilty. I don't want to hate you if you put me back in Collier Layne. And you will." I opened the door a few inches and peeked out. "You're scared, right? Afraid that I was in here hurting myself?" He grimaced as if I'd clawed his cheek. "Answer me, Nathaniel!"

"Yes," he said dejectedly. "Yes, you scare me. Are you proud of it?"

Perhaps it was better for all if he left without me.

33

THE MOSES CHRONICLES (2005)

The Big Enchilada

Almost four years after they first met, Alchemy insisted they have dinner at the Don's, a local Mexican restaurant in Culver City. Moses was already seated in a booth and reading a book when Alchemy slid into the seat across from him. "Sorry to interrupt. You look engrossed. What is it?" Moses held up the cover that read *The Disinherited Mind* and then placed it down on the table.

With the exception of a few goo-goo-eyed glances or thumbs-ups, the customers couldn't have cared less about the famous guy lounging in the crusty booth in the darkest corner of the room.

Alchemy ordered a large guacamole, three tacos, a shrimp fajita dinner, a beer, and a margarita all for himself. Moses was always impressed with his gargantuan appetite and his ability to remain damn near skeletal. Alchemy finished crunching down a chip with hot salsa and guac. "I do my best to keep Salome and Nathaniel away from L.A. because I don't want to tempt you without knowing what you want to do."

"Still nothing."

"You sure?"

"Butterworth says I have to do what feels right for me. I'm still healing, and then the real battle will begin. Ruggles has no idea how Salome will react. And I have no idea how I will react to her reaction."

"Sounds right. How's it going with Ben?"

"Eking along. The middle-of-the-night calls freak Jay out, and then she's cranky in the morning. I've started frequently sleeping on the futon in my room." Moses, thinking that might sound suspicious, quickly added, "Not that often. I mean we're... you know." He wasn't about to admit that their sex life had diminished considerably, a fact he skirted around even with Butterworth. "She supports the therapy. He and I are doing some traditional in-office work, too."

"You look healthy. Not so fragile."

"Doing some yoga. I'm lousy at it, but overall, doing okay. Blood tests have been good."

"Excellent... Any chance I'm going to be an uncle?"

Moses looked up and stared at the seaside painting on the wall. He was sorry he even hinted at the possibility during their talks while he was in the hospital.

"Sorry, Mose, I shouldn't have asked."

"We reconsidered it but..." He didn't finish his sentence. If he had, it would've gone like this: *I'm still afraid I'm going to die soon and I don't want my kid to be fatherless at three years old and I don't think Jay wants that responsibility and we're cold-shoulder arguing over nothing, which is not a good atmosphere and I'm going to be fifty and she forty*... Instead, Moses changed the subject. "What is so urgent about meeting up?"

"We're embarking on a world tour to promote *Noncommittal*. I'm leaving in October and I'll be gone off and on for about two years. It's the Around the World in 800 Days tour."

For the past two years, Alchemy and the band, with Absurda's replacement Silky Trespass, former guitarist of the Come Queens, had been touring the States. Moses and Jay did not mention seeing them when they played L.A.

"Have you discussed seeing your father with Ben?"

Moses didn't understand what seeing his father had to do with the Insatiables going on tour. "Yes, and according to Sidonna Cherry, this guy Lively said he is still willing to allow an audience," Moses said sarcastically.

"Laban Lively?"

"You know Lively?" Neither of them had mentioned Lively to the other before.

"Yessiree. We first met when I was a kid and I bit his ankle just before Salome stabbed him with box cutters."

Moses had read about this incident, but it had omitted Lively's name and Alchemy's biting Lively. He couldn't stop himself from grinning. "And you wonder why I'm afraid to see her."

"Oh, no, I don't wonder at all." Alchemy scrunched his eyebrows and shook his head. "She also managed to slice her hands before Lively slapped her unconscious and they took her away to Collier Layne."

"You saw all this?"

"Most vivid memory of my childhood. When they took her away was the last time I cried, until Absurda died."

"Alchemy, I'm so sorry."

"So it goes."

Moses rolled his lips together, pressed them against his teeth, and lowered his eyes. Each time he peered into the carnage of Salome's madness and the burdens her affliction cast upon Alchemy, he felt more deeply bonded to his brother than he could have ever imagined.

"So Lively is friends with your father?"

"Seems so. Lively insinuated that he was WWII military intelligence and they met during the war and continued a business affiliation ever since."

"Salome says Lively is CIA. What? Mose, you look distressed."

"I've been more obsessed about my father than anything else in my life. And now when all I must do is act and ask . . . I can't . . ." Moses halted, his words stuck in this throat. "Every time I seriously consider making plans to meet either one of them . . . I think about my mom, Hannah, I really miss her . . . and I become almost cataleptic."

"Shit, Mose. What I'm going to say might help you. Might make it worse."

"Wh-at?" A tremor crept into Moses's voice.

Alchemy gulped down his beer. "Mose, this is tough. Salome is going to have a major exhibition at the Hammer Museum. Some new work. Some old. Not happening for maybe two, three years. She'll be visiting often. I wanted to give you enough time to absorb it. Mull it over. Or get out of town."

Moses cupped both of his hands around his glass of lemonade. "Thanks. I think. Jay would've probably found out. I wonder if she's already heard rumors."

"It's bound to get around the art world."

"I've searched Salome on the Net and cross-examined Jay about her art. I wish Salome's parents were alive. Maybe I could have asked them about my 'death.'"

"Me, too. For lots of reasons."

"I'm still terrified of confronting her."

"Wish I could say your fear is unwarranted." Alchemy stood up. "I gotta use the facilities and get another beer and taco. You want something?"

Moses shook his head, overcome by a daymare:

Slipping and sliding along a jagged cliff, I walk into the sky, but instead of falling, I float-crash along. Suddenly, I begin to plunge through the atmosphere. I'm screaming but no words come out. I smash into the ground and my body, like a rocket, burrows deeper until I crash in a dark mine. Everything in my life is being sucked into the mine on top of me—Jay, our house, cars, clothes, books, and CDs. Someone is sealing the mine and burying me alive. From aboveground I hear the laughter of the dybbuk Shalom, —Don't miss your last chance.

Gasping for air, I yell, —To do what?

"Yo, Mose. Mose?"

Moses looked at Alchemy vacantly.

—I warned you . . .

"Whew. I'm surmising you've inherited the Savant dream-state gene."

"Suppose so."

Alchemy didn't inquire further, and Moses didn't want to hear any more about his inheritance. "Bro, brought you a beer. Sorry if I upset the balance."

"No worries. I appreciate the heads-up. So, can I ask a question about your father?

"Shoot."

"You think I should see her and Teumer, but you never want to see Phillip Bent again?"

Alchemy scarfed down another taco. "It's not the same. Salome is your mother. It might be good for her, since no one seems to know what really went down. She wanted you. And your other mom is gone. With Teumer, shit, I get that. It's hard for me to admit, but yeah, I wanted to meet my father. When I did, like I told you, he was a prick who has never changed. Fuck it, Mose, no one understands your hesitation more than I do. I know what it's like to be unwanted. I also understand that what I'm going to say is no fun to hear." Alchemy took his time and took two more gulps of his beer. "Salome never got over your death."

"I guessed that, only I'm trapped between guilt, curiosity, and fear of a rejection that will crush me. Let me cogitate."

"Sure." Alchemy lifted his beer bottle. Moses lifted his. Alchemy began, "To..." His eyes shifted toward the book still on the table. In a brotherly epiphany, they simultaneously said, "...the disinherited."

34

THE LAMENTATIONS OF MALCOLM TEUMER, I (2006)

Pleased to Meet You

Malcolm Teumer took pride in his ability to outwit and out-live the tormentors who had desired his death for nearly sixty years. If he were to die now, approaching his eighty-fourth birthday, his final word would be: victory. Still, he had been agitated when Laban announced that the second son of Salome Savant sought an audience. *Better him than Moses*, he thought.

The night before, he had watched the Insatiables' live Globo TV concert broadcast with three of his thirteen grand-children. Such noise. Not music. He left them for another room, where he muted the sound on the TV. He examined this Alchemy who roused and exploited the primitive needs of the masses with an admirable élan. Now Malcolm looked forward to their encounter.

He relaxed in the courtyard on his white cushioned chair centered amid the landscaped greenery. To his left, a fountain with seven naiads spraying blue water surrounded a statue of the spear-carrying Ares.

A guard notified Malcolm as Alchemy's limo passed through gate and made its way to his driveway. A servant escorted Alchemy to the courtyard. This vaunted buck with his pococurante gait, prominent chin, and frosty blue eyes was imbued with a magisterial assurance reminiscent of his mother. His muscular arms and taut upper body were highlighted by a tightly fitting soccer jersey given to him during the televised concert by Ronaldo, the Brazilian football star.

Malcolm stood up and the two men shook hands, taking each other's measure. Malcolm crossed his sturdy forearms across the chest of his short-sleeved, button-down green shirt. His frame was more roundish than trim, his white hair closely cut around the sides and back of his bald, freckled crown.

"Sit, please."

Malcolm offered him a cognac. Alchemy assented. They did not toast.

Malcolm asked, "What do you hope to achieve with this meeting?" His accent lilted lightly Germanic, and his words resounded with the bellicose syncopation of a chopping knife against a wooden cutting board.

Alchemy replied, "To see if there is any benefit in Mose meeting you."

"Acting as his savior was insufficient? Now you have anointed yourself the family unifier." Malcolm dismissed any pretense of politesse.

Alchemy's expression turned to one of slight amusement.

"You're implying what? That I'm upset because you screwed my mom? You grossly overestimate your importance in her life. You're just another slug in a very long line of unmemorable slugs she fucked and discarded." Alchemy paused, barely repressing a rueful smile. "I imagine a man of your instincts would be curious to hear how she remembers you."

"Your imagination reflects your ego's need, not mine."

Undeterred, Alchemy continued, "After I met Mose, I asked her about your relationship. She'd never mentioned you." Alchemy chose his words with precision. "She said she wished you were her best friend Kyle when you fucked. She called you a 'fiendish little man with the soulsmell of sour pickle juice.'"

Malcolm laughed jovially, as if he'd been complimented. "You should have been my son. You are hard. But he, he behaves like a weakling."

"Mose is not weak."

"If he were not so cowardly, he would be here instead of you."

"That is where you are wrong. It takes great fortitude to accept your emotional deficiencies rather than pander for love and recognition."

"Are you sure you are not speaking of your own situation?"

"Perhaps." Alchemy conceded the point and shook his head solemnly. He relaxed his elbows on the chair's armrests and clasped his fingers together in front of his chest. "Perhaps your ego is still smarting over the way Salome tossed you out because you loved her?"

"That assumes you believe I am capable of love."

"I've made only one assumption about you." Alchemy leaned forward, picked up his drink, swished it around his mouth, and then, like a Clint Eastwood avenging hero, spit it on the grass a foot to the right of Teumer's chair. "Nothing you've said so far leads me to believe you have any remorse for how you treated Mose or Hannah."

Malcolm stood up and grinned eerily. "Follow me." This insolent child needed a lesson in humility. They entered the house and walked into a room dominated by one of the untorn canvases from Salome's *Flowers, Feminism, Fornication* exhibit. "Wait here." He turned and left the room.

Malcolm returned in less than two minutes. He handed Alchemy a medal—a silver iron cross with a red, silver, and black ribbon. "For you."

"Why? Why do you have this? I don't want this."

"Give it to him, if you prefer. And these." He placed a slim sheaf of stapled and typewritten pages on the table. "Take them. Show them to your half brother. Or destroy them. The choice is yours. It seems you are now his keeper. It has been my pleasure to entertain you."

35

THE SONGS OF SALOME

No Exit Interview

The day Nathaniel departed, I took refuge in Orient. I didn't want to beg him to stay. Still, I wrote him often, and although I missed him, through autumn I contentedly flaneured about.

At Alchemy's Christmas break we flew to Paris and stayed at Nathaniel's flat on Rue du Cherche-Midi. The three of us would lah-di-dah to the Luxembourg Gardens, where we read Alchemy the French canon of subversive lit.

Nathaniel often convened with the Babacools, a group of aging or neo-hippies, at the Rond Point café for a nightcap or three. In another noncoincidence, one night Marlene Passant, the *Nouvelle Obs* arts writer, rumbled into the café flanked by two aspiring artists. She shed them and sat beside me. After ten nonstop minutes condemning America, praising me, and a candid admission, "I, too, have been incarcerated for unbecoming societal behavior," she fluffed her henna-colored hair and grinned like a feral cat. "I both detest and comprehend French sneakiness so I am sneakiest of all. You could use a viper like me on your side. Gibbon is selling the works you release to him too cheaply. You don't have an exclusive with him, do you?" I shook my head. Marlene was a surefire homicider with a soulsmell mix of shag carpet soiled with dried semen and freshly minted French francs.

She called the next day. "I secured a commission from a collector for forty thousand dollars. Do whatever you want. I have access to a studio on Rue de la Roquette that you may use." With a rush of adrenaline, I finished a *Scourge* painting: Delacroix's *Liberty Leading the People* with the face of Arletty (a famous pre-WWII French actress who became infamous because of an affair with a Nazi officer) as Liberty leading faceless Holocaust victims to the camps. On the painting I scrawled my version of the French motto: "Liberté, Egalité, Mendacité." Marlene and the collector were more than pleased. She paid me sixty percent rather than the usual fifty.

After Christmas I flew off alone to London, ostensibly to see an exhibition of work by the conjurer William Blake. My true motive was to infiltrate the spirit of Phil Bent, Alchemy's genetic dispenser. I located him through an executive at EMI, Bent's former record company, who arranged the meeting but warned me to expect "a rather decrepit and pitiful sod." I checked into the Hotel Russell Square, and the next morning I took the Underground to Earls Court. A gray and matted-haired *Macbeth*-like witch, with a golden front tooth, answered the door of the ground-floor hovel. If it weren't for his scraggly three-day beard, I might've thought it was his mother. He reeked of old sweat, hard snot, vomit, beer, cigarettes, and greasy wrappings of fish and chips. "Who de, heh, fu—Salome? Wha?" Next to him, Keith Richards would've sounded like Churchill. I didn't know if he'd forgotten our appointment or he was pretending. I blurted out, "You stink. Why don't you take a bath?"

He regained a speck of lucidity. "It's cold in 'ere and ain't got rot to 'eat up the water." The tub's heater only worked when you deposited some coins. "Maybe you could gimme a nice body wash. You always did get 'ot in a loo." He lamely reached to grab my right tit. I slapped his hand.

"The kid with yer?"

"Do you want to see him?"

"What the bloody fuck for?"

"Good goddamned question."

"That why you 'ere? 'Ow much is it worth to yah?"

He was collecting royalties, though perhaps not much, from the Baddists' records. "Fast Enough" remained a staple of oldies rock radio stations. Any money I gave him would go for heroin, pills, and alcohol. I muttered, "Nothing."

I cursed myself all the way back to the hotel. I wished he were dead. Terrified of the frailties he, and yes, I, too, had given to my son. I called the apartment. No one answered. I checked out of the hotel and left London a day early without going to see the exhibition.

I got back to the Paris around 8 P.M. Ana, the wife of the Portuguese concierge, was babysitting Alchemy. I found him in Nathaniel's office, which we'd temporarily converted into a bedroom, lying flat on the top of Nathaniel's desk listening to Captain Beefheart's *Trout Mask Replica*, which along with Brautigan's *Trout Fishing in America* Nathaniel had bought him for Christmas. I stood silently in the doorway until he sat up. My almost-thirteen-year-old-going-on-forty son turned his head and winked at me. I winked back.

"Do you like it?"

"It sure is different. Nathaniel told me I had to listen a few times before it made sense. I've listened to side one four times."

"And?"

"I'd like to meet the Captain and ask who he listens to."

"Maybe Nathaniel can answer that for you." I cozied up on the desk beside him. I hugged him, trying to exorcise the demon seed residue from Phil Bent that flourished in him no matter how much I wanted to deny it.

Nathaniel hadn't told Ana or Alchemy where he was going, only that he'd be home around midnight. I traipsed over to the Rond Point. From the window I spied Marcel, the reformed mobster maître d', pouring a drink into a glass for Nathaniel. Across from him fawned a luscious-looking girl. Jealous and thrilled, my instincts were to swoop in, pluck her from him, and devour her myself. I went back to the flat.

Nathaniel sauntered in close to 1 A.M. He told me he'd gone to see *Duck Soup* at the Pagoda cinema with some colleagues and then got a few drinks at the Rond Point. I didn't ask who the colleagues were. I didn't want to hear his wiggly words as lies or truth.

Nathaniel focused instead on my anguish and listened patiently as I told him about my disastrous trip to London. I realized how fortunate I was to have him instead of the

Bents, Horrwiches, or even the Holencrafts of the world. Then we fucked.

Overnight, my excitement at seeing Nathaniel flirting with a young hottie turned my spirits Savant Blue. I felt the pull of the dark matter. To Nathaniel, I pretended meeting Bent was the only cause. I had to confront him. Two nights before Alchemy and I were to leave Paris, Nathaniel and I went for dinner at the La Moule en Folie.

"Nathaniel," I began. His eyelids twitched. "The night I came back from London I saw you with a woman in the Rond Point. I don't care or want to know if you are screwing her."

He began tugging at his glasses. I clasped his wrists inside my hands. He tried to speak. "I, no—"

"Stop."

"But—"

"No! I've forfeited the right to know. No matter what you do, I will always be faithful to you in my fashion. I told you to go have affairs. But Nathaniel, first you came here without me and now there is someone else."

"Salome, there's no one else. A group of us went to the movies. We went for a drink after and then the others left."

I trusted his explanation. I also sensated a deeper disloyalty. "If I can't have you on my terms and that means I can't have you at all, it is my fault. Not yours. Nathaniel." My chest tightened, but I had to ask, "You have to tell me if you aren't coming back to New York when this semester is over."

"I don't know where I'm going next." His expression colorless, tone glum, gaze teetering into vagueness. Gravity Disease was beginning to infect his soulsmell with the deceitful scent of a rusty galvanized water pipe, and I was the cause. I fretted all through the night. All I could think about was removing myself from a life where I could hurt and be hurt by others — and if he were to desert me, I feared I'd end up inside Collier Layne.

36

THE MOSES CHRONICLES (2004–2007)

I Read the News Today, oh Boy

When he got home from the dinner with Alchemy, Moses asked Jay if she'd heard about Salome's upcoming exhibition. She admitted that she had, however she'd hoped it wouldn't happen so she'd stayed silent. (She remained mum about her visit to Kasbah's offices, where she confronted her "new" brother-in-law and testily explained that if he didn't warn Moses about the exhibition, then she would.)

This Salome news did nothing to dispel the discomfort that had infiltrated the home of Moses and Jay like an odorless California fungus over three limbolike years.

Moses had finally regained much of his strength. He had resumed teaching a three-quarter course load and doing research for his proposed book on Holocaust survivors and their relations to God. Despite adhering to an exercise regimen and healthy diet, the illness had noticeably aged him. His hair had grown back with streaks of gray. At forty, Moses's demeanor had retained an energetic boyishness, but by his late forties his being was characterized by a wizened frame, eternally puffy eyes, and an emotionally brutal fatalism that a long life would not be his, which earned him a new Alchemy appellation: Early Eminence Grizzled. At thirty-eight, Jay, who could still swim twenty laps with ease, was in the prime of her life. The Bernes & Allen consulting business forged ahead, spurred by a booming economy for the wealthy art-buying strata. With the outer trappings and inner dynamics of their postillness life evolving, Moses adjusted his Livability Quotient and now nurtured a commodious solitude within himself while subsisting on the little pleasures of life.

As the months rolled on, Jay spent more and more time attending to her business and socializing with clients. Unlike pre-illness times, Moses abstained from joining her, preferring to stay home or occasionally meeting with his "history pals" from graduate school. And Jay had stopped accompanying him to SCCAM events.

They resumed their usual summer and spring break vacations. In the past they had alternated on who chose the destination. Now Moses ceded the decisions entirely to Jay. More often than not, citing fatigue, he would remain in the hotel room reading while Jay toured, hiked, or whatever. Moses felt that as long as they spent dinner and evenings together, all was well.

During a spring break trip to the Grand Tetons, Jay announced that she no longer wanted to use birth control. "Moses, how about we let fate decide?" Moses, while making his usual case against fate in general, and specifically his worry about leaving her to raise a child alone if his cancer returned, saw Jay's body deflate. Joylessly, but wanting to please her, he surrendered. "Okay. Let's give it a shot."

Over time, Moses's resistance took a more passive form: He no longer initiated sex. When Jay did, he often found an excuse and said, "Not tonight." He tried not to worry over their diminished sex life until one night when Jay called from a MOCA party and asked him to look for the diamond pendant that once belonged to her mother. She could've sworn she'd put it on but now she hoped she forgot. He found it in her sock and stocking drawer, alongside a fairly new vibrator. How could he complain? Better she fantasize than slip off with another man—as long as that fantasized lover was not named Alchemy.

Butterworth and Moses explored the gnawing whispers of what other "meaningless" affairs Jay had withheld. Moses found no portents in any other past affairs, hidden or not, that could imperil their future; that responsibility fell upon his insecurities.

During one afternoon session, Butterworth, in an uninterrupted and evidently prepared speech, dismantled Moses's equivocations with unsentimental precision.

"Your parents' abandonment, your mother's death, Jay's dalliance with Alchemy—all are fixed actions beyond your control. You possess the power to change your perceptions and therefore their effects. Knowledge is power, but there are times when knowledge is painful and counterproductive. Is this the right time for you to answer some hard questions? Would it have served you better to be raised by an unstable Salome and an emotionally ill-equipped father? Would you be better off never to have met Jay? Or screwed her and left her and been alone when you became ill? Would you feel more masculine if you'd balled those coeds? You've chosen not to initiate a meeting with either of your biological parents. You've chosen to stay with Jay. The manner in which one perceives the past can alter the way one exists and acts in the future. When you got sick, you acted. You saved yourself. You can do the same with your past and your future.

"It will take time. The unconscious, with its diabolical intricacies, is the greatest trickster of all. This will be no Pauline conversion. Shedding habitual, unhealthy behavioral patterns, letting go of both the trivial and large hurts we all suffer, the envy of what others have or have done, and thus reordering perceptions and gaining acceptance—this takes immense time and incalculable effort."

Moses, shell-shocked by Butterworth's barrage, could only nod along with a spate of "I knows" and "I sees." In time, he accepted the challenges. Butterworth was right. It was not an epiphanic journey, more like a never-ending Escher maze with no destination in sight. But Butterworth's methods appeared to be more than Band-Aids on open wounds. Rarely did a new daymare slip through the sluice that emptied unmasked fears into his conscious mind. Months passed without falling under the spell of previous daymares. He slept less fitfully most nights, when Butterworth didn't call.

On a Sunday morning in October 2007, as he sat down at the kitchen table to eat his whole wheat bagel with light cream cheese, Moses picked up the *Los Angeles Times*. As was his habit, he read through the news section, then flipped to the Calendar section. His eyes immediately fell upon on a photograph of Alchemy and Salome, arm in arm in the Hammer Museum, under a headline that announced Salome's upcoming retrospective.

The moment of reckoning had arrived. Moses began hyperventilating.

Too agitated to wait until Jay awoke, he marched into what they still called their bedroom and hovered beside their bed, like an impatient child waiting for his mother to make him breakfast, staring and shuffling the paper until she reluctantly opened her eyes.

"What?" she mumbled sleepily.

He read aloud the opening paragraph. "You knew, didn't you?"

"I got a mailer with listings for upcoming shows last month. No idea about the article."

Moses bit into his bottom lip with his front teeth; he wanted to lash out. He couldn't. She'd heeded his wishes to keep mum about what she heard about the exhibit unless he inquired.

"Do you want to see her?" Jay asked as she put on her bathrobe and slippers.

"How can I not?"

"I have a plan."

"A plan would be good."

"If you want to wait until late January, the private opening is usually a few days before the public opening. Let's go as Mr. and Mrs. Bernes, art collectors. You can meet her and then see what you want to do next."

Moses's anger wilted. "That sounds reasonable. I'm going to call my brother."

While the Insatiables toured the world, Alchemy and Moses e-mailed often. They limited their correspondence to politics and culture, occasionally mental and physical states, but avoided intimate confessionals. As far as Moses knew, Salome and Nathaniel still resided in New York.

Now that the Insatiables had returned to L.A., Moses and Alchemy were planning to meet for dinner at a restaurant in Pasadena sometime before the Insatiables took off again in a few weeks. Moses didn't want to wait. He called Alchemy. His ire palpable, Moses didn't begin the conversation with preliminary niceties.

"Alchemy, I deserved a heads-up. You know I scour the papers."

"I assumed you'd decided not to deal."

"That's bullshit. You should have told me." In forming his new Livability Quotient, Moses had chosen to believe the show would never happen.

"Yeah, I'm sorry. I fucked up."

"Yes, you sure did."

"I can't undo it. She's gone but she'll be back. You want to know when? Ruggles has retired, but he's willing to come out here if you decide to meet her. But Mose, we, you and I, still need to meet before I take off."

"Why?"

"'Cause I have some stuff to talk to you about that might be better said in person."

"No, spill it now."

He paused. "Mose, well, fuck it—the *Enquirer* is threatening to do a piece about my sex life and . . . Jay, shit . . . They claim they got proof. No idea what they call proof. Mose, I wish all of this could've gone another way."

Moses simply said, "Me, too," and hung up the phone.

37

MEMOIRS OF A USELESS GOOD-FOR-NUTHIN'

A Room of One's Ownership, 1998–1999

It took a while for me and Absurda to stop doing the tiptoe two-step and become two dudes playin' in the band, able to party like the messy breakup never happened—and for me to feel like I wasn't gonna get tossed on my ass, outta the band and back in the deep end of the shitpool. Mostly them years was like one never-ending recording-touring session interrupted by some notorious incidents. We made five new records between '93 and 2000 and played more than a thousand shows. Some critics who loved us at first dissed us later, saying we was lucky to make it before the music biz fragmented and we only popped so big as a reaction to the synth-mope blandness of the '80s. Big yawn to them. Alchy was a constant geyser of songs, semen, and ideas. I used to think he must've been cranking up. Meth, 'roids, something. Nope. He'd often go three, four nights, gettin' maybe two hours of sleep a night before his eyes were protruding like burnt popcorn kernels and you couldn't mumble hello without him being disputatious. That's when he'd pop some tranqs.

Alchy's relaxation is sex games, and I can only partake after me and Absurda have uncoupled. I ain't usually a group sex guy, and I've stayed away from the porniest details of his sex-capades, but after a show in Dallas, this "mom" who Alchemy sexed before and three very hot and very young cowgirls want to entertain me, Lux, and Alchemy. We check what we call the Miranda Wrights of the young ones. For you who won't admit they watch cartoons, Miranda Wright was a female cop on Disney's show *Bonkers*. We use that as code when we think a potential may be too young or just plain trouble. The mom swears for them. Marty delivers a couple of grams. We get high and then Alchy says to the mom, "Come hither," so she strips and sits on the edge of the bed. He reaches into his suitcase and pulls out a rare Thomas Green beauty from the 1700s. For a lefty, Alchy sure loved his guns—for lots of uses. He points it at his head. "Savant roulette, anyone?" I freeze. Lux, who seen the sex stuff before, still gets twitchy. Alchy pulls the trigger. Zip. Mom slips the smooth barrel, which is like six inches long, into her mouth and starts gumming it. "'Happiness is a warm gun," he croons. Mom falls back on the bed and grabs the gun. Alchy kneels down and his tongue goes into overdrive and she's still suckin' 'til she starts coming. Fuckin' freaky.

Turns into one dead-dick-in-the-morning night. I ask him, the next day, "What the hell was that?"

"My mom told me to always please a woman before you please yourself. So, I do."

"Not that, I mean the gun thing."

He just smiles all mysterious. "Tonguing and gunning..." I always wondered if Salome told him about that, too.

Despite drugs being everywhere, Alchy only indulges if he needs it to close a sex deal. Me? You name it, I tried it. How else you play the road like that? Especially when we were traveling donkey class the first few years. Absurda was the only one in the band who got hooked, although, at first, none of us seen it that way. Not even Mr. Savant.

We all finally got hip to her problem being so destructive in spring of '98 during a six-month Euro tour. We'd already recorded most of *Blues for the Common Man*. Alchemy likes to try the songs on the road and come back and redub, remix, clean up, and maybe even redo or dump some entirely. It's going great 'til Absurda misses a gig in Naples. She hired a driver to take her and some Italian smoothie who latched on to her to Pompeii. She says some fresh iced tea made her sick. None of us buy it. Lux is so furious and worried his biceps is Nadling at warp speed. He insists we do a intervention and get her in rehab ASAP. Alchemy has a sit-down with her. She agrees to Sue, who is tour manager, rooming with her. Absurda don't miss none of the last six shows and plays great.

Back in L.A. we're working on the intervention. As an excuse we're gonna have a dinner to discuss the video for *The Ruling Class*, which is about half the world's population being under twenty-five.

I was crashing at Alchy's newest digs, a four-bedroom place in the Hollywood Hills. Salome and Nathaniel had moved into the guest house. Alchemy never finished furnishing any of his houses. He got closest after he met Laluna and had Persephone. This place was half empty and half filled with Dumpster-worthy shit that Salome used in what she called her art. Sometimes there was lots of crap I was scared to sit on, eat off, or even touch. He and Salome used to go on spending sprees, piling up art, books, and old records, and she drags home some weird shit like old clocks or rat skeletons. Alchemy is also beginning his life as the rock 'n' roll Bruce Wayne: money maven by day, politico by evening, and rock god by night. He starts Winsum Realty and we're his partners. He scopes condos and houses and land parcels so they meet his "aesthetic criteria." He dumped lots of 'em before the crash in '08 and we made plenty of dough. We donated some of the money and buildings to fix up in New Orleans after Katrina and New York after Sandy and an urgent care center in east L.A. Later, he starts Audition Enterprizes. We ain't partners in that but can invest on a case-by-case basis. I admire his good-guy shit, but I don't get involved.

I'm still carousing, and one night I got into a fistfight at Little Joy, the dive, and then did the Howard Stern show—me and him get each other, being two dudes from Queens who got out—live like 6 A.M. I get back "home" and Alchy is awake. He says, "Let's go see some stuff for Winsum. Or maybe for you." I don't like nothing he shows me, and we land at the House of Pies over on Vermont. I'm still sorta drunk—I snuck in my own bottle a scotch and poured it into my coffee cup, and he don't know I popped a coupla midnight runners as well. While I'm eating a pile of onion rings and fries, I notice Alchemy is consternated so I get all applesauce brained and admit, "I'm embarrassed to be so lame, I feel like all of this is a fake-out and I am a fraud and one day you're gonna ice me for something I don't even know I done, toss me out just like you found me, and it will all disappear."

He gives me a face like I gutted him with a knife and sits his elbow on the table and leans his chin against his fist. He don't say nuthin' for a few minutes. "We need to have this conversation, especially in light of Absurda's problems. There is no crisis that can bring you and me down. That is not going to happen with us."

"How the fuck you know that?" I say again, because I'm thinking of what I seen outside a Madam Rosa's and how, even though I'm cool with Absurda, I'm still pissed off. "What if I do something stoopit like Marty?" Truth was, Marty still worked for us.

"What could you say that would be so horrible? I know we could always work it out." He said that in his Alchemy-controls-all voice.

I'm still feeling like his looking for a place for me is some kind of warning, or maybe some Alchemy trap. That maybe he knows I seen him and Absurda, and he wants me to say something. But I never forget if it comes down to it, I'm the one who goes, so I say nothing and change the subject.

"Why'd ya pick me up in the first place?" All those years, I never done asked him. I didn't worry about not having shit 'til I had it.

"Coincidence is also opportunity. It's up to each of us to read the signs and make good or bad decisions." That was the hookie-dookie Alchemy in a nutshell. "Remember when I had that nightmare in the motel that first night?"

"Fuck yes." He had them after that, but I never got so spooked again. He later told me they was love and hate notes from his unconscious and he'd be lost without them.

"The way you reacted, I trusted you. I still trust you. My mom, contrary to the grief she gave you that day—"

"Still does."

"She blessed you with the Salome seal of approval. Said that you were no phony."

"No kidding?" I was flabbergasted. "I thought Salome always sized me up as some smelly sock you toss to the dog as a chew toy."

"Nope. One more thing you have to be sure about. Ambitious, you've made it to the big leagues, the toughest league of all. And no one, not I, your mother or father, or anyone can take that away from you except you. Besides, no lie, you are my street brother."

I swear to fucking God I was almost crying. That was the forthrighteous reason I ain't bought a place, at that time I love being with the band on the road and living with him, and even Salome and Brockton. They was my family.

38

THE SONGS OF SALOME
Humpty Dumpty

Back in New York, my mystagogues in limbo, bored, and horny as hell, wondering if it was over with Nathaniel, I lust-fucked a few young studlies. The satisfaction was short-lived. To fill the hollowness, I wrote Nathaniel a letter a day. He wrote me twice a week and called every other Sunday. He returned to New York for two weeks over Easter to meet an editor who wanted him to do a book about Bohemian Scofflaw twenty years on. I thought he would move back to New York. Not so. While he was attending a No Nukes rally in Berlin, the directors at the Free University invited him to come for a two-year lecturer stint. He wanted me, us, to join him. Ruggles encouraged me to go and be with Nathaniel. I could always come back. I was excited and wary. In almost eight years, I'd never been away from New York (or Ruggles) for more than two weeks.

We moved in early July to a spacious and inexpensive fifth-floor apartment in the Kreuzberg district, with cathedrallike ceilings and windows. Unpatched WWII bullet holes pock-marked the outside walls, and coffee and spicy odors from the Turkish café down the street mingled with polluted air that wafted from the East. I had my own room/studio with a bank of windows and a tiny Juliet balcony, where I'd sit and peer to the East at a group of forcibly vacated buildings, a reverse Potemkin village. (Nathaniel said the East German government kept those buildings empty because when people lived in them, too many tried to make it over the wall.) I imagined myself levitating, waltzing in the air above the watchtowers and the East Wall piled high with barbed wire like a black, thorn-filled rosebush sprouting above a barren field of land mines. The East, a lifeless, indecipherable blankness of the enforced silence smashing against the particles of neon light, bursting with possibility, in the encircled yet unbound West sector.

Though it was about a half hour from Kreuzberg, we enrolled Alchemy in the John Kennedy International School, which taught its classes in English and German. He showed a natural ear for languages and adjusted within weeks.

Nathaniel immediately immersed himself in the university life and in political groups in both East and West Berlin. He asked me to think about teaching some art classes. Think about it is about all I did. He and male his "colleagues" gathered on Friday nights for eating, drinking, and opinionating while the women sat like docile appendages. In what I thought was a sign of maturity, I suggested to Nathaniel that it was better for me to stay home with Alchemy because I might cause a scene. He wanted me to go. When one of them blabbered his claptrap, "The Wall is the great monstrosity of postmodern, postwar Europe," I answered, "You're wrong. The Wall is action. It's beautiful. It's the only true masterpiece of the twentieth century. True People's Art. Someday it will be the reason

communism dies. Maybe then you'll recognize your myopia."
They all pooh-poohed me. Ha. I was right. I cried in happiness when the Wall was breached, and in sadness when it was torn down in a tyrannical act of aesthetic demolition. They should've rechristened it the Wall of Freedom—refashioned it as a monument to man's stupidity and a gateway to the future. Now it's only a memory, destined to be a mythical Atlantis of art.

I started skipping the Friday night gatherings. I did accompany Nathaniel to the East, where he made connections with dissidents. Unlike the West Germans, most of them spoke almost no English so he always had to go with a translator. It thrilled me, until I breathed in the city's Gravity Disease. The Stasi, the ubiquitous East German secret police, served as the toxic communicators of the city's societal tetanus. Only the East's club scene had any attraction for me, and that held no interest for Nathaniel.

We began to live certain aspects of our lives separately, which suited both of us. I made my own friends. Among them were Arnost and Zdenek, or A and Z, two gay exiled Czechs whom I'd met at the Descungle nightclub. Owners of PhDs, A in art history and Z in poetry, they were overqualified Berlin taxi drivers. One night they took me to the SO36 club, and the twenty-two-year-old lead singer of the Wannaseeyas, Heinricha Von Priest—a tattooed, multipierced, multicolored-bobbed-hair, doll-faced Louise Brooks look-alike (yes, yes, it's true, Brooks claimed to have had an affair with Greta)—eased in front of me while I trance-danced to an early bootleg of the Bronski Beat, which was the HQ for the punk arty scene.

"Arnost claims you are Salome Savant." I nodded. "I've idolized you for years. I have a photo from *Art Is Dead* on the wall of my squat. Can you sign it?" Quelle hor-ror! Heinricha was young enough to be my daughter. At forty-two, I was a relic.

A, Z, and Heinricha became my emissaries to the epicenter of Berlin decadence, the legal clubs of the West and the illegal and underground—literally—of the East, which made the drug and sex scenes at Studio 54 feel as innocent as a Doris Day movie. Whips, cuffs, chains, poppers, and paraphilia party favors were the ho-hum accoutrements of Berlin nightlife. The Wall made it possible. Every day after I dropped Alchemy at school, either A or Z drove me to a different spot along the Wall. With my clunky video camera (until the batteries ran out), I filmed ordinary Berliners and tourists taking pictures of themselves with the Wall as backdrop. I shot prostitutes, pickpockets, skinheads, transvestites, drunks peeing and puking, old women who looked like they could be Gloria Swanson's sisters in *Sunset Boulevard*, the outcasts not only of Germany but all of Europe, who had migrated to Berlin.

I was excited by my cohort and with my film. Nathaniel was energized by his students and the political activism. He began work on *The Further Adventures of Bohemian Scofflaw*. Alchemy became precociously obsessed with his music. Every Sunday the three of us picnicked or biked in the Tiergarten. We were a happy family.

When winter descended, hooding the city like a death shroud, I became a walking hoarfrost corpse with camera; Zephyrus defeated by the exhaling breaths of Boreas, that for eons had trilled through the icy veins of Aryan falconers.

I took refuge in the steamy warmth of our apartment and surrounded myself with newspaper and magazine photographs from the Nazi era. With A and Z as my interpreters, I contacted libraries and individuals with personal archives—which led me to the trove of Klaus Grimmelshausen, whose uncle had been an official Nazi party photographer. Z and I took the train to Grimmelshausen's Nuremberg home. Sifting through the stacks of cataloged photos, I held in my hands, without consciously knowing it, what I'd been searching for—why I'd been brought to Berlin. My breath stopped—Hauptsturmführer Alois Brunner with his nameless adjutant, whom I recognized as the future father of my dead child, standing by his side.

I made copies of that photo and many others, and took them to Berlin. I sang to dearest Art, "You were right. I should've trusted you. You smelled his evil." I relived the civil war inside my womb, my DNA struggling—not to betray me but to cleanse me by strangling the oxygen from his offspring. Suddenly that long, suspended moment of misunderstood and tortured babydeath within me became quiescent, settled in the static of nontime. My Gravity Disease lightened; my soulsmell freed itself from the lingering guilty odor of infanticide.

I wanted to call Ruggles. No, that would be a defeat. He might want me to tell Nathaniel, and I wasn't prepared to tell him just then.

When Xtine came for a visit, I met her at the Zoo Station and we went directly to the O Bar. I placed the photo on the table. "Teumer." Horrified and anxious, she grasped my hand.

"Are you sure it's him?"

"Yes. I could never forget that face. And it's wonderful." I leaned closer to her and kissed her cheek. "It all makes sense. It's inspired me."

I showed her my first collages of me and Teumer, and so began the *Baddist Boys* series. I contemplated showing them then. I didn't. It was not yet the proper time. Instead of the collages, I presented another performance almost twenty years after *Art Is Dead*, a symbolic death this time. Xtine helped me construct a life-size body cast of myself. I covered its vag and nipples with gold stars. I installed the sculpture in a street near us that dead-ended at the Wall and encircled it with barbed wire, papier-mâché, and synthetic bones. Alchemy stood with Nathaniel and his colleagues, who gazed agog as dusk surrendered to the night. Heinricha's band played. Xtine began filming as I stripped down naked. A and Z bathed me in blood-red body paint. Between phrases on the wall—DON'T MESS WITH THE WONGS and CRIST DYED 4 U—I hugged my body against the West Wall and my silhouette merged into the celebratory mural, free from curators, critics, and pretension. Still dripping in paint, I lit a torch and set the entire installation aflame, dousing copies of the Teumer photo and Xeroxes of Duchamp and Greta with lighter fluid and flinging them into the embers. Their smoky visages commingled within the pyre. No one saw my tears as I danced around the ashes inseminating the Berlin night sky.

39

THE MOSES CHRONICLES (2008)

It's Alive!

As the January opening drew ever closer, Moses felt as if he were trapped in a horror movie where everyone awaits the coming apocalypse, but despite all the precautions, nothing can halt the onslaught. The *Enquirer* article was not yet scheduled for publication, while Alchemy's lawyers and PR people searched for a way to squash it.

His preparation included agreeing to Jay's plan, slightly adapted. Prior to the Members' Preview, there would be a lunch for fifteen, twenty prime movers, tastemakers, and close friends, which they'd attend.

On the Tuesday morning of the Hammer luncheon, Jay found Moses sitting half dressed on the closed toilet seat cover, hands pressed against the throbbing blood vessels in his temples, trying to clear his mind from the two Xanax he'd taken at 4 A.M. He'd dreamt that he was hanging upside down from a tree in Central Park while the rubber-hosed arms of whinnying cops flogged his back, and on the grass beneath him, his brother lay atop Jay as cameras snapped all around them.

"Moses, are you going to be able to go? You want some more coffee?" He didn't look up. She inched over to him from the bathroom doorway, already dressed in an olive green alpaca sweater and powder blue jeans. "Let's cancel."

"Jay, I'd prefer to go alone."

"What? Why?" Jay's eyes opened and closed and opened again in disbelief. Sure, they had some problems. Who didn't? But they were still a team. Bound by love. 'Til death do them part.

"Why?" Moses said just above a whisper. The cap blown off his self-editing mechanism, he spewed the unmentionable. "Why'd you have to fuck him? That's why. Were you fucking him while you were fucking me?"

Jay's insides clenched in fury and desolation, her emotions awash in a dizzying eddy of confusion. "I don't..." Unable to finish her sentence, Jay faced an ineradicable truth: No matter what he said, time had not healed this wound and in his heart he'd never forgiven her for sleeping with his half brother before they'd goddamned ever met.

Holding her head high, she turned and wobbled out of the bathroom, choking back tears, and retreated to the confines of her backyard office.

One hour later, upon entering the Hammer lobby alone from the garage, Moses was reassuring himself that, when Jay cooled down, she would understand that he attacked her out only of fear and insecurity. He hadn't meant it. He'd plead for her to have mercy on the man who doubts what he's sure of. And he was so sure she loved him. His thoughts stopped when he spotted Curt Scoggins, the gangly, curly-gray-haired curator with a tortoiselike neck, officially welcoming the guests. He pointed to the wide staircase. "Salome is upstairs. She'll take you through the show later." Moses inhaled and was submerged into the flash of a daymare.

A woman, head covered by a mourning veil, launches her baby carriage down a flowing waterfall above a marble staircase. It's Shalom, the dybbuk, singing softly, "99 crying babies on the wall..." A lifeguard rushes from behind to catch the carriage before it reaches the ocean. Shalom strips off her clothing and the lifeguard stops to watch. She cackles as the carriage crashes, and the baby spins through the air, disappearing into the sea. She sings on, "...98 crying babies..."

That same morning, as Alchemy downed his second cup of coffee, Xtine, who had flown in for the festivities, walked in from the guest house. "Your mother is in a nasty mood."

"No kidding. She knocked on my door after one last night threatening to boycott the entire week." He mimicked her peevish tone: "'I won't perform like an art monkey waiting to be fed some gruel by her museum keepers.' As always, her timing is excellent. Ambitious keeps calling me when he is drunk, leaving crazy, apologetic messages, or when I answer he just curses me out for being a two-faced prick. Mr. No Bullshit giving me only bullshit."

Xtine clasped his hand in hers as she had done since he was a little boy, when her hair was dark brown rather than white, her figure svelte rather than round, and she towered over him rather than coming up to his shoulders. They strode to the guest cottage. Salome was already dressed. Not in a flamboyant outfit or a pantsuit befitting an attractive woman of sixty-five. She had chosen a purple sweatshirt with its hood over her head, a black scarf around her neck, sunglasses, no makeup, too-short baggy brown pants, and work boots.

The Salome contingent arrived at the Hammer twenty minutes before the scheduled lunch. Tom Hayden awaited them in the lobby entrance; he assumed care of Nathaniel, his wheelchair-bound protest pal, and they commiserated about old times and present frustrations.

Alchemy's cell rang not two minutes after they arrived. He didn't pick up but waited for the voice mail message. "It's Jay. Moses is coming alone. We had a fight. He's in terrible shape. He can explain."

"Fuck. Fuck. Triple fuck," he said to no one and called her back. She didn't answer. Distracted, he entered the first floor's Project Room, which held the just-erected *Pillzapoppin'* and *Electroshocked Ladyland* installations. He hadn't found time to preview the exhibition. A 10'-x-10'-x-8' chamber, composed of thousands of multicolored psychotropic pills, which held a Salome-designed table connected to a mock ETC machine where you could lie down and be administered a mild shock to temples and ankles while the headphones played Hendrix's version of "The Star-Spangled Banner" at top volume.

"Try it. Experience a scintilla of the pain inflicted upon your mother." Alchemy turned to see that Salome had put on black silk gloves and powdered her face but still wore the sweatshirt and work boots.

"Maybe later."

"Brave boy." She took off one glove and pinched his arm, making sure her chartreuse-manicured nails dug into his skin. "It's no more painful than that."

He foresaw the karmic wheel spinning toward a long day that would unleash Salome, homicider. "Let's look upstairs," he offered as innocuously as possible.

The first four rooms contained a retrospective covering the gamut of her almost forty years of creative output. The last room housed never-before-exhibited silkscreen prints and collages. Immediately, Alchemy's gaze was drawn to the wall that read *Baddist Boys*. He examined the first print, a brownish-yellowish wash with Photoshopped images of his father and Salome in a rapturous pose inside a bathroom. The title card read *Getting Bent*.

"It's a funny piece, no? I won't sell it."

"Jesus, Mom, I've worked to keep this from the public for fifteen years."

"Oh, grow up. The fact that reprobate has survived so long augurs well for you."

"I wish you'd asked—"

"Asked what? Your permission?"

"Not asked. Informed."

"Consider yourself duly informed. My boy, when it suits you, you're as sensitive as a baby's ass," she hissed.

Ignoring her, he examined the second print, titled *Which Whore, Bitch?* His eyes caught sight of the third print. He froze at the image of a seminaked Salome, a gold star covering her vagina and a Jewish shawl draped over her shoulders and partially covering her breasts, holding a plastic bag in her hand, while she danced for a German soldier. In miniswastikas she'd scrawled "Arbeit Mocks Frei." The title card read *Mal de TeuMer.*

"Oh, shit," he mumbled. The veins in his neck pulsated as Mose, the art dealer Marlene Passant, the catalog essayist Frank Peters, and three others whom he didn't recognize approached.

Salome stripped off her sweatshirt to uncover a sheer purple blouse. She shook out her shoulder-length dyed lightbrown hair and wrapped a red scarf around her neck. Her eyes sparkled and her voice became filled with an almost youthful brio as she began to elucidate her work. "I could've done a few score more of my *Baddist Boys*, but I chose these lovely cads. I used photos of myself that Xtine had taken and photos that I'd taken or found that I then reconfigured."

Moses, nodding to the third print, squeaked out, "Who is the man in that piece?"

"His name was Malcolm Teumer." Salome paused, glancing at Alchemy, who slung his arm over Moses's shoulders. "I met him when I was a clueless teenager who loved to fuck. I still love to fuck, but I am no longer clueless. Twenty or so years ago in Berlin, I got the clues on Teumer. If you look closely at the piece, you'll see a fetus in the bag." As a group, they stared at the faded fetus. "We had a child who died in childbirth. When I discovered Teumer's past as a Nazi killer, I understood why our son needed to die."

The crowd hushed, waiting for Salome to say more. It became apparent she was done explaining. Soozie Daye, a local arts writer who often acted more like a groupie, asked the follow-up question: "Do you really believe it was better that the child died?"

"He died and I was given my son, Alchemy."

Moses didn't hear Salome's answer. He'd fled the museum. He called Jay on the way to his car. She didn't pick up. He left a message on her voice mail. "Please. I have to talk to you. It was worse than I could've imagined. I'm leaving now. I love you."

As he drove down the block to their home, he saw that Jay's Honda was gone from the driveway.

40

MEMOIRS OF A USELESS GOOD-FOR-NUTHIN'

Totem and Taboo Hoo, 1999

The day of the intervention I meander downstairs, after being out 'til dawn, minorly hungover. Alchy's sitting alone on a green wooden folding chair in front of a bridge table with three empty beer bottles, a three-quarter-filled one, two empty Cokes, an ashtray full of butts, and three chessboards. One was a computer game, one was a game he had going with Nathaniel, and the other was a "classic" game he was studying. The room had twenty-five-foot ceilings and skylights and this white marble floor that looked like a hockey rink with a bus-size couch in front of a monster-screen TV. A chair by some artist friend of Salome's named Longago, which hurt your damn butt when you sit down. A great sound system, of course. The Seeburg Select-o-matic jukebox from the '50s for those thousands of forty-fives.

I grab a beer and a pack of chocolate Hostess cupcakes and a pack of Twinkies from the kitchen and stumble into the living room, stuffing a cupcake in my mouth. Alchy yells, "Hey, Mr. Met, think fast," and he flings a baseball glove at my chest. I drop the Twinkies but hold on to the beer and catch the glove. "What the fuckaya doin'?"

He hands me a baseball. "Look at them."

They both was signed by Lenny Dykstra, who was on the '86 Mets World Series team, and Alchy knows I love the guy, who was nicknamed Nails.

"Whoa. Shit. Thanks." I pick up the Twinkies and plop down in a folding chair, down my beer and the Twinkies, put on the glove, and am throwing the ball into it.

"I was going to get you a bat, too. Thought you might find an unhealthy use for it."

He wasn't looking at me but at the chessboard.

"That game is so freakin' bor-ing."

"My mom claims it's a legacy from my grandfather. It's cathartic. Relaxing. It teaches me to be unemotional."

"You cheat? My grandfather taught me checkers. And how to cheat."

"Cheating defeats the purpose. You cheat when you play video games for hours?"

"When I get bored."

Nathaniel clomps in from the guest cottage and shoots me a glance that says I am messing with the order of the house, as if it's his, 'cause of my empty beer bottle and cupcake wrappers. As if Alchemy's mess and magazines was sacred. For a hippie dude, his life posture was never slouchy but grouchy-bouncy, except when he got drunk and he meowed about how life with Salome came crashing down on him.

He sits his lumpy ass in a folding chair. "It's the pinup boy for his de-generation. Always a pleasure to see your impudent leer."

"You head to the kitchen and earn your keep and cook me a omelet, and you won't have to see me."

"You two." Alchemy shakes his head at us. "Muzzle your stellar banter tonight. We have business." He spoke directly to Nathaniel. "Lure my mom back to your place before we get started." Nathaniel nodded. "It's your move."

Andrew, Sue, and the shrink arrive together and a few minutes later Lux comes with Randy Sheik. The Sheiks was always protecting their "franchise."

Everyone is there but the guest of honor. She finally shows up with Silky Trespass, who at the time is the guitarist for the Come Queens. They and Dress Shields, calling themselves the Mendietas, jam together off and on for years.

Around nine a cook serves up dinner, which is laid out buffet style on the dining room table. It's the only furniture except this giant Christmassy glass chandelier that Salome says was made special by some famous guy who also got one eye.

Most of us pull out the folding chairs or sit on the couch and eat in the other room. Alchemy has put on *Blue Velvet* with the sound off. Absurda's put on Jane's Addiction's *Ritual*, which I admit is one fine fuckin' piece of music. While we're eating, Salome and a chick Alchemy met maybe ten hours before parade in from the hot tub. Back in Flushin' we call those hookups "tramp-oline time," something to jump on all night and jump off of in the morning. Alchy frowned on me using that phrase.

The trampoline has covered up in jeans, sweatshirt, and flip-flops. Salome is slinking, still slightly wet, wearing a green T-shirt, no bra, orange sarong, with a towel slung over her shoulder. Barefoot. She was some kinda female Dorian Gray who must've had one of her paintings in the closet that looked four hundred fuckin' years old, 'cause her body is like a ticking sex bomb ready to explode. (Alchemy gave me that book after the Irving Plaza gig.)

When she's done eating, Salome puts on the Stones' "Miss You." She starts snake-dancing alone under the skylights in the living room. She forefinger wags at Alchemy and waves the towel like a toreador. He gets up and they are both shimmying their butts. I see where he gets some of his moves. They drift in and out in circles from six inches to six feet from each other. They are both mouthing the lyrics. Sick shit, man. Nathaniel, I peek at him, and even he is squirming and dripping in sweat. Lux and me give each other a look that says "I don't wanna see this." Absurda and Silky are whispering in each other's ears. They start dancing with each other, you know, how babes do to get guys hot. The trampoline is looking con-freaking-fused so she gets up and tries to butt in between Alchemy and Salome. They give her the homicidal Savant stare. She backs off. Everyone, even Nathaniel and me, is always an outsider when it comes to Alchemy and Salome. The two of them is swaying to the "oooh-oooh-aaah-aaah" and Mick's strung-out voice and with Isabella Rossellini on the screen and there's some very sexy vibrations in the atmosphere. Salome is singing really low, "...I miss ya, chile..." I am getting eroticized by all of this when my brand-new cell phone rings.

"McFinn. Nova."

"Yo, Franky Novalino. Long time, ya prick. How'd ya get my number?"

"Ya sister. That street corner sideshow would suck the anal warts off a the queer-ass pope for a dime."

She was the only one of my family to have that number. I told her not to give it to them but didn't say nuthin' about guys like Nova.

"Nova, insult my sister and break my heart."

"Hey, I was just dickin' wit' ya. Bonnie is cool. Ricky, listen, no jokin' . . ." I hear him breathing hard and halting. "I been shot and Jaw is dead." Jaw was a crackhead speed freak who'd been doing time in Dannemora. I didn't even know he was out. I hated that Nova is hanging with him.

"What the fuck you two do? No bull, Nova."

"We ripped off some Jew jewelers about six months ago. Big score."

"Nova, ya dumb knucklewit, those are the Jews with who you do not fuck."

"No lectures, hah, I'm in severe pain. We been hidin' out in Vegas. Somehow the bastids found us."

"Somehow? Jesus. Why didn't ya take a ad out on *America's Most Wanted?*"

"It was like they hired the Israeli secret service the way they come at us."

"What the fuck you want me ta do?"

"Put me up and get me a medic. Fast. My thigh been bleedin' for hours. Ya know I can't go ta no hospital. I'm takin' vycs for the pain. I'm parked in fron' a phone boot' in a Vons parkin' lot on Alvarado off a the Ten."

"Did you leave Jaw in Vegas?"

"No, he croaked on the way, so I left him on the side a some nowhere exit off a the Fifteen."

I'm thinking he is one lucky douche bag, 'cause Alchemy has access to a doc twenty-four/seven for Salome. "Okay. Don't fuckin' go nowhere. And don't call no one else."

"Ricky, I'll be in the Camaro."

"Be there in twenty, thirty minutes." I'm frustrated, but I can't strand the poor schmuck. He was one of the few dudes who stood up to my dad when he was beating the crap outta me.

I wave to Alchemy, who is now slo-mo soloing with the trampoline. He reads my face that says I got an SOS call. We step outside onto the front lawn. I explain the dilemma. His head's shaking in disbelief. Still, he gets it right away and surveys the options. "You go. Call me immediately. We'll meet at the Pantera." The Pantera been closed by then, but Falstaffa and Marty still live above it. "Don't use his car. If we can fix him up, maybe we can get him on a boat at the marina and out of here."

He follows me to my Escalade. "You aren't holding, are you? "No."

"Give me your knife. I'll keep it in the house."

I hesitate.

"Give it to me." I hand him my mettle. "Where's your Colt?"

"In my room."

Alchemy tells everyone I got an emergency but gives no other facts. He calls off the Absurda intervention for the night.

I race to the Vons and I spot the Camaro in a deserted corner of the lot. I bang on the fucking trunk. He don't move. I look in the window and start screaming, "Fran-kee, Frankee Fuckin' Novalino!" I think maybe he passed out. The door ain't locked so I reach in and—goddamn it, the poor bastard is dead. I kick in the side of his damn car. I'm embarrassed to admit, I want to toss my cell and get my ass outta there, but that's cowardly shit. I must do right by my man.

I phone Alchemy.

He says, very calm, "Call nine one one. You tell them this. Exactly this: He called you and said he was in deep shit. You tell them he said something about the jewelers, that they were after him. Only he never, never mentioned being shot. Got that?"

"Yes."

"Never to anyone. Not even me, ever again."

"Got it. I got it." We keep that under wraps 'cause if we hadn't, they would've jumped on us for not calling the cops right away, and we—I didn't need that.

Alchy is on top of the situation. Andrew and a shyster meet me at Parker Center that night. He gets the PR people ready because this hits the news big time, insinuating that I'm involved with all kinds of gang shit.

Alchemy was stand-up through everything. He never blinked. Or talked about tossing me out. At least, not to my face.

41

THE SONGS OF SALOME

Let's Not Make a Deal

After the performance I felt so high, younger, and more vital than I had in years. I was infatuated with Berlin life and didn't want to return to America. I needed to. Hilda, who was phobic about flying and had no curiosity about the world beyond Orient, turned down my invitations to join us for Christmas and then again at Easter, which upset me more for Alchemy than for myself. He and I flew back to the States for a month in July.

The city repelled me. I sensated that the inquisitions of friends or former fucks could undo me. I avoided Gibbon and the Hamptons, that summertime G-spot of the self-anointed elite. Xtine drove me to Collier Layne to see Ruggles; he was pleased with my "progress." I brought a copy of the Teumer photo. "It's real."

He raised his eyebrows and fingered his mole. "And?"

"I still mourn for myself and the child, only not in the same fashion. I found renewed faith my body. I forgive myself that indiscretion." He only nodded.

Before going back to Orient, I crashed for two days with Xtine. We avoided the downtown cliques and ate dinner at the Supreme Macaroni Company. After dinner, the summer air stifled and my head felt as if it were encased in a plastic bag while I gasped for breath. We lolled inconspicuously down Ninth Avenue back to the Chelsea. Before we entered the lobby, from behind I heard an unmistakable voice. "Salome! Salome, please wait."

Under the dim streetlights and headlights of the cars zipping across 23rd Street stood Lively with his saddle-sized sideburns and shiny cowboy boots. He hovered between the sidewalk and a double-parked black sedan. "Look, Xtine." I poked her with my elbow. "It's the archangel of Bad News."

"I'm sorry you feel that way."

"I do, Laban, so why don't you—whoosh—vanish."

"I have tried to help you in the past." Of course there was a reason he told me about Gus. "And I don't think what I have to say will qualify as bad news. Can we go somewhere to talk?"

"No."

He blew his meaty nostrils into a white handkerchief, stuffed it in his pocket, and shook his head in disgust at the sloth around him. "Suit yerself."

"So, surprise me with your good news."

"Do you know why Nathaniel chose to go to Berlin?"

"The delicate cuisine?" I asked. He almost smiled as his molten features relaxed. "That's not it? Hmmm. So tell me."

"I'd say it's due to his involvement with underground political groups in East Berlin. Smuggling money in and photographs out. Some of which were published in the West German magazine *GEO*."

I'd never read it. "I don't see how printing photos in a magazine is illegal."

"It is in Communist Germany. I'd like to help him."

"Your help he can do without."

"Perhaps. Perhaps not. In this case we are both on the same side. There's an old saw, my enemy's enemy is my friend. The Stasi is both of our enemies."

"You will never be his 'friend.'"

"Ally, then."

"You want me to help you to help him help you?"

"I wouldn't have phrased it in such a way, but yes."

"He'll never pass information on his friends to you."

"No need. His friends need funds. Supplies. They use a hand-cranked press to print their pamphlets. We can help them upgrade."

"Why should he trust you? Why should I?"

"Because I've never lied to you."

As beastly as he was, he believed that. His truths may have been false to me, but they were his truths.

"Laban, you're a deal maker. I have one for you."

"Shoot."

"I lost a child when I was fifteen."

His gaze squirmed away from mine. "Yes, I'd heard from the Bickleys. It was not my place to pursue any details."

"I have questions about the father."

He tapped the heel of his boot on the sidewalk and ground it on a now very dead cockroach. "Why do you think I can help you?"

"You're a spy, Laban. Finding information on people is what you do."

He chuckled, baring his oversized carnivorous teeth.

"You get me some information about him. Like where he's living. And I'll do my best to help you with Nathaniel."

"Let me see if there's anything I can do. No promises."

I asked if he wanted the photo of Teumer. He didn't need it. He knew more than I did about my own past.

42

THE MOSES CHRONICLES (2008)

Lovers Cross

Jay shielded herself behind the electronic curtain, unresponsive to Moses's plaintive e-mails and calls. She finally sent a one-line e-mail: "It's best I spend the night at Geri's." He considered a drive-by spy mission but dismissed it as too insidious. Alchemy called near ten that evening. Moses didn't pick up. He sat in his darkened room and listened to Alchemy's clipped cadence play on the machine, "Call me. ASAP. We need to talk."

Moses had no desire to hear whatever wisdom Alchemy wanted to impart. Anxious and restless, he called Sidonna Cherry, who answered in her typical playful fashion. "You becoming one of those PI junkies I need to put on retainer?"

"Gosh, I hope not. Just have some questions. When you researched my father, did you have an inkling of a sinister past? Is he dead yet?"

"I'll answer the second question first. I don't know. You want me to find out?"

"Yes."

"See, you are going to pay me again. In answer to question one, identity refashioning is not exactly unique in my line of work."

"Anything else you can find, and yes, I'll pay. I want to meet him."

"Oddsy bodsy, babe. I'll check if your ghosty pop is still samba-ing down Rio way at the same address."

Moses spent the night dominated by obsessive introspection and scrutiny, certifying all major "facts" of his heritage as fraudulent. He couldn't help thinking that Jay's fleeing implied even more portentous revelations. The next day, she finally e-mailed that she'd be coming by around eleven.

When her Honda pulled into the driveway, Moses feigned casualness. He loped out to hug her. Hair unkempt, wearing jeans and a tan blouse, sunglasses, and floppy straw hat covering her pallid complexion sans makeup, Jay shook her head as she brushed past him. "Inside." He trudged into the living room. The sun rays from the skylight above bathed the room, giving it an aura of airiness when strangulation would be more apt. Jay edged into the right corner of the white leather couch. Moses sat opposite, an unbridgeable two feet of space and an immeasurable gulf of hurt separating them. After all those years of seeming dormancy, the silent spores of the fungus *Lovegonelousy* had released their lethal toxins.

"Jay, I'm so, so sorry. Please say you're coming home to stay."

"I can't. Not yet."

"I'm begging you. Please forgive my idiotic jealousy. Don't you know how much I love you? I don't understand. Why did you have to leave?"

"Saying what you said and asking me not to go with you to the museum...Moses, *you* left *me*. You'd really already left. That just sealed—"

335

"I hadn't slept. I'd told you I'd taken too much Xanax. I was terrified. I apologized and begged you to forgive me, to come with me—"

"None of that undoes what you said, what you've been thinking. What you still think."

"Jay—"

"Stop." She had no intention of letting him reframe the events until she had her say. "Moses, I mean it, I feel like you left 'us' years ago. I've tried to bring you back."

"You feel wrong."

"No, I don't. You've become more and more distant. Whenever I brought up wanting a child—"

"I agreed."

"Agreed you weren't ready. I was ready! And then after I stopped using birth control—"

"Jay—"

"Let me finish. Since we met, I never wanted to be with anyone else. Not when you were sick. Not when you drifted farther away after your mother died. Not when you glared at me so spitefully when you found about...I never betrayed you in reality or emotionally. I hurt for your hurt, over Salome and your father."

"The nut and the Nazi."

Jay didn't acknowledge that she'd read his e-mail describing the scene at the Hammer. "Did you think I secretly pined for Alchemy? That I wanted to run away with him? That is so damn crazy."

"I was crazy. I plead temporary insanity."

"I had always wanted to spend the rest of my life with you. Not him. Not anyone else. You."

"*Had?*"

"I don't know. I can barely see beyond my next five minutes."

"Jay, please don't let this one misguided, monstrously large fuck-up destroy years of love and devotion. We, I, need...Come to see Butterworth with me. Or any therapist you choose."

"Tell me yesterday morning was the first time you thought those horrible things about me."

Moses bowed his head, thinking if she had told him of the affair the night they'd seen Alchemy's damn band, or if he'd never shared his daymares with her, maybe they wouldn't be in this position. But he knew that he was only scapegoating her for his neurotic behavior.

"You can't." She continued, "I don't want to imagine what else you've dreamed up about me."

"You know I think horrible things. Mostly about myself. Would it be better if I lied? Would you believe me? Would you stay?"

"That's just it. I can't trust what you say anymore. Maybe you only want me here because you're afraid to be alone, if the cancer strikes again."

"Absolutely false." Moses refused to fully accept what her words implied. "Jay, tell me you don't love me anymore."

"Whoever declared 'Love conquers all' was an idiot." Jay's voice pulsed with contempt. "I won't live with that kind of unspoken, lurking nastiness. Such pettiness! Moses, you always tried to protect me from the meanness, the disappointments in the world. Then you hurt me and disappointed me more than anyone. I wish you'd had an affair, or I'd fallen in love with someone else. That would be easier than this. I don't understand how we got here. I've never complained, at least out loud, that we hardly have sex. We had so much more sex when you were sick! I hoped when you went to Mexico last year that would change. We had sex two times in ten days. I couldn't blame your illness anymore. And when we do, sometimes it's like you don't want to touch me—"

"You couldn't be more off, please listen—"

"No, you listen. I've spent the last twenty-four hours crying my insides out. I dedicated my life to you these last years. After yesterday..." She sighed. "I'm empty."

Moses surrendered. He had no one to blame but himself.

Jay looked up, sniffing, rubbing her eyes. "Moses, about your father, I, well—"

"I've decided to see him. I have to find out a different truth, not Salome's version."

"Hey! Guys..." They simultaneously shuddered as they recognized Alchemy's voice. Neither had heard his car on the street or his footsteps walking up the front yard pathway.

Jay mouthed, "Did you know?"

Moses shook his head as he got up to open the door. Alchemy instantly saw the distress on Moses's face and, behind him, the evident shock in Jay's widening eyes. His almost breezy demeanor turned circumspect.

"Bad timing. But Mose, necessary after yesterday. It's essential you read this." He handed Moses a manila envelope that contained Malcolm's letter and the medal. Alchemy shot a solicitous glance in Jay's direction as she pushed herself off the couch. Moses spotted it. He failed to decipher their unspoken communication.

Alchemy tried to explain his presence and the envelope. "Look, this defies simple explanation. I saw Teumer in Brazil when we were on tour. He gave me this... Said it was up to me to give it to you or not. I think you'll see."

"Jesus Christ, now you see fit to give it to me?"

"Yeah, we fucked up. We decided it was—"

"We?"

"Yes, Jay and I—"

Moses swiveled his hips, and Jay's exasperated gape of horror met his look of confusion and disgust. "You've been seeing each other? Maybe I'm not so crazy after all."

In a rush to stop any further false condemnations, Jay blurted out, "Twice. Both times for less than twenty minutes. To help you. Alchemy wanted my opinion about the letter."

"And you told him no? And you knew about my father?" Jay nodded sheepishly. "Fuck, I can't believe this." Palms together, he squeezed the envelope between his hands. "So Teumer gave this to you for *me*?" Suddenly Moses's mood shifted from shame to self-righteous fury. He tossed the envelope on the dining room table. "Alchemy, I think it's best if you go."

"You sure? I guess, yes. It's all on me. Call me anytime. I had no inkling about yesterday. And Mose, I was better off without Bent. You were better off without Teumer. He's a really twisted guy."

"Yeah, great." Moses flicked his head and looked Alchemy toward the door.

Alchemy acceded. "I hope you can understand. If you need... Okay. See you."

Moses and Jay stood five feet from each other, stranded in their living room, drowning in a sea of incomprehension and despair. Jay ended the silence, her tone defensive. "Like I said, we met briefly, twice in the last, what, five years. Once when I found out about Salome's exhibition and I told him he needed to tell you or I would. And after he came back with the letter." She stiffened her posture. "And you are still so wrong to mistrust me. Wrong. Wrong. Wrong."

"Where'd you meet with him?"

"The first time at Kasbah. The second at a private opening at Gagosian Gallery."

"Did you tell him how to find Teumer?"

"No, Sidonna Cherry—"

"Did you tell him about her, too?"

"She worked for him and for Kasbah before she ever worked for us. Remember?"

"Now, I do."

"You should read the letter before judging me."

Moses stood at the dining room table and pulled out the pages. He shook out the envelope and the medal dropped on the table. "Jesus, what the hell?"

Jay frowned. "Never seen that."

Moses sat down. Jay put a cup of water for tea in the microwave. She didn't even bother to take it out when it buzzed. A saturnine heaviness settled in her chest as she leaned against the kitchen sink and waited.

43

THE LAMENTATIONS OF MALCOLM TEUMER, II (2008)
The Purloined Letter

Moses,

Since you have found me and your half brother, I assume by now you have met or will meet your mother. I want you to know me from my words, not from a distorted portrait painted by your mother's delusional accusations or Hannah's bitter renderings. I began this missive when Laban informed me of your intrusion. When it became obvious that you were no longer pursuing a confrontation, I decided to withhold it. Upon being notified of your brother's intent to meet me, this became the propitious time and manner to deliver it.

Inside every human, without exception, resides the essence of what moralists call evil. Herbert Spencer, in classic English linguistic perfidy, declared this drive to be the "survival of the fittest." I witnessed this exhibition of spirit by the delighted participation of women and children in acts of murder and debauchery. This empowering drive to vanquish and control is encoded in our blood and far outweighs courage or human generosity, or, for Christ's sake, loving thy enemy.

I hope (but doubt) that someday you will understand that the most profound gift I gave you was unlove. I revile the parsing of logic and language that is necessary to justify suffering as a corollary to *unconditional love from God and for God. The supreme human drives are self-preservation and selfishness. Greed, lust, envy, and desire for control are all forms of feeding the self. Love of a mate is only a manifestation of base needs to fornicate and control. Altruism is the lie of the self-deceiving.*

Moses, life is cruel. Failure is not acceptable, but it is also inevitable. It is your kneeling to failure that I find repulsive.

If your half brother's reconnaissance mission was only a prelude to your own visit, you must know who you are before you come: Moses, you are 100% Christian. Not a drop of Jewish blood flows within you.

I will tell you who I am and why you were left behind. I participated in the elimination of Jews and other putrid and inferior species. I served with honor as an aide to Hauptsturmführer Alois Brunner. After the war he and I worked in Major General Reinhard Gehlen's OSS/CIA–sponsored anti-Communist network. During Operations Paperclip and Applepie, I seized the opportunity to salvage the dreams of the falling Reich. I supplied Lively and Bickley Sr. with identities of SS officers who were Communist sympathizers (as well as a cache of Jewish gold and jewelry) in exchange for "bleaching" my war record, my entire history. I assumed the identity of a once baggy-eyed sad sack Jew who evolved into an unfeeling and unforgiving "victim." How clever, yes! I endured a defiling of my purity with a circumcision and tattooing. I traveled to America on a Red Cross passport. I strategically maintained my distance from Jews until my involvement with Hannah. Her childless predicament was fortuitous and left her susceptible to what I offered and the cover I needed. I always intended to leave her. It became necessary to expedite my plans when I was recognized. I resisted surrendering you until Laban and Bickley Sr.

forced me to make that choice—only if I left you would they continue to assist me in evading those who wished to put me on trial.

I see now it was the only choice—the right choice. I have followed your life as I have followed the career of your mother.

Hannah reared you in such a manner that makes you unfit to bear my name. You did not inherit Salome's beauty or tempestuous vigor. You are diseased of body and weak in spirit.

I heard you speak at the Skirball Center on a panel about the children of those who survived internment and their attitudes toward God. I asked you a question after the talk, "Where was your God then? Where is he now?" You could not formulate a cogent response. You circled around the question—as you must, because their God is not. He never was. These Jewish children have committed suicide or broken down because they are weak. Their parents were the strong ones. They survived without their God.

I was repulsed yet oddly proud when you went to Israel. The Israelis have earned my respect. They are more like Germans: They kill to preserve themselves. I wish you had remained there, enlisted in the army, and perished for your beliefs, as Israel will someday perish.

I saw you once more when we passed each other at the 3rd Street Promenade. You trailed a step behind your attractive wife. She is no doubt the lead dog. It is an affront to me that you have no children.

The first time I killed a man, I felt the superiority and triumph of my will. Murder and sex are inextricably tied together: Murder is a denial of creation and sex is the act of creation. True men live through our seed. The truest men understand the need to kill to persevere. Throughout history the powerful have taken the best women. I have taken many. After they have been taken, they are cast aside to lesser men. You are a lesser man who could neither kill nor procreate.

You have eight siblings. Two I left in Germany as I left you. Others live with me in Brazil.

Laban explained your disease and that you desired my help. I considered, but decided against introducing you to your half brothers and half sisters. They do not know you exist. I only agreed to see you to placate Laban, and because, at the time, I never believed you would survive more than a year. Yet, because of your brother, you are still alive.

I have no desire to meet you. But I do have one wish for you: Reward yourself with your newfound life and birthright. Be hard. Be my son.

44

THE SONGS OF SALOME

Still Born, Again

I was in the studio Dad had built for me gathering photos of Orient and of Kyle. I found one when she, Art, and I were secretly smoking cigars outside Donnie Boyle's. Alchemy was playing wiffle ball in the backyard with a friend when I heard him scream, "Mom!" Hilda was passed out on the back porch. Alchemy ran inside and dialed 911. I wrapped Hilda in my arms. I sensated this was her time to transmigrate to another world. I kissed her forehead, and even though she couldn't hear me, I said, "I will miss you so damn much."

The paramedics rushed her to Eastern Long Island Hospital. She'd suffered a mild heart attack. The doctors predicted full recovery but wanted to keep her for observation. I extended our stay by three weeks, for her sake and mine.

The night before her release, she died from "cardiogenic shock." I had sensated correctly. I felt myself untethering. I called Ruggles and he talked to me for almost two hours. He asked if I wanted to come to Collier Layne. I didn't. His words seemed wise: "If it was going to happen, and it was, isn't it better you and Alchemy were there? This way you were able to spend quality time together."

Nathaniel flew back for the funeral. He protected me from the odors of miniminded pieties whispered by Hilda's friends while they conveyed their phony condolences. Billy Jr. said he would sell the house and put the money in the trust. We took a few mementos, packed up books, records, photo albums and stored them in a neighbor's barn. The rest would be donated to charities.

One last time I climbed to the roof. Two great white egrets gracefully patrolled the bay, and I bid a final goodbye to Kyle, Art, Dad, and Hilda.

On the way to JFK, an irrecoverable sorrow gnawing at my insides, I asked the driver to stop at the cemetery. Alchemy jumped out and ran ahead of me and stood in front of Hilda and Dad's headstones. I wished I could've reassured him that although their heaven is a lie, there is DNA travel and Hilda existed somewhere where we could all meet again. Only Hilda and Gus weren't of our DNA and possessed no psychopomp powers. With his long, loose curls flopping over his reddened eyes, his hand touched the nameless headstone next to Dad's. "Who's under there?"

"Your brother," I said, as even-keeled as possible. "I was very young, only two years older than you are now, when I got pregnant. He died during childbirth. I never named him, but I wanted him to have a proper burial so he would be remembered."

Alchemy started to quake. So did I. I feared he was experiencing a mystical connection through me with his brother. We held hands and knelt in front of the headstone. He rubbed his eyes and runny nose against his red T-shirt.

"Was his father my father?"

"No. I met your father many years later. He lives in England now."

"I want to see him."

You could say that my impetuous stop at the cemetery was a coincidence that happened to change the course of our lives. Bullshit. Just as finding Teumer's photo was no coincidence. Both had to happen. I had to accept Alchemy's unwavering decisiveness, even as the ferocity of his determination startled me that morning. It always did, no matter how often I witnessed it.

Berlin reeked of death. Over the summer, Z had been diagnosed with AIDS and was interred in Auguste-Viktoria-Krankenhaus. He had barred visitors, preferring to be remembered as the smooth-faced man-boy rather than a leprous escapee from Kalaupapa. People listened to him because paranoia and AIDS were synonymous then; too many cowards thought even being in a room with an HIV-positive person was akin to a death sentence. I visited him almost every day.

I arranged a meeting between Alchemy and Bent. The bastard would see him only in exchange for £1,000. Nathaniel, who was attending a mid-September meeting of No Nukes organizers in London, flew with Alchemy and escorted him to Bent's Earls Court hovel, which he had actually cleaned up. The three of them ate lunch at a local fish and chips place. Although Nathaniel believed Bent was not high, he returned the next morning to check on Alchemy, just to be safe. No one was home. That evening, he returned to find Bent strung out, mumbling that Alchemy had taken off and not come back. Foolishly, we'd given Bent the money before the visit ended. Nathaniel taxied back to the hotel in a quandary, fighting his anticop instincts. Luckily, he found Alchemy, who'd run away, sitting in the lobby flirting with a desk clerk.

They were evasive when I asked for details. Alchemy simply shrugged. "I didn't like him. He said mean things about you and told me to ask if you had much fun in any loos lately." I held him close to me, wishing I could exsanguinate the blood of Bent from him.

Gibbon called from New York. He was coming to Cologne, and the skinflint even offered to pay for me to meet him there. A collector had offered $60,000 for a commission with the caveat that we meet first. I wanted Nathaniel to come with me, but he had classes and an appointment in the East. Reluctantly, I went alone. I checked into the hotel decorated in a fin de siècle gaudy opulence straight out of one of Greta's movies. I almost expected Wallace Beery to lumber across the lobby. Dressed in a white bodice tied in the back, a copperish chenille scarf, and a black leather miniskirt, I wandered downstairs to the dining room to meet Gibbon and his buyer.

"Salome, I'd like you to meet Mr. Malcolm Teumer, who has collected your work since your *Do Not Disturb* exhibition."

"Fucking holy fucking shit!"

Everyone in the dining room gaped at us. I collected myself. "Gibbon, please go. Leave Teumer and me alone. Wait in the lobby. This won't take long."

"What?" Gibbon jumped up and down in place. "No, I won't."

"Murray, I said go! Ask no goddamned questions." Teumer waved him away.

Once we were alone, I sat down and ordered a tea and cognac. "I guess Lively talked to you."

"Yes. This seemed convenient, as I have other business here."

"Attending an SS reunion?"

"Don't be silly."

"I'm not fifteen anymore. Don't give me some Joseph Beuys I-was-a-susceptible-youngster bullshit. You're both impostors in my book."

"I do not regret my service. And I see you have not lost an ounce of your fiery energy."

"You haven't lost an ounce of the superciliousness I once mistook for debonair manliness." Still ruggedly handsome, he was dressed meticulously in a dark blue suit. "Malcolm, no woman could ever be more relieved than I was that a baby of hers died."

"Salome, Salome, poor girl." He shook his head, leaned forward, and reached for my hand. I snatched it away. "He didn't die. That was a ruse we all agreed upon. Your parents, Bickley, and I. Our son was alive then, and he lives today."

I placed my hand on my belly and tried to feel the babydeath, or babylife. I started to panic, as if I were going to come apart and disperse into the dark matter. "No. No!" I threw the cognac in his eyes. I stood up and spilled the tea on his lap. He let out a room-piercing "Acchh!" I knelt beside him and pretended to dab his eyes with my scarf. "That is only a fraction of the pain I can cause you. Please, please call the police. I'd love to discuss your past with them."

The maître d' scampered to our table. In between his yelps, Teumer shook his head. "It...is...nothing. An accident."

I stood up and saluted, "Heil Hitler." I clicked my heels and marched into the lobby, where I told Gibbon that Teumer was a perverted stalker who I'd foolishly fucked. I ordered him to buy back all work of mine in his possession, even if I had to indenture myself to Gibbon for years.

Upstairs, in my hotel room, I vomited. I took some tranquilizers and called Nathaniel to confess the entire sordid mess. He heard distress in my voice and did his best to give me strength. "You and I together will face him. I won't let him hurt you again."

When I got back to Berlin (in another noncoincidence), Nathaniel told me he found Alchemy—almost the same age as me when I was with Teumer—having sex with two of Heinricha's friends. I envied Alchemy's freedom, the adventures ahead. I talked to him. "Sex is not good, it's *great*. Never let anyone make you feel guilty or dirty. Or shameful. Be kind. Don't lie. Treat women with respect. Treat them as your betters. *Use birth control.*"

I stopped going out. There'd been two deaths, and I feared another. My spirit, which once was enthused by Berlin, now became moribund. Nathaniel came to me one afternoon with a letter from Magnolia College, an all-women's school in

Virginia. He'd made the final list for a professor's position and they had requested he come for an interview. He'd neglected to tell me he'd even applied.

"Do you still want us to go with you?"

"Of course. If this job really happens, I will be able to provide some security for us, and for Alchemy."

"I still won't marry you."

"I never expect that you will."

While we waited for Magnolia's answer, I spent hours in my studio exhaling little drawings, reading, or just perched on my balcony dreaming into the Berlin sky. One evening I spied a woman, who must have been squatting, in a vacant building across the divide on the east side of the Wall. I tried to get her attention by turning on a spotlight above my head on the balcony, to psychically warn her that the East German police were coming to make one of their sweeps, looking for wall jumpers. She disappeared. I wondered if I'd reached her or if they'd caught her.

The next evening, I spotted a body zigging and zagging across the death strip. It was the woman I had seen the night before. The tower lights flashed. Orders echoed. I screamed, leaning far over the iron balcony. A barrage of gunfire. Howls of pain. She fell. Beside her—a baby. Its cries echoed across the Wall. I had to rescue them.

45

THE MOSES CHRONICLES (2008)

You're Gonna Make Me Loathsome When You Go

Moses and Jay both sensed the flammability of their situation yet seemed incapable of defusing it. Teumer's letter did nothing to alleviate the tension. Jay deflected Moses's entreaties to stay at their house, even if in separate rooms. Jay packed some items and went back to Geri's. Moses, forlorn and furious, remained alone in the house.

Teumer's letter, instead of extinguishing Moses's desire to see him, heightened it—he must meet the man behind that letter, the man who was half him. Moses asked Jay to go with him over an extended Presidents Day weekend. He hoped with her by his side he'd have the courage to confront Teumer and they could begin to repair all that had gone haywire with their life. Jay said only, "I don't think it's a good idea for us to go together."

She did agree to see Butterworth for couple's "almost conventional" therapy. They met in his office. Butterworth, sensing Jay's hesitation, said, "Let me hear why you're here, Jay."

Jay recited Moses's failings—and hers, too—not only of the last few days but the last few years. Moses shrank in his seat. Objectively, he understood the stresses on her—living with his illness, his heavier-by-the-day parental baggage and its aftereffects, her reasons for advising Alchemy to shield him from the psychic torpedoes launched in the letter—but he believed Jay had never adjusted her Livability Quotient to their new realities, and his outburst on the day of the opening unbalanced their tenuous equilibrium. When his time came to respond, he could only muster clichés—I'm sorry. I can change. We need to communicate better.

The session resolved nothing. Jay refused to return to their home. He offered to go to a hotel. No, she said, as if solitary confinement to the house was part of his punishment.

Before their third session in a week, Jay asked to speak with Butterworth alone. Moses waited in the outer office. When Butterworth summoned him and he entered, Jay averted eye contact—her eyes and nose were visibly red. Butterworth addressed them. "There are two reasons couples start counseling. One is to stay together. The other is to break up amicably. You are in phase two. I don't practice that kind of couple's counseling. I suggest you see someone else. I'll give you some recommendations."

Moses turned toward Jay; she blew her nose. "Who determined we are in phase two?"

"I did." Jay dabbed her eyes with new tissues, her body shrinking into a protective pose. "I don't know what I want. But it's not this. I need space."

"You've been saying we drifted too far apart. Now you need more space?"

"Moses, I can't outargue you, but I need time and space to think. To not feel guilty."

"I don't like it, but okay. I do understand why you didn't want me to see the letter. Parts of it anyway. I don't blame you."

"Yes, parts of it," she spat out caustically. She heard her tone, stopped, and took a sip of water from a paper cup. "You're angry. I'm angry. You're disappointed in me and I'm disappointed in you. Everything we had that was good, great really, feels spoiled." She leaned back and sighed. "I want to go now so you have time to talk to Ben yourself."

"Are you going home?"

She shook her head.

"Call you later?"

"Okay."

She left.

After a multiminute stare-off between Moses and Butterworth, Moses declared, "I want my pre-2001 life back."

"That kind of wishful thinking is a prescription for a never-ending encore of suffering."

"I want to stop this ache. I want to be happy. Not undermine my happiness. I can't give up yet."

Butterworth shrugged his muscular shoulders. "It's your choice."

"Do you believe Jay and I are in phase two?"

"The other day I asked you to try to understand why she advised Alchemy not to give you the letter, and I asked her to assume your position in regard to her fling with Alchemy. Neither of you could do it. My experience tells me when both people are trying to assert their rightness over attempting to understand, the road back is closed."

Moses changed the subject. "I'm scared of seeing Teumer, but I'm going. He could spurn me again. I have to take that chance."

Butterworth pressed his hands against his matted hair as if he were squeezing it dry. "That might help with your future. It's my opinion that it will not help with Jay. I've tried to guide you to a route that would free you from the self-imposed prison of a past that colored your present and colors your future. I failed. It's time we reevaluate our situation."

"What does that mean? I'm going to see Teumer. It's not my fault they didn't give me the letter."

"No. Maybe. Had you acted sooner or differently, neither of them would have had to make that choice."

"That's damn harsh. You said it would be a slow process."

"Yes. One must decide if time is being wasted. I'm not abandoning you now. In due time we'll take stock. If need be, I can help you transition to a more traditional therapist."

"Are you tossing me out because of Alchemy? Because it's a conflict? Did Alchemy tell you about the letter before?"

"That's confidential. Besides, I'm not tossing you out. I'm suggesting options. I've never discussed your therapy with him. That would be grounds for malpractice."

Moses limply left the office. At home, in each corner and crevice, he missed the presence of Jay. If she were there, if things had been the way they used to be, they would have laughed about his shrink getting ready to "fire" him.

In the following weeks, they e-mailed almost daily, but Jay avoided a face-to-face meeting. She cursed herself for being so selfish, but sometimes selfishness is a prerequisite for self-preservation. While Moses was out teaching, she picked up any necessary items. An actress friend of hers away on a shoot offered her a three-month house-sit, which she accepted.

Four days before Moses was to leave for Rio, Jay proposed to meet him at his every-six-months appointment with Dr. Fielding. Fielding revealed reassuring blood test results and announced that Moses had now passed the seven-year marker, which indicated that long-term survival was more and more possible, but that testing remained necessary—probably forever. Moses clasped Jay's hand. She didn't resist. He asked if she wanted to grab coffee or a bite. She demurred. She was meeting clients in less than an hour. They walked wordlessly to the Cedars parking lot. Jay stopped, waded in place. "I'm, um, over there." Her chin pointed toward the left corner of the lot. "So, see you. Good luck with, you know, him. I hope you get what you need."

"Me, too." Jay turned toward her car. Unprepared to believe that his marriage was over, Moses bolted to her side. "Jay, I still want you to come with me to Rio. Let's try. C'mon."

"I've thought about it. No, no I can't."

"Why'd you come today?"

"I had to see, to be sure..."

"If I'm healthy?"

"Yes. And I hoped my anger, hurt would go away. It..." Jay stopped herself. "I needed to see if this, separating, is right..." Her posture collapsed.

"Jay, it's not right. It's killing me that I don't know when I'll talk to you next. I talk to you every day in my head. Two hundred times a day. Can't you forgive me? Can't we try?"

"Not now, I wish I...I can't." Her eyes blinked rapidly, trying to fend off tears.

Moses silently vibrated with pain. What good would words do? Jay's emotions were now irreversible. Reason is powerless to repair the ruptured heart.

46

THE SONGS OF SALOME
Back to School

Nathaniel said I tried to scale the Wall as the police removed the bodies of the woman and her child. That memory is—whoosh—gone. The German doctors drowned me in Thorazine and shipped me back to Collier Layne. After a mercifully short vacation, I joined Nathaniel and Alchemy in Virginia, where Nathaniel had secured the professorship. It had a soulsmell of sunlit verdant fields fertilized with the entrails of dead slaves.

Often alone in the studio supplied by the university, unenthused to make art that would enthrall or enrapture, I fretted: Will my odyssey end in a tedious erosion into the nothingness of Harlottesville, Virginia? I became the Salome of Hilda's dreams, wearing the costume of the servile "woman," riding horses, gardening, and making dinner for the family, though Nathaniel was the better cook. Beneath this façade of domestic harmony—obeying the false boundaries of imposed time, emotionally and sexually bound by psychotropic cocktails—I became unrecognizable to me as *me*. And irrelevant to my beautiful man-boy who became a fleeting visage of teenage lust scampering among the adoring cadres. Worst of all, Alchemy started calling himself Scott at school. The ignoramuses had taunted him as "Chemistry" or "Al." I passively accepted this as teenage rebellion, though he appeased me by calling his band the Alchemists. He added new decorations to his room. Posters of bands and hot babes were replaced by one image on each of the four walls: a painting of Julius Caesar and photos of Indira Gandhi, Malcolm X, and Fela. Above, taped to the ceiling, a photo of the Plexiglas booth with Art Lemzcek staring at me as I blew him a goodbye kiss. He found the picture when he and Nathaniel unpacked stuff stored in Orient. Every time I tried to talk to him about the room, he rendered me speechless with, "It's *my* art installation." Intentionally or not, he made me feel so distant from my former lives in Orient and Manhattan.

New York might as well have been as far away as Jupiter. I refused offers to visit the city and no one visited us. Nathaniel, not entirely upset that I'd lost contact with most of my former party pals, attempted to attend to my desires and needs. His political zeal eradicated by what he called "the moribund American left," he often spent non-Magnolia time overseas. There, he was revered instead of reviled or forgotten. But those forays didn't sufficiently energize him to overcome his inability to complete his memoir or his new Scofflaw novel. So began the creeping stultification of his Gravity Disease.

I dissolved into a southern gentrified inebriation, like ice in an old Virginia mint julep on a sweltering July afternoon.

Ruggles, who I talked to at least once a week on the phone, demanded that my medicine intake be monitored at U.Va. Hospital. He and Nathaniel conspired to have Mark Somersby "befriend" me. Somersby had served as a resident with Ruggles at Collier Layne in the early '80s, but rather than pursue a career as a psychoslicer, he'd retreated to his Virginia family home where he assumed the role of the local foppish bon vivant who adored his drink. I nicknamed him Scarlett O'Somersby because of his carefully coiffed graying locks, delicate cheekbones and nose, blue eyes enhanced by eyeliner, a voice that pitched too high, and his often donned scarlet cape. I pegged him as too repressed to step out of the old plantation's closet. Yet only *he* encouraged me to make art. Any art. The closest thing to an oddball of my ilk, we became companions.

Alchemy would soon be deserting me for Juilliard and the delectable life of New York. Served me right for brainwashing him that New York is the center of the world. I descended into the caverns of deep Savant Redness. None too subtly, I tried to persuade Nathaniel to take back the New York sublet so Alchemy could live there and I could visit. He insisted that, at sixteen, Juilliard required Alchemy to live in the residence hall. Bullshit. Nathaniel long ago mastered the art of circumventing rules.

We "celebrated" with a BBQ on Labor Day, the day before Nathaniel would drive Alchemy to New York. He'd stay the week and see some old friends. Alchemy preferred to say goodbye to me here. I think we were all afraid of what might happen if I went to New York.

That night, my son and I strolled around the Magnolia grounds before sitting on the lakeside dock, feet dipped in the warmish water. Feeling a bit shaky, I expressed regret about our peripatetic life and asked if he had any regrets of his own. He teased me, "Not really. Besides, Mom, *stability* of any kind is not your strong suit." I laughed and asked him one favor. "Please, no more Scott. You are Alchemy."

He turned serious and his eyes gazed into a beyond. My son was no longer a teenage boy. Consciously or not, he had transcended linear time. His voice, inhabited by the DNA of lives past, echoed with such resolve and steely calculation that he unnerved me with his certainty. "No one who wants to change the world can be called Alchemy. And I intend to change things."

"Change what? You're a musician. An artist. You can do anything by being you."

He put his arm over my shoulders and nuzzled up close. "Mom, I am going to justify your faith."

I wish I'd believed in him a little less. Challenged him that night on exactly what he intended to change. Told him that whatever he did, even if it was hanging on a street corner playing his guitar for a nickel, it would satisfy me.

Back at the house, after Alchemy went to bed, I went into the dark bedroom. I stepped to the bedside, turned on my flashlight, and pointed the light at the sleeping Nathaniel.

"What's wrong?" he asked, panic in his voice.

"Why did you tell Alchemy to call himself Scott?"

He reached to turn on the nightstand lamp. I stopped him and kept the flashlight's focus on him. "Salome, I didn't."

"Maybe not directly. What *did* you say?"

"It was years ago. I vaguely remember saying, 'Do what you want.'"

"That's it? Be an honest man."

"We'd been musing about art and politics, and I joked that Abe, Tom, and Franklin were our greatest presidents, and guys with names like Grover, Ulysses, and Lyndon, not so much."

"Not funny. Did you encourage him to leave me?"

"No. Never. Still, it's healthy for him to get away from both of us."

"That's one man's opinion. Being around me is not unhealthy for my son."

Furious, I left a note, stormed over to the Magnolia stable, saddled up, and under the moonlight rode off into the Shenandoahs. I napped for a few hours in a meadow and returned when I was sure they were speeding up the Jersey Turnpike.

In the midst of a second night of fast-tempo sleeplessness, Frau Lou appeared and raged, "Don't you see that you and Nathaniel are reenacting your version of *his* parents' lives? Stop it, now!"

Over forty-eight frenetic hours I painted two series of twenty-four 6-x-6 V-shaped boards numbered 1–12, and then set them down on the floor using each piece as a number in a diamond-shaped clock. I painted "i deny time" and "be beyond time," "time kills in time" and "let's fuck time." I used Savant Red or Savant Blue for the backgrounds and white letters for A.M. hours and black letters for P.M. hours.

Finally finished, I collapsed on the cot in my studio. When my eyes opened, Somersby was kneeling beside me, his long eyelashes fluttering. "Nathaniel called. I raced over. He's been trying to reach you for two days and—"

"He presumed I'd done something unhealthy."

"Worried more than presumed. He's just being cautious," Somersby stroked my hair, knotted from dried sweat and paint, with his manicured fingernails.

"I need to wash up. I'm a mess."

"An undeniably lovely mess."

"Somersby, are you flirting with me?"

"I'd say more than flirting…"

Somersby turned out to be quite a bit more Scarlet Pimpernel than Scarlett O'Hara. We enjoyed a fun few days in my studio and his house, but never inside our house. Somersby assured Nathaniel that I was "doing just peachy," and I avoided talking to him. Hours before Nathaniel's return, we relaxed with an afternoon refreshment in the gazebo on Somersby's back lawn. He asked, "So?"

"So nothing. Was fun. Over."

He exhaled. Relieved. "I will talk to Nathaniel about my breach of honor," his tone lugubrious.

"So noble of you. Men! You always act like triumphant cavemen when you 'had' another man's woman. We fucked because I chose to do it. I decide if and when to tell Nathaniel."

When Nathaniel arrived, exhausted from the seven-hour drive, I threw my arms around him with genuine affection.

He drank a beer while talking about how Alchemy had already started a band with Amanda, who later became Absurda Nightingale. He asked if Somersby had taken good care of me.

"Yes," I said perfunctorily, although I could not look him in the eyes.

"How good?" He twitched and fidgeted as if he suspected something.

"Very good."

"What does that mean? Exactly." His right foot tapped uncontrollably against the floor.

"Polyamorously good."

He slammed the bottle on the counter and his voice trembled. "You did this because you're angry at me."

"You think I planned it?"

"Not consciously. You're too impulsive. But when you're angry, sex is your weapon. You seduced him to hurt me."

"No man gets seduced."

"By you, any man or every man can be seduced."

"Stop. I'm not going to see him again. Only I can't live in this backwoods. I can't. I have to move back to New York at least part time."

"Do you want to leave me?"

"No! Do you want me to repent? To admit I feel guilty? You want me to say you have saved me? Ha. I saved you. But do I wish I could be monogamous for you? Maybe. If I could change that one thing in me—maybe—but then I wouldn't be me. I'd be someone else and I don't want to be anyone else and if I were, you wouldn't have fallen in love with me."

"Impeccable Salome logic." To steady his trembling hands, he gripped the kitchen counter. Then he took off his glasses and rubbed his eyes with his palms and faced me again. I spoke first.

"You've hurt me, too." I didn't mean his Parisian fling—that didn't hurt me deeply—but his belief that Somersby or anyone could replace him, that scalded to my core.

He reached for a tissue from the box on the counter and blew his nose.

"Nathaniel, do you hate me now?"

"Of course not." He put on his glasses. "I don't want you to be anyone but you. I want only you, and for you to have what you want." He walked to my side and cupped my head in his hands and kissed my hair. "I'll serve notice that we're taking back the apartment after January first."

47

THE MOSES CHRONICLES (2008)

Child Is Father of the Man

Moses deplaned in Rio and took a taxi to a hotel in the Leblon section of the city. He ate dinner by himself at a churrascaria recommended by the concierge and spent the evening rehearsing his questions and the possible paths of the meeting.

In the morning, a hired car drove him to Alphaville, the walled and segregated wealthy community about fifteen miles from Rio. One thousand guards patrolled the city itself with its own parks, shops, and restaurants. At the north gate, the driver handed one of the guards a piece of paper with words written in Portuguese. "Please tell Malcolm Teumer that Moses is here." Addressing the driver, the guard, dressed in military-style uniform, appeared to say something akin to "only pre-approved visitors." Moses stuck his head out the window and made an insistent dialing motion. "Call him." After a brief phone conversation, the guard pointed, indicating they needed to pull to the side and wait. Moses leaned back. Breathed deep. Closed his eyes. Tried to visualize floating on a tranquil lake. The lake became a typhoon.

Ten minutes or so later, a scooter pulled up and parked beside the taxi. A muscle-bound young man in white pants and white short-sleeve shirt got off the scooter and motioned for Moses to step out of the car. He spoke to the driver in Portuguese. In broken English, the driver tried to explain something. Moses got the drift and allowed the man to pat him down and search the back of the car. He repressed a laugh at this ridiculousness—instead of enervating him, it relieved his tension.

Following the scooter, they passed garbage-free streets manicured lawns, immaculate parks, graffiti-free walls— practically a Hollywood movie set. They were a universe away from the simmering despair of the sunken shoulders of young women, the anger-clenched fists of street urchins, the stench of silent disease of the favelas, and equally distant from the multicolored explosions and the bikini-clad revelers of Ipanema dancing to the samba beat.

They pulled up to an off-yellow two-story stucco house. A woman in her early forties with neck-length wavy blond hair, hazel eyes, complexion as pale as his, stocky body dressed in jeans and flowery blouse greeted him at the doorway. She spoke in English with an accent lilted with the soft cadences of Brazilian Portuguese. "My father says you are the child of an old friend. I am sorry for the wait but João needed to come and show you the way."

"Not a problem."

"My father wanted to be properly prepared. He keeps to his Old World manners."

Sure, Moses thought, *Old World manners where you check your visitors for weapons.*

"I wish you had given us prior notice so I could have prepared some food or drink."

"It's a business trip, so I didn't know if I'd have time. Maybe if I come back again."

"That would be lovely."

He had imagined meeting his half siblings, but seeing his sister in the flesh still unnerved him. Sweat dampened the armpits and collar of his powder blue short-sleeve shirt. Born Jew or not, he still *schvitzed*.

"Please come in out of the heat."

"Thanks." He grimaced—she'd noticed. It wasn't all that hot.

"My father suffers from emphysema. So the visit may be short. He'll see you in his study."

She led Moses down a hallway. Art hung on all the walls. In one room, he spotted a Salome diptych, a 48" × 30" Savant Red and Savant Blue painting. They arrived in a sparsely furnished, dimly lit study. A desk sat in front of a window covered by red silk curtains, and bookshelves lined every wall; no art in here. Two red upholstered chairs, along with a folded walker and an oxygen tank, were arranged around a circular wooden table. A half-smoked cigar dangled off the lip of a ceramic ashtray. Moses and his half sister stood beside one of the chairs as Malcolm moved unsteadily into the room, followed by João, who eased him into a chair and then left. Moses remained fixed in place, assessing his father. Not a Mephistophelean grin or strikingly sinister eyes, but a face fleshy with mottled skin, bald head, a roundish body covered by a nondescript black suit, white shirt, and black tie. The plainness of the man almost stunned Moses. Then he heard his father's voice, a hiss that scalded like a white-hot branding iron meeting flesh. "Pleased to meet you. You bear little resemblance to your father or mother as I remember them." Neither one made a move to shake the other's hand. "Sit."

Teumer addressed Moses's half sister in Portuguese. She bent over and pecked their father on his cheek. She reached out her hand to shake Moses's. He could not resist; he felt her touch, held it too long, hoping—for what? Finally, he released it. "Have a nice chat. João will be outside if you need anything."

Father and son waited until they were alone.

"You received my letter?"

"Yes."

"Although it took some time, I am gratified you found the courage to disobey my wishes, to face me."

Barely able to form words, Moses asked, "She doesn't know about me?"

"Speak up. Talk like a man."

Moses repeated the question.

"Why should she?"

"So you assumed I wouldn't say anything?"

"Yes. And if you did? Would she care? I don't think so. Now that you are here, what do you want?"

Moses needn't ask about the letter or medal. He accepted them as mean-spirited, truthful, almost childish—yet effective—ploys to cause emotional turmoil. "Did you really think I might come here to hurt you?"

"One can never be too cautious. I don't know the depth of your hate or desire for revenge. After all, I was prepared to let you die."

"From the looks of it, you'll be dead soon enough. And I'm still here."

Teumer nodded his head, as if he approved of his son's combativeness.

"Who told Salome I was stillborn?"

"Not I. Laban and Bickley oversaw the mechanics of the birth and your delivery to Hannah and me."

"Did you rape Salome?"

Teumer laughed so hard he began to cough. João rushed in and handed Teumer a glass of water. Teumer waved off the need for his inhaler and spoke to João in Portuguese before returning to Moses. A minute later João returned and handed Moses a sealed plastic bag. "Open it. Look closely."

Moses delicately removed a piece of tissue paper that concealed a brittle black-and-white photograph—the teenage Salome, hair dancing in the Long Island breeze, head turned slightly to the right so her gaze denied the viewer eye contact, white shorts and a half-unbuttoned blouse, her breasts partially exposed. A man in a T-shirt, jeans, sunglasses, and a classic Borsalino hat, self-satisfied grin— Malcolm—beside her, right arm draped over her shoulder, hand cupping her right breast through the open blouse. "If anything, she seduced me. Your mother was voracious in her appetites."

Moses gripped the photo. He began to sweat again. He closed his eyes, waiting for rage or nausea or the lust for vengeance both he and Teumer expected to well in him. No, those virulent emotions remained almost inexplicably quiescent. He slipped the photo carefully back in the bag and held it out to Teumer, who refused it.

"I no longer have need for it. You keep it."

Moses placed it on the table and pressed on with his prepared questions. "Why did you behave so terribly to my mom...Hannah?"

"Circumstance and self-preservation. At first, I needed her. But you misinterpret my effect on her life. For almost three years I made her feel more special than she ever had or ever would again. I rescued her from a wretched ghetto life and introduced her to a cosmopolitan world she had only imagined, and where she remained even after I left. I had hoped to take you with me when I departed. Unfortunately, sooner than anticipated, let's say an old acquaintance recognized me in a Waldbaum's and caused a scene. So I immediately put into effect a contingency plan."

"Your Nazi name wasn't Malcolm Teumer?"

"No."

"You adopted it from a murdered Jew as your identity along with the story about leaving Temisvar for Germany?"

"Yes, something like that."

"What was your name?"

"Oh, I can't seem to remember."

Moses leaned closer into him. "What? You're afraid to tell me?"

"There is a fine line between courage and stupidity."

"And a finer line between semantics and a cowardly lie."

"Good. Good." They locked stares. "You are thinking you are not me, not like me—that you are better than me. You're clever but also a fool. You cannot escape being of my blood, just as I can disown but not dismiss you. I tried when you got sick. I chose not to save you."

This time, Moses could not resist reacting. "You didn't care if I died?"

"You were already dead to me."

"Not so dead that you didn't track my life. My whereabouts."

"When I lived in America, a Negro baseball player was famous for saying, 'Don't look back, something may be gaining on you.' His proposition is correct, but his conclusion indicated inferior thinking. Something *is* gaining on you, and you must look back to make sure it doesn't catch you. If it does, you must be ready."

"I've caught you now. Do your other children know about your past?'

"They know me as a good father and a provider. You saw her affection for me."

Indeed, he had. "You're so sure I won't expose your lies to them."

"You'd consider it ignoble."

Teumer had calculated correctly. Moses knew that the momentary thrill of causing his father embarrassment, if that were even possible, would solve nothing.

"What if I tell some Nazi hunters or official organizations?"

"The U.S. government does not want me or others like me exposed. You know that. You're a historian."

Moses nodded. He was well aware that the Reagan administration had put a stop to all pursuits of former Nazis living in the United States, and the policy remained in force.

"And I have been and will remain well protected here."

"Protected from others, perhaps. I've always wondered how cold-blooded murderers like you live with yourselves."

"What some call murder, others call natural selection. Don't scoff. Nature is a slow process of weeding out the weak. We sped up the process by selecting, in a most humane manner, those who over time nature would have eliminated. The weak must not inherit the earth or humanity will face extinction. We came close but were thwarted... for now. History is still on our side. As for my decision with you, modern medicine should only be used upon the sacred few. For the rest... let nature decide."

Moses shook his head. This man exulted in evils large and small, in the fastidiousness of the crematoriums and the personal cruelties perpetrated against himself and his mom. Moses had heard and seen enough. He stood up. "Even before I got your letter and found out about your monstrous life, I swore to myself not to behave like the emotional coward that you are." He winced ever so slightly at the thought of Jay and how he had behaved like a graceless coward. No, he couldn't punish himself right then. "I am so glad we finally met."

Moses moved closer. Teumer stared up at him, wetting his bloodless aged lips with his tongue. Moses picked up the envelope and took out the photo of his parents. He stared at it once more and placed it between his fingers as if he were going to rip it in half. "I don't have any need for this." He hesitated and dropped it on the table. "I'll let myself out."

Moses's invisible angel of torment had been transformed — not into a smiling seraph of lightness but a declawed demon. The ever-changing past once again became new, a future filled with possibilities of forgiveness or bitterness, compassion or heartlessness. The choice would not be easy, but it would be his.

373

BOOK III

The only consolation would be:
it happens whether you like or no.
And what you like is of infinitesimally little help.
More than consolation is: You too have weapons.

—Franz Kafka

48

THE SONGS OF SALOME

Boogie Woogie Bugle Boy

I've made an effort to tell my story in a linear fashion. Now this fallacious narrative of time has been undone by Mr. Parnell Palmer, government lackey, investigator for the Committee on Anti-American Activities. He showed up yesterday to "inquire" about the night of Alchemy's death. He claimed he wanted to issue a report stating once and for all his death was an accident and to squash all the "vicious rumors."

We met in Bellows's office. Palmer's unmowed-lawn eyebrows, tiny nose, lizardy neck, and bald head intrigued me. I sketched him while we talked. He eyed Dr. Bellows, who shook her head as if to say, "Let her do it." Until now, I refused to meet with any "official." What can they do? Lock me up? Ha. Palmer enticed me with the possibility of a visit from Persephone.

With more than a hint of incredulity, Palmer began by asking why my nurse had been off that night. I told him I had no authority to dismiss anyone, so I assumed Alchemy or Laluna gave her the night off because of the Super Bowl party. No denying that Alchemy and I argued earlier that day over Laluna's refusal to allow me to care for Persephone when they went on vacation. From the first, my relationship with Laluna had waned and waned farther. I wanted a grandchild, but I'd correctly sniffed her lack of enthusiasm for motherhood.

Palmer kept pushing me to defend my absence from the party. Reason seemed to bounce off his bald head. He couldn't understand why I always refused to attend that celebration of modern slavery and violence. I told him that I didn't leave my cottage or studio until later that night, when it was already too late. That was true in all meanings of truth.

"At times you have said that you and Mindswallow were both at your cottage when you heard Moses, Laluna, and Alchemy arguing. At other times you claimed you weren't sure where Mindswallow was. Which is it?"

"The answer is both. I heard bursts of their yelling when he banged on my door, while he was there. I'd taken some pills and was lost in drowsyland when Ambitious showed up. I'm sure he told you what happened. Why do you need me to confirm it? For all of his inverted thinking, he is not a liar. Nor, as he fancies himself, is he a killer."

"You have called yourself 'a homicider'?"

"What are you insinuating?"

"Well, first there was the 'performance' with Art Lemczek, then the incident where you stabbed Laban Lively with box cutters. And isn't it true you tried to burn Nathaniel by setting the house in Charlottesville on fire?"

"Exactly the opposite. A well-trained Pavlovian mind like yours is conditioned to bite only your enemies. I bite my loved ones—to save them. With his blessing, I saved Art from an arduous, painful death. That wasn't homicide. And I acted to save Nathaniel from himself."

"By setting a fire outside his locked room? Unique concept. Killing or trying to kill friends and loved ones. Perhaps you thought you were saving your son the nigh—"

I chomped at his hand. He flinched. "I also bite my enemies."

"And Moses was your enemy. Isn't that why you told Malcolm Teumer you wished your son Moses had died?"

"How do you know that? Malcolm Teumer was a liar. That's not what I meant."

"Maybe, but"—he pointed to Bellows's computer—"I can arrange it so you can listen to yourself anytime."

"You were taping my conversations? Or Teumer's? No matter what you want to believe, I did not kill my son. I'm done." I stood up and showed him the drawing—his eyebrows as tiny leeches eating away his face.

"Is that me?"

"Oh, yes. I need you to sign it."

"Why?"

"When you awaken tonight, you'll know why."

He mumbled "nutcase" and started packing his things.

Bellows knew me well enough to see I was joking, but not well enough to understand my motivation. Once Palmer left, I said to her that he was trying to intimidate me. People like him are afraid of anything that smacks of the extraordinary. I did what I could to intimidate him back. I admitted to her that I only vaguely remembered the fire. She answered, "We'll talk tomorrow."

So many memories are etched on my brain like ineradicable ancient pictographs, and others, so soluble, have been washed away by the waterfall of human aging and Collier Layne cocktails.

Too clear in my memory is the hollowness of the Harlottesville house. The shadow of my Somersby diddle-daddle ended the pretense of my adaptability to a southern belle jar domestic life. I hoped for a change in the slavish air when Alchemy returned at Thanksgiving. A vicious migraine struck me and ruined the dinner. After hours in my lightless room, I woke up feeling worn-out and unmoored. I stepped gingerly downstairs. Deep into their drinks, Alchemy and Nathaniel were talking intensely while listening to the Louis and Ella sessions. I halted in the hallway and overheard Alchemy ask Nathaniel, "Why do you put up with her antics?"

Antics? I jammed my jaw shut.

"A question I have asked myself, oh, a thousand times. I think she's as beautiful as the day I first saw her in Max's. She's an artistic genius and, at the same time, a child who needs me to take care of her. Her moral compass may seem askew, but she's never been a phony. She is exactly who she presents herself to be. And she may not see it, and you may not see it, but I need her."

"I see it but I don't totally get it."

"So much of what I struggled to achieve is being trampled by the forces of regression. If it weren't for Salome, I might've fallen into my cups and given up. When she is her best self, she acts with absolute faith in her abilities, in mine, in yours. When she is in a red or blue period..." His voice trailed off. "The year in Paris, when you two stayed in New York, I was miserable without her. I took this teaching gig because I thought it would help us. Ruggles thought so, too. We were both wrong. What can I say? She drives me almost as batty as she is"—he laughed—"yet I always love her madly."

"I can't imagine life with my mom and what it would've been like without you. I won't ever forget."

How could he not understand how much I'd done for both of them by being with Nathaniel?

I eagerly returned to New York after the New Year while Nathaniel stayed in Virginia. It turned out disastrously. AIDS had denatured the city of so much vitality. Many friends had moved. Or died. The art market had crashed in '87, Gibbon closed his gallery and now relaxed in style in the Hamptons. The Whitney Biennial curators, who I'd previously brushed aside, now rebuffed me. Leslie Tallent penned a piece on the younger artists I'd influenced, which made me feel like a has-been. I spent some nights with old friends like Xtine and some new ones. And too many alone. My nonstop movable feast of the '60s and early '70s seemed to have settled into an antiquated garden party with cocaine on a cracker as an hors d'oeuvre. Instead of burning down the castle, these kids lined up around the block to get inside.

My son's busy life didn't include me and my "antics." Absurda, or Amanda, as we called her then, and I adopted each other as surrogate mother and daughter. When I received the invite to Blind Lemon Socrates's imminent-death-from-colon-cancer requiem/extravaganza at Alexander Holencraft's new apartment in the Dakota, I asked Absurda to be my date.

Mostly, I enjoyed the night. I dressed accordingly in ankle-high, rust-red boots, a short but not too short maroon dress, and a half-length silver faux-fur jacket with a pink boa around my neck. I did not enjoy the questions: "Where have you been?" and "How are you?" I asked instead, "How do I look?" The answer was fucking fantastic.

Socrates, with two teenage boys on either side of him, leaned on his cane. The poet Noma Moma Dada read a tribute, and the French filmmaker Matsa Brie announced the upcoming premiere of a documentary on Socrates's life, before introducing the icon of honor. Socrates dropped his cigarette into his scotch glass and listened to it fizzle out. "I have spent my life attempting to halt the urbane decay that many of you represent," he said, inching his long neck tauntingly toward a gaggle of young admirers. "I leave you with one thought: If you care more about riches or material goods than about virtue...then I have failed you. And you will fail yourselves." He shook his head indignantly, as if he foresaw his fate as the forgotten.

Holencraft yelled, "Thank you, Socrates!" and everyone began drinking again. I felt a pinch on my ass. I turned, ready to slap the offender. His body shriveled and colorless, I wouldn't have recognized Raphael Urso, except for his Willem de Kooning eyes bulging out in flinty disgust at the world. He laughingly said, "Whoa, there, Salome. Where's Brockton?"

"Virginia."

"Let's do what we shoulda done years ago."

"Raphael..." I snapped my middle finger against his forehead. "That's all I ever wanted to do to or with you." Ever good-humored, he laughed. Alchemy, with a female friend, unexpectedly showed up. "I'm going to talk to my son."

Absurda had seen him, too, and we arrived by Alchemy's side at the same moment. Absurda and Holencraft were exiting stage left for a night of indoor sports at the Stanhope. I witnessed a furtive exchange of glances and pursed lips between Alchemy and Absurda. He hummed, twinkle-eyed, "Do wah diddy diddy, dum diddy do..."

I'd never previously decoded the telegraphic signs of desire and denial tapping between them. I sensated the specter of Gravity Disease tainting her soulsmell of suede shoes and a champagne bottle's cork. I wasn't sure if the aura of Alchemy hindered or helped her. After a time, she left for California. No matter; she couldn't truly escape her disease, or him.

New York and I seemed to be vibrating at different frequencies. I found it harder and harder to venture out alone. My immune system began to wilt from loneliness, and the psychic temblors of another bout of Gravity Disease sent me retreating to Harlottesville and Nathaniel's (mostly) nonjudgmental empathy. I counted the days between Alchemy's school breaks and waited for a stirring from my psychopomps.

During the Christmas break of Alchemy's junior/senior year (he was graduating in three years rather than four), we traveled to New York and all decamped at the 3rd Street apartment. Nathaniel intended to talk to him about his postgraduation plans. I didn't care what he did. Watching the evening news one night, Nathaniel flew off on a predictable tirade about the impending invasion of Iraq and the brainwashed public. Alchemy seized the opportunity he must've known would come.

"Nathaniel, you taught me that when Nixon abolished the draft he did more to undermine the antiwar movement than anything else because it removed the threat to the middle-class and rich kids and their parents."

Nathaniel nodded.

"You used to quote some French guy, 'To resist is to create. To create is to resist.' I think it's a good motto in art and in life."

Again, Nathaniel nodded. I sensed something off, but he caught me completely by surprise with what he said next.

"I enlisted in the army. I'll be going to boot camp in July. I will resist creatively and create with resistance. And it'll look good in the future."

Nathaniel clasped my hand. I pulled it away. "Future! What future is that? Do you want to kill yourself to hurt me? To sacrifice, waste years shooting at people! This isn't the fucking best way to rebel against us."

"Mom, stop shrieking. Do you think every decision I make is because of you? You are so narcissistic. I'm making my own choices now."

Nathaniel tried to be reasonable. "Alchemy, the way to protest a war is not to fight in it. It's—"

"Nathaniel," I cut him off. "Alchemy"—I lowered the volume of my voice—"I haven't dedicated my life to you so you can die in a war started by two egomaniacs with penis problems."

"Mom, don't make this about anyone else, you're still making this about yourself. You always make it about you. Whether it's ten minutes of almost great sex in a Porta-Potty or—"

"Stop. Stop. My son cannot be this cruel." I got down on my knees and begged him not to punish himself—to punish me, in some other way. Whatever detours I made, how foolish my actions seem, the greatest accomplishment of my life was having him as my son. Still on my knees, my voice a beaten whisper, I said, "Someday you will ache like I ache right now." Alchemy's face implacable, I pleaded with Nathaniel, "Please. Please don't let him do this. Stop him."

Nothing could sway him. In July, Alchemy left for Fort Bragg.

Then came the fire. Bellows told me that, according to Dr. Ruggles's records, I set the *Let's Fuck Time* pieces afire in the pit outside and then set some of the older *Pearl Diver* drawings afire in the hallway. Nathaniel and I suffered smoke inhalation and his hands suffered minor burns. Guilty and ashamed, Nathaniel agreed with Ruggles to send me back here. And I became forever unfree to walk the streets on my own.

49

THE MOSES CHRONICLES (2008)

The Social Medium Is Not the Message

Sctfree1: mose, you there?

Moses wasn't sure if he wanted to talk now. Since returning from Rio, he'd sent only one e-mail to Alchemy, detailing his meeting with Malcolm. Though he did miss their talks, messaging, and e-mail exchanges.

Sctfree1: ok, call me later.

Moses did not want to speak on the phone.

MThead23: Yes, I'm here now. What's up?

Sctfree1: last night the chameleon mom took the form of a grand inquisitor. she asked who was that masked man at the hammer who left during my talk? meaning you.

MThead23: Geez. It's been months.

Sctfree1: months, years, they mean nothing to her. i said you're a collector whose parents were holocaust survivors.

she sniffed like maybe she didn't believe me. i didn't push it. she's a freak.

MThead23: Freaks me out. You think she knows?

Sctfree1: don't think so. she's never given one clue she knows any more than what she's always believed happened.

MThead23: OK. Tell me what form she next takes.

Sctfree1: maybe now is the right time for you to meet her? you and jay come up here?

Moses took a long drink from the bottle of water on his desk.

Sctfree1: ???

MThead23: Thinking. Still absorbing all the changes. The good, the less good, and the awful. I don't think Teumer can do me any more damage. Salome...she feels, very present.

Sctfree1: get that. when you're ready, say the word.

Again Moses hesitated before typing.

MThead23: The word is if I do see her, it will be without Jay.

Sctfree1: whatever works best.

MThead23: Jay and I, we're not working so well anymore. It's been hard on her with all of my shit. We're taking a break.

Sctfree1: wow. i'm sorry. you wanna talk? in person?

MThead23: Not now.

Sctfree1: soon. i'm in need of your eminence grise expertise. lotta questions about the nonanswers blowin' in wind.

MThead23: Send an e-mail. I have to go.

Go where? he thought.

The tunnel of love, as Moses and Jay had once affectionately nicknamed their home, now suggested a dank, abandoned subway tunnel. His and Jay's bed was as welcoming as a water-soaked electrified third rail. Divorce papers he didn't want to sign and decisions whether he could afford to buy Jay's half of the house or sell and move awaited him after finishing his day at SCCAM and making the enervating drive from Pasadena to Venice. He spent hours reliving his meeting with his father. With each passing day, he felt better about how it had gone. He did not feel better about how he'd behaved with Jay. As a child, he'd sworn never to desert Hannah and that promise was kept. But he had failed miserably with his wife. He hadn't physically abandoned her, but she was right—emotionally he had sealed himself off. He began to see that somehow his fear of his father had translated into behavior that helped ruin his marriage. He blamed no one but himself. Moses understood that free-floating fear and hate caused only self-destructive reactions. He could never attain peace of mind by hating, by being afraid. His least-troubled hours were spent in the classroom, re-creating the triumphs and tragedies of histories past, or gabbing in the cafeteria with his students while marveling at their youthful optimism.

He often procrastinated in his windowless basement office in the humanities department. All signs of his married life erased as efficiently as Malcolm Teumer's war crimes past. Gifts from Jay no longer hung on the walls. Photographs of Jay with her head resting on his shoulder, which he'd featured prominently on his desk, now removed. He wondered if anyone had noticed.

The answer arrived one April evening when Moses, lying on the chocolate-brown office couch, was interrupted by a tapping on the closed door. He pushed himself up, rubbed his eyes, and opened the door to find Evie-Anne Baxter, an MFA music student who needed to pass his class to fulfill unfinished BFA requirements, flashing her evanescent smile. "Saw the light on under the crack. You mind?" Evie wore a white midriff T-shirt that left her belly and tattooed shoulders exposed. She closed the door and plopped down onto the sofa. She dangled her sandaled feet over the sofa's arm, wiggling her toes. Moses propped open the door, his standard policy, before sitting upright in his swivel chair behind his desk across from the sofa.

"You're here late." Evie yawned as she spoke. "I could use a nap. Or a beer."

"I'm still marking midterms."

"Yeah? When my parents divorced, it was like, hell on my dad. He stayed late in his office, too."

Taken aback, Moses paused before issuing a flat-voiced, "I'm sorry to hear that." Clearly, his impending divorce was common knowledge.

Evie sighed histrionically. "I'm not doing great in your class, am I?"

"Great...No." Moses turned around in his chair and pulled out Evie's test paper from the stack. He reached to hand it to her but she didn't move, so he placed it back on the desk. "You received a C-plus on your midterm."

"Evie and tests, like bad combo. I need to get at least a B to keep my scholarship. What can I do?"

Moses issued his stock answer: participate more in class, study harder. Unable to veer his eyes away from her exposed skin, he asked, "If not that, what do you propose?"

She answered eagerly, "I propose you and I go for a drink and talk about it someplace less stuffy and more fun."

"Evie, that's not appropriate. Besides, I'm not a fun guy these days."

Evie sat up, jutted her lower lip like a sulky child, and then sang, ad-libbing the last words, "*How ya gonna keep 'em down on the farm after they seen Paree...or spent some time with me...ee?*" He had begun his lecture on the Jazz Age by playing that song. "Not appropriate? Maybe for you, but for the other profs here, this is like the Harvard of horndogism. What're you gonna do tonight? Like, watch the History Channel? C'mon." She waved her hand to say, *Let's go.*

"You're obviously paying attention, so please participate more. That'll help your grade." He showed her to the door.

In the following weeks, Evie flitted in and out of class carefree as ever. Moses avoided prolonged eye contact or speaking to her alone in the halls. He realized he was acting as if something unseemly *had* actually passed between them.

In late May, the semester was officially over and all were preparing for the summer break. Moses was staring at a text from Jay asking him not to cancel the meeting with his divorce attorney again, when Evie knocked on Moses's office door. "Hey, Professor T, you got a minute?"

"Sure."

Leaving the door open, Evie sauntered in, stood in the middle of the room, and grinned. "Thanks for the grade."

"You did extremely well on your final exam. Scholarship intact, I presume."

"I studied hard. And I did really love your class. You're the first guy that ever made history like fun. Hey, my band is playing at the Smell tonight. Evie and the Bralasses. I'd love it if you came. Some of my music profs are coming."

Moses demurred. "Previous plans." He did have a meeting with his divorce attorney.

"Another time, then."

Moses mumbled, "I don't think so."

"Professor T, don't you get it? Your marriage is *history*."

Annoyed, he asked rather curtly, "How do you know about that?"

"The Itch List knows everything." The Itch List was a student-only Web site, which apparently carried more information than just about teachers and their classes. "I like older dudes whose faces have life lived in them. And you're so smart." Evie spread her arms, with her palms at forty-five-degree angles, and bowed her head as if she were onstage. She held the pose for Moses, who stared at the green lace top that didn't do much to hide her freckled breasts, and she pronounced, "It's my abandoned child thing. My dad—my mom kicked him out for good reasons—after a while he decided he didn't need to see me or my sister."

"I'm sorry. It's terrible when parents punish their kids for selfish reasons."

Evie shrugged. "So, tonight?"

Moses thought, *Evie, you need to be around men your own age. I'm not a cure for your problems.* "I'm sure you and your band are terrific. But I can't."

With the semester's end, Moses found himself adrift in space and time without the usual soothing summer routine. No vacation with Jay. No visit to New York to see Hannah and old friends. Mostly he ate takeout or frozen dinners alone in the empty house. Sometimes he felt so lonely he wished for a solicitor to call. But when he'd meet with friends, he almost always wished he had stayed home.

He found himself languishing in memories of his Jay-life. He thought about returning to Budapest, where the inexplicable out-of-body vibrations of the dead entered his body, tears welling unwillingly in his eyes, as he sat in the Great Synagogue desecrated by the Nazis and their minions in the Hungarian Arrow Cross. What foolishness—that out-of-body idiocy—for a descendant not of the slaughtered but of the slaughterers. If he returned, he'd be looking for an entirely new set of clues to his past. No, he couldn't go back.

The land mines exploded, the shrapnel of divorce lodged in his lungs, he reflected on his new identity and what the cancer had wrought: Was he no longer the same person? For centuries, Jews had pretended to convert to Christianity to save themselves. Others had converted out of belief. How had that changed them?

How would this change him? He had often been perceived as a type—a transplanted New York Jewish intellectual. Would he unconsciously surrender his invisible yarmulke and unmask a secret identity previously unknown to himself? No, he was still Moses, only non-Jewish, motherless, unmarried yet unfree. A lost man with a surfeit of wars still raging in his soul. Would he even find peace in the arrival of eternal nightfall?

Moses cursed Butterfield for his sly way of giving up on him. He began therapy with a psychologist in Santa Monica. After one disappointing afternoon session, he drove to Bergamot Station, hoping to find Jay perusing the galleries, as she often did for her clients. He drifted to the café, took a seat in the outdoor patio, and scanned the parking lot and open spaces, pleading for his soon-to-be ex-wife to pass by, when, from behind, he heard a cooing voice. "Pro-fessor..." He recognized Evie's voice as she approached and stood by his side. "You mind? Or is this off-limits, too?"

"Please. Not at all."

Before she sat, she pulled her sweater over her head, and Moses stared at her tattered, sleeveless T-shirt (it read THE JAM). "Getting hot."

"So, Evie, what brings you so far west of the 405?"

"Stalking you," she teased. "C'mon. I came to see Exene Cervenka's collage exhibition. One of my idols. She was the lead singer for X."

"Someone once dragged me to see X after I first moved to L.A."

"Knew there was a hip dude hidden under that buttoned-up shirt. That why you're here?"

"No. I'm here because . . . I was hoping to run into my wife."

"Sorry. I'm not her. But you got me. You believe in fate?"

"No."

"Dude, you sure know how to charm a lady."

Moses half laughed. "Evie, I am glad we've run into each other. I did not handle our last conversation particularly well. You mentioned problems with your father, and I was hastily unsympathetic."

"You were."

"I'm sorry."

"Apology almost accepted. How about we finalize it and go someplace less oinky for a real drink . . ." She reached for his hand and dragged him out of his chair and toward her car. He resisted. Why? She was damn cute. Seemed kind of goofy. He had nothing to go home to. He needed to change his life and he still regretted his youthful timidity with women. So . . . he surrendered and suggested Chez Jay, the forty-year-old dive of the older "hip" crowd. There was little chance either his students or Jay would see them there.

A few hours later, dizzy, besotted by liquor and lust, Moses found himself laying out his credit card for a room at the nearby Loewes Hotel. Once inside the room, Evie, in a series of swift motions, slipped her iPod into the room's player and turned up her band's CD. She pulled her T-shirt over her head. "Evie, I don't . . ." She thrust her breasts in his face, which Moses found himself kissing frenetically before she slunk down between his legs. She unzipped his pants, dismissing Moses's halfhearted admonishments.

"Tastes good."

Moses, enthralled at being seduced so boldly, suppressed his rising panic.

"Professor T"—she giggled, pulled off her jeans, and sat on the bed—"now suck me then fuck me." She put her legs on Moses's shoulders and gently pressed him into a kneeling position as she lay on her back. Moses surrendered. Consequences be damned.

A few hours later Evie woke Moses. She was already dressed.

"Geez, how long have I been asleep?"

"Not that long. It's only ten. Sorry, but I have to go."

Nonplussed by the sight of this young woman he hardly knew standing over him in a hotel room, Moses mumbled, "Oh, okay. I guess."

"I'm meeting my band at eleven. I don't want to have to explain why I can't make it." Evie bent over and kissed him. "That was very nice. And don't worry, Prof"—she pulled her hand across her lips as if zipping them shut—"our secret. Maybe next time I'll stay, if, ya know..."

"Yes, I think, yes, I would really like that."

50

THE SONGS OF SALOME

The Collector

I want to be grateful—my son's stardom and wealth unshackled me from Collier Layne and Billy Bickley Jr. But I'm not. Do not condemn me yet.

For almost three years I wandered in the haze of grainy, bleachy fumes caused not by the fire but the embalming fluids of a "new" psychotropic concoction that clouded my mind. I was Lady Tiresias trapped in asphodel, visited by stygian visions of the first son undead, the descent of Nathaniel, and Alchemy's death by envy.

When Ruggles finally reconfigured my drug regimen, I emerged from my exile. Alchemy appeared with the guttersnipe Mindswallow in tow, on their way to L.A. We'd missed celebrating Alchemy's twenty-first birthday. I was so thrilled to see him.

Unfortunately, the immediate joy was tempered by the mention of Billy Jr., who'd "summoned" Alchemy to a meeting. Alchemy told me that after the Lively box cutter performance, as part of the deal not to prosecute me (which everyone had hidden from me) and put me in Collier Layne, Greta had appointed Bickley Sr. as my official guardian and trustee. She wanted no more to do with it.

Nathaniel's marriage proposals now made sense. If we'd married, instead of the Bickleys he could've attempted to become my guardian and keep me out of Collier Layne.

Bickley Sr. died in 1989, after my incarceration and just before Greta's death. Evil Billy Jr. became my guardian and trustee, so he controlled the dispersal of funds. He and Ruggles successfully completed Alchemy's army hardship discharge. Ruggles hoped that freeing Alchemy would be healthy for me. But during their meeting, Billy Jr. explained that with the discharge papers completed, when Alchemy turned twenty-one and was no longer in college, there was no legal obligation to give him another cent, and besides, he needed to conserve the money to keep me in Collier Layne. And then he almost giddily added that if the trust ran out of money he'd personally drive me to a "public dump."

After he dutifully relayed the bad news, we spent the afternoon laughing and reminiscing about good times. Those precious few hours with Alchemy brought me such joy. As we walked to the lobby, he sensed my onrushing despair and promised to return to rescue me.

Good to his word, Alchemy used his signing bonus to sic the Sheik's lawyers on Billy Jr., and my son became my guardian and gained control of the trust. He moved me to L.A. I lived in his newly bought home for a bit. Nathaniel took a sabbatical and joined us when the Magnolia semester ended, and we (and the first of many "nannies") moved into a small rented house in Silver Lake.

From the first time I visited L.A., the town's ballyhooed clichés of eternal sunshine, apocalyptic winds, and lemming-like pursuit of froth and fashion spoke a language of living that eluded my sensibilities. Its soulsmell of a smoldering surfboard, drive-thru ice cream, and tattoo and gun parlor sensated me with intestinal panic.

I tried to live my life as Salome the artist, not as mother of superstar. I thought about finally exhibiting the *Baddist Boys* collages, but my psychopomps' undulating warnings whispered, "Too soon, too soon." I listened.

I prepared a smaller exhibition for the Grand Dame of the L.A. art scene, Lily Fairmont. As the title of the show, I truncated the Diogenes quip, "It's not that I am mad, it is only that my head is different from yours," into *My Head IS Different*. Using the garage in the Silver Lake house as a studio, I painted a series of portraits of other Collier Layne vacationers. I defined them with quasi-abstract squiggly profile lines, color, and brushwork. I can't say I made one intimate friend during any vacation. I never had a single violent or sexual interaction with any other guest. I only watched and listened. I've purposely refrained from detailing the barbaric and profane treatments of group therapy, electroshock, and mind-raping drugs given to others. It is not my right to tell their story. I wouldn't want any of them to reveal their version of mine.

Some days after the opening, Lily called. Her voice dripped with her sardonic tone, "Honey, two not at all amusing elderly gentlemen want to buy some pieces." I asked her to describe them. They were standing right there, so she held out the phone. I heard the unmistakable voices: Lively's slow-winding-lariat-snap drawl and Teumer's strident Teutonic grumblings. Lily, the anti-Gibbon, agreed that certain people should not have my work. I asked her to put them off and have them return the following afternoon.

The next day, nurse-nanny number one drove me to the gallery. She waited in the car.

I arrived before them and hid in the back room. I watched as she denied them the paintings. Teumer was bloated, rounder, and no longer even vulgarly sexy. Lively, hulking as ever, appeared uneasy. Teumer kept trying to change Lily's mind and she kept insisting, "Honey, there's not a chance."

Unexpected reinforcements arrived in the form of Absurda, Mindswallow, and Pullham-Large, who had missed the opening—not that I cared. They were dropping by before going to a recording session.

I uncloaked myself and emerged from the office. I mouthed to Lively and Teumer, "Stay there," while I draped the others with histrionic hugs. Absurda and Pullham-Large perused the pieces in the back of the gallery. Mindswallow leaned against the front wall, drinking a beer; art interested him about as much as football did me. I turned to face my nemeses.

"Pig meat sweat! I smell pig meat sweat fresh from the inferno."

Teumer sneered at me. "This is how you welcome your old friend and lover?"

"Malcolm, if I could undo only one night of fucking, I'd undo the night alone with you."

"Oh, it was more than one night. And our offspring lives here in Los Angeles. Would you undo that, too? Perhaps we should go visit him."

The repressed vision of our son alive arose from the foggy years I was under Ruggles's drugs. I almost believed him. I stared at Lively. "He's lying."

"'Fraid not."

"Mr. Mindswallow?"

"Yo."

"Do you understand the piety-filled corrupt language of liars? It's the language of those who reek of pig meat sweat." I heard my voice nibbling at the edges of hysteria. So did Teumer. Expecting me to hit, spit, or tackle, he slid back next to Lively. I edged toward them. Teumer raised his right arm. In a flash, Mindswallow snatched his wrists and arched his arms behind his back. "Not a smart move."

Teumer whined, "Let me go!"

"I ain't into hurting an old man, but I let you go and you try something, I'll hit you so hard it'll knock your gonads into your mouth."

Lively pacified the situation. "No need, son. Let go of my friend, and we'll be on our way." Mindswallow released his grip. I stood between Lively and Teumer, put one hand on each of their arms, and walked them to the glass doors. "Never a pleasure doing business with you two." I turned and smooched Mindswallow on the lips. "Absurda, you're a lucky woman to have such a chivalrous killah bee by your side." Mindswallow yawned.

Nurse-nanny drove me to the ocean. After a stroll on Venice Beach, on the way back to Silver Lake we detoured to the Sunset Boulevard recording studio. Pullham-Large paced nervously outside the control room. Without my asking, he fetched Alchemy.

Alchemy, smoking, looking displeased, slowed his walk from harried musician to concerned-and-in-control son as he approached me. "Mom, you all right?"

"The sand and salty air sanitized me after the filthy exhalations of Lively and his friend who came to the gallery. I'd like to move closer to the ocean."

"What did Lively want? Maybe I can help."

"His friend's a collector and wanted to buy some pieces. I don't need your help."

"Okay. Dinner sometime later this week?"

"Yes. Go back to making music."

So, you see, my seeming bratty ingratitude has warrant. Instead of gaining me my freedom, Alchemy's fame tightened the noose of dependency around my neck. When a child becomes father to the mother, the ceremony of innocence is drowned.

51

THE MOSES CHRONICLES (2008)

I Prefer Not To

Moses got up before 6 A.M. and took a taxi back to Bergamot to retrieve his car. When he got home, he turned on his computer hoping for an e-mail from Jay, but no. To his surprise there was an e-mail from Evie. She'd sent it at 5 A.M., probably when she was first getting to bed. She asked if they could meet the following night. Moses answered from his private e-mail. They met at the Marina Hotel, a somewhat run-down and inexpensive hotel used mainly by flight crews because of its proximity to the airport, and where there was scant chance of being noticed. They ordered room service, had sex, and watched *To Have and Have Not*, which Evie had never heard of, much less seen. Moses told her how the forty-five-year-old Bogart and the nineteen-year-old Bacall had met while making the film.

"That why you picked this one?"

"Partly."

"I'm twenty-six, not nineteen. Guess she had daddy issues, too?"

"I don't know."

"Professor T"—she didn't like calling him Moses—"you're like an old guy, but I wouldn't be with you if you were a clown."

Moses looked confused.

"You haven't heard that?" Moses shook his head. "C-L-O-W-N. Creepy Lecherous Old White Nympho. It's what we call some of the teachers."

"Well, I'm flattered, I think."

Thus their afternoon encounter turned into an affair. He'd wait for her to contact him—which she sometimes did two days in a row and then not for four or five days. Still incapable of embracing any notion that life has a bottom, Moses allowed himself a dollop of hope that Evie's arrival, however dubious their "relationship," signaled at least a lull in his descent.

Things continued in this way—erratic, guilt-laden, yet invigorating. The attention of such a young and attractive woman began the repair of his frayed ego. Moses spent much of his time reading and going to the movies alone. One of his old college friends, who taught at Columbia, encouraged him to start writing down his ideas comparing the revolutionary years of 1848 and 1968. He never got past jotting a few notes and listing the books he'd need for research. He perused a long proposal that Alchemy had sent him outlining ideas for the Nightingale Foundation, which he envisioned as both beneficial for society and as the jumping-off point for entering the political arena. He wanted Moses's input.

At the end of July, Evie and Moses met at the Marina Hotel—he still didn't dare see Evie at his home or hers. They watched *The Palm Beach Story* from bed while Moses rhapsodized about Preston Sturges (he relished the role of cultural mentor). Then Evie nonchalantly put forth a question Moses had expected for some weeks: "You told your ex-wife about me?"

"I'm not officially divorced. Very soon, though. And no, not yet."

"Hey, no prob. I've told none of my friends or other lovers about you."

"Best way to go for now." He was relieved not only by her circumspection but also that she had other lovers.

"How about your brother?"

"Who?"

"Isn't Alchemy Savant your brother? Figured you might exchange, you know, stuff. Guys being guys."

"My *half* brother and I are not exactly on a 'guys being guys' terms. I haven't seen him in months."

"Be a playa. Show me off to him! Show off my music! You got more PILF points than you know."

"PILF?"

"Professor I'd like to fuck."

He laughed silently, but with some pride, at the idea of Moses the Lothario. "Let me think about it."

"If it's so upsetting, forget it."

AlchemyAlchemyAlchemy, his name compressed and shrank Moses's balls. "Maybe I'll send him a download of your music."

"Great. Great."

"No promises."

Asking Alchemy for any favor was anathema to Moses. Instead he called Andrew Pullham-Large, who said to send it over. He also informed him that the *Enquirer* had "agreed" to leave him and Jay out of the story. They couldn't substantiate the innuendos about Alchemy and Jay. Alchemy had threatened a prolonged lawsuit regardless of the cost. This earned more of Moses's gratitude.

Pullham-Large e-mailed within two days. "Not for us. Tell her to keep at it. Too much Bikini Kill/Sleater-Kinney, not enough Evie-Anne Baxter. If you have any other suggestions, always looking for exceptional new talent." He forwarded the e-mail to Evie.

Later that night he checked his in-box and there was a reply from Evie. "Cum on, intro me to your brother. They'll listen to HIM." Just below it was an e-mail from Alchemy. He wanted to meet the following week to pick Moses's brain about the Nightingale Foundation.

Moses didn't answer either e-mail that night.

In the morning he found another e-mail from Evie. "C'mon, Moses. What's wrong? Are we still good?"

Moses, despite his desire to help, couldn't explain the situation to Evie. He had decided that when he and Alchemy met, he'd see if the proper moment came for him to slip her into the conversation. He didn't want to tell her because it might unduly raise her hopes.

Evie, there are complexities in my relationship with my brother that preclude me from pursuing this with him right now. I want to support you, only in this specific request it is not possible. Please understand. I love your music and your company.

Her peevish response: "If you really love my music, what's so complicated you can't send him a cd?" Moses answered with a brief e-mail saying he'd give her more details (although he wasn't sure what he would say) when next they saw each other. She answered "OK" without setting a date for "when next" they'd see each other.

Unlike previous years, without Jay and now not hearing from Evie, Moses relished the start of classes, so he was not displeased when he received a call in mid-August—a week since hearing from Evie—from the secretary to Robert Slocum, dean of the Humanities Department. The dean requested a meeting without giving a reason.

Immediately after hanging up, Moses's regret over Evie's recent silence escalated into runaway paranoia. He imagined that Evie had lodged an official complaint. He pored over and deconstructed all of the correspondences between them: no way to deny a relationship, yet nothing tawdry or disrespectful. They'd begun sexual relations *after* she had completed his course and fulfilled her BFA requirements in compliance with SCCAM's notoriously lax faculty-student relationship policy. Moses supposed she felt betrayed and that his behavior would lead to dismissal, suspension or, at best, probation. The hope that his life's descent would have a long lull was a gross miscalculation.

52

MEMOIRS OF A USELESS GOOD-FOR-NUTHIN'

Freudian Slipper, 1999–2001

In 1999, we were at the top of our game as a live band and
Blues was on the way to becoming triple platinum. We skip
the group intervention, and Alchemy accompanies Absurda to
a recovery tank in Minnesota. We postpone the video and the
tour. I go to Queens for a few days for Nova's funeral. When
Alchemy gets back, me, him, and Lux do some recording and
jamming in the studio while waiting for Absurda.

After ninety days, Absurda prances up to Beverly Hills
beaming like a farmer's daughter in a "Got Milk?" commercial. Her hair is growing out and her skin's all peachy. Holding
her hand is a guy who she hooked up with while he was rehab-
bing for Oxy, Perc, and booze. Claims he is a surfer. He hands
me an embossed card that says "Hugo Bollatanski, Esquire,"
which Alchy says is a fancy way of saying lawyer. He breezes
around all tan and wearing a white suit. Dude surfs about as
often as I climb Everest.

Absurda is raring to play, so we shoot *The Ruling Class* video
and all but finish *Multiple Coming*. In the summer we head out
for more months on the road supporting *Blues*.

Hugo buckles his belt to Absurda and hops on the tour bus. He and Alchy is always yack-yack-yacking about the upcoming election. I despise all the smarmy fuckers. Even though we play a benefit for Gore, I don't tell them if I voted it would've been for Bush Jr.

In the middle of the tour, Hugo decides he needs to be Hu-Gone and will relocate to D.C. to work with some political types. Absurda acts like it's cool. I know she's bleeding, so I warn Hugo not to dirty-deal Absurda. The next day, Absurda, during the preconcert meal, pulls me over so no one can hear us. "Ricky, you surrendered your right to intrude into my personal life when you broke up with me. I can take care of myself, thank you very much."

For the next few months, Hugo flies in and out regularly and Absurda seems good. When we arrive in D.C. for two shows at the Cap Center, Mr. Suavola is in the dressing room with flowers and chocolates. I'm thinking I may have to do some reevaluating. Then Absurda don't show for the sound check for the second night. Can't reach her nowhere, so we head back to the hotel and the chambermaid lets us into her room. The two of them is in bed and they ain't moving. Towels laid out on the floor that stink of crack smoke, a few Percs on the bathroom sink, and empty bottles of bourbon and Tylenol PM. Alchy dials 911. Lux is trying to slap Hugo out of his stupor. I kneel by the bed. I feel Absurda breathing. I lift her and carry her to the shower. The paramedics show up and zip 'em off to the hospital.

We cancel the rest of the tour and Absurda reenters rehab. Me and Lux go home to L.A. Alchemy goes to New York to hang with Salome and Nathaniel. He comes back just before

Absurda gets out of rehab again. This time, her sister Heather comes to babysit. In early 2000 we start recording most of *Noncommittal*, which we're gonna do in three months. Faster than anything we done since *More*.

After an all-night session, Marty is driving me and Alchy to this seventeen-acre spread, fifteen of which is woods, that Alchy is buying in Topanga for under $2 million cash. Once you turn off Topanga Canyon, you gotta be Davy Crockett to find the place. It's a mile or so drive up this twisty road through the forest 'til you get to the very cool three-story, five-bedroom main house built back in the '20s. He shows me "my" room on the second floor. On the grounds is an ancient two-story dance hall, which is a fancy name for whorehouse that he is refurbishing into a guest house for Salome and Nathaniel. We walk down this path to what was once a stable, which he is converting into a recording studio. I'm looking out for snakes when Alchy decides to stick his dick in my business again.

"This may not be the optimum opportunity—"

I cut him off. "Don't futz around. What's on your mind?"

"That's why I love you."

"Why I love me, too. So what?"

"I sense there's something still unfinished between you and Absurda."

I been percolating on that idea myself, only every time I think about making some move, or even talking to her about us, I hear, "Oh, thank you, Alchemy," and I get that pukey feeling.

"No, we done our thing. Besides"—I'm thinking I need to come clean with Absurda before I finally tell him what I seen—"I'm enjoying the fruits of being an Insatiable." He can't retort nuthin' to that. I hear him rolling the saliva in his mouth like he wants to spit, but he only nods.

We do some gigs on the West Coast just to try out the new songs, then come back to L.A. for some remixing and maybe rerecording for *Noncommittal*. We plan the release to coincide with a world tour starting in fall 2001. We ain't back two days when Alchemy gets a hysterical call from Salome. Brockton had a stroke and is in bad shape. He jets back east before his mom flies off to biddy-bip land.

We decide it's hiatus time. Me and Brewer finally team up for "The American Van" spot, which was an absolute gas. One afternoon at the Malibu Market, I eye this very young-looking preppie girl wearing a skirt and V-neck yellow sweater. I shoot her a half smile. She don't react, so I'm moseying back to my car when I hear her razzing me. "Hey, you." I turn around. "Yes, you, creep! You some kinda freak? You want to *kill* me?" I been aggressed on by plenty of drunks. That PLEASE LET ME KILL YOU T-shirt caused me shitloads of problems, but mostly I handle it without muscling up. This girl gives me the shivers. I hadn't done nuthin' squirrelly. I can't fight her. She sure don't want no autograph. Then she is laughing so loud everyone is gawking at us. "Mr. Tough New Yawker, Ambitious Mindswallow, never figured you to have such small balls."

"You figured right the first time. You can check for yourself anytime you want."

"I think that's *premature*. That another of your specialties?"

My brain locked. I'm back to being a Queens dork.

"C'mon, tough guy, think you can handle me drink-for-drink at Moonshadows?"

I give her the Miranda Wrights. Her name's Bryn Smith-son and she's just turned twenty-two and her address says Lincoln, Nebraska. She seen us when we played the university in Lincoln when she was seventeen. She went to Pepperdine and now works for Pfizer pushing legal drugs all over SoCal and Arizona. We start hanging out. Over Christmas, Bryn heads home to Nebraska. She don't ask me to join her. I wished she had so I could say no. I'm not thrilled about meeting anyone's family, especially hers, who is religious Christians.

The idea of seeing my own family gives me a rash. Absurda don't want to see hers neither. Lux is off on a trip to Europe and South Africa. I find out Heather is gone, so I invite Absurda, Marty, and Falstaffa to hang at the Topanga compound. I clean out any sign of Bryn 'cause I want to keep it from Absurda that I am an "article" for the first time since her.

On Christmas Eve we order up food from Gelson's market. Absurda is not indulging in any substances. Later, the two of us are sitting on outdoor chaise longues in front of the living room fireplace when she zings me.

"So, I heard you're dating a teenager."

"What?" I fake ignorance.

"C'mon. Sue saw you trying to impress her at the Ivy. Flea saw you at the Lakers game. Ricky, stop Nadling. You afraid I might tell her how you acted like an A-one asshole when you broke up with me?"

I'm thinking it's finally time to get a few things straight.

"I been meaning to tell ya, that night outside Madam Rosa's, I saw—"

"Stop. Ricky, there's nothing to discuss." I'm too familiar with her Fond du Lac frigid face that says I ain't getting nowhere. "You got drunk and high and you messed up."

"What about you and—"

"I said stop. Yes, I was high, but don't you dare put this on me. I did nothing to cause you to act like such an asshole."

"I want to explain what happened, ya know."

"I know what happened and you already explained plenty. You didn't love me anymore. You wanted to fuck other women. That hurt. I waited and waited for you to realize it was *your* loss. You didn't. I did what I had to and moved on."

I sit back and finish my beer. I tap the empty bottle against my forehead.

"Ricky, don't. I'm long over you."

"That's good. Maybe." I decide it's best I say no more.

"No maybe about it. This is going to sound mawkish, but despite what people say, you're a softie underneath that coconut shell who acted like a shit because you didn't know how to break up with me. I know you love me."

She's never gonna admit, or maybe she was too high to remember, what she done. If I start something, then it's gonna lead to a shitstorm with her and Alchemy, and I end up the big-time loser in every way possible: no Absurda and no band.

The next night, as she's preparing to leave, I'm dying to ask her to stay. I walk her out to the lot, and she tosses her bag into her rebuilt ruby red Spyder. She comes up to me, puts her hand on my cheek. "Ricky, we said goodbye last night. I think I better...go now." I don't say nothing. I just watch her drive off.

Bryn comes back for New Year's. We go to a dinner party for thirty or so people at our lawyer Kim Dooley and her boyfriend's, who is chief counsel for Kasbah, Hollywood Hills place. Absurda shows up on the arm of Fred A. Stare, the lead singer of the Vegan Junkies. I am not pleased. Fred A. is a real junkie. The three of us is making small talk and Fred hands me a card from the Church of Cosmological Kinetics. "You should come to a meeting. Getting kinetically purified helped me. Absurda came to her first meeting just yesterday." I look at her like, *Are you kidding me?* I can't believe she'd spend one second in the Church of Cockamamie Ideas and buy that bullshit from their slimy leader, Godfrey Barker. He sucks on young wannabes and celebs with drug or other problems.

Three nights later, the phone rings around 2 A.M. This is gonna sound hookie-dookie Alchy-like, but before I even answer, I *know* Absurda OD'd. Silky Trespass found her. They were supposed to be guesting with the Pussycat Dolls at the Viper Room. Before Silky's finished talking, I am cursing and shaking—I punch a fucking hole in the bedroom door. I am so freaking pissed that I didn't see this coming. And cursing myself out 'cause I didn't ask her to stay at Christmas.

From her little druggie-rep case, Bryn pulls out some tranqs. I take a couple and down a few beers. It's on me to call the guys. I never heard Alchemy so without nuthin' smart to say.

Lux arrives in Topanga by 4 A.M. He calls Mr. Akin, who goes ballistic. Lux listened coolly for about twenty minutes before he says, "Mr. Akin, I'm sorry but it's time to hang up." Her mom sobs and sobs, "Mandy, my baby. Mandy, my *baby*." She wants her to be buried in Fond du Lac.

Later, me and Lux are drinking and sorta reminiscing, and I says, "Lux, I feel like a piece a garbage for dumpin' her. I feel like I shoulda been able to stop this."

"We tried, man. We all tried."

"I never asked you, if like any time, Absurda and Alchy ever did it or anything?"

His big hands wiped his forehead. "The answer is not as far as I know. And, Ambitious, Absurda's gone and you're worried about who she dated?"

"Yeah, it's screwed up. Only, well, I seen things that tell me Alchemy was happy when we broke up."

"Just the opposite. And let's stop this shit right now. She didn't OD because of you. Or Alchemy. It happened and we all have to live with it."

Alchy meets me, Lux, Andrew, and Sue—we didn't let anyone else come—in the hotel in Fond du Lac where he stayed years before. I catch that his eyes is spinning from the netherworld, which means he ain't been sleeping, which is worse for him than when he has a screamer, 'cause whatever is "gestating" is fixing to come out. I give him a few Percs so he can get through the night.

The funeral's at the church, which was ridiculous 'cause she don't believe in no religion. Alchemy and her brothers give the eulogies. Her girlfriends from the Big Gulp Girls show up. Mr. Akin is bugging Andrew about who gets her royalties and who is in her will. Her mom starts shrieking at me and Alchemy. "You did this to her! You pretended to be a good boyfriend! And you"—she slapped Alchemy across his cheek—"you promised me you'd take care of her. I hope you both rot in hell!" Mr. Akin comes running over and gives us a stare like you best not touch her, which neither of us would've ever done. Mrs. Akin turns to her ex-husband. "Now you want to play hero? You're the reason she ran away in the first place!" She grabs Heather's hand. "Let's go home. The rest of you—all of you—just stay away."

At the hotel, I drink 'til I pass out. In the middle of the night, I hear Alchemy having one of his screamers. I fly down the hall and bang on his door, because we got a long-standing pact that I'm the one who checks on him.

I hear some whispering before he lets me in. A pair of woman's shoes, dress, bra, and panties is on the floor. I close the door behind me and a head peeks out from under the covers.

"Alchemy, don't say nuthin'!" I don't want to hear him finesse his way outta his one. "Heather, get dressed. This ain't never happened." Me and him—he's still got no clothes on—glare silently. Heather comes out of the bathroom and I open the door. I point. She scurries down the hall. I slam the fucking door on my way out.

No one says nuthin' at breakfast. Absurda's brothers drop by. I expect trouble. Nope. They want to drink with us. After four double schnapps a piece and a lotta mealy-mouthed ass kissing all around, they leave. I follow Alchemy to his room. He thinks I'm going to bust his balls about Heather. He starts packing his suitcase. "Get it over with. Say your worst."

"You just gotta fuck every chick no matter who gets hurt, don't you? Didn't you do enough damage by screwing Absurda?"

He stops packing. "Nothing ever happened between us."

"Bullshit. I heard her and you outside Madam Rosa's that night."

"I have no idea what you're talking about."

"That's a motherfucking lie."

"No, Ambitious, it's not. Whatever you think happened, didn't—" He seems so totally cool. I'm kinda half crying, half got the crazy blood-rushing shivers, and it just happens—I flatten my fist against his face. He stumbles back and lands on his ass. "You're such a schmuck. I heard Absurda thanking you while you was twirling your half-nig—" I don't finish.

"Well, I asked for your worst." He don't look pissed or surprised.

53

THE SONGS OF SALOME

The Burning Bushel and a Peck

The tangible allergen of my ghost-child contaminated the Los Angeles air, and my psychic dyspepsia worsened. After years of beating myself up over the youthful betrayal by my body, followed by the acceptance of my body's justifiable killing of our child, I lost my ability to sensate the truth. Was this person, who Teumer claimed to be our son, real or fake, dead or alive? Lively had left his phone number at Lily Fairmont's gallery. I called. It rang into oblivion.

I couldn't voice my unrelief of the child's possible existence to Nathaniel or Alchemy. Both of them, anxious at my brittleness, assumed it came from Lively's visit. Each time I tried to speak of it, the words choked me into silence.

Alchemy offered to buy us a home back east. We chose a two-story 1930s stone house on Cove Road on Shelter Island, a more pristine and isolated midpoint between the two forks at the end of the Sound. With his partners, Alchemy bought a three-story building on West 26th Street and Eleventh Avenue. They converted the basement and two floors into a women's shelter and made the top floor an apartment for Nathaniel and me. Ruggles grudgingly agreed that I could forgo twenty-four-hour supervision for now. An aide came to check on me three times a week, and she and Nathaniel signed off on me taking my "normal" pills.

While he watched over me, an unforeseen bout of Gravity Disease infected Nathaniel, caused not by politics or my behavior but by the recognition of his dependence upon Alchemy's generosity. Alchemy placed the deed to the Shelter Island house in Nathaniel's name, and it highlighted his near pauperism. In thirty years of railing against the rampant selfishness of the wealthy, whenever Nathaniel had extra money he gave it away. He had donated the proceeds from the sale of the family home to a defense fund for death row inmates. Because they supplied a free house and other perks, Magnolia didn't pay a grand sum, and he left before he could accumulate a pension. The advance he hoped to get for writing his memoir never materialized. He never made a dime when subletting his New York apartment, which we let go. Nathaniel supplemented our "Alchemy income" with adjunct teaching jobs at Stony Brook and Suffolk Community and occasional speaking gigs, but it was his self-esteem that needed supplementing.

He found invigoration in the rumblings of the antiglobalization movement, whose leaders idolized him. He spent weeks working the phones (and learning to use e-mail) preparing for the Seattle '99 protests, which made him positively cheery.

Murray Gibbon and Marlene Passant opened the Gibbon-Passant gallery not five blocks from the apartment, and I scheduled a show. Inspired by the autumnal colors, I painted a series of Savant Red and Savant Blue abstracts on Plexiglas. I kept the edges sharp in honor of my past, and titled the exhibition *The Beauty of My Weapons*.

The Insatiables, at the peak of their popularity, were conquering Europe. When a radio station spread the rumor that Alchemy would fly in for the opening, Marlene and I decided to take advantage of my progeny's fame. Not that there weren't poseurs and frauds thirty years before, only now it seemed like New York openings were funless and filled with nonstop monkey chatter that gave me a case of external tinnitus. We sent out five thousand invites for the private Friday night opening, announcing a mystery guest. Hundreds arrived to find only blank walls and me, in my disguise as Dr. R. Mutter McGuffin, dean of the Dept. of the Theoretical Arts, behind a desk, selling MFA and BFA diplomas in the Myth of Fine Arts and Bachelor of False Advertising for $9.99. Some people got really upset. Most took it with good humor and enjoyed the free wine and beer. I sold them all. Gibbon snickered, "At least nobody died."

The "real" opening happened the next Saturday. The show garnered my first review in New York's self-anointed paper of record. A rave. The beginning of my art world redemption. You disappear for a while, live long enough, have a celebrity son, and a new generation of "critics" replaces the former slanderers. Every painting sold within a week.

Two days after the Bush coup of 2000, Nathaniel and I took the jitney to the city so he could help organize some protests. The country's passivity enraged him. *Mother Jones* magazine asked him for a piece. He tried to write from the perspective of an aging Bohemian Scofflaw, in hopes that would spur him to write a follow-up to *Tag*—and perhaps make some money.

The afternoon he left for the post office to mail the piece, I took the subway to meet a displeased Gibbon and Passant at the Odeon. I'd sold a Savant Red painting for $100 to a broke young couple. In the middle of Gibbon's tongue-lashing, my cell rang. Nathaniel had collapsed and an ambulance sped him to St. Vincent's Hospital. I began to get hysterical—Marlene grabbed my arm and led me outside. Gibbon followed. We hopped in a taxi. I explained to Marlene that the ER doctor at St. Vincent's had scarred my face with his ineptitude and I'd vowed never to set foot there again. This time the ER doctor, Neil Downs, who smelled like hot apple cider, competently assessed the problem, sent him for tests, and called in a neurologist; he'd suffered a stroke.

I sensated this was not Nathaniel's time to leave me. I called Alchemy in Los Angeles. He was coming immediately. Xtine rushed over and stayed with me until midnight. I crawled into the empty bed in the semiprivate room and slept. After a few hours, the hospital's spiritual Clorox odor awakened me. My brain feeling swollen, I left for a walk.

Winter, with its low smoky blue-gray clouds, like a silkscreen backlit by the city's neon gleam, insinuated itself into my body and drew me to the seminary on 21st Street. The gardens were normally open to outsiders for only a few hours in the afternoon, but I'd made friends with the dormitory guards, who let me inside. I watched my breath as I meandered around the courtyard. I closed my eyes. I prayed to the sky for Nathaniel's recovery. Suddenly, I felt blood dripping from my nose.

I sat on a bench, tilted my head back, and patted it with the edges of my scarf. From my breath's icy-hot vapors appeared an unfamiliar DNA ancestor.

— Shalom, my scion out of time. I am Margarita.

— Why have you never appeared before? Where is my Salome?

— I am Salome's daughter. She sent me because I have a special message and mission for you.

— Have you come to take Nathaniel?

— No.

— Then why?

— When Salome and our family's first father lay together, I became the child "untimely ripped" away to save his purity. My mother and I never found each other until it was too late. If she had found me, and he had known of me, he would never have allowed himself to be slain. You must stop it from happening again.

— What do you mean?

— Find your firstborn. Yes, he lives, and do what you must to assure our family's destiny. Because one must live and one must die. And one has been chosen.

— Why? What? I don't understand.

— Salome, murders do not happen suddenly. They gestate over years... and then they happen suddenly. You are their mother, you must be the one.

A guard found me on the ground beside the bench. He helped me inside, where I washed my face and warmed up. I caught a taxi back to the hospital. Soon Alchemy arrived, looking haggard, still anticipating I'd crumble or Nathaniel would leave us. My steadiness surprised him.

Dr. Downs explained the MRIs and MRAs indicated that, in all likelihood, Nathaniel would be facing a long recovery. Alchemy took charge, getting Nathaniel a private room and private nurses. After three days, they sent Nathaniel home to 26th Street.

Alchemy stayed in New York to help us out. But he also needed to work. He began producing an album by Cyrus P. Turntable. At home, he and Nathaniel spoke until Nathaniel became too frustrated and tired—the stroke had damaged his speech—about the short- and long-term ramifications of the Bush coup d'état and how this fracture in the democracy would help revolutionize the outdated system.

When the *Mother Jones* piece came out, Alchemy read it to us aloud.

"'The swell of change, once so tactile, seems unreachable and our dream of a new enlightenment has become an American Inquisition converting the baby bombers and flower babes, war-fragged vets and suburban protest kids, civil disobedients and civil rightists, same-sexers and sexual sublimators into a class of overfed complainers. This is the moment to reconsider the past and remake the future and *awake and sing* once more!'

"Damn, Nathaniel, I think the coup inspired you to catch Scofflaw's voice."

Nathaniel's eyes veered toward me, and he struggled to say, "Thank your mother. Without her help... she is the artist and chameleon in more ways than one."

Yes, my son and I are chameleons. My heart hurt for Nathaniel, who could only be himself.

One afternoon while physical and speech therapists worked with Nathaniel, Alchemy took a smoke on the enclosed terrace, which faced an unused ramp of the old West Side Drive. We meditated on his future and mine. In my body, in my DNA, I sensated that Margarita told the truth and Teumer had not lied.

"So, when you become the Political Savior, are you intending to call yourself Scott?"

"You'll never forgive me for that, will you?"

"I want to make sure I'm not going to have to forgive you again."

"I'm forever Alchemy."

"Do you ever think taking care of me and Nathaniel would be easier if you had a sibling?"

"I haven't thought about it."

"Do you wish your brother had lived?"

"What kind of question is that?"

"So you'd like to have a brother?"

"Where are you going with this?"

"Nowhere. Sometimes, because of what happened with him, perhaps I became too protective. Overbearing."

"Yes. And no. I'm sure some people would be appalled that you encouraged me to have lots of sex. And others would've been proud that their kid enlisted in the army."

"Yes. War good. Sex bad." On that note, he took my motherly advice and went out for the night to find himself some sex. I sensated he had no idea that his brother still lived.

As the holidays passed uneventfully and the new year began, I duped myself into complacency. I buried thoughts of my undead child, as I had buried him decades before.

Just as I thought we'd begun to recalibrate toward a filial equilibrium with me—who would've guessed—as part-time caretaker of Nathaniel, Absurda succumbed to her Gravity Disease. Alchemy went into shock. That night he spent hours on the phone with Mindswallow and Lux, and all these record company PR people and managers. I wanted to scream, "Stop! Mourn. Cry your fucking eyes out!" The vicious ether began to envelop us, and I feared the family disease would strike him. Neither of us slept all night, and in the morning, as he prepared to evade the locusts swarming outside the building to go to Fond du Lac, he promised me, "Mom, I'll be back right after Absurda's funeral."

He didn't come right back. He sent Falstaffa and Marty to move me and Nathaniel back to Topanga. I didn't object. I needed to be with my son. I needed to protect him.

We settled into our guest house on the compound, and I found two Teumers in the L.A. phone book, Jane and Moses. No Malcolm. I timed my first reconnaissance trip for the day before the Insatiables played their Absurda tribute show. Alchemy would be too preoccupied to track my whereabouts.

My nurse drove me by Lily Fairmont's gallery to check on some possible sales and then to this Moses's home in Venice. We parked two doors down from the small house. I told the nurse it was the home of an old boyfriend and I wanted to spy on him. She didn't think that odd at all. I

walked around the front and inhaled the soulsmell of mor-
bidly bland steamed white rice.

The morning after the Troubadour tribute show, I stopped
Falstaffa as she was bringing some beers and breakfast to the
recording studio. Alchemy'd been in there alone all night. I
brought in the tray. Alchemy lay on the floor, pillow under his
head, staring up at the skylight. Surrounded by the weapons
of musical destruction on one side and the Beretta he kept in
the studio on the other. I placed the tray on the floor, picked
up the gun, walked up the three steps to the console board,
and returned it to its usual spot. I walked back and lay down
beside him. I stared up, squinting at the morning brightness.
For many minutes neither of us spoke.

"Mom, I fucked up bad. I didn't save Absurda. I've pissed
off Ambitious. Lux seems fed up. I don't care if I never write
another song."

Gravity Disease, I understood. Suicide from self-pity, I
couldn't abide. "Do you feel sorry for yourself or for Absurda?"

"Both."

"Mindswallow and Lux can take care of themselves. The
world can survive without another of your songs. I can't survive
without you. Take some time. You need to protect yourself."

He soon sought sanctuary in the monastery, which offered
me the opportunity to pursue my mission without any interference. My course of action not quite set, I called for a taxi. My
nurse intervened. Alchemy had left instructions not to allow
me to go anywhere alone. I sent the taxi away. Two nights later,

while everyone slept, I slipped out and down the path that led to Topanga Canyon Boulevard. I wanted a ride to Venice Boulevard. From there, I'd make my way to his house. I never even made it to PCH. Yes, I'd taken a bottle of Haldol and borrowed the Beretta from the studio—only as precautions. Misinterpretation of my intent landed me back here.

And then, in what was surely no coincidence, a week or so before I was finally allowed to leave Collier Layne and rejoin Nathaniel, I found a copy of *People* on a table in the lobby, with the sidebar headline "The Sexy Savior." My insides shredding as every new word pierced and twisted itself into my body, I wondered if, as Margarita warned, my moment to save Alchemy had passed. I resigned myself to a life bracketed by the death, pretend or not, of my two children. For I lived Moses's death for decades before his resurrection, and I lived Alchemy's murder long before it occurred.

54

THE MOSES CHRONICLES (2008-2009)

Smile, You're on Candide's Camera

Moses surveyed his room, the few items left to be packed. The house would go up for sale next week, and he was moving to a one-bedroom apartment in Marina del Rey. They'd split the house money and their savings. Jay asked for nothing else.

His mother's menorah rested on the almost empty shelf next to the plain white envelope where he kept his father's medal. A large plastic bag filled with rubbish and a half-filled box with mementos sat on the floor. He grabbed the envelope. Held it tight. Tossed it in the box. He just couldn't throw it out. He blew dust off the menorah and spoke aloud, "Hey, God, an eight-day-a-week miracle up your sleeve so Jay will come home? Nah? No answer? 'Course not."

Outside, a car honked. Moses placed the menorah in the box and grabbed his sport coat and the binder with the proposal and his notes on the Nightingale Foundation. The driver proceeded to Musso & Frank in Hollywood.

Already seated in a leather booth in the back room, Alchemy finished autographing cloth napkins for two teenage boys. He signed three more napkins and put them on the end of the table. If no one else came over, he'd leave them.

He got quickly to his agenda. "What'd you think of the foundation proposal?"

"Looks promising. It can do a lot of good and it will set you up for the political leap."

"Good things from the foundation. Great things from the Nightingale Party, which is the endgame." Alchemy finished his vodka and ordered another, along with a glass of wine for Moses. "How much they pay you at SCCAM?"

"Fifty-eight and benefits. Summers off. Why?"

"That's it? Come work with me."

"Doing what?"

"I need someone I trust to oversee the foundation's everyday workings. You're the only person since I've been 'famous' who never asked for money or special this or that. I heard about the girl's music you sent to Andrew. You didn't put me in that spot."

Moses hadn't been sure what he would do in regard to Evie. If she had made an official complaint, would introducing her to Alchemy get her to withdraw it? Alchemy just made the decision for him.

"Mose, I'm going to *need* your knowledge and smarts when we go political."

"There are many people smarter and way more experienced than me in working the political game."

"I'll hire them when the time comes. None of them is my brother." Alchemy took a few purposeful gulps of his drink. "Tell me if I'm right about this, during the revolution, Washington used as his motto 'Victory or Death.'"

"I'm not sure if it was his motto. He did use that phrase as the password during the crossing of the Delaware River. One would have to say 'victory' and the other had to answer with 'or death' to get by."

"Good enough. Now, what I'm going to say, I don't want to sound like I'm complaining. I'm not. My mom was taken from me when she flipped out at the gallery and stabbed Lively and herself. When I was thirteen and living in Berlin, she tried to jump off a balcony so she could climb the Wall. Both times I stood by helpless. When I turned twenty-one, the Bickleys maneuvered to take away the small money in the trust earmarked for me and I couldn't get my mom out of Collier Layne. I had no prospects. No backup plan when we started the Insatiables. It was all or nothing. If we made it, I promised myself two things. First, I would take care of Salome and Nathaniel."

He took a few gulps of his vodka.

"Now, I've kept that promise as best I could. I made a second promise to Nathaniel and myself—to find a third way politically. It's now time to start that process. I only know how to do things all the way—victory or death."

With that, Alchemy laid out his offer. He would set aside money in a trust for lifetime health insurance, a $100K salary, and if Moses's cancer returned, or if it just didn't work out, he'd still get paid until he recovered or found another job. But more than the money, it was an opportunity to be part of history, not just teach it. "Think about any questions. I got to take a leak."

When Alchemy returned, Moses posed a more immediate question. "Where's Salome living?"

"Here some, and Shelter Island. Nathaniel is not doing so well."

"Sorry to hear that. There's more to evaluate, and if I take this, it'll be time to end that charade."

"Agreed... Mose, should we talk about Jay?"

"No need. Lot of divorces after cancer. And our failure had nothing to do with you. End of story."

Alchemy nodded.

Moses continued, "Alchemy, there *is* something we need to discuss. If we're going to do this, and continue our relationship on any serious level, you can never again lie to me in words or by silence. If I sign on, and I find out any more subterfuge, I walk."

"Mea culpa. I shouldn't have seen Teumer behind your back. And I should've given you the letter. I fucked up."

"No more BS?"

"My word. Mose, it may not seem that way, but I'll be indebted to you. I need you. We will do great things together."

Could either of them live with that debt? Alchemy had given Moses a new life. Now he was offering him a new life. Again.

"I'll ruminate. We'll talk again."

Two days later, on Friday afternoon, Moses met with chipmunk-faced Dean Slocum in his office. They sat opposite each other, separated by a black coffee table covered by academic journals.

"Moses, doubtless you've suffered through years of trauma. You look healthy. How are you feeling physically?"

"Pretty good."

Slocum nodded. "I asked you here because Charles is stepping down as chair of the Humanities Department on Monday." Before Moses could ask why, Slocum stopped him. "I'll explain another time. The chair is yours. I need your answer by Sunday night."

Moses pretended to cough and covered his mouth, repressing a giant-size hee-haw of relief.

"This is gratifying. Only my brother, who is extraordinarily persuasive, wants me to work with him."

"You know serving as chair comes with a bump in pay and benefits."

"It's not about money. Sure, it matters. But this is more about how I want to spend the rest of my life."

"I understand that. Only Moses, a tenured position is one of the most secure jobs in the world. Family businesses are notorious for their contentiousness."

"I'll mull it over and get back to you by Sunday."

Slocum was no fool, and he made his appeal to Moses's insecurities. Moses didn't want to make the decision out of fear. After his illness, divorce, and skirting career suicide with what he now considered the foolish misstep of Evie, he desired—no, needed—to change his life.

On Saturday he called Alchemy, who answered, his voice impatient, "Mose, what's up?"

"Bad time?" Moses asked.

"Yep. This'll be what'll it'll be like to work with me. This is also why I want you. Most people don't listen. Don't hear anything in my voice. You did."

"I'll take it."

"Fucking excellent. Better than excellent. I'll call you tomorrow and we'll get the damn thing started."

Faster than Moses could have imagined, Alchemy pushed him into action. Moses met with heads of other foundations before setting up the nonprofit with the help of Alchemy's lawyers and accountants. They raised the initial endowment with contributions from the Insatiables and their business partners. Alchemy pledged a good share of his net worth of $300-plus million, including his shares in Winsum Realty and Audition Enterprizes, which were invested wisely in new technology and media, as the bedrock of the endowment. Unlike in many nonprofits, he and Alchemy were determined that the vast majority of the money would be spent on needs, not frills or waste.

They chose an abandoned motel building that Alchemy had bought and refurbished on the corner of Inglewood's La Brea Avenue and Regent Street for the Nightingale office. Moses handpicked the small staff, taking to his role with a natural aplomb. His gait transformed from a bedraggled slouch to one of, if not quite preening, a man sure in his position. But he showed no arrogance. Quite the contrary, his elasticity in dealing with different personalities made him a compassionate boss.

The night of their first fund-raising gala at the new offices, Alchemy slid up beside Moses. "From the time we took our little trip from the monastery to L.A., I felt like we'd do great things together someday. And now, this is just the beginning."

55

THE SONGS OF SALOME

If I Had a Hammer

After returning from the monastery, Alchemy brought Nathaniel east, fetched me from Collier Layne, and tucked us away in Shelter Island, assuaging his guilt by offering the spoils of his wealth, before scurrying back to L.A. for "urgent business."

Gravity Disease had robbed Nathaniel of his zest for fulminating and denied him his role as my protector. Our relationship worked because he reasoned to me in spoken words and I translated his words into sensations. I unreasoned to him in emotions and he put them into the logic of his spoken language. His stroke left his mind lucid, but even after therapy, he had slightly impaired speech and he often needed a cane. His reliance on me for everyday needs strained the unspoken expectations of how we balanced our us-ness as nothing had before.

I went out to the porch to drink my coffee and sit with him one morning. The pitter-patter of the spring drizzle seemed to fall in rhythm to the sound of Coltrane's *Ballads*, which played on the small cassette player he'd never abandoned. Normally, he'd either be reading or waiting for our nanny to deliver the newspapers. Eyes closed, he swayed in his rocking chair. On the table beside him was a shoe box full of letters. A separate bunch held in a rubber band from his protest pal and mentor, Dave Dellinger, who had died earlier that week, sat on his lap.

I grabbed a cushion from a nearby chair, placed it on the wood floor, and knelt beside him. With my open mouth I tasted his still pure soulsmell, tinged now with the odor of promise lost, like the yellowing, fraying pages of an old paperback book.

I, too, was bereft of inspiration. I took down the mirrors in the house because I couldn't bear to look at my withering beauty. When I did go out, I suffered the indignity of the younger hotties stealing the carnivorous grins that were once mine. Like my mother before me, I was slipping into reclusiveness. Even worse, my powers as a sensate morphologist, worth more than physical beauty or youthful vigor, were blocked.

When the tape ended, I got up to turn it over. Nathaniel began speaking mournfully, though not bitterly, of the pernicious calories of junk food, junk culture, and junk news that had hastened his slide into irrelevance and impotence. His once grandiose plans had become less grandiose with each defeat, and he now had only two plans—one to live out his days and one to die.

"Don't do this to yourself," I pleaded. "You've contributed more than anyone could ask. Let's take a trip. No political or art agenda. Let's take off like two young kids with nothing to do but loaf around."

"I've never been a very good loafer."

"*I've* always been a great high heel."

His smile said he understood my message better than I did.

"Salome, if you need to go, please go. I've never wanted to constrain you and I don't want to start now."

I did feel constrained. No matter, I couldn't desert him. Yet, high heel that I am, I could heal neither him nor myself.

Nathaniel found the perfect way to halt our breaking apart. He invited Frank Peters, a critic I'd met years before through Greta's old friend Betty Parsons and who'd reviewed *My Head IS Different* for *LA Weekly*, to visit us when he came for the Hamptons Art Fair. Nathaniel suggested it was time for a Salome Savant career retrospective. Peters agreed. He put the wheels in motion by getting in touch with Curt Scoggins at the Hammer Museum. With all the meetings, conference calls, and e-mails, I was becoming overwhelmed. Nathaniel came to the rescue by acting as my go-between. He took over the logistical arrangements—he'd adapted to e-mail and texting. I carefully went about choosing what I wanted to show and making new work.

While assembling a catalogue raisonné and a list of my major collectors, Scoggins discovered that Teumer and/or Lively owned seven of my pieces. Nathaniel, none too cheerily, relayed this news. I cursed Gibbon for not getting them back when I'd asked him to in Germany.

Nathaniel told Scoggins that Teumer was an old flame who'd remained obsessed with me and it served everyone's best interest not to contact him. We didn't need his pieces.

Truly, though, I hated that my creations were in Teumer's unclean hands. I got in touch with young Bicks III. Unlike his father, he possessed a warmth that he must have inherited from his mother. Bicks III spoke to Lively. He and Teumer had bought the pieces through their import-export company, and when they dissolved their partnership the year before, Teumer took outright ownership of the art. Not two hours after speaking to Bicks III, Teumer called from Brazil. He'd lend the pieces for the Hammer show but would never sell them back. My answer: Forget it. About to hang up, he took the conversation in another direction.

"We're quite fortunate to have a son so worthy of us."

"If he exists, I've never met him."

"I don't mean *our* son. Your son Alchemy and my third son."

He bragged how Alchemy visited him in Rio and he'd given him "a letter for Moses." He sounded so smug when he guessed Alchemy hid that news from me. He magnanimously volunteered to travel to L.A., not easy considering his age, but he'd do it so we could introduce ourselves to "our son."

"Fuck you, Malcolm."

"Anytime, my dear."

Soon after, Teumer sent me a copy of the letter he'd given to Alchemy. And it was then, when Nathaniel found me preparing to burn the damn letter, that we had a huge fight. I finally admitted to Nathaniel that I'd known about Alchemy and his newfound brother since my last stay in Collier Layne when I read the *People* article. It astounded him that I was able to keep mum. But my admission exposed Nathaniel's lack of loyalty to me. While I was locked away in Collier Layne, he, Alchemy, and Ruggles decided against telling me this new truth. Despite his conflicts, ethically Nathaniel had to respect Alchemy's wishes—or so he said. I gave him hell followed by days of silence. When he finally apologized, I demanded he show me the same ethical rectitude and keep my awareness a secret from Alchemy. And Nathaniel also said, whether to appease me or out of sincere belief I don't know, that if this son were alive and happy in his life, that not seeking him out sounded reasonable.

It's been over sixty years and I can still feel the tincture of evil sweat and scum that infiltrated my soulsmell when his seed impregnated his beastly odor into me. And I was foolishly naïve to think our conversations were secret. After the interrogations by the CAA's Parnell Palmer, I've assumed the government was always wiretapping me, Teumer, or anyone connected with Nathaniel. Palmer wants to talk to me again. I will be prepared this time. I shouldn't have ever considered believing that he wants to quiet the rumors—no, he wants to smear the memory of Alchemy. I asked Bellows to set it up with this caveat: I insist on a visit with my granddaughter, Persephone.

56

MEMOIRS OF A USELESS GOOD-FOR-NUTHIN'

Lost in Space, 2001–2003

On the plane ride back to L.A. from Fond du Lac—one of the few times Alchy booked us a private jet—I sit in the back by myself. And I get fucking drunk. I can't believe what has happened. I never felt crappier in my life. I lost Absurda, and now I feel like I lost the best friend I ever had—even if he swore he ain't done what I know he done. I don't know where I'd be without him. I am so fucking confused.

Falstaffa comes to pick us up at the Santa Monica Airport. I just trail behind everyone. Alchemy stops and waits for me. "C'mon, man. You coming home?"

"I'm, well, you know. You sure?"

"Your room will *always* be your room."

I go, but I'm still feeling not right. Salome and Nathaniel are living in the guest house, and Nathaniel, who is getting worse and some days he can't walk without help, he still razzes me about being "the Estragon who came to dinner." I tell him he's the washed-up Rev who's gonna be extragone off a cliff if he don't shaddup. I ain't fond of staying in Bryn's condo 'cause the lip flappers tip off the paparazzi. We spend some nights in Absurda's Rampart place, which she left to me. Only me. The hood is still too dicey for the paparazzi to hang out.

About a month after Absurda's funeral, we hold a memorial concert at the Troubadour. I'm reeling like someone stabbed me in my good eye. I get high. It don't help my ornery mood and I get in an argument with Salome. Hugo Bollatanski shows up, and I'm on my way to throw him out when Alchemy steps in. "Let it go. He's trying to make amends. We all have to let the bad blood go." He means me and him, too. But his speechifying during the show—he makes her drug use and dying into a reason to legalize all drugs so the government can tax and control it—fuckin' pisses me off.

After the show, me and Alchy get in a stare-down duel. I wait, and then I says, "You making Absurda a poster child for drugheads wasn't right. Not tonight." He lights up an American Spirit and the match flashes and it's like it lit his eyes on fire, a voodoo doll gold and brown. Lux pulls me away. Me, Lux, and Bryn walk to my car. I'm wondering if Alchy told him anything. I ain't said zip. Not even to Bryn. Lux asks Bryn to get in the car while me and him talk. He says, "Ambitious, you and Alchemy, man, I don't know what went down in Fond du Lac, but whatever it was, you guys need to make peace."

"Yeah, it's on him, too."

"No doubt. But Absurda wouldn't want the two people she loved most in the world to stop talking because of her."

I mumble, "Lux, I need some time. Me and Bryn are going to Cancún."

"Take whatever time you need." He opens his arms and bear-hugs me.

The trip away was a good escape, but I still ain't sure what my next move is gonna be. The Topanga place is near deserted when I return. Salome is back in Collier Layne after getting caught leaving the compound with Alchemy's Beretta to do who the fuck knows what. Nathaniel is confined to the guest house with his nurses. Alchemy's disappeared into a freaking monastery. His version of a biddy-bip-bip farm.

I feel jumpy staying in Topanga. The Rampart house is too fucking packed with boogeymen. I put it on the market and rent a place in Hollywood Hills for a few months. Bryn kinda moves in with me but also keeps her condo 'cause she don't want to stay alone in my new place after we hit the road.

When Alchemy reappears in L.A., he tries to keep under the radar 'cause of the shit with his new brother, Mose. But the media catches on and makes Alchemy a bigger hero for saving Mose's life. Alchemy plays it all modest in public. To me, he brags how "intelligent" his "professor brother" is. For months I keep asking to let me meet the mysterious Mose, and he keeps avoiding it. I figure he's embarrassed by me.

We're also dealing with the Sheiks selling Kasbah to the Germans for gazillions. That kinda helps reunite us, 'cause we gotta decide if we are going to continue as a band, and if we are, how we deal with this takeover. Lux invites me and Alchemy to his parents' place for dinner so no outsider will bother us. I'm kinda nervous about going there. Feeling ashamed, but I got no choice.

We eat dinner with the Bradshaws in their dining room. It's kinda tense. I ain't saying much. On the wall across from me is two pictures. One of MLK and one of a sorta black, dark-eyed Jesus. Made me think of the pictures of JFK and a white blue-eyed Jesus that Granny McFinn kept on her dining room wall. Lux was about as religious as me, but he was trying to be the peacemaker.

After dinner, Big Lionel and Mrs. Bradshaw go to their bedroom.

Lux steps up. "Straight out, I want us to continue. Not for the money or the women. For the music. For what we've done and can do. It's not going to be the same without Absurda. I'll never stop missing her. But you two need to stop acting like bratty teenagers." Lux was never afraid to call out Alchemy (or me, for that matter), and Alchy always took it from him. "I love being an Insatiable. Or we can all go do our thing elsewhere."

I realize Alchy has said nothing to Lux. Still, I want him to speak first.

"We have to continue as a band. I have to continue now." He turns to me. "Ambitious, what I did with Heather was flat-out wrong. I wish I could undo it. And maybe you wish you could undo some things, too. But we both did what we did because we hurt so damn much and acted in ways destructive to each other and to ourselves."

That don't get to the heart of it, but if I start in again about Madam Rosa's and what happened in the hotel in Fond du Lac—I can't live with Lux hearing any of that—that's a road with only one way out. I don't answer them directly. "Okay, guys, what's our strategy on this merger bullshit?"

For what feels like forever, we have all these dumb-ass meetings about our new deal. The chill between me and Alchy has warmed, especially after we start jamming. We're looking for a new guitar player after I decide to stay on the bass.

After the German takeover is done, we all have our gourds full of lawyer bullshit. It takes us a while to get going, but I'm excited to hit the road for a U.S. tour, which will bank millions. We settle on Silky Trespass as guitarist. Everything is first class. We're as popular as ever, only we don't hang out that much. Me and Alchy get into it big time one night in front of Lux and Silky, 'cause he wants to add a bunch of lefty antiwar songs to the set list. I am one hundred percent against it. We don't agree about the war in Iraq or even Afghanistan. I says, "What the fuck? They blew up the Trade Center, and you ain't no pacifist, so what's your problem?"

He gives me some spiel about war is not the way to make peace and because they kill innocent people doesn't mean we should. He wants the world to love us. I don't give a damn what the world thinks as long as they keep their bombs to themselves. Suddenly, he gives me this condescending smile. "Sometimes, we have to think about how things affect more than just ourselves."

"Just because you think you doing good for others, don't mean you ain't doing it for yourself."

He sighs overloud and says, "Okay, say that I'm doing for myself. I'm also doing it for others."

He writes "Dyin' to Be Your Hero," which is a good song. We play that one the rest of the tour. Only I'm feeling it ain't really settled between us.

57

THE SONGS OF SALOME

The Loneliness of the Long-Distance Runner

Alchemy gallivanted across the world's stages for much of the year as I prepared for the Hammer retrospective. Xtine flew out to help with the assistants I had hired to build the *Pillz-apoppin'* and *Electroshocked Ladyland* installations. Nathaniel argued against exhibiting the *Baddist Boys*. I had to because I knew that, like a curse I must expunge, no longer could they remain repressed in the unconscious attic of my studio.

Before the show opened, the spate of publicity certainly alerted the spawn of Malcolm. As the day approached, I felt myself teetering, unsure of where I might fall considering some of the eruptions at previous openings. Alchemy, with an uncharacteristic lack of intuitiveness, sniped at me for acting histrionically when I threatened to boycott the various openings. I dared not reveal that I'd found a picture and profile of the Pretender on the Web site at the university where he taught. I kept it undercover in my studio and spent far too many hours trying to commune with him through our DNA, hoping one of our mutual ancestors would bring us into contact and prove he was of my blood. He remained apart from me.

During one of the preopenings, from the Hammer's second floor, I watched as the crowd entered. He slithered into the lobby by himself. I recoiled when he and Alchemy shook hands like...old bros. I made my way unsteadily to the exhibition hall and started my talk right in front of the *B Boys*—and the two of them.

I saw nothing of me in his face. I inched closer, and closer still when he asked a question. I hesitated before answering, for in his eyes—not the luminous optimistic multicolors of Alchemy's eyes, but ominous hazy gun-smoke gray—I sensated his innards crumbling as the vision of my assignation with Teumer and my relief at his unbirth unfurled within him. His palpable pain flustered me. Again, I tried to commune with him. He fled the museum.

The morning of the official opening I awoke at sunrise. Haunted by my failure to carry out my Margarita mission, I'd slept little. As Alchemy began his cooldown walk after his morning jog around the compound, I joined him. I asked him about the man quizzing me about the *Baddist Boys*.

"An acquaintance. Collector. Why?"

"I got a whiff of a familiar, unholy fragrance. Pig meat sweat." I lied to gauge his reaction. He frowned but didn't take the bait.

"He's a very smart guy. History professor. I think he and Nathaniel would get along."

"How did you meet him?"

"His wife used to work with Kasbah. I met her first." His answer turned out to be perfectly true and perfectly untrue.

"I didn't see him with anyone."

"I guess she had other plans."

He wiped his forehead with his T-shirt and his eyes narrowed ever so slightly. "I have to shower before you impugn me with having an unholy fragrance."

I sniffed the air. "No, just man sweat. Go. I have to help Nathaniel get ready."

The opening completed the reversal of my art world reputation from the misogynistic imprecation as hysterical woman artist who fucked her way through the world to what became, in Scoggins's validation, "an underappreciated, often misunderstood visionary worthy of our veneration and awe." I attempted graciousness and welcomed his plaudits, as my atoms attempted to flee my corporeal body. I hid behind Nathaniel and his wheelchair, which he needed for longer outings, most of the night. I only insulted a few people. During the four-month run of the exhibition, other opportunities to move the show presented themselves. I committed to nothing.

When it was over, with the Insatiables preparing to tour again, despite my embracing by the L.A. art community, Nathaniel and I preferred to return to New York. I never sensated how foolish that move would turn out to be.

58

MEMOIRS OF A USELESS GOOD-FOR-NUTHIN'

Going, Going, Gone, 2003–2006

Back in L.A. after the tour, I'm hanging at Kasbah. I see Alchemy in a face-off with a slinky familiar-looking lady in the corner by one of the fake oases. I intrude. He introduces her as "Jay, my brother Mose's wife. We're discussing his long-term follow-up treatment." His way of telling me to get lost. I was about to bounce when Randy shouts, "My brother needs more art!" Whoa! I remember her. Me and her never talked much 'cause we had nuthin' to offer each other.

Later, when me and him is relaxing in Buddy's office, I says, "Man, that is wazoo wild shit. Your bro know youse two did the shimmy an' shake?" I ain't sure they did, but it's a good bet.

He rubs his fist under his nose and he says, dead cold, "There is nothing to know. L.A., within its various circles, is a small town. They're both in the art circle."

"What the fuck's that got to do with anything? I bet she got into artfully circling her limbs around all things Alchemous."

"Don't be a jerk. I'm telling you we were friends. She was more interested in my mom's art than me."

I'm thinking he is protesting too much, and being his "friend" didn't mean shit. Soon, I find out why I'm right about them and why he don't want me to meet Mose. I was at the Key Club jammin' with some local L.A. guys. After the show, some scumsucker paparazzo tracks me down in the bathroom. He says he's pitchin' a piece to the *Enquirer* on "The Insatiable Sexual Appetite of Alchemy Savant." I says, "So?"

He says, "I need you to ID some of the women in these pics and tell me if he had sex with them." He shows them to me and one of them is Mrs. Mose and Alchemy all lovebirdy-like back in the '90s. I tell the fucker to get very lost. Fast. Not that I care much about Mose or his wife. I just hate them papa*ratz*i.

Then the pap threatens me: "If you don't help me, I'm going for a story that you're a no-show cheapo father."

I should've told you this already. I got a son from a trampoline break in St. Louis about six years before. I don't even remember the girl's name when she contacts me, which she does after the kid, Ricky Jr., is already born. The test proves he's mine and I pay child support but, I dunno, I never seen him.

I clench my fists so the pap sees, and I say to the ratfuck, "Run the damn article. 'Cause I will never, ever help you."

Sue and Andrew have already heard about this guy trying to dirty me if he can't get to Alchy. They advise me to see Ricky Jr., who lives with his mom, a nurse. It turns out to be a great thing. Thankfully, he's a cute kid. Nuthin' like me. His mom married a decent guy. I spend lots of time with Ricky Jr. over the years and we are now pretty close. He's getting ready to go to law school next year. Ain't that a sweet switch.

I tell Bryn about Ricky Jr. and she is cool, until I say maybe we should have a kid. She is so not into that. I propose that she quit her job, come on the Euro tour, and we get married. She don't say nuthin', just scrunches her nose. I fucking offer to quit the band. She not only smacks me down, she breaks up with me. I was her *trampoline*.

I dive into a drug and drink binge the second we land in London and don't quit all through Scotland and Scandinavia. I don't give a rat's ass that everyone is "worried." We go to Paris for a show at Parc du Catherine Deneuve or something like that. At the after-party, this actress, Camille Javal, who been in the film *Paris by Night*, says she is going to audition for the *Friendsy for You* video, which we are going to come back and do at end of the tour, 'cause Alchy wants this young French kid to direct it.

Camille has these juicy lips and a deep-throat voice that's so sexy I got a hard-on listening to her coo my name. While we're touring the rest of Europe, me and her talk all the time. I dunno why, but she's the first person I feel okay to tell about the Madam Rosa's shit. And how bad I feel about everything. It was a good choice 'cause she don't condemn me or nuthin'. "It's good to love so hard that it nearly breaks you," she says.

I start staying at her flat when we get back to Paris. The Frenchy director rejects Camille for the main female part. I put it to Alchemy, "Since when do we, meanin' *you*, let anyone else call these shots?" Alchemy says it was a mutual decision with him and the director. I say, "C'mon, give me this one." He's kinda embarrassed, but he tells me Lux, Silky, and Andrew don't want her neither.

I figure I'll talk to Lux on my own. Maybe I can change his mind. He says if Alchemy agrees, it's okay by him.

A couple of nights later, Alchy plays me this new song "Mysteries and Enemies."

Lying at the corner of suicide and loathing
when she slipped her hands down my clothing
smile as sweet as Judas's gun moll
eyes glistenin' like a midnight Manhattan snowfall
Her voice lured me without a sound
"I'm your mystery and you're my enemy"
as I crawled into the well-trod garden
of her pleasure mound

I ask, "So you think Camille's doing me just to get the part?"

"What makes you think this song is about you?"

I don't answer.

Before we start shooting, me and Camille talk about the video. She says rejection's part of the business and she's fine with it. I ain't so fine. I say to Camille that we'll get married the next day—then they have to give her a part. "Ambishoos"—I loved the way she said my name—"that is very kind but a bad reason to marry. We are fun together. And you are a better man than you think. I feel you don't really love me." And wow, she is harsh, but she is right. "Please, don't be angry wheez me, but no one who loves you should marry you. Not now. Even eef you fight, you are too much in love wheez Alshemie. You need to break from him before you are free to love so strong like you did wheez Absurda."

I don't say nuthin' to Alchy or no one else. We shoot the video and head home. I'm sad about leaving Camille. She gives me one last piece of advice: "Don't be impulsive. Break when you feel strong."

Before recording more songs for *Dieseasee* and starting the South America and Asia tours, we take a little time off. I've given up the lease on the Hollywood Hills house, and Alchemy says I can stay in Topanga. I accept but don't plan on staying. Alchemy is preoccupied with Mose, Salome, and Nathaniel, who had more strokes and talks so slow it ain't even fun jousting with him.

Andrew calls me up saying Alchemy is buying a building in downtown L.A. for Winsum Realty. I answer, "You never ask me before. Just do it." He says Alchemy thinks I should check it out. Bastard knows me so damn well, 'cause I love it. I end up claiming the top floor for myself. While it's getting fixed up, I take a trip back to New York. I spend a little, very little time with my mom and sister. See some old guys from Flushing. I jam nights with some guys from '70s and '80s NYC bands. It's fun and we talk about doing some recording together.

And get this, they built a condo on the site of the puke-filled Gas Station club where I slept outside as the good-for-nuthin' Ricky McFinn. I buy myself an apartment.

The whole time, I'm doing some heavy reconsidering about my future. I am feeling pretty good about myself. So when Alchemy summons us to regroup in L.A. to start planning the tour and recordings, I've decided, after almost fourteen years, it's time to cut the cord. Alchemy don't try to dissuade me. Just says, "If that's your decision, I'll have to accept it. Lux asks, "So, what's your plan?" I'm ready for that. "I been playing with a bunch of guys from New York and we're talking about doing something together."

Later, when we're alone, Lux says, "Are you sure about this? It's cool to play with other guys, but it won't be the same."

"Lux, it ain't been the same with us for a while. For now, I'm good."

I call up a coupla the NYC guys, but they end up punking out on me. So I take a trip to see Ricky Jr. When I get back to L.A., I call Lux about hanging out some night. He can come check out my new place downtown. He says he can't do it. They've finished auditioning bass players, chosen one for the tour and are rehearsing like mad.

I hang up the phone feeling like, *Holy fuck! What the fuck have I done?*

59

THE SONGS OF SALOME

Into the Mystic

I told Bellows a few more times that I had some information that would interest Palmer and his committee of investigators. He ignored Bellows's bidding for a visit with Persephone.

I sing to Persephone, as I sing to Nathaniel.

I found him. Napping, I first thought, in his wheelchair on the porch. I tilted his head up and removed his glasses. I kissed his lips one last time. His face laden with Gravity Disease. The last years offered so few rewards. He felt like his life's work had been debased. He willed himself to stay with us and experience my Hammer retrospective, which delighted him.

That morning on the porch I breathed, for the final time, the purity of his soulsmell. It spread from his essence to his corporeality, and suddenly—the Gravity Disease lifted. His face appeared almost youthful. Tranquil.

I lay down next to him. His left hand was draped over the chair's side. I held it in mine. With the ministrokes coming more and more frequently, he had left me a note a month before. "No wishing you'd not done this or had done that. Make more art. I treasure the life we lived together."

I awakened Alchemy with my phone call. "Nathaniel's gone. I'm okay. I just need you to come here from wherever you are."

And he did.

As Nathaniel wished, we buried him in Virginia beside his parents. There was a memorial service in New York City. I didn't go. The tentacles of the dark matter beckoned. I resisted. Alchemy, before going back on the road, stayed with me and then Xtine. Ruggles, now retired, visited briefly. No one could replace Nathaniel. I've never stopped missing him.

60

THE MOSES CHRONICLES (2009-2010)

Obey My Voice, and Arise

Moses often speculated that as memory compresses and expands, time slows down and speeds up almost inexplicably. For when he reflected upon the year immediately following his operation, it passed in an elongated and vivid slow motion, and the next years felt compressed, swiftly passing into indistinguishable, barely recalled moments, interspersed with incidents that expanded to significant and memorable in the present or in retrospect. And now, today, almost a decade after finding his brother, Moses girded himself as time nearly stopped. Salome was on her way to the foundation.

The pseudoreasons for this visit were to get her approval on how her work and Xtine's photos were to be used to decorate the walls and to review the final applications for the first Nathaniel Brockton Fellowship for Political Activism. Since her few oblique comments after the Hammer opening, she had never hinted at even suspecting the truth, so Alchemy and Moses decided that Alchemy should not broach the subject of Moses's existence with Salome ahead of time.

This latest attempt to meet had been delayed not by his illness, pathos, divorce, or the perpetual recording and touring of the Insatiables, but by the passing of Nathaniel Brockton and Salome's descent into self-imposed isolation at the family's Shelter Island home.

Moses scoured Nathaniel's obituaries for insight into his mother. He found precious little. Moses admired Nathaniel's devotion to his ideals, but he didn't think much of *Tag*. He wondered if Salome had ever mentioned him to Nathaniel.

Moses paced around the office, occasionally glancing at the tantalizing Suzan Woodruff abstract on the wall. He'd hired Jay as a consultant to furnish and decorate the offices, in hopes of keeping her close to him. Foolish move. Of course she was sympathetic when he relayed the events of the Teumer meeting. But she glided over his hints at attempting reconciliation. Whenever she left to meet someone—he couldn't ask who—the wound breached and bled.

Although they e-mailed a few times a week, and spoke on the phone erratically, they'd last met at the office three months before. He had told her about the upcoming "Salome summit." How he wished she were beside him now.

His friends pushed him to end all contact with Jay, to lower the unattainable standards set by his rose-colored vision of her. They encouraged him to start dating. He placated them by going on a few setups, which "didn't work out." After the Evie misfire, he understood that he couldn't approach sex as a good meal, gratifying yet disposable. He was terrified that, literally, he wouldn't survive another failed relationship. So Moses made one simple decision: He would remain alone. It never occurred to him that his emotional retreat imitated his mom's behavior. Hannah, too, had forsworn the risk of romance after the rejections by her first husband and Teumer. With no child to love, the Nightingale Foundation became the recipient of Moses's adoration and passion.

Ten minutes before Salome's scheduled arrival, Moses began to feel faint. He texted Alchemy: "Call it off." No response. Moses paced—*I should leave. I should call Jay. No. I can't.* He scurried into the bathroom, doused his face with cold water, and took a Xanax.

He decided to wait in the conference room. It was bigger and safer than his office. Moses stood in front of a wall where a series of Jasper Johns prints hung. They'd been donated to the foundation by Salome's onetime dealer Murray Gibbon, after he met with Alchemy's lawyers, who'd uncovered some dubious accounting practices. In time, they would be auctioned off.

Moses heard the front office door open. He peeked out from behind the door. "In here!" he screamed too loudly. His eyes focused on his mother, dressed for the winter cold of New York in a camel hair coat. She rewound a flaming red scarf around her neck before slowly removing her tan leather gloves and stuffing them in her coat pockets. Alchemy said something to her that Moses couldn't hear. With the elegant Savant sashay, which had bypassed Moses, they entered the conference room. Moses retreated to the far side of the marble table.

"Mom, I want you to meet Moses. He is the driving force as well as day-to-day operations runner of the foundation."

Moses planted his hands flat against the tabletop to still his trembling. The maneuver didn't stop the fast-spreading *schvitz* stains under the armpits of his light blue button-down shirt.

Salome began to sing: "I just saw the devil and he's smiling at me..."

Despite weeks of role-playing with his newest therapist, Moses's armor melted away. Past became present. He stood in front of his mother at the age of fifty-three, suddenly an infant—defenseless and bereft of language.

"What? Stop." Alchemy recognized the tune. Indignant, he glared at his mother, who glared at Moses, who looked bewildered. Salome unfurled the scarf from her neck and wrapped it around her fist as if loading up to land a right cross.

"You think I don't know about your *blood* sucking?"

Moses and Alchemy glanced at each other. Alchemy mouthed, "Oh, shit." Her ability to keep her awareness a secret flabbergasted Alchemy—and rendered him momentarily speechless.

"Alchemy, how did this *Moses*"—Salome's voice was witheringly derisive—"beguile you?"

"We're brothers. It's an incontestable fact."

"If I taught you anything, you know that there are multiple truths, but there is no such animal as an 'incontestable fact.'"

"Mom, listen to me," he pleaded, "he is my brother and your son."

"I've lived fifty years with the loss of my child and lost he shall remain. I'm leaving."

Alchemy stood beside Moses as they watched their mother make her way toward the door. Alchemy patted Moses on the back. He said resolutely, "You are my brother." Moses wished he could dissolve and fade into a faraway cosmic soup. He managed a what-can-you-do? shrug.

"I'll be right back."

Alchemy followed Salome to the car and asked the driver to take her home. She got in the backseat. "Traitor," she hissed.

"Mom, we can talk about this later."

"Not to me you won't." She closed the door. The car drove off.

Alchemy returned to the conference room holding a bottle of Grey Goose taken from the office fridge. He held the bottle by the neck in one hand and two glasses in the other.

"Mose, I never suspected..." Still unable to find any words, Moses waved away Alchemy's placations. "She's a fanatical maker of myths that become even more unshakable when the myth is exposed." Alchemy poured a glass and swooshed his vodka like mouthwash before he swallowed it. "It's small consolation, but at least you had Hannah and she loved you."

"It is more than consolation. It was a treasure and I'm so grateful for that."

"Mose, you understand quantum physics?"

"Only sort of."

"I thought I did. I just met Amy Loo and Spencer Frieberg, from riteplay.com, the music site, and we're investigating making quantum computers. When they whip out their equations..." He smiled sardonically. "I love the idea that anything can appear one way and then another depending on how you look at it. Salome is right about this—all truth is subject to interpretation." Moses flinched, unable to suppress a sudden feeling of betrayal. "When we first met I was really laid low by Absurda's death. Remember, you asked me if I believe in God?" Moses nodded, not sure where Alchemy was going with this. "I didn't answer because, well, I had no answer. I spent many hours meditating on that question in the monastery. No matter how I looked at, I couldn't make that leap of faith." He finished his vodka and poured another one. "Ambitious, searching for a reason, blamed me for Absurda's death. In the monastery I realized that when reason fails—and it always fails when tragedy hits—everything and anything can be blamed on someone else or the 'mysterious ways of God.' Shit, Salome is proof that reason is irrational and the irrational is reasonable.

"Mose, even with everything I have in life, the emptiness, the terror of the nothingness, it can paralyze me. I realized my aim is finding meaning in life in a world without God."

"I've always struggled with that. When the cancer hit, the struggle to understand why became as hard to comprehend as the cancer itself. I accept I may never grasp the reasons for my cancer or Salome's behavior. Or plenty of other things."

"Maybe. I didn't try to find you, but I'm sure lucky you found me. Look at your situation and your bad health. What if I hadn't been born? Or you couldn't find me? Was it worth finding out all of this shit? If you hadn't..."

"...I'd probably be dead."

"So is the pain of tonight worth being alive?"

"Right now, not so sure. Last week and next week, yes."

"Drink, please. It'll get you to next week faster." They both took a gulp. "I'm not sure what any of this means ultimately—" Alchemy's cell rang. "Can I take this?"

Moses nodded and half listened. "Yes, still at the foundation. Laluna, I'll see you tomorrow. Promise."

Alchemy hung up. Moses didn't ask who was this Laluna on the other end of the phone. He thought she'd be gone in a week.

"I think it might be smart if I get back to Topanga and make sure Salome doesn't do something unhealthy."

Alchemy finished his vodka, apologized again—he should've handled it differently—and then left.

Moses thought no matter what they did, this is how it had to turn out. A bit drunk, Moses returned to his office and placed the Insatiables' *Blues for the Common Man* into the CD player and played "Invisible Party."

It's not the mental dissection
Or the lack of introspection
But being blessed and lucky
That gets your ticket to the
Invisible party

He poured another vodka and called the only person he believed ever understood him. She didn't answer. He left a message saying the "outcome" of summit Salome was the inverse of meeting Teumer; this now topped his disaster list. His cell phone rang back almost immediately. He answered quickly with an enthusiastic, "Hey!"

"Moses?" He heard the unexpected voice of Sidonna Cherry. "Got no answer on your home phone so thought I might try this. Got a minute?"

"Yep, still at work." He tried to hide his disappointment. "What's up?"

"I have an automatic search on Teumer, and, well . . . Teumer died a week or so ago."

Moses's immediate reaction was no reaction. "Moses, I'm sorry. I can e-mail you a translation of the Brazilian obituary."

"No reason to be sorry. And the obit, I'm sure it's one big lie. Maybe later." He didn't feel like explaining the evening's events. "Thanks much. I have to go."

He took another drink. Finally, his eyes began to close and he nodded off on his office couch. He awoke sometime after midnight. His father was dead and he didn't care one bit. He felt no relief, hate, or sorrow. Was that awful? No. Since meeting him, not for one second had he regretted their lack of relationship. At least in that one space of his life, Moses had found peace.

He sat at his desk and checked his e-mail and phone messages. Nothing from Jay. He logged on to his Facebook page. No message there either. He pulled up Jay's page and saw she'd posted that she'd be attending an opening at L.A. Louver. She should have been home by now. He checked her information: Her status had been updated from "single" to "in a relationship."

61

MEMOIRS OF A USELESS GOOD-FOR-NUTHIN'

Under the Bridge, 2006–2009

Lost in la-la land without the Insatiables, and them New York guys blowin' me off, I start boozing and drugging. I call Camille, who is in Montreal shooting a TV thing. She sounds truly happy for me, and not a little pleased that I took her advice and left the band. And she's sure I'll eventually find my way. I do find my way to celebrate with her in Montreal. It's a fun time. But when she's done, she flies off to Paris and I head back to L.A.

I spend my time playing video games and getting blitzed. One night I puked and then passed out in the lobby of the building. After the janitor wakes me, I sit and talk to him for an hour. I got nowhere else to go.

I get a call from Andrew saying the Sheiks need me to sign some papers. After a long night of drinking, I show up at Kasbah and proceed to conk out on the floor of Buddy's office. I feel drops on my head. I open my eyes and Randy Sheik is holding his damn wiener in his hand. He and Lux are cracking up. I scramble up and am about to turn out Randy's fucking lights when Lux starts squirting me with a water gun. I wanna be pissed but I gotta laugh, too.

Alchy shows up. I ain't seen him much. Immediately, he asks to talk to me alone. The paper signing was only an excuse to get me there. He starts yammering that he can't lose me like he lost Absurda. He has an idea that I should record an album of cover songs. He'll even produce it when they get back from touring if I want. The Germans will give me an advance to do the album. I say thanks, but no thanks.

Things didn't go better for me. I take a walk one night over to Skid Row, which ain't far from my place. I ask a couple of them guys if they wanna party. I take out my bottle of scotch. I got so drunk... we must've gotten into some fuckin' fight. I woke up in a back alley all bruised and banged up, five hundred bucks and my wallet gone. I say to myself, *Do I really wanna end up a good-for-nuthin' gutter rat dead in some backstreet?*

I get my shit together, and Andrew helps me put a bunch of guys together to record *Pedestrian Tastes*, which turns into my band Ferricide. Andrew and Sue get us a contract with the Germans. When the Insatiables come back after their six-month tour, I ask Lux to play on a few songs and he does. I don't ask Alchemy 'cause he's put on his Good Samaritan costume, which interests me about as much as going ice fishing in the raw.

Then I start what becomes almost three years of touring or recording with Ferricide. When the Insatiables tour, they sell out arenas; I play for two thousand people. It don't bother me as much as you'd think 'cause I like running my own band. The guys, who is mostly young, look at playing with me as a big deal, not like I owe them something. I picked the producer and road manager. We don't make much money but enough so

I ain't losing any. It was good times, and positive for my head, but I'd be lying if I didn't admit to missing playing with Lux and Alchy.

I still ain't found no one who I want to be an article with. In off time, I play the good dad and hang with Ricky Jr. But at the end of three years, I'm damn tired of the road. I'm not sure what I'm gonna do next, I just know sittin' around for too long is no good for me.

Alchemy is getting consumed with the Nightingale Foundation, and the name don't please me at all. I got a call from Buddy Sheik asking me to meet with Mose and him. Maybe I can contribute to the foundation.

Alchemy's damn sneaky about keeping parts of his life separate when he wants to, but I'd met Mose a few times over the years. We never hung out or nuthin'. He was kinda cool in a twerpy Jerry Seinfeld way, if that makes sense. He don't Fancy Dan his smarts, but he sure knows a lot. He and Alchemy don't look much alike except around the mouth. Girly lips. Mose got light eyes and is balding, and must never step in the sun 'cause he's superpale. Alchy calls Mose his "half brother." When a writer asked Alchemy, "Which half?" he answered, "Whichever half I choose." Him and Mose roll their eyes and nod their head just a tic if you say something they think is idiotic and they don't want to actually call you on it. It was freaky since they wasn't raised together.

During the meeting, I see how tight Alchy and Mose has become. Alchy gets pissed when I tell him I ain't in the donating mood. Mose is cool and says, "I get it. Drop by the new offices anytime and see what we're doing. Or if you have some special interest, we're open to all ideas, especially with working-class kids." He made me feel kinda guilty. Buddy shows me the tax advantages and eventually I donate plenty over the years.

As I'm getting ready to leave that day, Alchemy says that me and him should talk soon. I says, "Sure, but it's on you to call me." I ain't holding my breath.

62

THE MOSES CHRONICLES (2009-2010)

I Don't Vant to Be Alone

Moses accepted the outcome of Salome's Nightingale office performance with nary any self-castigation, only a bemused cringe. His adjusted Livability Quotient consisted of consciously sublimating his anxieties and finding satisfaction in managing the foundation, which remained his only social outlet. He jokingly called his new situation "existential everydayness." Overwhelmed with Insatiables business, Alchemy involved himself when called upon to show up for fundraisers, drop a note to a donor, or sign off on budgetary priorities. Moses sent a nightly e-mail apprising him of the day's news. Rare as Alchemy's presence in the office was, he generated a palpable excitement when he breezed in, assembled the staff, and invited them to the tiny Café Largo. He and Lux, billing themselves as the ProTeans, were doing a private showcase with a guest guitarist.

On the night of the show, the Nightingale contingent and select members of the media milled about, waiting for Largo to open its doors when, ten feet from the entrance, a shriek and a command—"Owww! Let me go! You don't own me!"—silenced the anticipatory buzz. A rattily dressed, muscle-bound man was twisting the blue, pink, and black hair on the girl's head. Moses summoned his stern professor's voice. "Stop that! What's going on here?" The reply: "None of your damn business" and a punch to his chest. Moses tumbled to the sidewalk. Alchemy, followed by Sue and two bodyguards, streaked out of the club. The man, cursing with pathetic bravado, slinked down the street. The fracas quieted. Alchemy yelled, "Thanks, Mose!" and hustled the girl into the club. Sue helped Moses get up. "You just rescued their new guitarist."

The ProTeans appeared on the unlit stage. Alchemy announced "Laluna," and a lone spotlight shone on her. Laluna's fingers twisted the guitar strings into the ominous opening notes of "Exile's Revenge." Laluna was slim but no waif, with thin lips, small, slightly crooked teeth, tiny copper piercings in the corners of her bottom lip, high rounded cheekbones, and a nose with a light bump (perhaps from being broken). Her outfit mashed four decades of fashion into one: calf-high white suede boots, pink Spanx with nothing else covering her butt, a sleeveless pink cowl-neck sweater, peace sign earring hanging from one ear and her "Gypsy Cross" from the other. Laluna's axe-wielding energy and flair added a beautiful menace the band had lacked on stage since Absurda's passing.

Laluna's brash performing presence gave way to taciturnity once she retreated backstage. She hovered behind Sue, holding the neck of a beer bottle. Sue formally introduced Moses to Maria Lopez Appelian, nicknamed Laluna.

Laluna managed a barely audible, "Thanks, for, you know."

"I didn't help much until reinforcements arrived."

"You need to be careful, man. My father could've killed you."

"Your father?"

She nodded.

"Better me than you."

"Guess so." She shrugged and took a hefty gulp of her beer. The conversation petered out until Alchemy appeared.

"Mose, didn't you just love our guitar angel?"

"Sure did."

"We have to get together soon. I'll call you."

Stunned and perplexed, Moses stared squinty-eyed as Alchemy and Laluna slipped out the back door. Sue's gaze followed his.

"Believe it or not, Mose, the man of a million trysts may finally have found true love."

"When did it start?"

"Let me see, it's been so long." Sue's exaggerated pause emphasized her sarcasm. "A month. Maybe two. Since she crawled out of her stroller."

"Just how young is she?"

"Eighteen or nineteen. They've rented a 'safe house' to hide from her Neanderthal father and Salome. Even *I* don't know where it is."

Cynicism over the durability of their relationship prevailed among the Insatiables' inner circle. You could count Moses among the cynics when he visited the "safe house," situated on a dead-end block in Eagle Rock. Laluna's mom, who was not much older than Alchemy and still quite attractive, answered the door. She cooked them dinner but, despite their entreaties, chose to eat in front of the TV in her room.

"We're buying this house for her mom"—Moses caught Alchemy's use of *we*—"and giving the old grump some bucks."

"My father's idea of how a dowry works."

"Hey, my mom paid for Bent to see me. And then he sold me to some old perv."

"And my father...kinda wanted me dead..." Moses chimed in.

Laluna's eyes opened, aghast.

"He failed. And despite them, or maybe to spite them, we're all still here."

Laluna raised her beer bottle, "To family values, we gotta love 'em."

Moses asked if Alchemy had "christened" her Laluna. "Nope. Mose, okay if I call you that?" Moses nodded. "As a child, my paternal grandfather, who didn't speak much Spanish, loved the sound of the words. He said they reminded him of the 'sad smile of the cloud-covered moon.'" Moses could immediately see what the uncle meant.

After more alcohol and more stories, at evening's end, Laluna, her understated humor and empathetic warmth emerging, said, "Mose, thanks for making this easy."

Moses sensed a deep intimacy between Alchemy and Laluna that bypassed the twenty-year age gap. They converted him from cynic to believer.

Soon, Laluna officially joined the band and took up residency in Topanga, and "LAlunamy" became a fixture of the gossip columns and blogs.

It didn't take Laluna long to notice that Moses infrequently came to Topanga, and when he did, Salome was gone or retreated to her cottage. Alchemy judiciously parceled out the details of Moses's past. When pressed, he said, "It's Moses's business to tell you, not mine."

Laluna took the initiative to find out. She met Moses for lunch at the foundation. Never one for long-winded diplomacy, she straight-out asked, "What's up with you and Salome?" Moses did his best not to demonize Salome or heroicize Hannah. He tried not to sound too self-pitying and he purposely omitted the details of Teumer's inglorious past. The confession was not cathartic, only depressing. "I'm sorry, Mose. Sucks. Terrible. You and I, we got to work together. Salome, she doesn't get with me either."

"How do you mean?"

"She was horrible to me when we first met. That's why we took up in Eagle Rock. She hasn't been great since I moved in full time, and yesterday she slipped me this"—she shook a letter in her right hand—"under the bathroom door while I was showering, before she and Alchemy left to meet some art types. Look."

Using four different-colored pens and in a neat curvaceous script, Salome had written:

Alchemy needs to rear you, his girl-child, without me to siphon off his time. Taking care of both of us requires too much of his energy. I wanted to help you. Educate you. Be maternal in my fashion. You rejected me.

Despite my utter terror, it is healthier for us all if I return to Collier Layne. I want the two of you to thrive.

"Have you shown it to Alchemy?"

"Not yet. I'm thinking of moving back to Eagle Rock with my mom until we start the tour next month."

Moses advised her, "It's hard to tell when Salome is being cunning or reacting from someplace she can't control. I think she's motivated by the belief that she's Alchemy's ultimate protector. Not that he is hers. Talk to Alchemy. *You* have leverage. Play Salome's game. Stop her from putting a wedge between you."

It turned out to be excellent advice. Alchemy, while reaffirming his love and commitment to always take care of her, made it obvious that Salome would lose a throw-down with Laluna. He gave his mother an ultimatum: Temper her demands and be more accepting of Laluna or they would make other living arrangements. Salome chose to stay in Topanga with the nurses he hired.

Laluna called up Moses to thank him. "Maybe, you know, if things get better with Salome and me, I'll be able to return the favor someday."

63

MEMOIRS OF A USELESS GOOD-FOR-NUTHIN'

Semper Fie, 2009–2010

I'm surprised when, maybe a month after the meeting at Kasbah with Mose and Alchemy, at around 2 A.M. one summer night—me and Ricky Jr. are watching porn—Alchy calls. He says we must powwow. It's more than a year since we seen each other one-on-one, the longest since we met. Week or so before I seen him on Larry King. He don't apologize for his excesses. King asks if he is a "conflicted millionaire." Alchemy quips, "more like hypocrite millionaire." King busts out laughing and kisses his butt. "Why I love this guy. Why the world loves Alchemy Savant." I don't get how Alchemy pulls off that Regular Joe act. I go on TV for two minutes and come off like a jackass.

I head over to the upstairs private room at the Broadway Bar, which the owner keeps open for friends after the official closing time.

Alchemy's eyes are high stepping to the biddy-bip-bip beat. He gets up from the couch and hugs me. I push him away. All-cuddly Alchemy gives me the creeps. "I missed you." I don't respond in kind. We get some beers and go out to the empty balcony that overlooks L.A.'s Broadway.

"So, 'sup?" I ask.

"You ever think back and wish we'd never made it so damn big?"

"Nope. Never."

He laughed. "Of course you don't. Once, when I was at Juilliard"—he stops for a minute taking his personal detour to Collidascope Land—"Absurda and I went to see Richard Thompson at the Ritz. We were standing in the back of a packed house while the first act was on, and Thompson slinks in and stands beside us. He's so nondescript no one else recognizes him. An hour later he is blowing everyone away with his playing. I promised myself that that would not be me. Sometimes, I wonder if that wouldn't've suited me better."

I don't think he regretted being him. Only he ain't exactly lying neither. He always worried that whatever got Salome would get him, too. Maybe he didn't have to be a rock star. Only him living a normal life was about as likely as me winning the Mr. Congenial award.

"You didn't ask me here ta get my opinion on that."

"Silky's left the band. You hear Laluna's joining?" I nod. "Lux and I want to do a free concert at the Grand Canyon. Then a farewell world tour. Call it quits after twenty years. We need you. We never found a permanent replacement for you." This is true. They used session guys or friends in the studio and different hired hands on the road.

I don't want to answer yet. "Whataya gonna do if you quit music?"

"I'll always make music. No touring. Different stuff. I want to dedicate myself to the Nightingale Foundation."

"C'mon, you're going into politics."

"Maybe."

"Liar."

"Yeah."

"And you call me the ambitious one. Or maybe you was being sarcastic. Damn, taken me all these years to get it." I'm wondering if the time is right for me to go back. He downs another beer in one go. From his pocket he takes out his iPod and hands it to me. "Put it on and listen."

I do.

"Man, this ain't saying enough, but that's the most insane and beautiful three or four minutes a music I ever heard—fuck—I never heard nuthin' like it before."

"It came to me in my sleep and I woke up and just played it. Absurda gave it to me from out there..."

"I don't buy that otherworldly shit." I hand the iPod back to him. "When you are dead, you stay dead. No damn spirits is creepin' around."

"Probably. Only I don't know what I don't know... It's eight years and I am still plagued by what we could've done for her."

I keep it zipped. I learned that from him. Sometimes saying nuthin' is as meaningful as saying something.

"Hey, look, I'm really sorry about what went down with us."

I know he's talking about the shit that went down at Madam Rosa's. I just nod as if to say, *so fucking what?*

"Are you finally ready to listen and believe me instead of blowing up and punching me before I can finish talking?" He closes his eyes and opens them, expecting me to bust out all gooey.

"I never doubted what I seen and heard, and it means what I think it means."

"Listen to me, Ambitious. Absurda and I were taking leaks outside. But you're right, she was thanking me—she was grateful for all she believed I'd done for her. The band and all. And, well, for bringing you into her life."

"This ain't no Alchemy creation to make me feel like shit?"

"After all this time you don't think I can come up with something better than that to make you feel like shit?" He's trying to joke, but his eyes, his body got the look of helpless sadness that I seen that first day years ago when he had to leave Salome in Collier Layne. In all the time I know him, I seen that look maybe five times.

I finish my beer. "You and her?"

"Never."

"What about, you know, what I..." I couldn't bring myself to say it. I done beat myself up plenty over that night. "I'm sorry. I dunno—"

"Look, I get it. And neither of us will ever forget it. But we all have ugly shit in our heads. The guy I love as Ambitious Mindswallow—and I felt this from the day we met—is one angry motherfucker fighting against himself, who screws up...a lot, but in the end, you do the right thing."

64

THE SONGS OF SALOME

The Holy Trinity

When the Insatiables returned home after their latest tour, Alchemy asked me to fly back to L.A. I thought because, with Nathaniel gone, he wanted me to be with him. No. He wanted to lure me into an ambush. Somehow he believed I remained unaware of his DNA infusion to this "Mose." That I had not overheard conversations between them about the foundation. I regretted my necessary malevolence to the unstillborn son—I couldn't embrace him. I awaited the mystagogue Margarita to give me strength and guidance while the polar forces of ether and gravity ripped me apart. By denying his existence, I hoped to force Alchemy to choose between us—I couldn't imagine he'd side with him over me. I hadn't anticipated the power of the third player in their newly formed alliance.

Laluna. A graceful faun bathed in the microbes of stealthy determination and youthful ignorance. She addressed me with cordial respect I didn't want and quickly dismissed me. She enchanted him with her beleaguered smile hissing with a touch of the homicider, and her sullen eyes that demanded his protection. She possessed a spectral sensuality that didn't suppress her soulsmell of a rag doused in lighter fluid—intoxicating and toxic. She rejected my initial offerings and made me a pariah in my son's home.

In a grand gesture, a few months after she had ensconced herself permanently in Topanga, she decided to act like a concerned member of my family. She invited me for tea in the main house. It, too, was a trap. After small talk went nowhere, she zeroed in on her true reason for the invitation.

"I'm sorry if it didn't go well when you met Mose."

Of course, my son and the woman he lived with shared intimacies. "What business is it of yours?"

"It's my business because I love Alchemy. You love him. Moses loves him. And Alchemy loves the three of us."

"Do you love me?"

"I would if you'd let me."

"Laluna, the real question is, Can you only love someone if they let you?"

The question flummoxed her. She answered with an indirect accusation. "Mose, he's a great guy. Accepted me right away. Only, whenever your name comes up, his body clenches as if he's preparing to be punched in the nose. I know that feeling, I felt it most of my life with my father."

I now presumed Alchemy had instigated this meeting and conversation, so I decided to end it there and exile myself to my cottage, understanding that Laluna had usurped my position with Alchemy.

I got two guards to help me empty the bottom floor of all furniture except one black and one white director's chair. I painted the walls, ceiling, and floor Savant Red. I couldn't talk to Alchemy, so I wrote him a letter. My nurse hand-delivered it.

> *I have never given a damn if anyone thought me a "vicious virago," "a cold cunt," "crazy," or "talentless" (though I have been called all these things). I cannot live with your condemnation of me as a heartless mother.*
>
> *It is impossible for me to describe my lifelong travails, still I will see him if you desire it... Someday you will understand that my actions are justified.*
>
> *And I will reach out again to Laluna.*
>
> *I can't bear you hating me this way. Or in any way.*
>
> *I can't.*

I waited. I told myself, *Patience...* Two nights later, I was talking on the phone to Xtine—she believed Alchemy would never desert me—when Laluna knocked on the door. "Xtine, I've lost. Call you later."

Disoriented by my red cavern, Laluna sat in the black director's chair. Alchemy was "worried" about me. She asked to come in his stead. Both of us donning a mask of deceit, we issued apologies that we didn't mean. She for her insensitivity and seeking to intervene where she didn't belong and I for overreacting. Laluna followed up with a further false olive branch.

"We're leaving next week, but when we come back, I want us, just you and me, to spend time together."

"Let me ask you this. Why do you seek my companionship?" She squirmed in the chair. Her lips scrunched in one direction and her nose in the other. I reminded myself that she was barely twenty years old and uneducated in the distorting mirrors that reflect one's own, often ineffable, multiple motivations. "No need to answer. Let's agree that I have never been that warm to you. Let's also agree that you have been wary of me." She nodded. "The reason you want to befriend me has little to do with your empathy for my situation. Or interest in my life or my art. You want to please Alchemy. That is good. It's the same as if I see him—it will be to please Alchemy."

"If you mean Mose, Alchemy hopes you see him because you want to."

"I don't. But I would see him to please Alchemy. And therefore, because that is the wrong reason, I won't see him."

I'm not sure she understood, but I continued anyway. "You and I getting along will make Alchemy happy. We both want that. If he is happier specifically because you and I have a relationship, that ultimately benefits you. But does your relationship benefit him? In the short term, yes. In the long term, I predict your relationship, if it lasts, will hasten his Gravity Disease."

She gaped, perplexed. Gravity Disease would be inexplicable to her.

"Laluna, to paraphrase your own words from the other night, I will let you love me, for now. And I have begun by confiding this to you."

She thanked me but volunteered nothing else.

The three of us ate dinner together, and our conversation consisted only of shallow, enervating non sequiturs. The morning they left, I found a note under my door.

I could never hate you. Often mystified, sometimes frustrated, always loving. I am glad you and Laluna talked. You have to give each other a chance. This will be our last tour. I need to spend time with you as a son and as Laluna's mate and not as an Insatiable. Love, Alchemy

I found no solace in his words.

65

THE MOSES CHRONICLES (2012)
Selective Affinities

The Nightingale Foundation Prize hosted a funding soiree at the Palos Verdes home of Thessalia Bambucos, widowed courtesan–turned–queen of an Internet media empire. As the evening wound down, Alchemy tapped Moses on the arm and said, grave faced, "We need to a take a walk." Alchemy's one blue and one green iris seemed to have expanded, leaving almost no white in his eyes. Moses nodded and Alchemy went to thank Bambucos. They moved outside and silently began to walk down the street.

Moses assumed Alchemy wanted to continue their discussions for the transition from foundation to political party. Alchemy planned to use the foundation as the facilitator — affecting individuals' lives with their programs while delivering their message that America needed a new path, a third way. Alchemy's grandeur without grandiosity, his well-disguised drive that verged on monomania, and his total belief in *e pluribus unum* would eventually culminate in his running for the presidency in 2020.

Once they were far enough away from Bambucos' home, under a darkness sporadically illuminated by lights beaming from behind the curtains of the wealthiest strata of America and the yellow-orange hue of Alchemy's cigarette, he asked Moses, "Your phone still off?"

"Yes." Moses, who as a kid imagined that the people on TV could see him through the screen, shared Alchemy's paranoia that the government possessed secret technology that could hear conversations through any live phone. Alchemy had told him Loo and Freiberg were working on just such a technology.

Alchemy puffed hard and then spit a gob of phlegm on a manicured lawn, more like a lawless rocker than a political candidate. "Look, I needed to talk because, well, Laluna and I want to have a kid. Yeah, yeah, I know what I said years ago. Go ahead. Give me shit."

"I will. Just not now, because that's terrific. I'd love to be an uncle." The longer Alchemy's relationship continued with Laluna, the more Moses had anticipated a change in Alchemy's no-kid plan.

"If things go right, and you have a lot to say and do in this, you won't only be an uncle..."

"What?" Moses's voice raised an octave. "You don't need my permission."

"This super sex god can't make his zygote float."

"Come again?"

"It won't solve the problem if I do." Alchemy snickered. "My zapper has no zip." They reached an empty private tennis court, and Alchemy flopped back against the green fence.

"Mose, this is the most embarrassing admission... We've been *trying*. Fertility docs and mystical potions. All failed. Laluna is blaming herself—wrongly—because her mother had multiple miscarriages before having her and then never could conceive again." He pushed back harder against the fence, which rippled around the court, and then he melted toward the ground. Moses crouched beside him.

"You once needed my help. Now, we need your help. I need you to come up to Topanga and do the herky-jerky. Your seedlings will be put in the doc's test tube and implanted into Laluna."

"What the eff? You want my sperm?" Moses felt as if he'd been slammed in the head and was suffering a concussion that left him bewildered and off balance. Deep emotional barriers impeded him from immediately processing the implications, the lifelong impact of becoming a surrogate donor.

"Yes, but I also want you to keep this between us."

Surrogate donor *and* anonymous father. "Wow, this is beyond unexpected."

Alchemy detected the ambivalence in Moses's voice. "If you need time or aren't cool with this, I get it." He pushed himself up using the fence and stood tall. "Laluna doesn't know the plan. I prefer to get your okay first."

"Yeah, I can see that. But why me?"

"You're my brother."

"Half brother."

"Given our respective fathers, our mother is the good half. How's that for absurd?"

"Scary, too. You know me, I'm a deliberative thinker."

"Sure. Take your time. But not too much."

"I'll answer soon. But please, sound out Laluna."

"Mose, I've contemplated the enormity of this request. I still needed to do it. I'll talk to Laluna. Only, if you decide no, tell me immediately. Please."

They walked back in silence. Moses still reeling.

The more he thought about it, the more Moses realized he'd abhor living as a father not just in absentia but not as a father at all. He couldn't articulate or justify his feeling that there was something unseemly in the request. He tried to convince himself he should be honored that Alchemy had chosen him. And, of course, he owed him.

Alchemy relayed to Moses that Laluna was shocked by his admission and his plan, but that once it sank in, she was all for it. For now, she preferred not to talk about it, which suited Moses just fine. Moses felt Alchemy's urgency and desire. And he also understood his desire for ultimate secrecy.

A week after the initial conversation, Moses, still not totally committed to agreeing but leaning that way, made an appointment to have his sperm tested at a Pasadena clinic, where there would be no way to trace what he was doing back to Alchemy. The doctor happily reported to him, "You're a lucky man. Your sperm seem undamaged by the cancer or chemo. They're plentiful and spry for a post-fifty-year-old."

The following Wednesday, Moses drove up to the Topanga compound. Alchemy ambled out to meet him in the driveway. "Save a life. Give a life."

"Let's hope."

He masturbated in a downstairs bathroom. His semen safely in the prepared cup, he placed it on the sink counter and swiftly left the compound.

Alchemy slipped into the bathroom and fetched his brother's seed. He passed it to the new fertility doctor, who believed it was Alchemy's. Laluna got pregnant on the first try.

66

MEMOIRS OF A USELESS GOOD-FOR-NUTHIN'

Hello, I Must Be Going, 2009–2012

You know by now I ain't no philosopher and I see life as mainly about some chicks or dudes, some family shit, having money or no money, and then you die. You can dress it up in fancy duds, but that's the deal. Alchemy ain't no different.

Before I meet Laluna, I peg her as another hungry honey trap. When I meet her at the Kasbah offices (though they is owned by the Germans, the Sheiks keep the offices) and I give her the once-over, I'll never forget it, 'cause she looks *different*. Wearing a yellow sundress with smiley face apples and oranges on it, a big floppy yellow old-lady hat, no makeup at all, and sparkly-faced like Courteney Cox in the Springsteen video, only with the piercings in her lips and a space between her two front teeth—she bangs the bell as the hottest ten possible. And whew, when she catches me gawking, the sparkly smile goes to a glare that could've shrunk Johnny Wadd's dick from twenty paces. Alchy introduces us and she acts like our stare-down never happened. At first, I was suspicious of her and sometimes I'm thinking she is jealous of me and Lux because of our histories with Alchemy. Nope. She's too hip for that. I seen Alchemy and Laluna when they was practically babies, I mean she was a teenager, and if I believed in reincarnation they'd be the reason 'cause they was wiser and understood more shit at twenty than most people ever do no matter how long they live. I ask myself, "Why them?" It's not just being smart. Lucky is better, and they was, but that's not it. Neither is having messed-up folks, 'cause that's *normal*. I met her father, who is an Armenian gang guy from the Valley, and her mom, who he whomped on for years until Laluna and Alchy got her to divorce him. She was a really nice lady who came on tour with us for a while. She made us homemade meals and acted, I dunno, like a real mom. Unlike Alchy, who has his Collidascope Land moments, and he always acts like he can fix everything, Laluna always has at least one foot planted firmly on earth, but inside she also got a Collidascope of her own, so to speak. At first, that combo worked for them.

Still, Salome master mindfucked Laluna from day one. Any moron could see Laluna loved and idolized Alchemy. Guess that was Salome's problem. She makes a rare drop-in to a Pro-Teens gig at the Smell, wearing a T-shirt with Absurda's face on it, which is most def a shot at Laluna. Alchy keeps Salome away from most of our gigs after that.

I told Laluna that it was great to play with her. Best since Absurda. She answers so serious, her voice so low, "I'm happy to hear that. Only I wish not this way. No one can replace Absurda." Maybe not, but Lux and me understand we done recaptured that special connection where Alchemy sees what each show, each audience needs, and without ever having to say a word the three of us *feel* how to follow him. We record *The Great Awakening* and then hit the road and we bank mucho dinero. It was almost heartwarming to see Alchy head back to hang with Laluna. Raunchy rock partying didn't appeal to her. The rules of their relationship is a mystery 'cause Alchy, I don't think, ever fully quit floozying and I got an inkling she sneaked her share on the side though I never caught her, and she sure never came on to me.

I'm the only one not in a steady relationship. Lux has settled down with Leanne, who is a TV producer. One night after a show in Stockholm (Alchy always insists we stay at the Grand Hôtel there), Laluna is in bed already, so us three is sitting in Lux's room drinking when Alchemy says, "So guys, what's it like having kids?"

Lux taps his hands on his legs like he's preparing for a drum solo. "Ball-bustin' hard, you want mine?"

"Fuckin' goes double for me since I came late to the party." Then we crack up and give the thumbs-up. Lux says it's the best thing he's ever done but it is also the toughest. He and Leanne, who don't want kids, have had some major throw-downs about how to deal with his kids from other women.

"Why?" Lux asks. "You and Laluna thinking of hitching and diversifying your portfolio?"

"I don't need my mother's lectures on the evil power structures of marriage, so no to that. Kids? I'm thinking about it. My mom says she'd like a grandchild."

That don't surprise me about Salome as much as you might think. Feeling naughty, I volunteer, "Wit' all the fucking you done, I can't believe you don't got one already. You playing the secretive Alchemy? Like you hid your father all them years."

I been giving him shit about the big clam-up over his father and how he guilts me 'cause *I* don't see my folks hardly at all. He was so pissed when Salome showed paintings of his dad and Moses's dad without telling him first. He admits nuthin' in public about Bent or Mose Sr., only kind of hints that it is all just "one big Salome fantasy."

"No. No secrets. Just lucky, I guess. One other thing, Sue's got interest in us doing the halftime show at the Super Bowl. Before you get excited, I'm voting no."

Him and Nathaniel, even though they like football, they also hate it. Salome calls it "Super Barbarian Day." Still, I says, "Why the hell not do it? That's like two billion eyeballs watching us. And you watch the damn thing!"

"Yes, and I am mad at myself for watching."

Lux is revved, too. "C'mon, Alchemy. If this is our last go-round, what a way to go out."

He is ready for us. "We've never sold our music for ads, and this is a secular holiday that's bigger than Christmas, only it sells the religion of American corporatism and false patriotism. And the NFL owners have a plantation mentality." And yackety yack. When he gets on that high political horse, there is no knocking him off. Even though me and Lux are so into it, it's a no-go unless we can change his vote.

Alchy gets a call from Laluna, who wants him back in the room. I start wagging my finger and I mouth, "Come home to Mommy, little boy." He smirks, but he seems happy, so what the fuck, right?

The next night I says to Laluna, with Alchy and Lux standing there, "You also voting to pass on the Super Bowl?"

"I'll vote yes if I can sing 'Fuck Like a Woman.' Uncensored." It's one of the few songs Absurda used to sing lead. Laluna never asked to do it before. It got the lines "Preachers say I'm gonna end up in Hades / only it's them jocks-of-all-trades / who got the morality disease / 'cause I will fuck who I please…"

Laluna is acting more rock 'n' roll than any of us. Alchemy, grinning, says, "See, that's why I love her."

Funny, though, later that year when we're back in L.A. for a hiatus between tour legs, he invites me and Lux up to the Topanga house to watch the Super Bowl to see what "we're missing out on." That what you call irony? That year, the party is only like ten of us. It starts what becomes his and Laluna's Super Bowl party tradition.

We changed the sked so the Grand Canyon gig is our final show, which Alchemy says is a true celebration of America, and we make the show free for the two hundred thousand people who show up. HBO broadcasts it live. We take a helicopter up to the top of the mountain and I remember Andrew teases him, "I can see the multitudes…Alchemy, are you going to consume them all tonight?"

"Maybe yes."

We open with a new song, "Beat Attitudines":

Declared peace/got war
Kissed the moneychanger,
Befriended the mocking deranger
Lay between the virgin and the law

Turned wine into water
Who ended up teaching me more?
It's always love
We're searching for

Got cheeks to turn/money to burn
The meek got no net worth
Rich claim it's theirs by birth
Made swords into stock shares
Gave away my golden chairs
Wandered forty days in the sand dunes
Sold my sermon on the mount
They asked for a discount
I sung my American tunes

Dropped my pants/did my peace dance
Prayed for mercy
They treated me worsely
Beautify and rejoice
We are the saviors of tomorrow
'Cause we got no choice
Live in happiness with your sorrow
And don't hang me up
'Cause I will let you down ...

Some rabid believers call that song blasphemous. Me,
I think it was blasphemy that we burned through so much
money on that concert 'cause with all the permits, lawyers, and
cleanup, it cost us like three million bucks.

When we return to L.A., I am still hoping Alchemy'll change his mind and we'll do another record, and then, who knows? I don't see him much because I'm hangin' with Ricky Jr. in New York 'til I get another death call. Falstaffa passed from the hep C. We knew it was coming, but it still sucked. I wasn't even forty yet and I buried too many good people. The funeral is one major-league bummer. Me, Lux, Alchy, and Marty are the pallbearers. (A week later, Alchemy pays off Marty with $250K and asks him to "retire." He never forgot Marty's trashing Absurda to me all them years before.)

I think it's kind of strange, 'cause even though she don't know Falstaffa like us, Laluna don't show and I'm questioning if they broke up or she caught him, well, being Alchemy. Before we head out, he asks me and Lux if we can come up to Topanga the next Monday.

We meet in the studio. Laluna ain't there. He has three bottles of Cristal on ice. He's almost beaming, which is not what I expect. "Laluna is pregnant. She's had a tough few weeks. Doc came yesterday, and it's three months and all looks good. We're announcing it soon."

Congrats all around and we pop the bubbly and we each take swigs from our bottle. He puts his down and picks up his guitar. "I got a new one. Come to me last week. It's called 'Know More.'" He starts playing before singing. It has a real slow, bluesy feel. Me and Lux get what it means, but he says it anyway. "When Laluna is up to it we'll record a coupla more songs. And that's it, I'm done. No reunions. No nuthin'." He takes a few giant gulps from his bottle. "I've accomplished everything I ever wanted to do in music as the Insatiables, and I couldn't have done it without you two."

When Lux goes to take a pee, I ask about that stuff he played for me a couple of years ago.

"It never came again. I'm waiting. Anyway, I'm not sure I'd ever release it."

Even after twenty years, he don't always make sense to me.

67

THE SONGS OF SALOME

Tryx Are for Kids

L.A. felt purgatorial. New York resonated with the vacant chair that was Nathaniel. I wanted love. If not love, I'd settle for great sex. In the last years with Nathaniel I was left to devices of self-fulfillment. I needed my orgasms. I did not want sex to become a memory or fantasy. I considered hiring a younger male nurse. Ha. Too *Sweet Bird of Youth*.

Alexander Holencraft phoned that he was in L.A. for a week. He asked to meet for dinner in West Hollywood. He greeted me at the restaurant entrance with overblown flattery about how young I look. Even in the dim light, in his disintegration I saw my own. He took my hand. I followed him to the table. We were not alone. Persistence brought me Willibrordus Ildefonsus Ignatius Verdonk, a chief curator at the Stedelijk Museum in Amsterdam. His name was virtually unpronounceable, so I called him Tryx. We'd met briefly during the Hammer show when the Sted bought *Pillzapoppin'* for their permanent collection. During Nathaniel's illness, I'd ignored Tryx's missives, so he hounded Holencraft to reintroduce us. As a twenty-six-year-old grad student traveling in Berlin, he'd seen my performance by the Wall, which ignited a twenty-five-year fantasy.

He wanted to make a documentary about me. With his soul-smell mix of sawdust and soldered silver, I had found a man who wanted to fuck me and who I wanted to fuck.

We set about to make the film *Remembrances of Things Past and Future.*

Tryx became my accompanist in Amsterdam and New York, choosing art, getting new photographs, and doing interviews for the doc. I could never reveal my mystagogues, so when questioned about my creative method I showed them a never-exhibited painting of red, white, and blue stripes with one word written in each stripe with ministar shapes: *Dream. Listen. Sing.*

I chose the music we used over Xtine's montage of videos she'd taken of me working over forty years and mixed in some old photos of Dad's. Alchemy did an interview that was funny and sweet about how I inspired him to be an artist. That's when he wrote "Savant Sensation Bluz," and he also picked other music.

Laluna did not contribute. Our relationship remained unflourished. Alchemy announced his retirement from touring and from the Insatiables. A few months before the opening and preview of the film, he flew to Amsterdam to tell me of my impending grandmotherhood.

Stunned. Overjoyed. Speechless is how I reacted to the news. Without sentiment, Tryx and I parted. I returned to L.A. after the huzzahs over the exhibition quieted. I needed to infuse my granddaughter with my songs.

68

THE MOSES CHRONICLES (2013)

Try, Try Again

A few months after the birth of Persephone, Alchemy and Laluna's daughter, Moses took a day off from the foundation and motored up the 405 to the Skirball Center to attend a day-long symposium expounding upon the works of concentration camp survivor Levi Furstenblum on the twentieth anniversary of his suicide. In spite of, or perhaps because of the past years' revelations, Moses's fascination with the Third Reich's craven depredations continued. How different his questions for Furstenblum would be now than if they'd met fifteen years before.

He sat in a middle-row aisle seat as the panel began debating the meaning of Furstenblum's views on forgiveness and redemption. The moderator began with a quote from Jacques Derrida's essay on "unforgiveness" followed by a passage from Furstenblum:

Forgiveness is not earned, achieved, or bought. It is like love and ascends of its own volition. One can strive to comprehend unspeakable acts, but one cannot will forgiveness. There are those who live by the maxim "Forgive but don't forget." I find that phrase disingenuous. When

I say that we are all capable of evil, I do not mean to imply any belief in the concept of original sin—to be human is to receive and inflict misery. Despite impulses of vengeance toward my torturers, and here the difference in our humanity is critical—I did not demand their death. I am not a murderer. Accepting that too is necessary for forgiveness. When released from the camps, I experienced the misery of perplexity and callousness in the actions of friends and family. Forgiveness came to me for them. For the murderers, who never asked for it, I wait.

As Moses listened, he thought about how the burden of his anger and frustration had dissipated, and he had come to forgive the failures and mistakes of Hannah and Jay—those he loved most. Even for the unstable Salome, whose responsibility for her actions was suspect. His father hadn't sought it, yet somehow he felt he had achieved forgiveness for him. His own search for self-forgiveness remained ongoing. And then, just as she was drifting away on the lightness of forgiveness, the moderator loudly announced, "Time to break for lunch," returning Moses to reality. He made his way to the back of the room. Then he stopped, heart aflutter, mouth agape. Had Furstenblum's words conjured the image?

"Hi," Jay greeted him, almost too jauntily, and moved closer to gently embrace him as she whispered, "I hoped you'd be here." His arms fell limply to his sides. Disarmed, Moses asked, "Eat something?"

"Sure."

Even after four years of divorce, they still e-mailed, if only sporadically. Jay would inquire at least once a month about his health. Jay's mom had finally passed away ten days before, after years of not really being present, and Moses had sent flowers and a card to which he received a thank-you e-mail.

They filed out of the room, and he followed her toward the cafeteria. Her once midback-length hair was now cut to the nape of the neck. "Let's sit and talk first." They veered off to cement benches and sat under the shadows of the Santa Monica Mountains.

"Jay, why didn't you just call or e-mail that you were coming?"

"I was afraid. I don't know your situation."

"I'm not situated." Moses noticed Jay's slightest exhalation of relief. He refrained from asking the reciprocal question.

"With my mom passing..." Her voice trailed off and she sighed. "I just wanted to see you."

"I am so sorry about your mom."

"She's better off. I'd been missing you and thinking about you. And whenever my father complained about the 'burden' of my mom, I thought about what we went through together. And I wished you were in Miami by my side." Moses didn't offer that if she had asked, he would've been on the next plane. "Moses, we shared something so rare, and we blew it."

"Yes, we did," Moses said hesitantly.

"Moses, what are you thinking?"

He didn't say what he was thinking. Death and mourning leave one so vulnerable, and although it is not uncommon, it is a treacherous time to seek to rekindle the embers of love lost. His desire to hold her, swear his enduring love, stalled at the barrier of the unknowable. Can this past be recaptured, a present restored, a future remade?

Instead, constrained by the memory of his outburst that signaled the death knell of his marriage, he offered blandly, "I need to grab a bite and then I'm going back in. You staying?"

"Is it too late for forgiveness?"

"Neither of us can answer that now."

"Will you call me so we can answer it together?"

Moses recalled a graduate school history professor of his who scoffed, "The idea that most people claim to be brutal realists proves the opposite. Most of you fall into one of three categories of gullibles: those I classify as the less gifted, the willfully ignorant, and the perpetually delusional."

For much of his life, Moses considered himself to be among the brutal realists. Later, he conditionally reclassified himself as willfully ignorant. Finally, he descended to the perpetually delusional. He researched and discovered that almost 10 percent of all divorcees remarried or lived again with their former spouse. He found no information detailing for how long or whether they stayed together.

He invited Jay to the premiere of a play written by Nightingale Grant recipient Hilaria Diaz. *The ICEman Cometh* was not O'Neill's classic play but one portraying the plight of illegal immigrants. Moses thought that if he and Jay were to make a go of it, both of their Livability Quotients needed reformulating, and that formula now included his relationship with Laluna and Alchemy and his nonrelationship with Salome, all of whom would be there.

Alchemy and Jay greeted each other with amiable if jittery hellos. Laluna, who disguised her awkwardness in public appearances by feigning boredom, flashed a rare radiant smile of welcome. Jay took a bathroom break during the intermission, and Laluna, after edging her way to Moses, shifted her eyes in an exaggerated side-to-side toward a loitering Salome, who suddenly darted up the aisle. After they watched her disappear into the lobby, Laluna leaned over and whispered, "Mose, it makes me really, like really happy, to see you with someone."

Throughout the evening, his emotions roiled—desire, resentment, distrust of Jay's motives and his own, and the facile hope that love really could conquer all. Jay wanted to go out after the show. Moses claimed fatigue and asked if they could meet later in the week. They did, at an Indian restaurant on Pico. Over appetizers, they made small talk about the difficulties of her work after the economic crash, his contentment working at the foundation, and his mixed excitement and angst over establishing the Nightingale Party. Moses, blinders off, saw Jay at forty-five years old with tiny crevices arching out from the corners of her eyes, the crinkling of her lips, hair dyed to hide the creeping gray, glasses necessary to read the menu. To him, she sparkled as attractively as ever.

Between the appetizer and main course, small talk over, Moses took the plunge. "Jay"—he took a gulp of his water—"I don't believe in more than incremental changes in our essence.

Whatever you loved about me before still exists, and what you *didn't*, that does, too. I am still the guy you no longer wanted to be with that day in the Cedars parking lot."

Jay took a sip of her white wine.

Moses consciously chose not to push the Alchemy button by spitting out what he was thinking: *I am never going to be a big enough guy to say, "So glad you screwed my brother."* He understood all partners lie, deny, omit, rearrange, and censor to avoid hidden relationship land mines. Only now, he couldn't locate the danger line separating honesty and mean-spiritedness, so he continued cautiously. "The monstrous thoughts that stream into my head, well, I have to believe that everyone has them, only my filter is thinner than most."

"I know that. But I can tell, just in the way you were at the play, I can feel even in our e-mails—you have changed in some way. Somehow seeing your father helped you."

"I guess so, as horrific as it was. I'm sleeping better. My daymares, they're much less frequent."

"It's not like you ever kept your, um, daymares a secret. I just didn't think they included *me*."

"If I could control them, I would have."

"Moses, whatever it was that made us work so well for so long, to be silly and feel safe, I never found elsewhere. With us, I never felt alone. Not until, you know. And Moses...You?" Jay pressed her lips together, awaiting his response.

"I pretty quickly adapted to being alone. My life mostly revolves around the foundation and my brother and—you know they have a daughter?"

"Sure. Your niece."

Moses bowed his head and moved the bread crumbs and bits of spilled rice in a circular motion on the white tablecloth. He knew he must tell her, even if this truth reopened the wound that helped destroy their relationship, even if he risked losing Alchemy's trust in him. Moses unbowed his head and stared into Jay's eyes. "Persephone is *my* daughter."

Her expression transformed from quizzical to shock when she realized he wasn't joking. Moses explained the sequence of events. Jay nodded ever so slightly, still half disbelievingly, until Moses pronounced, "I am not delusional. I am not making this up. Persephone will never know. I am now complicit in my family's, all of my families', cycles of deception."

"My God. Moses, this must be impossibly difficult for you."

"It is and it isn't." What he wouldn't admit to Jay, and only belatedly admitted to himself, that the least flattering of his reasons for agreeing was it allowed him to feel superior to Alchemy in this one way. "Laluna and Alchemy don't make me feel like an outsider. So far, at least. Persephone will get all the advantages of being rich and enjoy the love of a mother and two fathers." He shrugged. "Jay, I don't know how to say this or if this is the wrong time or what is going to happen, but when I was so scared and lost, I always looked to the time with you to keep me awake and alive."

Jay clasped Moses's cold and shivery hands in hers, thinking, *My Moses, abandoned by his parents, and yes, abandoned by me. We only wanted to love each other and failed.* And so she said, "Moses, come home with me tonight."

69

MEMOIRS OF A USELESS GOOD-FOR-NUTHIN'

Flushing Flashback, 2013–2015

In my second Insatiables afterlife I don't see Alchemy or Lux much, and one more time I'm trying not to drown in a shit hole of my own making. I gigged with other dudes, but it don't have the same fire. If Ricky Jr. ain't visiting, all I do is play video games, watch sports, and try to stay away from losers who only wanna get high. I can't find no woman I want to stay with for more than two days. Or maybe they don't want to stay with me. I'm so bored I visit my brother and father in upstate New York so I can see the house my money bought and what they do with the $2K a month I still send them.

I hardly recognize my dad slothing around with a belly and balloon-size face and like three strands of gray hair. He still spits and snarls like he wants to stick thumb tacks in your eyes. My brother is a massive mashed potato blob of tattoos and half his teeth are gone or chipped. The two of them and my brother's girlfriend all got DUIs so none of 'em should drive. We take a few days' vacation in Lake George. My treat. We're cool until we get back to the house. We're all pretty wasted and watching some story about the pervey priests on TV, and my brother's girlfriend says it's a Jewish conspiracy against the Catholic Church. My father laughs, "Ya idiot, they just followin' tradition because Jesus and his pals was a buncha Jew fags and Mary Magdalene was the first fag hag."

I said, "Shut up, Dad. I got no more patience for your dumb-ass ignorant shit."

"Oh, look at my liberal son with his Negro, homo, and Jew friends. You talk like some faggot girly man."

"Dad, I said shut the fuck up. The best thing I ever done was get the hell away from you. You fucked me up good with your ignorant bullshit."

"I always knew you was a pansy-ass pussy who wishes he was a nigger. I was too fuckin' soft on you. I should whip your ass right now."

I'm ready to shut the fucker up for good when my brother's girlfriend starts screaming words that ain't even words 'cause she's so wasted. Lenny claws her into their bedroom and two minutes later she wobbles out. "Lenny's dick gone plurp. Ricky, ya wanna fuck me?" Lenny starts cracking from the bedroom like a typical no-sense-making drunk. "Ricky, ya better not fuck my woman."

"Don't worry, I won't."

"Why not? Ya too good for her? We're gonna settle this like real men." He passes out before he can crawl five feet.

It's clear why I done my best to ignore them all these years. I drive back to the city the next day and, surprise, I discover my father "borrowed" my credit card and cell phone and bought $15K worth of computers, phones, and big-screen TVs online. I can't press charges, so I pay.

Back in L.A., I meet Alchemy and Lux for dinner and I ask about reuniting. No chance. They bug me to regroup Ferricide. I figure I'll try it. I get two former members and two new kids and we write songs and some covers for *Performance-Enhanced Death Drugs*, which we call *Pedd-o-file*, and pisses lots of people off—which was fine by me. We end up having an indie hit with a cover of Mott's "Rock and Roll Queen," which the music blogs say is my subtle shot at Alchy. As he might've said, "not consciously." Anyway, Sue and Andrew set us up for a tour, and we hit the road.

About six, eight months into the tour I run into Lux at a hotel in Austin. He's drumming for Buddy Guy. I miss him, and after my show I head over to the blues club where he's at and join the jam. Then me and Lux retire to the bar and we're BSing about the best and worst times, the bomb scares and near riots. I ask why he is doing this because he can't be making much money.

"Yeah, but playing music is all I ever wanted to do. Some guys are doctors or roofers. I'm a drummer."

"Music's the only thing I'm any good at. I wish Alchemy didn't give us up for politics. Why can't he be like Bono or even Billy Bragg, speechify about peace and brotherhood bullshit, donate money, and still make music?"

"You're asking me to explain Alchemy?" No one can explain him, I get that. "He loved being famous and the girls and shit, but I'm not sure he enjoyed the success the way we did. The band, in its way, was part of his bigger plan. He's not a musician, he's *Alchemy*."

He spoke truth. I drink up and get another beer. "Lux, the worst was Absurda dying."

"For all of us. The night of the funeral, after you went to bed, Alchemy asked me to stay up with him. He was having, I guess, a minibreakdown. I've never seen him so vulnerable, before or since. He couldn't stop shaking, saying he was as weak and nuts as Salome and *he* was going to check into Collier Layne. He kept saying, 'It's all my fault. I should have seen this and fixed it.' And shit, when Heather came over—" I shook my head. "Yeah, I know. I wished I could've stopped them. What was creepiest of all, he kept calling her Amanda."

"Why didn't ya ever tell me this?"

"Didn't seem right. If he wanted, he would've told you."

"Think him and Absurda was in love? Like really *in love*?"

"Falling in love was not part of Alchemy's big plan back then."

70

THE MOSES CHRONICLES (2014)

Seeing Is Disbelieving

Almost naturally, as if there could be no other outcome, Jay and Moses once again became a couple. They took beach walks, went to movies and art events, and spent most nights at her condo. Only the barrier of meeting his new family, which he'd erected after the evening at the theater, stayed the cementing of their second-time-around relationship.

That afternoon, Jay was picking Moses up at noon at his acupuncturist (almost sheepishly he had begun a regimen as part of his recovery: acupuncture, a strict diet, yoga, and weight training). They were driving up to Topanga for lunch with only Persephone and Laluna, which suited Jay just fine. Alchemy had zipped off to San Francisco to meet with Frieberg and Loo, the Internet whiz kids behind riteplay.com. Alchemy's Audition Enterprizes had supplied the seed money and became a major stockholder, and Google was making an offer to buy the company. Salome was in Chicago, accompanied by Tryx, where she was giving a lecture and receiving an honorary degree at the Art Institute.

They entered the hidden drive located about seven minutes up Topanga Canyon Boulevard from PCH. Fifty yards deeper into the woods, they stopped at the guardhouse manned by graduates of a Nightingale jobs program for former convicts, before driving up the half-mile private road. Jay parked the car in the large circular driveway.

In the garden, on her knees with a beer bottle by one side, Laluna tended to her flower bed. Dressed in woolen leggings that looked as if they were patched together from thrift shop sweaters, a thigh-length orange flannel shirt, short hair porcupining chaotically, no makeup on her smooth, tanned skin, Laluna struck Jay as carefree, young, and successful—yet her large, oval brown eyes seemed to deflect the gaze of anyone who stared too long and exuded an almost defiant aura that warned the uninvited to keep their distance. Jay guessed that it was the tension between vulnerability and stubborn independence that attracted Alchemy so ineluctably to Laluna.

Jay couldn't balance her fluctuating emotions. Jealousy, because Laluna and Moses shared a child, hesitancy because Laluna seemed to float in her own world. Yet Jay found herself wanting this young woman's approval.

Moses picked up and hugged Persephone, who settled happily in his arms. "Say hi to your auntie Jay." The greeting instilled a special sense of security in Jay about her future with Moses. Persephone tucked her head shyly into Moses's chest. Jay noted Persephone's pale skin and light brownish hair, like Moses's, and her hazel eyes that looked like neither Moses's, Alchemy's, nor Laluna's.

Laluna waved to Moses and washed off her hands with the water hose. She and Jay shook hands. Moses carried Persephone as the four strolled along the gravelly paths winding around the grounds, until they stopped in front of Salome's studio.

"Jay, Mose says you're a fan of Salome's art." Jay nodded. "You want to peek inside?"

"Love to but..."

Moses had never been inside. His eyes darting anxiously, he muttered, "I don't know."

"C'mon, Mose." Laluna glanced at Jay, her first sign of kinship. "*We* know you want to. We'll protect you from her evil spirits." Laluna turned to her daughter. "Perse, honey, you want to visit Granmamma's studio?" She nodded emphatically. "Perse sits or naps with her while she's working."

Laluna dropped her empty beer bottle into a recycling bin and took Persephone from Moses, and with her free hand pushed open the two glass doors. "I call this her 'mad room.' She gets mad when anyone goes in without her permission, but when you do, it might drive *you* mad."

Laluna held the door. Jay, then Moses, stepped gingerly into the first of three 750-square-foot spaces with twenty-foot ceiling and multiple skylights. They were engulfed by scores of clocks. Clocks with numerical signs and in languages ranging from Old English to Arabic to Chinese. Clocks with no numbers at all. Some hand-carved in wood, some one of a kind, some purchased at Ikea. Others made of cheap plastic or various forms of cast metal. Two clocks made out of rocks. One sundial on the floor. A seven-foot-tall wire spiral clock. A slew of wristwatches side by side: Salvador Dalí with his mustache as the hour and minute hands, Annie Oakley with six guns as the hands, Smokey the Bear and another with Jesus on the Cross. A replica of an ancient Greek water clock. From hundreds of years old to digital. Three cuckoo clocks. Not one clock ticktocked. Salome set and then disabled each clock to the moment she got it. In bold two-foot-high letters, scrawled across the floor in red chalk: THE END OF TIME STARTS NOW.

"Got no idea what she intends to do with this stuff. She's told me she doesn't believe in time. I look at this and, hmm... Who am I to question her?" Laluna led them behind a black curtain into a space of equal size, without windows or skylights. Paints, brushes, signs, books, rocks, twigs, stacks of torn wallpaper, coins, movie posters, piles of newspaper and magazine images, Kewpie dolls, Indian Ganeshes, an old, empty gumball machine filled with tiny pebbles.

Laluna clicked on a remote control and a TV nestled in the corner started playing. The images began with Salome's youthful, near-perfect face morphing into its present profile, marked by the vicissitudes of age and madness, followed by images of her creations melting and distorting in a distinctly trippy fashion through various stages of her career. The soundtrack played splices of the Insatiables' "Savant Sensation Bluz," Miles Davis's "Blue in Green," and Davis's version of Lauper and Hyman's "Time After Time." A half-delighted, half-frightened squeal erupted—it sounded as if it might be coming from the video, until they heard "Unc Mose!" They hurried through another black curtain to the back room, where Persephone stood beside a nude life-size body caste of Salome, and was staring at the never exhibited collages, done in *Baddist Boy* style, of Salome and a man dressed in Nazi uniforms. They were holding a baby that they were either throwing into or pulling from a fire pit. The baby's head was a photo of Moses taken off the SCCAM Web site. Across the top, in skeletal letters, she'd scrawled "Child Sacrifice?" Moses eyed Laluna and signaled, *Time to go.*

Jay clasped Moses's hand as they speed-walked back to the main house. They avoided speaking of what they'd seen. They ate a late lunch on a glass patio that overlooked the Pacific. Laluna kept nudging Persephone to eat her lunch instead of play with it. Moses offered support. "My mom said I never ate much until I was ten or so." Laluna's stare fixed on her caprese sandwich. Moses quickly changed the subject. "I hope Alchemy gets what he wants from Spencer and Amy. Those teen titans of the tech world could really help the foundation."

"Yeah, I guess." Laluna opened another beer and took a gulp. "So, Mose, you're Alchemy's political guru."

"I wouldn't go that far."

"I would. I got a question, and don't bullshit me. Is what he wants to do with the Nightingale Party a total waste of energy and money? He's so obsessed. I start out talking about what to eat for dinner or rewatching *Battlestar Gallactica* and he finds a way to talk about 'the third way.'"

"If I thought it a waste of time, I wouldn't be so involved." Moses started to list their agenda: changing the health system from "Medicare for the aged" to "Medicare for all," taxing all religious institutions like businesses, redefining the Patriot Act. Laluna quickly looked bored. "I'm not exactly sure how or if we can do it, or what he expects. Not exactly."

"I guess that makes two of us. When you know, please tell me if you think he's going to make a fool of himself. You'll tell me? Promise?"

"Promise."

After they finished lunch, Laluna unexpectedly announced that she had to leave. "Got a meeting in town with Jack Crouse. He's a fan." Crouse, perhaps the most famous movie star in the world, possessed charisma and appetites equal to Alchemy's. "His friend, who calls himself Swami Barker"—she rolled her eyes as if to say *whatever*—"wants me to do some music for his video."

"Godfrey Barker? High priest of the Church of Cosmological Kinetics?" Moses tried to repress his distaste.

"I don't know." She shrugged. "If he's a jerk, I can pass. Stay as long as you want. Take a swim. Or a spa. I'll be back in a few hours. The nanny can watch Perse. Enjoy the sunset. There's plenty to drink."

Jay wanted to take a swim, so Laluna showed her to a room with a selection of bathing suits.

Laluna swung back to the patio where Moses, paying no heed to the majestic views of the Pacific, was checking his iPhone for the latest news. "Hey, Mose, you'll know if the world explodes."

"I guess I'm as obsessed as Alchemy. Always was."

"Look, I'm sorry I talked you into going in, you know, there."

"Should've been prepared when entering Salome's Fun House without a ticket."

"Sooo right. What's with Salome and that guy in the uniform? Hadn't seen that before."

"That man was my father."

"Holy shit. Was he really..."

"Yes. Alchemy never told you?"

"Neither did you, and he said he doesn't know that much about him. Since he doesn't know that much about his own father, it made sense."

"Neither of us know that much."

"Jay looked so upset for you. She's cool. So, you guys getting married again or what?"

"Don't think so. No need. I'm keeping my own place. I think it's better for now. Mine's small and a mess, but I like it. She's okay with that."

"I got this feeling that you and Alchemy, well, you have the same idea that a house is a place to sleep and take cover, but you kinda live elsewhere."

"I've gotten more like that."

Laluna took off. While Jay swam in the heated pool, Moses sat beside Persephone in her room and she showed him her drawings. After which Moses sat with her while they ate dinner. They returned to Persephone's room and Moses read her a bedtime story. When he kissed her good night, she meowed, "I love you, Unc Mose. Come back soon."

Back at Jay's condo in a quiet pocket of Century City–Rancho Park, while Jay slept, Moses fretted deep into the night over what he'd seen inside his mother's studio. *Get over her denial.*

I'm fifty-seven years old. I can't get over it. I tried. When I saw her studio, I thought I was going to have a heart attack. Why is she treating me like this? Why? Because she is NUTS. What did I ever do to her—except live? Maybe if she knew the truth about Persephone she'd change. Love me. No—she'd hate me more.

Over a breakfast of scrambled egg whites and whole wheat toast, Jay said, "Persephone's face just lit up when she saw you. You think she has any clue?"

"No. I just spoil her. That's what uncles do." He sipped his coffee. "Jay, I'll be forever sorry for the way I acted. I'll always blame myself that we never tried for a child. No excuse, well, sort of an excuse, but it's also true, with me being sick and all, I was afraid I'd pass it on. Or die. I couldn't handle it."

"I didn't handle it so great either. I wanted what I wanted and I couldn't, I refused to see your side of it. So, yes, and no. I'm sorry and I'm not. Worst thing is listening to people with kids who think I'm a failure as a woman for not having kids. Or they have divine rights because they have kids and I'm some childless witch." She paused. She remembered that he *had* a daughter. "Sorry for, ah, just a pet peeve."

"No, I get it."

"Moses, I can't dwell on my regrets. I'm gladdest that we're back together." Still, she wondered: Would Moses have agreed to sire Persephone if they had not split up? If they'd had a child? What would have become of Moses if Salome had raised him? What if she had never slept with Alchemy? No, she couldn't allow herself to venture too far down those roads.

She and Moses were together again, Persephone gave him joy, and he and Alchemy were friends *and* brothers, and that is all that mattered.

"Me, too." Moses smiled wanly and took her hand in his. Almost as if he read her thoughts — that looking forward was essential to Jay's Livability Quotient.

71

THE SONGS OF SALOME

Crazy Like a Fox

Louise Vulter: So, why do you want to get involved in electoral politics?

Alchemy: When I lived in Berlin in the '80s with my mom —

Vulter: You speak German?

Alchemy: Badly. Living abroad helped me gain a wider perspective on the world. From our apartment, my mom and I watched a woman on the east side of the Berlin Wall attempting to escape to freedom — the tower guards shot her.

Vulter: That must have been traumatizing.

Alchemy: It left an indelible impression. When Gorbachev allowed the wall to come down, it was an act of great political courage that changed the course of history.

Vulter: Aren't you forgetting someone?

Alchemy: If you mean Reagan, I will concede that point for now, for the sake of my larger argument. *Politicians* achieved it. You can influence the ways of the world from outside standard power structures, but it must be from inside that you institute a vision for the future.

Vulter: And one of your visions is downsizing our nuclear arsenal by eighty to ninety percent. That is worrisome. It is not a vision shared by patriotic Americans.

Alchemy: As a patriotic American, I am worried, too. But our worries need to change, as do our visions. We are almost twenty years into a new century and we are still behaving like it's 1989. There are hundreds of better ways to use our power to keep America safe and strong. When I served in the army —

Vulter: Yes, yes, you volunteered to serve, only to quit early when family connections —

Alchemy: Louise, I'm not sure where you're getting your information, but my mother's health was in danger and as her only living relative —

Vulter: By danger, I know this may be hard, but you mean her hospitalization for mental illness?

Alchemy: Yes. I enlisted so I could serve my country in Iraq. Unfortunately, for many reasons, my mom's doctors urged, no, *demanded* I come home. I love my country, but I love my mother more.

Vulter: As well you should.

Alchemy: I want to return the focus to my vision of a future for America, and I'll be happy to come back to speak about mental illness and its effects on a family, but first, I'll say this. My mother's problems should not be equated with my seeking the counsel of a therapist, which helped me immensely in understanding and coping with her illness.

I'm not sure what most disturbed me, Vulter's discursive nuance-free style or my son's "my mother, the nutcase albatross" insinuations.

Laluna and I watched the cable news broadcast in the main house, another of our attempts at filial piety. Things went sour when I quipped, "At least he didn't bring up my 'troubles' after the woman was shot." Laluna picked up Persephone from her blanket on the floor where she'd been tapping on a tiny computer screen like a modern Etch A Sketch. "Time for bed. Kiss Granmamma good night." Laluna didn't like Persephone to hear a word of my vacation history, as if it would contaminate her. Only in my studio would she allow me to be alone with Perse. She wouldn't let me babysit at night without a nanny in range. When Perse got older, she damn well was going to hear all about it from me. (I'd tell her now, if Parnell Palmer would allow me to see her.)

I didn't demean myself by offering to take Persephone upstairs and sing her to sleep, only to be rebuffed. I watched alone as Vulter zinged Alchemy about his "Socialist dogma" and desire to close the stock market. He parried the attacks with aplomb. "Don't misquote me—I said I'd shed no tears if we could do away with traders and bankers who prey on the middle class. I made a fortune by taking risks on ideas I believe in, not companies that cut workers' salaries or fire people to aid the bottom line. I am all about creativity in all forms and profiting from it and using that money to do good." Nathaniel would have been proud.

Laluna returned during the audience Q&A. A jealous prig was asking Alchemy an insipid question about why he lived with a woman twenty years his junior. Next to him I glimpsed a familiar face.

"That woman"—I pointed at the screen—"do you recognize her?"

"Sure, it's Jay. She lives with Mose. He's probably backstage."

"So you know her?"

"Yeah. She's cool. It's not like we're BFFs or anything. I see Mose more than I see her."

Ah, yes. I remembered at a Nightingale-sponsored play, just before the curtain came up I caught a glimpse of him, mealy skinned and slinking down the aisle. My first reaction—another setup. Thankfully, no one attempted to force a confrontation. During intermission I followed the woman, who was clearly with him, and tapped her shoulder just outside the restroom. Startled, she spun around. "Are you *his* wife?" I asked.

"That is none of your business."

Her eyes shredded me with hatred, and for that I admired her. "You love him. That is good."

"You are missing out by not loving him."

I stared now at the TV. Laluna had muted the sound and was already texting someone. As the credits rolled, I saw Alchemy, Vulter, him, and his wife talking and laughing together.

I waved good night to Laluna, who barely waved back. I walked to my studio, Margarita's words circling above me: "You are their mother, you must be the one."

72

THE MOSES CHRONICLES (2015)

So Cynosure of Yourself

After years of debate, exploratory research, and financial planning, Alchemy had dived into assembling a "professional" political team that would aid in his run for the presidency in 2020. Alchemy was seriously considering hiring Dewey Winslow to be his chief political consultant, but before making a final choice he wanted Moses's opinion.

Moses drove alone to Winslow's Dana Point home. He and Alchemy welcomed Moses to the wing of the house that served as Winslow's office. In his pink Lacoste shirt, Gucci glasses, and a caterpillar mustache, he impressed Moses as someone who'd spent his childhood summers partaking in the Newport, Rhode Island, regatta. A modest five foot six and muscular, he assumed a larger presence by thrusting his chest forward. Alchemy introduced him as the "best political consultant in the business."

"Patronizing me already? And why not? With everything I'm going to do for you." Winslow guffawed. They took seats around a table carved from an oak tree trunk, which he quickly explained was not taken down for logging but had been damaged during a lightning storm. It was laid out with snacks and two pitchers of iced tea, two pitchers of lemonade, and two open bottles of white and red wine. Moses noted the photographs on the walls of Winslow with Nancy Pelosi, Barbara Boxer, and other California Democratic luminaries.

Winslow began with his prepared remarks. "Moses, your synopsis of third-party movements is impressive, as is your analysis of how, in the last elections, more people, both white and nonwhite, stayed home than voted for either candidate. Your hypothesis that they did this not because they were uninterested but because neither candidate enthralled them opens the door for us."

He took a few gulps of lemonade and continued, consciously directing himself toward Moses.

"Alchemy already made it clear that he does not want a 'spin doctor.' I prefer to call myself a 'contextualizer.'" Moses took out a pad and pen from his frayed brown leather briefcase. Winslow stopped him. "Sorry, no note taking, no tapes today. Questions?"

"We want to undo the status quo. You are the establishment. The last time any national third-party candidate got anywhere, and Nader doesn't apply here, was Ross Perot in 1992 and he soon fizzled out. Why are you doing this?"

Winslow, unperturbed, shifted from his effervescent prattle-patter to a measured imperiousness. "My father was an air traffic controller fired by Reagan in '81. He couldn't get another decent job, tumbled into a sinkhole, and never dug himself out." Winslow's face didn't betray a scintilla of emotion. "I've worked within the establishment for over twenty years. The 'great hopes' of my party have let me down. As

Alchemy says, we need a twenty-first-century Social Contract. Is this venture risky? Sure. What defines failure? Not getting Alchemy elected president, not establishing a third party—or not pursuing the dream?" He sipped his lemonade again. "I'm not looking to make friends. I got one." He nodded toward a white cat sleeping on a large pillow in the far corner of the room. "I honestly don't know what 'winning' means here. I just want to help."

"Whatever it is, what is your 'winning' strategy for us?"

Winslow picked up a sealed plastic bag and tossed it to Moses. "Open it. Take a close look." The bag contained four cloth wipes, which Moses examined skeptically.

"It says here, 'Four Fabulous Colors, Red, Green, Blue, and Yellow.'"

"And?" Winslow challenged him.

"Um, they're all blue."

"Correct!" Winslow laughed loudly. "Back in the late '80s I was the kid gofer at AMACON Worldwide ad agency on a campaign for these wipes. We used all four colors in the ads. In the stores, only one out of every ten bags had four colors. The rest, all blue—it was so much cheaper to produce. They sold hundreds of millions, ninety percent of them blue." Winslow caught a subtly skeptical glance between Moses and Alchemy. He dropped the wipes angle, and his tone became more serious. "Lincoln said, 'You can fool some of the people all of the time, and all of the people some of the time, but you can't fool all of the people all of the time.' That's where Abe got it wrong. You only have to fool fifty point one percent. With a third party, you need even less." He turned toward Alchemy. "My aim is not to fool people but to persuade them that you are the all-American great leader that the country needs now."

Moses understood it wasn't essential for him to like Winslow. They needed someone like him. And Winslow was about to make it even more clear why they needed him.

"Alchemy, despite you being what I call 'a public domain celebrity' for over twenty years, my guess is you got a few skeletons I'll need to deal with. Music is a dirty and corrupt business, but it's the minor leagues compared to politics." A woman knocked on the door and entered. "My partner, Elizabeth Borden, the pretty face and charming personality of the organization. She is also the finder and keeper of the skeletons."

Borden wore light red lipstick on her thin lips and a navy blue pantsuit that epitomized seriousness. She passed folders to the three of them and sat in the fourth chair. Winslow resumed. "Drugs? No problem. The Nightingale Foundation programs negate prior indulgences. Years of therapy? I can turn that into an asset if you don't mind me referencing your mother's past."

"Fine, within limits."

"We'll need you to verify what's in here and fill in what we've missed." Borden spoke in a clipped tone.

"Candy Rappa?" Winslow looked up from the pages and whistled.

"She'll help with the porn vote—it's um, huge." They all looked at him quizzically. "Bad joke." Alchemy grinned.

"Tonguing and gunning?" Winslow asked, befuddled.

"Just a little harmless sex thing."

"Hmm." Winslow angled his head to the left and then to the right, as if he were working out the cricks in his neck or maybe his thoughts. "Sex is not harmless, but Clinton proved it need not be fatal. It's the Tiger Woods–Derek Jeter duality. Tiger Woods presented himself as the faithful family man while diddling everything that moved. The public turned on him, and he never recovered. Derek Jeter never claimed to be anything but a playboy. He's a hero to men, and women still love him." Winslow purposefully paused. "Most Americans will accept you if you present yourself as who you are. They hate lying, hypocrisy, and bad judgment. An affair with a porn star raises questions of judgment. Still, I can handle that." Winslow leaned forward in his chair, his voice almost mellow. "The affair with Absurda when she was with Mindswallow, and, I'm sorry to bring this up, but one other affair, with uh, how should I put this—"

"Jay," Moses interrupted him. None too thrilled with hearing Jay mentioned in the same conversation as a porn star, he clenched his fists and uttered the necessary assurance. "It happened before Alchemy and I met and, although I hope it doesn't come up, if it does, it won't be a problem."

Alchemy flashed Moses a thank-you smile before interjecting, "No matter what the rumors say, I did not have sex with Absurda before, during, or after Ambitious and Absurda's relationship."

Winslow inhaled, his cheeks expanding and then slowly contracting. "There's a story, apocryphal or not, but apropos. Early in his career, Lyndon Johnson spread the rumor that his opponent slept with pigs. Johnson knew it was a lie, but he said, 'I only need him to deny it.' Denial gives a story credibility and forces me to do plenty of extra contextualizing. Look at all the time and resources wasted on the idiocy of the Obi birther bullshit. The Kerry people totally misplayed the Swift Boating assassination. I follow the axiom, 'Do unto others before they do unto you.' My job is to find the best narrative to give you credibility by contextualizing her extensive sexual history—"

"Find another way. I liked to fuck. Absurda liked to fuck. We fucked a lot—separately. End of story. Equality in fucking without judgment is one of the reasons I'm doing this. Real equality in all forms—legal, financial, and moral—for all."

Alchemy turned his gaze slowly to each of the people in the room so they fully understood: He makes the rules.

Moses pulled a paper from his briefcase. "Religion worries me more than sex. I took this from Jefferson in a letter to Richard Rush: '...religion, a subject on which I have ever been most scrupulously reserved. I have considered it as a matter between every man and his maker, in which no other, & far less the public, had a right to intermeddle.'"

"Moses, that's good but too heady for the everyday sound bite. It's my job to simplify."

Borden had been sitting mum. She eyed Winslow, who gave her the go-ahead. "Speaking of religion, your biggest liability may be Laluna's budding relationship with Godfrey Barker and his church. What exactly is the nature of the relationship?"

Alchemy answered perfunctorily, "Jack Crouse persuaded her to do the music for a Cosmological Church video."

An unsatisfied Borden continued, "It's poison. You have to end it. If you don't, I have advised Dewey that we cannot sign on."

Alchemy, visibly bristling, got up from his chair. "You mind?" He lit a cigarette, took two puffs, and then stubbed it out in an empty ashtray.

Moses never anticipated Winslow turning them down for this reason. "Dewey, it hasn't hurt Crouse's career."

"He's not running for political office. There are certain things you can't sell to the public as a politician." He veered his gaze from Moses to Alchemy. "You both need to consider the extreme challenges of this undertaking, from every conceivable angle."

"Challenges?" Alchemy opened his arms and held out his hands. "No problem. The impossible is the least that one can demand. I don't know any other way."

The meeting ended. Alchemy walked Moses out to the front of the house. "Thoughts?"

"He seems good. You checked him out thoroughly?"

"Yes, and still checking..."

"The one thing they didn't, you know. Maybe there are *other* things?"

"There are and I will tell them over dinner."

Moses understood that with Alchemy, everything was on a need-to-know basis—and there were things he didn't need to know and was better off not knowing.

Unsure of himself, Moses still pressed the point. "Persephone."

"You tell anyone?"

"No."

"Not even Jay?"

"No one." He suspected Alchemy would be unhappy but okay with him telling Jay, but he knew he would not be okay with Moses's breaking his word. And so, betraying everything life and history had taught him, Moses deluded himself into believing that telling this *one* lie was less destructive than the truth.

"Then it's only you, me, and Laluna."

"Right."

"Mose, we're crossing the Delaware. You know the passwords."

Driving back to the Laguna hotel, Moses reflected on his brother's role as pop icon gone political. In our culture, he thought, stars live a far different reality from the rest of us, a reality where rumors become truths and where what is seen by others is *the truth*. All else happens in a vacuum where there is no identity without others to give one definition. Alchemy understood that he, as Alchemy Savant *star*, thrived in a public reality consisting solely of the external and the immediate. He constantly needed to reassure the public that *his* future was essential to *our* future. In this age of multiple, uncertain realities, stars are the existential heroes of our time, and stardom allowed Alchemy, and even the skeptical Moses, to believe in the reality of the impossible dream.

73

MEMOIRS OF A USELESS GOOD-FOR-NUTHIN'

Spittin' Image, 2016

After a year and a half of touring with Ferricide, I get back to L.A. I don't see Alchemy except on TV, so I don't expect it when he calls me up and says me, him, Lux, Silky, and Laluna need to meet. He wants each of us to pick two older Insatiables songs and do an intro and we'll release them off our Web site as a free download.

I show up early 'cause I'm interested in, well, snooping around. There's a slew of cars in the side lot and I wonder if I got the wrong day. The huge room where the projector use to be is now a banquet room. Also they added on a small screening room. Waiters are serving drinks and hors deserves. I pop open a beer. Alchy is spieling, circled by a bunch of political groupies. "My aim is to usher in the postpatriarchal. I want the world to be a better place not just for my daughter, but for all daughters no matter their race, religion, or lack of religion. I don't mean just by picking a woman for VP. Of course that is important. I don't want to change biology. I love being a man. But I often wish I'd been born a woman..."

He meant all that crap. Only Alchy, if he'd been born a woman, she'd still be a control freak.

I see Hugo Bollatanski hovering over the buffet table. He got gray hair and a droopy face. I don't care if Alchy has forgiven him for the shit he pulled with Absurda, I'm thinkin' of giving him an old-fashion McFinn hello when some dude taps my shoulder. It's Spencer Frieberg with Amy Loo next to him. We never met and they want to thank me 'cause Audition Enterprizes put up money for ritevway.com, the microblogging site. I ponied up for that one, 'cause I passed on riteplay.com, which caused me to make like five mil to Alchy's hundred mil. I wonder if they'll still be Alchemy fans when he starts taxing them at ninety percent! They introduce me to Elizabeth Borden and Dewey Winslow, who is Alchy's political pals. They ask if they can conversate with me sometime about Alchemy. I say sure, but not today.

I excuse myself and check out the house. It's the only place Alchemy has lived in for more than a few hours before thinking about moving. Laluna supervised some renovations like the glass patio and making the third-floor two bedrooms into one big one for them and building a playroom for Persephone, and her toys and shit is everywhere. No doubt about it, they love and spoil that kid. He moved the Select-o-matic and a couch into one of the downstairs rooms that has piles of books and magazines on the floor. Looks like he inherited Nathaniel's filing system. Instead of his collection of old music mags like *Trouser Press*, *Creem*, and *Punk*, I now see politico mags.

I want to investigate my former room, so I start up the staircase when one of the ex-con security guards puts his up hand, "Sorry, off-limits." There's a photo of us on the wall from about '98. "See that? Not off-limits for me." He steps aside. For years, "my room" hardly been touched, but now I guess Laluna fumigated me out of there with a paint job. There's nuthin' in there but one double bed and a coupla dressers.

I'm heading down the hallway when I hear Mose and Laluna coming up the stairs. They're laughing and all buddy-buddy. Mose is saying, "I agree we have to act together, and do what is best for Perse." They clam up the second they see me. Laluna gives me a hug. Me and Mose shake hands.

Persephone rushes out of her room and jumps in Mose's arms and kisses him. "Unc Mose, come in here, I want to show you my crayon box and crinkly paper Granmamma gave me."

"Okay, honey, but I only have a few minutes. Your daddy and I are working today." He nods to me and they go into her room.

I says to Laluna, "You hiding out from the do-gooder I'm-better'n-you brigade?"

"Not my kind of peeps."

"Mine either."

"I do have to make a brief appearance." She sticks a finger in her mouth like she wants to gag.

"How you dealing with all this shit?"

"Mostly, I don't. I do what I want. He's always bouncing ideas off me. That's fun."

"Yeah, he always wanted my 'perspective.' I knew he always wanted this but I still don't get it."

"Like he says, if someone with his money and influence won't do it, only the assholes will."

I prefer not to opine on that one, so I says I'm gonna go hang out in the studio.

"Ambitious, give me thirty minutes and I'll meet you. We can kick around some tunes. Figure out our choices for the promo."

On the way to the music studio I see Salome in the space between her cottage and her art studio. She's relaxing on a lounge chair under an umbrella, reading a book. Her hair is gray streaked and not as long as it used to be. Her face got some old-age lines, but she's looking pretty good.

"Is that the still-infantile-but-no-longer-an-infant known as Ambitious Mindswallow? Sit down," she orders and places the book under her chair next to her flashlight. I pull up a lounge chair. "What brings you up to our cozy hideaway?" I explain that I'm early for an Insatiables meeting, and ritzy politicos ain't my type.

"You know the only place to spit in a 'ritzy' man's home?"

I let loose on the ground.

"No, you silly boy — in his face. Only this ritzy man is my son."

"What I hear, he may not be so ritzy after tossing his fortune into this political Dumpster."

"I commend him for it. It's what he and Nathaniel always planned, had he stayed with us." I know better than to talk politics with Salome, so I don't say nuthin'.

"I am upset with you, you know why?"

"I thought you was always upset with me, so, nope."

"Specifically because I never heard from you after Nathaniel moved on. For all the teasing, he was quite fond of you."

I did feel shitty, only I'm not sure how to handle those things. "Alchemy said the funeral was private. And, Salome, Nathaniel died years ago and you seen me since."

"I could explain to you that there is no such thing as time." She let out her loony tunes laugh goin' up the scale. "There is no statute of limitations on expressing sorrow."

"Why is there no such thing as time? I'm starting to feel old."

"Tell me, how often do you think about Absurda?"

I says, "How do you mean 'think'?"

She pats me on the head. "Nice to hear how you remember her, but that kind of fantasizing has nothing to do with time. I can't divulge anything of such import to *you*." She laughs loud. Salome is still as biddy-bip as the day I met her. And I still feel old, and Absurda is still dead.

"Speaking of the once dead and still alive, is my son's so-called brother here?"

I'm perplexed for a second. "You mean Mose? Yeah, just seen him before I come over. Was with Persephone and Laluna."

"Damn it. I may have to go and put a stop to that." She stops. Looks up. "Beware, we have an intruder."

Standing about ten feet away is a woman who looks like Salma Hayek. "Hi, I'm Carlotta, I planned today's event and I'll be supervising the annual Super Bowl party."

I wonder if she can get us a serious football pool, instead of Alchemy's usual pools on the over/under on how many times the announcers call the players "heroes," coaches "geniuses," and compare football to war.

"Laluna asked if there is anything special you would like to eat or drink today or on Super Bowl Sunday."

Salome waves her toward us. "First, my son should ask me, not you or Laluna. I don't blame you. You don't know better.

I'm good today, thank you. I will *not* be partaking in the Super Bull festivities. You like football, don't you, Ambitious?" Before I answer, Salome says, "What about you, Carlotta?"

"It's not my favorite sport. I have to get back, but if you change your mind anytime between now and the day of the party, I can bring you what you want." She hands Salome a card and starts back down the path.

"Cute, yes? Good smell, too. Hello, Ms. Solano!"

"Shhh." I'm shaking my head. Yeah, that worked.

"Please come back!" A little startled, Carlotta turns around. "I want you to formally meet Ambitious Mindswallow. You know who he is?"

"Of course." She shoots me a party-planner smile.

"I've known him since he was a teenage killah, and I can sense he's got, to use his oft-stated phrase, 'a hard-on' for you."

I'm mumbling, "Oh, shit, Salome, shaddup."

"It's no coincidence you arrived while he was visiting with me. Please, give him a chance." She's pushing me out of the chair. "Get up. Go with her."

I know better than to rile up Salome, so we start walking back to the house. I says, "I'm sorry. Salome is ... different ..."

"Is she right?"

"About what?"

"Don't play stupid."

"Well, yeah. I'd love to ask you out."

"It's not proper to socialize while I'm working. Take my card." She swallows me with her big brown eyes and big breasts, and I am a goner.

74

THE MOSES CHRONICLES (2016)

The Revolution Will Be Digitized

Securely reunited, Moses joked to Jay that he hadn't been, well, less unhappy in years. They laughed at his reluctance to say the word "happy" without the prefix "un." Whatever the reason, the passage of time or repression, the Jay-Alchemy affair no longer ignited his jealousy or feelings of inadequacy. When Jay attended a Nightingale function, she and Alchemy exchanged pleasantries and that was it. Mostly, Jay and Laluna sat together or hid in a corner. The two of them got along well, actually liked each other, but their differences in age and basic interests kept them from reaching out for a closer relationship.

Moses threw himself full force into expressing the Nightingale Party's philosophical and political goals as talking points for the press, or young candidates they hoped would vie for local positions, laying the groundwork for Alchemy's 2020 presidential run. Professorially speaking, "philosophy" and "talking points" remained incompatible, and some of his former colleagues at SCCAM reproached him for crossing enemy lines from academic to political operative. He countered, or maybe rationalized, by saying they're just different forms of educating.

With Alchemy staking a huge chunk of his fortune on the party's future, all other sacrifices became trivial. Moses remained both somewhat apart from and overseer of those who ran the analytics, local offices, advertising, polling and everyday PR flackery, Web and social media. All heads of the departments sent him weekly summaries, which he put into one-page summaries for Alchemy. The Nightingale Party occupied the same building as the reduced-in-size Nightingale Foundation.

Laluna, who claimed no special interest in delving into the netherworld of Cosmological Kinetics, had finished the music for the video and bid Crouse and Barker adieu, which satisfied Winslow. Borden asked Moses for his permission to speak to Jay. Less than jubilant, Jay agreed. Moses asked Borden not to send him a copy of or even notes of the interview.

The rumored Alchemy-Absurda relationship and the possible blowback from the unpredictable Mindswallow still rankled Borden. Moses asked what specifically worried her. Oddly, she clammed up. He took the bait and pressed Alchemy, who, exasperated, told Moses, "Get Cherry on it if you want to." He called her. A few weeks later, she informed him she had a tape he needed to hear. Moses asked her to send it to his home.

Alchemy and Louise Urban Vulter, who had jumped from right-wing media rabble-rouser to junior senator from Arizona, were in the middle of a ten-day barnstorming tour. Their next stop was at the University of New Mexico in Albuquerque, and Moses decided to go.

Vulter and Alchemy were vying to become the voice of the disaffected and disenfranchised. Vulter had tamed her belligerent style and presented herself as a representative of "*my silent minority, working- and middle-class real Americans.*" Of late, she'd made veiled references to breaking away from the Republicans and establishing the Reformation Party, which not only lessened the chances of Alchemy being branded the spoiler but also increased his chances for the future. Moses noted to Alchemy that the last time four serious candidates ran, Abraham Lincoln became the sixteenth president with thirty-nine percent of the popular vote.

In the ten minutes before they appeared on the stage, Moses observed the playful rapport between Alchemy and Louise. They'd found common ground that surprised them both: Alchemy's expertise in shooting guns, which he'd learned as a teenager in Virginia, Vulter's Insatiables fandom, and her reputation along Prescott's Whiskey Row as "one hell-raisin' bawdy babe."

The audience's questions showed a preponderant interest in all things Alchemy, from his opinions on other bands to his political positions. Vulter, sensing Alchemy taking over the evening, reverted to her go-to issue and jingoistic persona, unleashing an anti-Islamic fusillade.

"Alchemy, your fandom is a nice subject, but what of your plans to dismantle our nuclear arsenal? How do you propose to stem the Islamic tide? One that would ban your music, prohibit your lifestyle? We're idly witnessing this imminent peril threatening you and all the faithful. I demand we use all of our power to save *our* American way of life. The attacks on our institutions and governmental systems are not cyberterror — they are cyber*war* waged by Islamic technojihadists. Suicide bombers without the suicide. *I* know how to win this war. Singing a nice song won't do it."

Many in the audience applauded passionately.

Alchemy, measuring the temperature of the crowd, began to sing: "Oneness though many / in this land o' plenty..." The audience joined in: "we are the ones who are proud to share / open your arms if you dare."

"C'mon, Louise, join the rest of us. Don't be so stodgy," Alchemy teased, fully aware that Vulter would not appreciate being called "stodgy."

She joined in: "Let's have some fun / all hail E Pluribus Unum Wampum."

When the auditorium quieted, he began again, "Now, don't we feel better? Seriously, Louise, I don't disagree that this is a major problem for now and the future. A song won't stop a real or cybermissile, but it can make us stop and think about what we share, so that the missile isn't fired. Taking an eye for an eye, or four eyes of theirs for one of ours, isn't a solution. Better to change cyberswords into cyberplowshares."

Back in the hotel, eating a room service dinner, Alchemy listened to the Cherry-supplied recording with his usual insouciance:

A woman's voice: "Oh, my God... Oh, my, my... Oh, baby, let me..."

Alchemy: "No wonder... they call you gums."

"Jesus fucking Christ. Yeah, that's me and Absurda. I forgot all about that. Goes back to when we were at Juilliard. All of us were taking turns faking sex with each of the others in the room. Somebody edited out their voices."

"You want to talk to Borden? Maybe give Cherry the names of the other people there?"

"I'll try to remember who they were."

"How is Mindswallow going to respond if this gets out?"

"He, Carlotta, this new woman he's been seeing, Laluna, and I had dinner not long ago. I think he's over being pissed at me. I'll talk to him." One of his three cells rang. "Hi, Louise, yes it was a good night. What's up?"

Moses motioned asking if he should leave. Alchemy shook his head. "Yeah, saw it. What can we do? Can't promise no more songs." Vulter was vexed by the local TV news station playing only a sound bite of the audience singing. "I'll call the station and ask them to add something. Okay? And yeah, I say take it."

When he hung up, he explained to Moses the real reason for her call. "The bigwigs in her party offered her a spot on the new Committee on Anti-American Activities. She's ambivalent. Her libertarian and 'security' instincts clash."

The repeal of the laws that allowed the CAA to investigate and legally incarcerate American citizens by a star-chamber-like process, along with rewording and perverting the original intention of the Cyber Safety Acts, were central to the Nightingale Party's mission.

"You kind of like her, don't you?"

"She's more thoughtful, and funnier, than those on our side think. Sometimes she panders too much, and I wish she were a little less —"

"Intolerant? Anti-Islamic?"

"Rigid. Mose, she and I could be a formidable team. Don't go apoplectic. Never going to happen. We'd never agree on who should be on top"—a wisp of a smile crossed his lips—"of the ticket..." Moses laughed. "Mose, I got a more serious question. What do you think of shifting tactics, so I go for California governor next year? I can win. Then we go presidential in '24."

"I'm thinking it's an idea to consider for not very long. Unless it's a total disaster, the '20 election sets the stage for '24. If you run for president and don't win, that's expected—we go again in '24. Run for governor and don't win—you're branded a 'loser.' If anything, having no record is better than a blemished one. What brought this up?"

"I got a feeler from the Independence for California peeps. They already have a half million signatures for the ballot initiative. They'll file when they reach a million. They're in search of a standard-bearer with name recognition and clout."

"If that's the case, then this is the worst idea since the initiative to make California six states. IFC wants California, Washington, and Oregon to secede and get Vancouver to join in a union to form a loose association with the U.S. and Canada."

"I know what they want."

"Then how can you?...It's akin to the Articles of Confederation, which failed. It's nuts. Impossible."

"Really?!"

Moses always marveled that in Alchemy's world "impossible" did not exist. He also saw that instead of getting tired, he was getting juiced and ready to riff deep into the night.

"Okay, Mose." He was standing now and circling around the room. "I'll talk to Winslow about the tape and IFC when I'm back in L.A. Get me more info on IFC and who's giving them money."

"Sure. I'll do some other research, too."

"But Mose, follow my reasoning here. You're the one who told me America is fracturing. That the three West Coast states have more common interests and beliefs than their neighbors in Arizona, Nevada, and Idaho. You're the one who said the three coastal states are among the best options for ringing up good numbers. That's fifty, sixty million people, and they have an economy that would rank among the largest in the world. Didn't you say that somehow these rifts need to be repaired or it could lead to permanent fractures? If I'm gov when it cracks..."

"I said *maybe* in fifty or a hundred years, because all empires run their courses. Not in five or ten years. I believe you can begin the repair we need now."

"Revolutionary change starts in the head, but it's the feet that make it happen. One can look back a thousand years easier than forward fifty. Be futurific and march forward."

Alchemy closed his eyes and seemed suddenly far away.

"Alchemy, what? Where are you? Say what you're thinking."

"That shit with Louise and the Muslims. Makes me crazy, too. But all this religious posturing has made the line separating church and state all but disappear. I'm going to make it reappear. Whether it's for governor or prez, you know it's going to come up again and again. I want to get out in front of it. And 'spiritual but not religious' is liberal bogusocity."

Moses was beyond wanting to argue with his brother. He wanted to go to bed, but Alchemy was in the zone.

"Mose, you're a progressive politically. But a true progressive has to make leaps in every direction. You still can't extinguish that niggling belief. I said belief, not doubt. Ninety, ninety-five percent of the time you don't believe in God, but a secret little piece of you still isn't sure."

"I doubt, therefore I am." A slight deprecating smile crossed Moses's face.

"I doubt, but still act, therefore I am. We're forty, fifty years into the new world of the digital age, and with the right vision we are on the cusp of a new political and social order. It took Christianity two hundred and fifty, three hundred and fifty years to become the historical force that dominated the last seventeen hundred years. Within seventy-five years of Gutenberg's invention, Luther and the Protestant Reformation took hold and undid the monolithic power of Catholicism in a timeframe that seemed, to them, unimaginably fast. The quantum revolution is not the future—it's the present. We're not in the Industrial Age anymore. It's the Cyber Age, and 'cyberplowshares' can take us to a new era where religion and nationalism are as archaic as idol worship and the steam engine. A man or a woman working with a binary device, not some papyrus or Gutenberg Bible—a believer in humankind's power and intelligence, will lead us to a Promised Land without God. Or to extinction."

75

MEMOIRS OF A USELESS GOOD-FOR-NUTHIN'

Ringolevio One Two Three , 2016–2017

I send Salome flowers and a note that I am truly sorry about Nathaniel. I also thank her for being Salome, 'cause Carlotta Solano ain't like most of the women I dated. She likes people and people like her, and she is as sweet as I am not sweet. She's thirty-one and never been married. Not a rock 'n' roll chick. Not even a fan of the Insatiables. We click in and out of bed, and she ain't no honey trap counting my bankrolls.

Her parents are still married and live in the same house in Cucamonga they bought when she was born. Her father works in a local air conditioning/heating repair business and her mom worked part time at the local school so she could be home with the kids. Carlotta moved to Eagle Rock after goin' to U.C. Riverside. Brother works in the AC business. They don't treat me either special or like a scumbag who is boffin' their daughter.

I feel like I swallowed a redbrick sandwich the day I propose. She jumps like ten feet in the air, which is the fucking answer I been waiting for. Carlotta don't want some *Entertainment Weekly*–style shindig with a fire-eating mariachi band and parachuting mermaids as bridesmaids. We get hitched over the Memorial Day weekend in her folks' backyard. Her dad won't let me pay for zip. I nix a church ceremony but I find a priest who agrees to perform the service for a donation. I invite my sister and my mom. Carlotta talks me into inviting my dad. I do not invite my brother. I warn them all to behave, which is like asking a monkey not to shit in the jungle. Ricky Jr., Lux, and Alchy is my best men and witnesses.

After dinner, Carlotta's pop makes a real nice toast. He asks if anyone else wants to make one, and Salome stands up. That gets me Nadling at super speed.

"I believe that the institution of marriage should be abolished, yet, as the matchmaker of this union, I accept the blame."

My mother blurts out, "I'll remind ya a that when Ricky fucks up." Carlotta is sitting between me and her mom and I see her squeeze her mom's hand.

"He won't, but if he does, they met at *my son's* house."

Alchy raises his glass toward Salome. "I'm always the beast of your burden of blame."

Salome sticks her tongue out at Alchy. "Many years ago I told a snarky little boy that he needed to grow some balls to become the Sancho Panza my son needed."

"Of evil," I yell. "Sancho Panzer of evil. I had to ask Alchemy who he was."

"Yes, yes, I did say that. I was wrong. You were not evil, just splenetic and misguided. And you became a great Sancho. Alas, you have been replaced by another…" She gives a sideways twitch at Laluna and we're all waiting for Salome to compliment her. Uh-uh. Alchemy looks like someone just barfed in his soup. "Ricky, you're not society's stereotypical ideal of a husband, but hell, I'm not society's ideal of a mother, so... Carlotta, you are blessed with the good fortune to have found a courageous and loyal partner who will always watch over you."

After the toasts and before dessert, my slobbering and soused dad starts poking Alchemy about Vulter. "She's one smart lady. Make a damn good president." He thinks this proves he ain't no sexist even though he says, "I'd sure like to give her 'a Real McFinn' night." Alchemy's so slick at playing drunks, he treats their moronic postulations like no one ever uttered them before. "You're right about her. Louise loves a good party, and she's smart and warm underneath."

Salome's antennae goes berserk and it's uh-oh time. She gets right in Alchemy's face.

"Underneath what? You can't trust her. She talks out of both sides of her mouth and she's lying from each side."

"How the hell would you know?" My dad is gearing up his nasty. Salome can match him nasty-for-nasty no problem.

"Nathaniel scouted behind enemy lines and listened to her radio program. I watched her on TV with Alchemy. Complex ideas confound her and her supporters."

"We all can't be a gen-ie-us and a crazy bitch like you. Or a millionaire commie like your son."

"Your simple-minded insults prove my point. You're a parasite who lives off your son, who Alchemy rescued from his misbegotten life, which, in effect, means *you* live off Alchemy the commie."

Alchemy slings his arm over Salome's shoulder and edges her away, which don't stop Mr. Must Have the Last Word. "Ya gotta be dumber than a Flushing cockroach to spend a dollar on that crap you call art!" Me and Alchy exchange frustrated sighs. I say, "Dad, shut the fuck up or you'll be on a plane in two hours."

Just as they're serving the cake, Laluna tells me that Persephone isn't feeling well so she is leaving early. Alchemy is sticking around. I got an idea that ain't the only reason she's gotta hop. Laluna gets that Salome was jabbing her as much as complimenting me, and she's PO'd 'cause Alchemy don't back her up that *she* is a great Sancho, which is the trap Salome set. No matter what he says, he can't win.

Carlotta walks Laluna out to the driveway. Alchemy is off in the corner of the yard with Salome, who says real loud, "She's now the leader of the Salome defamation league." I start to go toward them. For once, I'll play peacemaker.

Lux cuts me off. "Don't, bad move."

"Yeah," I says.

Then he teases me, "Who would've thought a once skinny little shit like you, with two bucks and a torn T-shirt to his name, would one day land such a great woman as Carlotta?"

"Who you callin' 'once' skinny?"

He pinches my belly through my shirt. "Okay, okay." I say, "but I know the real reason you shaved your head, and it ain't just for the look."

He says real stern, "What're you implying?" Then he cracks up. But he got me thinking, since I left home, I do got one *wonderful* fuckin' life.

76

THE SONGS OF SALOME

Say the Secret Word

My ancestors deserted me when I most needed them. To complete or abandon my Margarita mission was my question. Why? Why must I be the one? Yet, although I could not reach him through my DNA, I had sensated that night in the office that he was my son—and Margarita was right, his reappearance boded ill for Alchemy. I forced myself to drop by a few political or foundation events at the house. He was never there. I made an effort to be more solicitous of the entity known as "LAlunamy," hoping to glean more insight. When they rehearsed and recorded their album *Chansons*, often with Persephone by my side in the studio, I offered only kudos. I never criticized or asked if I could contribute. Or admitted my hurt when Alchemy allowed Laluna to choose another artist to do the art accompanying the text after I offered to help. I began to think that never seeing *him* again was no coincidence, and the completion of the mission might be unnecessary.

That changed after Mindswallow's wedding. Before we dressed for the festivities, I went to fetch Perse for a morning constitutional. Laluna was in the kitchen talking on the phone. I got a cup of coffee and sat across from her at the butcher block counter. She pulled at her lip piercing, her anxiety tell. "Okay, Got to go, Jack. Send me the download."

Sometime back, Laluna had come to my studio with Crouse and Godfrey Barker. Barker was a bloated-cheeked, potbellied blowhard whose uniform of silver-gray silk kurta and white pajama pants gave him the look of an irony-free '60s TV sitcom hippie, an unctuous purveyor of airy-but-not-airy-enough "science." I faked serenity as I showed them around. He paused in front of a *Baddist Boy* collage of the Pretender and Malcolm. "Ah, yes, I remember seeing them at your Hammer retrospective. I don't remember this particular one. Is it for sale?"

"I didn't exhibit it. And no, not to you."

He bared his teeth and smiled haughtily. "It's not for me."

"Who?"

"Someone I think you would approve of. Can I take a cell phone picture?"

He did. I never heard from him and never gave him another thought—not until that morning in the kitchen on the day of the wedding. Sounding a bit defensive, Laluna told me that Crouse wanted her to try scoring his new film.

"That's nice." I said. "Where's my granddaughter?"

"Alchemy is driving her to Mose and Jay's for the night. She loves being with them." She sounded far too self-satisfied. "Alchemy will drive us to the wedding."

I let it drop.

Except for the petulant Laluna, who left early to pick up Persephone, and maybe Ambitious's Neanderthal father, everyone had a swell old time. Alchemy beamed, elated for his true brother. In the car ride home, I broached the necessary topic. "I've been considering, maybe, that night in the Nightingale office—I may have let my myopia overtake my empathic impulses, with, you know"—his name choked in my throat—"him."

"You mean my brother, your son, Mose?"

"Yes."

Instead of compassion at my suffering over the turmoil of my lost child, my attempt at making peace elicited an accusatory question. "And now, years later, how do you intend to correct that myopia?"

"You and he are close. His wife seems to be friendly with Laluna. He spends time with Persephone. Maybe a family get-to-know-you session." My tactic was clumsy—I hate clumsy—my words sounded like someone else was speaking them. I backtracked. "I'm sorry. Maybe this is the wrong time. We can talk again and I'll explain how, from the moment of his conception, his life affected mine in only the most excruciating ways."

No sympathy. Only a lifeless, "I'll talk to him."

Alchemy never spoke his name again in my presence.

77

MEMOIRS OF A USELESS GOOD-FOR-NUTHIN'

Two Wrongs Don't Make a Wright, 2017

I forget about Elizabeth Borden 'til she e-mails me about a meet. I double-check with Alchemy. For a guy who spent so much energy fogging his personal life, this told me how much he wanted to do this shit. And wanted it from day one.

I meet Borden at the Kasbah offices. Right away she sticks a confidentiality agreement in my face that "prohibits" me from "disclosing to any individual" what we talk about. I sign it Ricky McFinn, which ain't been my legal name for years.

She starts with Nova's death and shows me phone records that I called Alchy before I called the cops. "Fuck, this was like a hundred years ago. He told me to call the cops and I did."

"What were Alchemy's relations to Ana Perez, who you knew as Falstaffa, and Martin O'Malley and their drug business?"

"He never did no drops. You gotta know he believes all drugs should be legal but that don't mean he supports using them. Matter of fact, he threatened to boot my ass out over my intake."

She's like a zombie with a voice that sounds like it's giving GPS directions. I got no patience for her bull, so I volunteer that I been in jail, punched people out, been banned from my share a hotels and restaurants, ingested boatloads a drugs, and who knows what the fuck else she would disapprove of, but I ain't running for nuthin', and it got nuthin' to do with Alchy.

She asks if Alchemy ever propagated the idea of a revolution. That's a laugher. I tell her that from the first day I met him he says how much he loves America. Since he made three, four hundred million bucks, even if he's gonna piss it away, I says, "What the fuck is he revolting against?"

Borden don't smile. "Do you know he met with Malcolm Teumer when you toured Brazil in 2006?"

"Nope. He was always meeting all kinds of people that I passed on. That some relative of Mose?"

She don't answer. Next up is "some of the women" in Alchy's life. This subject does not thrill me. "Judging by his relationship to Laluna, would you say he has an attraction for very young girls?"

"Who don't?"

She frowns. "Did he ever have relations with underage girls?"

Her attitude sounds like she got some info. "What do you think?"

"I think I asked you a question."

"Young ain't underage. And if you know Laluna, she was never young."

"What about Miranda Wright? Did he have relations with her? Mr. Mindswallow, why are you laughing?"

"'Cause you shoulda been a comedian."

I don't explain Miranda is someone Alchemy created as a signal for us, 'cause I'm thinking that may sound more suspicious. I say Miranda was a young groupie I never met. She don't give up. "So, did he have had relations with her?"

"My rule was if you think he fucked someone, then he did. So, probably yeah. Ask her."

"Is it true that you and Alchemy and sometimes Lux, you engaged in group sex with the same women?"

"Lady, you sound pretty damn pervey."

"Should I assume that is a yes?"

"Assume what you want."

"Okay, one last inquiry. What do you know about the relationship between Jay Bernes and Alchemy? How long did it last?"

"By 'relationship,' you mean how long did they hook up?"

"That's not what I said."

"What did Alchemy say?"

"He didn't. We spoke to her."

"She told *you?*"

"I didn't say that."

"I guess this confidentiality agreement goes one way, hah? I don't know squat about Mrs. Mose and Alchemy."

"Let's talk about Absurda and Alchemy and their relationship. How long did they date?"

"That's now a second 'last inquiry.'" I stand up. "And who says they dated?"

"I can't tell you that. My purpose is to protect Alchemy. Did the three of you orgy?"

I walk up to her and bend over so our noses is almost touching. "My purpose is to protect Absurda. The answer is NO." I pick up that agreement and rip it to shreds. "And I hear any shit that don't please me, that'll be your partner's face. So, Little Miss Scuttlebutt, you best be fucking careful."

78

THE MOSES CHRONICLES (2018)
Twilight of the Idols

Moses did his best to avoid any more face-to-face meetings with Salome in any incarnation — live, cinematic, or papier-mâché. In past years, Salome's possible presence, more than his disinterest in sports, led him to pass up the annual Super Bowl party. He thought this year would be no different until Alchemy texted that he was dropping by the office the Monday before the Super Bowl to invite the staff to the party. Alchemy also said he wanted to meet Moses in his office.

"I need you to come Sunday. Salome will stay in her cottage or leave altogether. Jack Crouse wants to donate a million to the Nightingale Party. I told him no. Maybe the foundation could use it. He also invited himself to the party."

"I read that Crouse is now one of Barker's handpicked 'seers,' so I guess, even if it goes to the foundation, you need to speak to Dewey."

"It gets trickier. Last night, we messed around with ideas for two new songs based on Salome's latest drawings for *Pearl Diver by the Black Sea.*"

"Are you thinking of re-forming the Insatiables?" Moses had suspected that someday Alchemy would miss making music.

"No. While we were playing, and I thought it was going really well, Laluna brings up that Crouse and Barker had come to the house to discuss doing a remix of the soundtrack she did for a new video. They convinced her to try their secret m-edit-ation orientation. It 'revealed' that despite having it all in the material world, she is 'unfulfilled.'" Alchemy's voice betrayed his exasperation. "I asked her again, 'Do you want me to quit politics?' She claims she's on board as long as she doesn't have to campaign. I asked if she changed her mind and wanted to join Lux, Silky, and Mindswallow, who are setting up a summer tour. She said no. For the two of us do a follow-up to *Chansons*? Possibly. Take a vacation? Yes, she wants to go far away from here, and without Persephone." Moses had sometimes suspected that Alchemy steamrolled Laluna into having a child before she was ready. Regardless of how much she loved Persephone, maybe that had sparked Laluna's restlessness. "And no, Mose, I have not been messing around."

"Is she?"

"She says no. I asked if she wanted to spend some time away from me. Am I being too cloying or too patriarchal? Not at all. She does exactly what she wants. If anything, she's spending too much time *without* me."

"Alchemy, I'm sorry. You should take that vacation. We'll hold the fort here and leave you two alone. And if there's anything else I can do, just ask."

"Thanks. I'll rent a place far away where we can record some songs, just chill. If all goes well, when I return I'll declare for the presidency in '20."

"I'm sure you and Laluna will work it out. Take as long as you need. But I have to say that Laluna taking up with Barker and Crouse again—not good. If you don't tell Winslow before he finds out, he may quit. We can't afford that now." Moses, lips tight, hesitated.

"Mose, what? I see you thinking."

"I'm asking you now, as your brother, one last time, please consider again the negative possibilities of this campaign."

"Mose." Alchemy's one blue, one green eye drilled into him like twin laser beams. "You can step away. I can't. I've spent many nights awake, speculating on every risk imaginable. I've crossed the Delaware. I've set the boats afire. There's no turning back."

Three days before the Super Bowl, Moses was in his office reviewing Alchemy's schedule and what would be the best time for him to take a long vacation. His phone beeped with a text message from Sidonna Cherry, whom they now kept on retainer. "Go outside. Now. Open the package in your office." A messenger, standing astride her motorcycle, helmet still on, handed him an envelope, which contained a burner phone and a piece of paper with a handwritten note.

It's a free country if you can pay for it.

After the 2000 election, American democracy is in a struggle for its survival.

America has aided and abetted the overthrow of at least a half dozen legally elected governments since 1953.

The Pasadena IVF
Miranda Wright

He recognized the phrases as comments he'd made while teaching at SCCAM and the name of the clinic where he had his sperm tested. Miranda Wright meant nothing to him. A few minutes later, Cherry called on the burner.

"Moses, the Committee on Anti-American Activities has been holding covert investigations, and you and your brother are among those on their hit list."

Naïvely, he had never fully comprehended the breadth of the CAA's audacity.

"How do you know? Why are you telling me?"

"Because I'm getting a goddamned subpoena."

"What the hell? Are you sure? Why?"

"They don't have to tell you that. But Parnell Palmer, the CAA chief investigator, and his creeps are not nearly as stealthy as they think they are. They started sniffing around me because I'm working for you. I sniffed back. They won't get shit from me."

"Thank you."

"Don't tell me any more. Talk to Alchemy. Toss the phone. I'll send another one next week."

The next day, Moses went to Cedars-Sinai to take his required every-six-months blood tests. Then he and Alchemy met for lunch at the Pig 'n' Whistle.

"Mose, how'd it go? That's doozie of a bruise on your forearm."

"Yeah. Happens. No results yet. I'm feeling okay. Lately the void is emptying into a bigger void. And this is why." He showed him the paper Cherry sent over. "According to Cherry, the CAA is investigating us. Who is Miranda Wright?"

"No one you need to stay awake worrying about. I also talked to Cherry yesterday."

"Maybe the CAA knows about the Pasadena IVF, the doctor who tested my sperm before, or the doctor who injected the sperm?"

"So what if they do? The Pasadena clinic has no connection to me. And my doc never knew I gave him your sperm. Mose, this is terrific. My—our—approval ratings are through the roof. Those appearances with Louise definitely helped. Cherry is right, we are scaring everyone."

"They've scared me back."

"Intimidation is their business. I won't blink first."

"Should we ask Cherry to do more recon?"

"Hold off. You rest. I'm going to need you more than ever. And don't worry, I got this."

79

MEMOIRS OF A USELESS GOOD-FOR-NUTHIN'

Dancing in the Dark, 2018

Me, Lux, Silky, and a few friends been jamming at the Echo, billing ourselves as the Ables 'cause we're working on touring together in the summer. We asked Laluna. She ain't into it. I'm hoping she changed her mind when she calls me the Friday before the Super Bowl. I ain't going to their party, 'cause I don't want Carlotta to work for Alchy (I want she should quit altogether). It's real curious when Laluna asks me to meet the next day in Elysian Park at Fix for coffee.

I get my double espresso and stroll to the patio, where Laluna is singing and playing behind a paper sign that reads NOW PLAYING — MARIA. This Maria got long blond hair, sunglasses, and no piercings in her lips. Not doing our stuff but some trad Gypsy music. She warns me off with a shake of her head. I sit alone. I give a coupla youngsters an autograph and take a pic with them. Most people in L.A. are cool about leaving you alone after that.

Laluna don't take off her wig when we walk down Echo Park Boulevard. I ask why the hell she's in disguise and say if she wants to play we can all jam, with or without Alchy. Again, no thanks, and she tells me she enjoys the anonymity. She's done "being a 'star.'"

"Laluna, what's Alchy say?"

"Call me Maria." I don't know if she means just for now or forever. I ain't going there. "I don't need his permission."

Her phone rings and she looks unhappy and declines. It rings again two minutes later. "Jack, I can't talk now... All is good. I'll see you at the party." She shoves the phone back in her pocket. "Ambitious, stop making that face. I'm exploring many new things and kinetic m-edit-ation is one of them."

"Lal—Maria, I don't know Crouse and I ain't as smart as you or Alchemy, but that fucker Barker is a con man supremo. Alchy can blind you with his spieling, but he is genuine. He ain't no scambooger."

"I appreciate your concern, but I didn't ask you here to discuss that. Do you know any woman or women Alchemy was in love with?"

"Nope."

"Never in all of those years?"

"Nope." She seems like she don't believe me. "Only him, best I ever met at keeping secrets." Except maybe Laluna. "Is Alchemy fuckin' around on *you*?"

"No."

I eyed her.

"Ambitious, I am certain he is not."

I buy that now because he'd never risk losing Perse. She, more than Salome or Laluna, is his kryptonite.

"What do you know about Absurda's abortion?"

"Just that she had one when she was sixteen and still living in Fond du Lac."

"That's it?"

"Yes. What's goin' on?"

We walk a bit without her answering. I figure she'll talk when she is ready, which she does. "Nathaniel donated his papers to Magnolia College, and Salome couldn't bring herself to look at them, so Alchemy and I dug our way through thousands of pages. He never threw anything out."

She hands me a crumpled piece of paper from the Riverhead Abortion Clinic, dated November 13, 1996, and the name Amanda Akin is typed on the top. I'm guessing Laluna don't know that is like six weeks after we broke up.

"Look at the emergency contact."

It's faded, but it reads goddamn Nathaniel Brockton?! That makes no sense. She never would've fucked him. Or him her. "You show this to Alchemy? He say it was his?"

"He was there when I found it. He and Absurda weren't ready to raise a kid. Because of the publicity, Nathaniel went with her."

Damn it. After all the time when he finally convinced me the shit between us was my fault, he was fuckin' lying to my face. I wanna go crush the bastid's head.

"Why you showin' this to me now?"

"Just come to the party tomorrow."

"Where the fuck is he?"

She clamped my wrist. Held it tight. "He's out of town on

political business for the day. Please, please don't contact him before." I'm sizzling and she can see it. "Come late if you can't control yourself. We'll talk after everyone else leaves. I need to settle some things once and for all."

"You ain't the only one."

80

THE MOSES CHRONICLES (2018)

At Close Range

Alchemy's call interrupted Moses and Jay's leisurely breakfast at the Saturday morning Venice farmers' market. He was calling from the Santa Monica Airport before jetting to Arizona for an impromptu meeting with Vulter. He anticipated Moses's question. "I am not partnering with her." He needed Moses to meet their lawyer Kim Dooley later that day at his apartment, not the offices or Jay's apartment. "Things are happening fast and more is going to happen. See you tomorrow. And don't be late. Don't be late."

While waiting for Dooley, Moses paced in his small living room. He stopped by the mantelpiece that held Hannah's menorah and his father's medal, constant reminders of his reconfigured identity. He still called himself a secular Jew, but the changes in his identity manifested themselves in the most unexpected ways—when he heard the subtle anti-Semitic slurs that popped up too often, he rebutted them with the authority of the outsider instead of the defensive stance of the "victim." He'd always wished he could tell his mom about the meeting with Teumer. She'd be proud. How lucky he felt that she raised him. At least he didn't have to explain the wild complexities of Persephone's birth to Hannah and why she would be, but couldn't be, a grandmother. Most of all, he hoped he had finally lived up to Hannah's expectations that he act like a mensch.

Dooley was all business and no questions allowed. The documents she presented named Moses chair of the Nightingale Foundation board — replacing Alchemy — and assigned him, along with Alchemy, as cosignatory of its financial disbursements. He was also named cotrustee on Persephone's and, astonishingly, Salome's trusts. He was removed from all official positions with the Nightingale Party. Moses assumed the CAA investigation necessitated the suddenness of these changes.

Louise Urban Vulter, with her sunbaked freckled skin not covered by makeup, hair not in its typical bun but in a '50s-style pageboy, and dressed "Arizona" in jeans, flannel shirt, and cowboy boots, greeted Alchemy as he deplaned from a private jet at the Scottsdale airport. She seemed a bit taken aback; he was looking less and less like a youthful and fearless Apache warrior and more like a ravage-featured, once proud Indian now confined to the Whiteriver reservation. Nobility and optimism did not guarantee success — in fact, more often the opposite occurred on the political battleground.

On the ride in her Range Rover to the Scottsdale Gun Club, they resumed their friendly barb-tossing rivalry. Vulter chided him because his love of shooting didn't stamp out his desire to ban so many types of guns. He kidded her back, asking why any true hunter needed a semiautomatic weapon. The talk turned serious when they arrived at her private parking spot and stood face-to-face outside the car.

"What's so important you had to fly to Arizona to take target practice for an hour?"

"You took the CAA assignment, right?"

"Can't tell you anything about it."

"Okay, I'll tell you. You received a report saying Miranda Wright and I had sex when she was only fourteen and she got pregnant and I paid oodles of cash to cover up the affair and her abortion."

The corners of Vulter's mouth twitched ever so slightly. She tilted almost imperceptibly back on her boot heels, forcing a glacial expression.

"Thank you."

"Alchemy, for what? I can't help you."

"You can lie but you can't hide..."

"*...When you're standing naked at my bedside...*" Vulter laughed, blushing, as she sang an off-key version of the line from "Eight Is Just Enough," on which Absurda and Alchemy shared the lead vocals.

"Louise, why'd the IRS and your committee stop looking into Godfrey Barker and his church?"

"Who says we were?"

"Fine, you weren't. Who most wants to discredit me so I go away?"

She shrugged.

"C'mon, play along."

"The desperate and strategically shrewd mainstream Democrats. I got the same scared types in my party."

"Exactly. Barker gets big funding from Hollywood Dems. Louise, I'm going to help you. Next week you will receive some damning information on Mr. Barker and his associates. Use it wisely."

"To what do I owe this honor?" She leaned forward, coyly provocative.

"I'd like you to quash the upcoming subpoena on my brother. And don't tell me it's not happening."

"It is and I seriously doubt I can stop it. There are people on that committee who don't trust me because of my relationship with you. Fact, if news of this meeting gets out—not good."

"For either of us. I don't understand why you need to subpoena Moses. Or Sidonna Cherry, for that matter."

"Let me put it this way: You've stood naked by many a bedside. And yet, truths remain hidden. And mysteries still abound."

BOOK IV

I spin so ceaselessly
Or did I lose my sense of gravity . . .
Some strange music draws me in . . .

—Patti Smith
(German concert, 1979)

81

THE MOSES CHRONICLES (2018)

The Magic Mountain

The party began under a cloudless sky, another ideal seventy-six-degree SoCal January day, the kind that inspires envy in the rest of the world and lures millions, who too often disregard the unwritten warnings of man's covenant with nature.

Valets took the guests' cars, and an experimental solar-powered van shuttled everyone up the hill. Thirty tables with ten chairs each, and four outdoor TVs dotted the grounds: two tuned to the game, one playing *Horse Feathers* and the other *North Dallas Forty*. Twenty solar-powered heaters would warm and illuminate the area next to each table if, as the sun set, a slight chill entered the air. This spread qualified as modest in high-end L.A. circles, where $25,000 events were rated bowling alley worthy. The waiters circulated outside offering appetizers, and inside were two banquet tables filled with main courses. Everything was organic and locally grown or raised, except for Twinkies and pigs in a blanket, which were a concession to those with a Mindswallow-style palate. *Apocalypse Now* blared in the small screening room while the game played on a large-screen TV in the living room.

Jay and Moses, among those who were allowed to park up the hill in the driveway, arrived at kickoff. Moses's transformation from professor to boss did not subdue his feelings of fraudulent outsiderness in any large gathering. He understood that the currencies of the cliques that formed this party were money, fame, and power. Beauty and intelligence were commodities, bought and sold like art or SpaghettiOs. He couldn't help feeling more like a SpaghettiO in this menagerie of famous faces and heavy hitters, who, on the surface, appeared as an anachronistic mix of old and young, staid and hip, all brought together by the catalytic bond of Alchemy.

With balletic grace, Alchemy glided among the guests: Euge Baltzer, aging metal rocker of the band Samureye; Romy Milton, granddaughter of a major pet food mogul and sex tape "star"; Chipper Ronan, machine tool heir and aspiring screenwriter; riteplay.com founders and Nightingale Party supporters Frieberg and Loo, who donned football jerseys with DIGITAL DRUID printed across the back. Laluna—in a low-cut powder blue San Diego Chargers jersey, blue-and-white-striped leggings, orange high-top sneakers, black hair growing longer—locomoted aloofly about as the marginally engaged hostess of the festivities.

Moses and Jay chose a table at the outskirts occupied by some of the younger guests who worked with the party or foundation. Moses looked at the Insatiables crowd: Lux and his wife Sue, Andrew, Kim Dooley, and two of the Sheik brothers. He zeroed in on the group fawning over Crouse and Barker. He and Jay exchanged glances while listening to two of his

Nightingale "kids": "Crouse sure is pretty." "Yeah, pretty stupid to be hooked up with that Swami Barker."

Jay spotted the graffiti artist known as Krankey. Moses nudged her. "Go. I'll let you know when I need you." Moses watched Jay grab a second glass of champagne off a waiter's tray as she made her way toward Krankey. Behind her he saw Barker being escorted to his meeting with Alchemy.

As he entered the cluttered office, Barker seemed to be addressing, possibly praying to, the gaudy silver insignia necklace that hung to the middle of his kurta, bequeathed to him by the church's deceased founder. Alchemy shook his head, dismayed. How could anyone, especially Laluna, take him seriously? Alchemy pointed to a chair.

"No. I'll stand. I've been expecting your little reprimand. You can't tell me not to talk to Laluna." Barker's voice took on the yogi-esque air of the unruffled transcendent.

"Not my intention."

"I'm glad to hear that."

"Last week Laluna brought you to my mother's studio again. You proceeded to lecture her that psychiatrists and psychotropic drugs caused her illness and that if she and Laluna joined your church, you 'guaranteed' the tension between the two of them would end. True?"

"Let them undergo Cosmological Kinetic purification and I'll be proven right. Your problems with Laluna and your mother far exceed your abilities to fix them."

"Perhaps. But it is my problem, not yours. Your problem is dispensing disreputable information to the Committee on Anti-American activities about me that you insinuated came from Laluna."

"That's slanderous. I've never talked to anyone on that committee. Don't blame me because you're jealous of Jack's relationship with Laluna."

"I don't. I blame you for being a charlatan." A scene with Crouse and Barker, messy as it might be, suited Alchemy just fine. It would leave no doubt that their association was one-sided. "You can see Laluna whenever she wants, but you are not welcome here or anywhere near my mother. Tomorrow morning a judge will be granting a restraining order against you and you'll be properly served."

"What? How could you? I'll fight it."

"Go ahead. Enjoy the festivities." Alchemy exited, leaving the door wide open behind him. He addressed a muscular security guard stationed in the doorway: "Dave, please escort Mr. Barker downstairs."

Moses took a sip from his water bottle, and suddenly, for the first time in months—a daymare.

I'm sitting alone in the back row of a roofless Budapest temple. It's pouring but I can't move. Beside me appears the dybbuk, Shalom, dressed in a black T-shirt and black jeans. She touches my cheek.

—Moses, now is the time.

—For what?

—Redemption.

—I have done nothing wrong.

An apparition hovers above her.

—Moses, she warns as he lifts her away, doing nothing wrong does not mean you have done something right. Act and I will love you in the dimension of forever.

The apparition exhales. A fiery gas bubble pops and sends sparks through the air.

—Act and feel my blood surge within you.

"Unc Mose." Persephone climbed onto the chair formerly occupied by Jay. "I want to show you the pool I painted with Granmamma." Persephone led him to the cordoned-off side of the house and the empty pool, its floor and walls a psychedelic mishmash of colors. She fingered a necklace of papier-mâché "Black Sea" pearls. "She taught me a song she made up." Persephone, giggling, sang, "*Black Sea pearls are worn by little girls, who take trips around the world, and get a big kiss and find their bliss...*" She stopped and ducked her head against his thigh. "I forget the rest. Granmamma says I am a better drawer than singer."

"I think you're aces at both." Moses's phone beeped. A text from Alchemy: *Winslow. Now.* "Perse, honey, I need to talk with a friend. Let's find Auntie Jay. Wait with her and I'll be back in a jiffy." They found Jay talking with Krankey, who was hoping she could get him past the security guards to meet Salome. They had orders not to let anyone near her cottage. Moses exhaled, "Jay, game time."

The "jiffy" took longer than anticipated, and Perse, restless, asked Auntie Jay to take her inside so she could play with her newest art-making computer program. Laluna caught up to her on the second-floor landing and stopped Jay outside the doorway to Persephone's room.

"I need to ask you a big favor." Jay nodded. "Did Mose tell you that Alchemy and I are going to take a three-week vacation by ourselves?"

"He mentioned something. Costa Rica? Maybe Argentina? Either sounds great."

"We're still checking. But we also want Perse, if you're okay with it, to stay with you and Mose. I'd like it if you'd stay up here."

"That's not a favor, that's a pleasure. Moses would love it. But up here for a few weeks, with Salome so close?"

"I wouldn't do that to Mose. She's been getting crazier. When she heard Perse might stay with you, she said, 'I won't allow it.' Don't worry, she can't stop us. I, we can't have her here anymore. I wrote some music inspired by her *Petra Sansluv* drawings. Salome said they have a 'larcenous and putrid soulsmell,' whatever the hell that is, which disqualifies them from being played for '*my* granddaughter with *my* drawings.'" Jay winced. "She and Alchemy will decide if Salome's going back to Collier Layne or her own place."

"If that's the case, I don't see any problems. Except, after that long a time, it might be hard for Moses to give her up." The champagne had disarmed Jay's usually stringent self-editing skills. "His relationship with Perse makes him so happy, but it also hurts him."

"Hurt, Mose? Why?" Laluna looked perplexed. "Because of the way Salome treated him?"

"No. Not that. It's so goddamned hard for him to keep up the pretense of 'Uncle Mose' when he's really 'Daddy Moses.'"

Laluna pushed Jay almost too forcefully down the hallway. "Who told you that? Moses?" Laluna crossed her arms across her chest and scratched her fingernails against her forearms.

"What?...Wait...Shit." After disobeying the Savant Code of Omertà, Jay flailed haplessly, seeking to forestall the now inevitable firestorm. "I'm sorry. I'm drunk. Yeah, Moses, he must've dreamed it up."

Laluna said coldly, "No, no. I don't think he did."

"Hey, Mommy." Perse walked into the hallway and Laluna and Jay stared at the blue-gray-eyed, stubby-legged Persephone. "Can you come help me?"

Moses spotted Dewey Winslow schmoozing with Chipper Ronan. Winslow now sported a goatee instead of his sliver of mustache, and with his gold-framed glasses he looked more like a professor than a professional political shark. Moses signaled to him with his eyes. Winslow placed his glass on the tray of a passing waiter and sucked traces of mustard off his fingers. He and Moses moved away so as not to be heard. Moses began filling him in on the morning's polls that had Alchemy with a seventy-plus percent positive Q rating, with only twenty-three percent negatives among all groups and economic and education levels—higher than anyone else in politics.

"Yes, excellent. Fantastic." Winslow's unimpressed tone didn't match the exuberance of his words. "What's Swami Gotcha-by-the-Balls doing here?"

Moses explained the circumstances of Crouse's donation offer and Barker's presence. "Alchemy's turning down the money and taking care of this once and for all. He'll be here in a minute or two."

"Too fucking late. Pics and tweets of that two-bit rainmaker and Laluna are spreading across social media." Winslow pursed his lips, nostrils pulsing, as he clasped Moses's shoulder with his right hand. "You do remember my warning about associating with Barker?"

Moses removed Winslow's hand. Ignoring his question, Moses posed one of his own. "By any chance were you subpoenaed by the CAA?"

"No. Why?"

"Alchemy and I were notified that we're on their hit list."

"Holy shit. Why wasn't I told?"

Moses exhaled and tried to slow his rapidly beating heart. "Alchemy decided to wait until he or I could tell you in person. So I'm telling you now."

"I need a drink." Winslow strode toward the bar. Moses followed him until Alchemy cut them off. The three of them stepped a few paces down the path leading to Salome's cottage.

"Alchemy, if I'm to do my job, I must be kept in the loop."

With equanimity intact, Alchemy informed Winslow of his newest plans. "Okay. There's no need to get peevish. Here's what you need to know. I met with a CAA member only yesterday. As a result, I've decided to align with the IFC. I'm not

going to run for the presidency, but governor, backed by them."
Moses gaped at Alchemy but sensed that he should stay silent.
For now.

"You're joking," Winslow said.

"Not for a second. I've also proposed to talk to the CAA in
an open forum."

"They won't agree. You don't know who you're fucking
with."

"Oh, but I do. I always know who I fuck. And who is fucking me."

Winslow hesitated. Stepped back. "I'm not sure what
you're implying, but you're fucking yourself by aligning with
the IFC."

"That's the way I'm going. If you still want to be involved,
I'd like that. If not, no worries. We have to go."

Alchemy ambled away, Moses by his side. "Why didn't you
consult with me about this governor business?"

"Because it's bullshit. Winslow or Borden or maybe both is
the leak. There is no Miranda Wright. Never was. I planted that
with them. *He* sicced Barker on Laluna."

"What? Winslow's playing us with all that noise about
Barker? You sure?"

"If the news about the IFC leaks, then yes, one hundred
percent. I've already sent IFC a private and dated letter—they
will get it Tuesday—explaining why, although there is much I
support in their platform regarding the climate, the environ-
ment, I do not support their ultimate goal. We'll drop it on our
app and Web site. And we need Cherry's help in digging out
who is giving Winslow his marching orders."

"Is this why you had me sign those papers?"

"Mose, you need to slow down or maybe speed up on the vodka. You look a little peaked." Alchemy moved closer. "Relax. You can leave now if you want."

"I think we'll do that."

"I'll explain everything in detail tomorrow. It's all for the best." Looking over Moses's shoulder, Alchemy spotted Crouse and Laluna side by side, clinking their beer bottles as if making a toast. "Call me tonight if you need to."

Alchemy walked over to Laluna. Moses was scanning the crowd looking for Jay when Barker cut him off. They'd never officially met. "I'm Swami—"

"I know."

"So you'll understand my, let's say, advice. If you're smart, you'll reason with Alchemy to stop that restraining order and allow me to see Laluna without his interference."

"Why would I do that?"

"Because you're the good German, and good Germans know when to change sides."

"What are you talking about?"

"I think you know exactly what I'm talking about."

Moses answered, quietly assured, "I'm smart enough to know that threats and unfounded smears are the weapons of the desperate and the vanquished."

"I agree." Barker bowed slightly. "It is not I who made the first threats. As a historian, you'll also agree that truth is a powerful weapon for the victorious."

82

MEMOIRS OF A USELESS GOOD-FOR-NUTHIN'

Double or Nothing, 2018

All night I'm stewing. Don't sleep. I go first to Malibu with Carlotta to the party she's working. At halftime, I zip down to Topanga. Laluna catches me right away, huddles me away from the crowd. "You Maria or Laluna today?" She enemizes me with the dick-shrinking glare like she done the first day I met her at Kasbah. "Hey, was just joking."

"You're going to behave, right?"

"Yeah, yeah." I get me a beer or three. I go commiserate with Silky 'cause we're having a problem finding us a lead singer for our tour. Silky says she seen a lady who has chops.

Some young babes snuggle up to me. I'm a dopey dick-for-brains male, only when I'm an article, I am a faithful one-woman guy. Can't help myself, though, I still charge my rocks with some harmless flirting now and then. I was too antsy to even play.

I find Lux. I tell him I have questions and he best not lie to me.

"Ambitious, I'm hurt." He's only being half sarcastic. "I don't ever lie to you."

"Did Alchemy and Absurda ever, you know?"

"Christ, man, no. I told you before, NO."

"That night at the after-party at Madam Rosa's, when all the shit went down with my brother at the Plaza, before I left with the girls... I seen the two of them outside with his wang dangling and she was squatting down wimping, 'Thank you...' That's when I lost it and, well, ya know."

"Look, man, it's years ago, and if they did, they did. Absurda's gone. Carlotta is terrific. Alchemy's with Laluna. Let it go. Let...it...go."

He eyes Laluna talking with Barker and Crouse. "What's up with that?"

"I seen her yesterday and she's trying to figure some shit out. She don't wanna be 'Laluna' no more. She and Alchemy, they're both different but not the *same* different, ya know what I mean?"

"I hope she figures out to stay away from those guys."

Laluna waves and wishes a "ta-ta" goodbye to Barker and Crouse. Alchy appears outta nowhere and fucking hugs me. He's acting strange, too. Tells me he's so glad I made it, that I'm still his "brother," and sometime me, him, and Lux should sneak in to see this new Insatiables cover band. I'm nonchalanting like nuthin's wrong. His eyes is open too wide, them brown pupils is spinning their netherworld dance. I figure something is gestating, and I'm guessing he knows something is up with Laluna. He gets a call he "has" to take. I yell after him, "Bet life was easier bein' a plain old rock god." He laughs.

I tell Lux I'll catch him later 'cause I need to talk to Salome. I'm not ten feet down the path when Laluna races up. "Don't bother her today." She says Salome's been behaving extra biddy-bip, even for her, and they're moving her to her own place. "We'll all meet in the studio after everyone clears out. Come by then." Laluna ain't her usual unflappable superhip chick self. As pissed as I am, I try to be a good guy. "It'll work out. Ya know Alchy, he can fix anything. He'll fix this."

Most people are only half watching the game. Mrs. Mose is so drunk that Mose has to hold her up as they stumble over to the house. All the shit that's gone down with them, I'd start drinking, too. Well, drinking even more. I call Carlotta, who don't answer. Must be working. I leave a message I might be home late. I'd bet five grand on the over/under, so I watch the game with some guys who is also actual football fans. And wait.

83

THE SONGS OF SALOME

Before a Cock Crows

Parnell Palmer and I, with Bellows by my side in her office, held a computer TV chat because he still has more questions and I had more answers. Screens are hindrances to any sensate morphologist, but I acceded when Palmer agreed that Persephone could soon visit with me. There is a not so minor catch. She is somewhere in Eastern Europe. I tried to wheedle Perse's exact whereabouts and the time of her expected return. He stonewalled.

Palmer began this cross-examination by asking if I'd heard Alchemy and Laluna arguing about her consorting with Godfrey Barker and Jack Crouse. I hadn't. Crouse was so bland and inarticulate—worth maybe one fuck.

Through the screen, I recounted to Palmer what transpired on the day when, a few days before their football party, Laluna brought Crouse and Barker to my studio for a second time.

Barker began by apologizing for the collector he thought might want a *Baddist Boy* collage, who had passed. This was news to me and gave me a taste of his entitlement, since I'd told him I wouldn't sell it. He suggested I do a commission for their new church in Hollywood. I said thanks but no thanks, which provoked an attack from Godfrey the Enlightened. He said the antipsycho drugs "stulted" my artistic growth and caused me to become even more "unstable." "Truthfully," he said, "I offered the commission as a favor to Laluna." He smiled arrogantly. "You haven't done anything exceptional in years."

Laluna blanched.

"Barker, I don't need favors from her or from you, and I take insults from vulgarians like you as compliments."

Too self-absorbed to notice Laluna's discomfort, he lectured me on the benefits of Cosmological Kinetic therapy, which would "purify" my demons and "open" me up to create "monumental" art again.

Crouse chimed in too enthusiastically, "It's great! Really great! You should try it!"

I paid no attention to him and addressed Barker. "Exorcisms of any kind do not intrigue me. I am my demons."

"It's not an exorcism. Purification puts you in touch with those demons and then you'll embrace and control them. Ask Laluna. You two would become much more simpatico and mutually supportive of each other, and of Alchemy, instead of jousting rivals."

The only impediment to improving my relations with Laluna was her imposing upon my relations with Perse. If she'd stopped that, we'd have been just groovy.

Palmer had listened through the screen without much comment. I heard his muffled voice speaking to someone off-screen. Then he swung his axe.

"So you didn't say to Barker that you'd burn his church before you'd ever create art for it?"

"No. Why would I? I might've implied that cavemen had superior aesthetics."

"Salome, no need for me to delve more deeply into your memory lapses and actual past pyrotechnics. I'm more interested in a conversation between you and Laluna that took place the evening before the party. You threatened to use whatever sway you had over Alchemy to tell him that you sniffed that she and Crouse were having an affair, to stop her from surrendering Persephone to Moses Teumer's care for a month."

I explained to Palmer that it wasn't a conversation. I didn't threaten her. I *asked* her about Crouse. She didn't hold her fire. She spit out, "Unlike you, I would never fuck someone behind the back of the man I love." Explaining myself to her was futile. I tried a new tactic. She'd written a few maudlin songs to accompany some new Petra Sansluv drawings. Initially, I was reluctant to partner with her. Still, I suggested we plan an exhibition/concert together. I begged her to let Persephone stay with me and the nannies when they went on vacation. She just bobbed her head from side to side. That meant "Drop dead."

84

THE MOSES CHRONICLES (2018)
Hat Trick

Unsettled by the machinations of Winslow and Barker, Moses, vodka in hand, returned to his former seat at the now empty table. He need not be an ace deducer of silences to read trouble in Jay's herky-jerky walk as she returned to the table holding two glasses of wine. With some difficulty, she managed to sit down. She drank down one of the glasses. "You'll have to drive. Oh, Moses..." She blew her nose in a napkin. She picked up his icy-cold vodka glass and held it against her forehead as she talked. "Salome is trying to stop you from seeing Persephone. And she went off on Laluna, saying she isn't fit to raise Perse. They're at war and I'm not sure who is going to win."

Moses let out an overly loud, "Fuck that." He took the vodka glass from her and downed it in three gulps and stood up. Jay, almost relieved, thought Moses meant to speak to Laluna to find out more. Jay could only hope that Laluna would ask Moses about Persephone and save her from confessing her breach.

Moses marched down the path leading to the cottage, composing the first words he'd ever speak to his mother. He heard muffled music. He knocked on the door. Ten seconds later he knocked again. Harder. The music lowered, and she appeared in the doorway as he'd never seen her in photos: in a paint-splattered orange T-shirt—her arms, bony thin—white cotton pants, a pink kerchief around her neck, complexion translucent, skin almost scaly. Her spirit, though, showed no loss of vigor, no signs of surrender to aging or fatigue. "At last, you made the pilgrimage. Sorry, it's too late, my overture expired."

"What overture? You did everything in your power to deny me. And you're trying to deny me Persephone."

Salome deliberated before taking a step toward him and shutting the door behind her. "I tried to reach you through our DNA. When you didn't respond, I determined you are not truly my son."

Undeterred, Moses countered, "I am your son. I'll never figure out why you hate me because I *didn't* die. If my father was *that* evil...This is not about him. It's not even about you and me. I'm not foolish enough to doubt you can make me bleed again. I accept, finally, that there will be no happy or even sorrowful sunset moment of reunion. We share only this—an unhealable rift."

Salome touched Moses's left cheek with the crinkled skin of her fingers. For the first time since his birth, her flesh met his flesh. It did not burn. Nor did it heal.

"I am sorry and also I am not sorry," she said. "More often than anyone likes to believe, our choices are made *for*, not by, us."

Moses refused to rebut her excuses. "Laluna is Persephone's mother, not you. You don't have the power to deprive me of seeing her."

"Teumer was wrong. You do have balls. Oh, yes, ever benef-icent, he sent me a copy of the letter he gave Alchemy for you."

Moses's head bowed. Eyes closed. Mouth parched. Tongue thickened. So much of his life remained lost in a miasma of obfuscations and misconceptions. Salome reached out and tilted his chin upward. "For the good of all, for all you believe in, release yourself from Alchemy and let him fulfill his des-tiny." Then she clapped her hands at the air between them. "Moses..." — she said his name, her son's name, not with deri-sion but compassion — "stay." She disappeared into the stu-dio. She returned holding a tattered red beret. "I only met my mother one time. She gave me this. I bequeath it to you. Now please, please leave us." She placed it delicately on his head, turned, and retreated, locking the door behind her.

85

THE SONGS OF SALOME

Sweet Savor

The explanation of my meeting with Laluna and Barker did not cause Palmer to temper his inquisition. Thinking always of my Persephone, I continued my account.

After his morning run on the day of the party, Alchemy stopped at my cottage and plaintively explained again that he and Laluna needed time alone and away. While they were gone, I might not be able to stay in my cottage or in the main house. He said Persephone would be staying elsewhere. I asked with who. He acted as if he hadn't heard that Laluna and I had already argued about it. He did make it clear that when they returned, he and Laluna preferred if we'd all talk civilly about a possible alternative living situation for me.

"And you passively agreed to that?" Palmer asked.

"Laluna owned his balls. That trumps all other weapons."

Through the screen, I felt Palmer's condemnation. "When we first talked, you admitted that you gave Moses a hat when he came to your studio. Why'd you do that?"

"A lot about that day is hazy." I'd made a mistake with that admission. Too late.

"It seems so. Why'd you give it to him?"

"An impulsive act."

"So we agree that you are susceptible to impulsive acts. Given that your fingerprints and DNA were found on the weapon, perhaps shooting your son was another of your impulsive and hazily remembered acts."

He didn't pose that as a question.

"I didn't shoot my son. I didn't. Lots of people's fingerprints and DNA must've been on it. Moses. Laluna. Alchemy. Mindswallow. Fuck you, Palmer, that's it. Until I see Persephone, we are done."

"Yes, now about Persephone and Moses—"

"There is nothing to say about them. Nothing."

I couldn't tell Palmer that I gifted Moses Greta's hat as an act of mourning, and also relief, because I sensated cancer cells growing inside him. Yes, cancer has a very particular smell. I sensated that Moses would soon die and Alchemy would be saved.

86

THE MOSES CHRONICLES (2018)
Enormous Changes

With both Moses and Jay too drunk to drive, and Jay feeling queasy, they climbed the stairs to the second floor. They
passed Persephone's room and headed toward an open door
at the far end of the hall. The lone double bed was untouched.
No suitcases from possible overnight visitors. They entered.
Jay used the adjoining bathroom. Moses checked his phone,
which had been vibrating. He opened an e-mail marked
"Urgent" from a Nightingale media watcher. Moses pressed
the link and the screen opened to *TMZ*. One of their "cor-
respondents" had staked out the Topanga Canyon Boulevard
entrance to the Alchemy compound and posted a video "interview" with Crouse. He stuck his head out the window of the
Mercedes to answer questions.

"Jack, Jack, how was the party?"

"The Super Bowl party is super. The Nightingale Party
is a disaster. Alchemy is a brilliant rock star and a lousy
politician. He asked me to join him in supporting the California secession movement. How silly is that? Love the

guy, but he should stay out of politics and stick to music and... *very young girls.*"

"Stay tuned."

Moses forwarded it to Alchemy with a note: "You were right."

"Please put that away." Jay parachuted onto the bed. Moses lifted one leg to the edge of the bed and balanced himself with the other against the floor. Jay rubbed his back. "There was more," she said, her words slurring slightly. "I screwed up. Laluna, I think, I'm not sure, but maybe, somehow she didn't know about you and Persephone. Now she knows."

Too dispirited and anxious to react beyond frustration, he simply sighed. "What does that mean?"

"It means I'm pretty sure that Alchemy lied to her, and to you. What's this?" Jay pulled the beret from his back pocket.

His phone rang. Laluna's name flashed on the screen. "No, Moses. Please." Jay patted down her hair and pulled the beret onto her head. "Fits."

He didn't want to talk about his mother. Not yet.

"Let me" — glassy-eyed and grinning, she snatched his phone, turned it off, dropped it on the floor, lay back, and reached to tug him down on top of her — "satiate... you..."

Years before, Jay's jesting words could have spurred jealousy or despair. No more. Moses thought, *Sure, why the hell not?*

87

THE SONGS OF SALOME

The Not So Long Goodbye

After my reborn son's intrusion, the eviscerating, unseen light was drawing me to the dark matter. I dug a small fire pit behind my cottage. I lit some scrap paper and twigs. I gathered up photos of *Art Is Dead* and the Teumer *Baddist Boys* collages and carried them outside. I didn't hear Alchemy until he stood beside me.

"Mom, what are you doing?"

"I had a visitor."

"I saw." The belated rampaging of Gravity Disease had transformed his effervescent blue orbs into wary slits encumbered by sadness. His delicate, unblemished skin turned blotchy and rough-hewn. "Mom, you don't have to burn them."

"You never conveyed my offer for a family get-to-know-you session? How can you let Persephone stay with him instead of me? Why, Alchemy why?"

"It doesn't matter now. After tonight, you won't have to worry about him staying here while we're away or his coming here to visit."

"Is he sick again? I inhaled a serious case of Gravity Disease."

He didn't answer. "Mom, don't fret. It's all taken care of." Alchemy picked up the pieces and placed them in the studio. He returned and scooped some dirt, and we watched the fire die before it really got started. "I love you, Mom."

I thought, *In the end, he couldn't betray me.* I was so pleased.

"Got to say goodbye to the last people cleaning up and then tuck Persephone into bed." He turned to leave.

"Kiss her good night for me. Tell her I'll come to see her in the morning."

88

THE MOSES CHRONICLES (2018)

Strange Interlude

After their twilight frolic, Moses and Jay both conked out. Down the hall, Alchemy finished reading Persephone a bedtime story. He clasped her tiny hand tightly in his. "Perse, honey, Mommy and I are going on a trip very soon. Uncle Mose and Auntie Jay will take care of you. Would you like that?"

"Yes."

"Mommy and I will call you every day."

"What about Granmamma? Is she going?"

"No, just Mommy and I. Granmamma is going on her own vacation."

Perse's bottom lip drooped sulkily. Alchemy tickled it with his pointer finger. "Daddy, d-on-on't…"

"We'll be back sooner than you can sing, 'Petra Sansluv found her pearls.'"

"More."

"'At the bottom of the Black Sea / if you climb the Black Pearl tree / you can make a wish / to the Pearl Tree fish…'"

Persephone's eyelids shut. Her lips formed into a smile, her breathing soft and peaceful.

Moses's head snapped forward. He sat up. Head between pillows, Jay snored away. Grabbing his clothes, he dressed in the bathroom and turned on his phone. There were two missed calls from Laluna, an e-mail from Sidonna Cherry to him and Alchemy, and a follow-up from Alchemy, which now included Lux, Dooley, Warfield, and Pullham-Large with the subject: *Defcon 1. This will drop at midnight unless we can stop it.*

"Oh, fuck, what now?" He read the section that Alchemy had copy/pasted into his e-mail.

SpeedFeed can report that the Senate Committee on Anti-American Activities has issued subpoenas for Alchemy Savant and his brother, Moses Teumer. Among other things, the senators want to speak to the brothers regarding their ties to the deceased, unrepentant Nazi war criminal and father of Moses, Malcolm Teumer. Our sources, who requested anonymity, report that the brothers constructed an intricate maze with the singular purpose of confusing anyone seeking to understand the family relationships. We can state that the brothers visited the Sr. Teumer separately in Brazil. Salome Savant, mother of Moses, maintained relations with her lover until his death. Moses Teumer, a former professor of history at SCCAM, was well known among his students and colleagues for his profoundly anti-American lectures. Alchemy also has ties to the IFC, which has at least one member affiliated with white supremacist groups in its hierarchy.

Although not yet officially part of the CAA investigation, SpeedFeed's independent sources allege sexual swapping among Alchemy Savant, his live-in partner, Maria Lopez Appelian aka Laluna, Moses Teumer, and his ex-wife, Jay Bernes.

Moses cursed under his breath. "Oh fuck fuck fucking bastards. LBJ pig-fucking hell." He read Alchemy's response, which was underneath the SpeedFeed report.

If they pub we go full force. High road denial/attack strategy? Get me booked on the morning shows. Mose, we need target points. Think about appearing w/me on at least one show. We only have a few hours. Know you guys only just got home, but we may need a midnite meet. More soon.

89
MEMOIRS OF A USELESS GOOD-FOR-NUTHIN'
Sins You Been Gone, 2018

I never cared less about winning a bet. Stragglers are dragging their butts getting out. Laluna is hiding in the kitchen with the cleanup crew. Alchemy has disappeared. Lux, who's been hanging with me, gotta take off. I'm so tense I ain't feeling no buzz from the booze. I pass by Salome's cottage and studio. No lights. It's getting chilly so I go wait in the recording studio. I grab a beer from the fridge and open the skylight and keep the ceiling lights low. Strum a few chords on an acoustic. I'm not feeling it, so I sit at the board and tinker. I see something labeled *33 Visitations*. Sounds like what Alchy gave me in the bar the night we kissed and made up. I see the two of 'em coming. They look like the *Titanic* and the iceberg steaming at each other, only I don't know who is which one.

Alchy don't flinch when he sees me. He turns all loose limbed, using his I-can-solve-the-world's-problems-just-'cause-I'm-me voice, and asks, "So, what is the crisis?"

Laluna hands him the paper from the clinic. "Tell Ambitious what you told me."

He stares at me, shaking his head. "You won't be happy."

"I ain't happy now, so stop bullshittin' and start talking."

"We were both taking a piss outside Madam Rosa's. Absurda told me she was pregnant." He's standing to the left of me. Laluna jams her jaw tight and is letting him talk. "I told her we'd cancel the rest of the tour because you'd want to stay home with her...Although there was no reason, she was thanking me. She was pretty emotional." His and Laluna's unwavering eyes are X-raying me. I feel naked, like we're all naked. "Yeah, Ambitious, it was yours."

"Is this some Alchemy slick scheming?" I say all full of bravado. Only my bones know it's truth.

"What could she do, after you ran off to the Plaza and ended it like you did?"

"That got nuthin' to do with you not tellin' me. Motherfucker, you shoulda told me. How the..." I hated the sound of my whiny voice.

"I gave my word to Absurda."

Thinking he's settled it with me, he slides next to Laluna. He is like six inches taller than her, only they feel the same height. She backs away and walks up the three steps behind the console, like she can't stand to be near him.

I ain't satisfied. "Alchemy, why the fuck—"

"Ambitious," Laluna cuts me off, not raising her voice, her body shaking, full of quiet rage. "Ambitious, he's telling you the truth. It's impossible for him to have a kid of his own. He lied to me. To everyone. Persephone's not his—she's Moses's."

I'm so torched, and in my own head, what she says don't sink in. "Why the fuck did Absurda tell *you* first?!" I smash my fucking beer bottle against the wall. The pieces fly everywhere.

"Ambitious." He reaches for me. I spin around, still squeezing the bottle's neck, ready to mince-meat his pretty face. Laluna bulls herself between us. "Go. Cool off. This is between Alchemy and me now." I sense that it's best I take a hike 'cause I never, not once, ever seen her even close to crying 'til that second.

90

THE MOSES CHRONICLES (2018)

AU 79 1850F

Finding no one in the house, Moses frantically searched outside. He spotted the recording studio's lights and headed down the path. While walking, he sent his response e-mail to everyone else. He heard Mindswallow cursing to no one outside Salome's studio. He kept walking and typing.

> Must somehow stall SpeedFeed for 48 hours. Get best lawyers. Dispelling lies postpub could prove fatal. Brazen act of pubbing w/o asking for reaction indicates suicide bomber job. Meeting Alchemy now. Call ASAP.

Orange-yellow lights streamed out of the open studio door. Voices crackled like sparking electric wires. Their fury quieted as he passed over the threshold and into the studio.

Laluna spoke first. "Mose, I'm glad you're here."

"Me, too. Mose, tell her. Tell her Persephone's *mine*."

Moses was ready to do battle with political enemies over the SpeedFeed smears, not with Alchemy over Persephone's paternity, Jay's betrayal of his confidence, or the fact that Alchemy had broken his word again. Certainly not his own role in the whole mess.

"Go ahead, Mose, tell me. First, take a good look at your brother, the god of cool." Her voice punched out with contempt. "America's savior. The big man reduced to groveling so his brother covers for him."

Moses, wobbly and uncertain how to answer, moved deeper inside, sidestepping strewn instruments. He halted between them. He sighed and bowed his head for a second, and regained enough composure to speak. "I can't. Alchemy, I'm sorry."

"What?"

"Laluna knows the truth."

"Mose, how could you?"

Laluna answered for him. "He didn't. Jay confirmed what I didn't want to believe."

Moses felt obligated to defend Jay. "She didn't mean to, it just—"

"What? Mose? You told Jay? You lied to me?"

"You lied to me first. You swore you'd told Laluna."

"*Boys*, it doesn't matter who lied first. Or last. I'm taking my daughter away from *all* of you. Tonight. For good." Through the skylight, a moonlit silhouette of Laluna's face glistening from her silent tears.

Suddenly, the invulnerable edifice that was Alchemy began to topple. Not from the calumnies of his enemies; those he could repel and master. No, the dream-deniers of time and truth arose, leaving the invented past in ruins and annihilating Alchemy's imagined future. Moses reached his right hand toward his brother, a sign he loved him, that they'd work it out somehow. Alchemy's eyes—drained of their luminous energy, now dulled and static—closed.

601

91

MEMOIRS OF A USELESS GOOD-FOR-NUTHIN'

Sealed with a Judas Kiss, 2018

I'm pounding on Salome's door. "We gotta fucking talk!" She yaps back, "Give me a fucking minute. I'm coming!" She opens up, wearing only a nightgown, pointing her freakin' flashlight in my eyes. I push it away. "Salome, no Savant slime-speak, whattaya know about Nathaniel and Absurda's abortion?"

She leans against the doorway. "Oh, poor, poor Ricky." She's puts her fingers through my hair and pushes it off my forehead. "It certainly wasn't Nathaniel's abortion. Amanda needed our help and love, and we gave it to her."

"I woulda helped her if she asked."

"Why would she, after you tossed her away like a tattered hand-me-down doll?"

"Alchemy say it was his kid or mine?"

"I never asked. It didn't matter."

"Like it don't matter if Laluna is tellin' the truth and Persephone ain't his but Mose's, and that's why they're movin' you outta here for good."

"Not Alchemy's?"

"No. Moses's."

She jumps to the obvious conclusion, which I'd blanked on before 'cause I was so whacked over my own shit. And like she's thirty, not seventy-five, barefoot and in her nightgown, she takes off, flying down the path.

92
THE SONGS OF SALOME
Nonny, Nonny

Mindswallow's fierce knocking invaded my sedative-induced state and, in his fury, he revealed the duplicity between Moses and the succubus. How could they do that to my son? How could Alchemy conspire with them to remove me not just from their home—but their lives? How? Running down the path, my bare feet began to bleed and I heard Margarita: *Now, Salome, now.*

93

MEMOIRS OF A USELESS GOOD-FOR-NUTHIN'

Had to Cry Today, 2018

I chase Salome. I catch her and she says, "Don't stop me." Ain't no point. I trot alongside her. It sounds sorta like it's chilled in there, and I'm thinking Alchemy done worked his magic one more time, when fucking Salome, so freaking amped, bursts ahead of me and tackles Laluna and is clawing at her face. Me and Alchy dive in and pull her off. She tries to kick me in the nuts. I wrap her in my arms. Laluna, still on her knees, stares at Salome like she's gonna rip her eyes out and feed 'em to the coyotes.

"Mom, Ambitious is going to let you go. You done?" She nods. I do. Carefully.

Alchemy extends his arms to Laluna and helps her up. Mose starts wiping her cheeks with his shirt.

Laluna asks for some water. I go get a bottle from the fridge.

Out of my good eye I see Salome's tiptoed up to the console. "Salome, what the—?" The others turn. Too late. The Beretta is aimed at me.

She shifts her sights to Mose and starts singing, "*Say, hey, the mother not only rises / she also surprises...*"

Mose, he dares her, dead cold, "Do it. Do it." She cackles. Me and Alchy flash eye contact. Salome, she nuzzles the gun at her head, shrieks, "I can't! I must!..." Alchemy takes off with a superhuman leap and soars up and over the console. Laluna, Mose, me—we charge at them. In midair, Alchemy clutches Salome's hands in his—and fuck...

94

ALCHEMY OF THE WORD

Ach du Liebestod

One shot. Wonder.

Pop's music make me. Sing. Do I wake? Ever. Never. More. I Savant to be. Alone. Full scream. Ahead! Row your row your boat gently down the sleep stream, verily, verily, verily life is but an American. Dream.

Laluna comin' down, down. On you. In me. On we. Ennui. Woman, behold. Let yer Savant bluz people go. Go free. Go. Down Mose, go down. To the crossroads. Beg a ride. Promised Land. Denied.

Salomay, she say—Get Bent. I'm crying.

Owed to my Nightingale. Beautyless and truthless. All you need. Is. Had to run. Home. Home run. Take a loss. Do away with pity and party, party. Bacchanalian slide. 'Tis not the meat, 'tis the notion. Jump trope.

Persephone! You are not mine as I was yours. I die…for you. You be MTease. Mal Comes. Say Ha-nah nah nah nah, nah-anah nan-anah nana-anah-yaweh. I cry. Lalunabye.

Moseying down the stream merrily, merrily 'til. Hannah No Mo' Ma and Pa Mal ain't no faux pas nor no po'fa so la tee. Duh-oh.

Do you know how to lonely? The Mose knows.

I prez pro tempus fugit of the California Dreamin' society. No fun. Sing. I am. Too largesse to be. Tell me. No lie. Dance!

Roll roll, up roll up to the American history mystery tour. To. Roll down. In paradise. Whoa! No rocks in the soul. Time to stroll. Blessed be the satiable man. J'ai faim. Je t'aime. I thirst.

I consum-ate myself. Oh, soul-o mea culpa runneth over my desire. My kingdom come. Pray. No way. To who? You voodoo to do Yahweh diddy derri-dum derri-do derri-dada. He say, who we baby, 'oo we? Won't you let me take you on a See cruise? See the zeits. No zeit und sein. To sein or not to sein, sin?

Happiness is. Sing. That's the same old song all nich nacht long. Don't nail me down, for I stigmatter at heaven's door. Knock, knock. Who's there? Apparent. Apparent who? A par-ent who's not there is a parent only in name. Apparently. A child with no name is.

Salomay I ask you a question? Momism? Ism-ism ism go schism miss'im, miss'im go gism, fee fi ego-ism. Cry. All God's isms got no rhythm. Go get 'em and construct destruct. My spirit. Mama committed. Songless.

Re-Greta all or nothing. Sing. To auld angst synecdoche be. Forgot. Forget me. Not.

Can you see the real me? Doctor. Awopbopalopbopa-bigbang-messy-eye-complex. Pfft. With a simper.

My last chants. Dies Irae. Deus Vult. Oy gevalt. Sing. Forsaken. I go. All fail down. Madness over method. Style over song. So it began. So it ends. Dead is art. It is finished.

I am. Dying to love. My child. Child of love. Love child. Perse-honey—live my. Dream. Sing. They know not what. I do. Do you? Ricky. Mose. Mom. LaLoon! Bang, zoom. Go boom.

Still. Dead. Arise. Arise And sing.
    For me.

95

THE MOSES CHRONICLES (2018)

Awake, Awake, Put on Thy Strength

Jay dressed and went to wash her face in the bathroom. On the floor she noticed a folded piece of paper that wasn't there before. She picked it up and unfolded it—across the top it read "Cedars-Sinai Medical Center." She scanned the blood test results and Moses's highlighted platelet count: forty-eight thousand. It had dropped by seventy-five thousand, WBC count 17.1. She didn't know exactly what those numbers meant, except that it wasn't good. Not good at all. *I'm such a fool*, she thought. Too paralyzed to ask, Jay had denied the message of his bruises, his increased night sweats.

Clasping the note, she sped back into the bedroom, grabbed the beret, and tiptoed as fast as she could downstairs. Finding it deserted, she checked their car. Still there. She tossed Salome's beret in the backseat.

She spotted a guard and asked, "Moses?"

"Think they're all at the music studio."

She steeled herself. *Be strong for Moses, no matter what the—*

An echoing crack.

She took off down the path.

A piercing cry.

Legs churning now faster and faster, until Moses, splashed with blood, bowed over Laluna, who cradled Alchemy's half skull in her hands, pleading, moaning, "Oh, my God, oh, my God, please, oh, God, don't die, you can't, I didn't, I won't, couldn't…" Mindswallow was pinning the thrashing Salome to the ground.

Jay crumbled. Moses went to her and raised her up.

"Take Persephone to your apartment. Get her to bed. No TV, phone, or computer tonight. Don't call anyone but me." She yearned to hold him so tightly that they would spin back to a time before he ever met Alchemy. Trembling, she murmured, "Oh, Moses."

He embraced her. His blood-drenched body staining hers. He gently pushed her away, held her by her arms. "Jay, someday, maybe in a few months, maybe next week, maybe, who knows, after I'm gone — Perse must know *everything*. No more lies."

And so it was promised.

MEMOIRS OF A USELESS GOOD-FOR-NUTHIN'

Rashomonstrosity, 2018

For seconds after the shot, it's like time stops. I hear nothing and I'm standing there paralyzed. Then I yell at myself, *You ain't been hit. Fucking do something!* I empty the damn gun so, what the fuck, ya know.

Salome is muttering manically in her private lingo and swinging her limbs every which way. For the only time in my life, I hit a lady. The first slap does nothing. She spits at me. I knock her out. Mrs. Mose swoops in and out in an instant. Laluna is hysterical.

Mose says to me, "This was an accident. Salome flipped…" I finish for him, "…because she is Salome."

"Can you?" He stretches out his arms. Together we lift Salome up, and he holds her in his arms. "Call nine one one. It was an *accident*," he says again, but in such a way that I wonder if he seen what I think maybe I seen…who pulled the fucking trigger.

THE MOSES CHRONICLES (2018)

Cries and Whispers

Persephone gripped the staircase banister. Shivering. "Auntie Jay, I had a bad dream. Daddy didn't kiss me good night, he kissed me goodbye."

"Oh, honey, it was just a dream. You're awake now. I'm here."

She whisked Perse back into her room. The nanny, in her robe, stumbled up the stairs. "Please throw some clothes into Persephone's backpack. Fast." Jay bundled Persephone in her blanket.

"Where are we going? Where's my mommy and daddy?"

"They're together. They'll be busy for a little while. Your daddy asked me to take you to our house tonight." Jay enveloped Persephone in her arms and chest, trying to empty the fear coursing through both their bodies.

Holding the backpack in one arm and Persephone in the other, she dashed to her car and buckled Persephone into the backseat. Persephone reached for the red hat beside her. "Granmamma's."

"Yes, it was a present from her to . . . Uncle Mose. He wants you to have it." Jay shut the door and hopped into the car. She started the engine, took two heavy breaths—in and out—then pressed on the gas pedal and carefully drove down the private road. She turned onto Topanga Canyon Boulevard, cautiously taking the tight curves, until she'd made it a quarter mile down the road. Then she pulled to the side and waited as police cars and ambulances roared past her and up the mountain.

His mother felt weightless in his arms. Moses felt weightless, too, as if her body had evaporated into the ether and transported them to the cottage. Moses gently laid his mother in her bed. She opened her eyes, blinked. Her lips moved. No sound. Her eyes shut again. He waited.

Nothing. Nothing more from her to him. His heart aching, forever broken, Moses began to weep.

OUTRO

Can you take me back where I came from?
Brother, can you take me back?

—The Beatles

98

MEMOIRS OF A USELESS GOOD-FOR-NUTHIN'

That's All, Folks

The medics drug Laluna, who can't stop crying and screaming. I give my story to the cops.

They send Salome back to Collier Layne. I ain't seen her since.

The funeral is back in Long Island. I don't remember much, and sorry, I don't want to. Me and Lux do the eulogies. Fuckin' brutalest thing I ever done in my life.

Mose, he steps up big time. Him and Mrs. Mose kinda babysit for Perse and Laluna 'til the cops officially declare it an accident. Laluna can't take no more bullshit, so she and Perse disappear to Hungary or Romania. No idea when she is coming back. Andrew and Sue, everyone turns up the heat on the SpeedFeed bullshit. They ain't no better than the paparazzi. It was Mose, goin' on TV just one time, acting all classy and calm, that got SpeedFeed to do a complete retraction and apology. Still, I learned a long time ago, people will believe what they wanna believe.

Mose officially shuts down the Nightingale Party, but some followers are keeping it alive on the Net and with meetings. He keeps the foundation going. I seen him at Kasbah working with the Sheiks on money stuff, and he looks not so good.

None of us ever speak about that night. Don't goddamn matter what I seen or even think I seen, 'cause Alchemy is dead and nuthin' gonna change that.

It ain't no fun, but I gotta admit I spent a lotta time hearing Absurda's voice from that Christmas Eve when she came up to Alchy's Topanga place. "I waited and waited for you to realize it was *your* loss. You didn't. I did what I had to and moved on." And blaming Alchemy for what I said and done. You know by now that I do what I do and move on with no grousing allowed. Only I'm gonna be living with this shit for a long, long time. Maybe forever.

That's it. What I've told you, every damn word is the truth as I seen and lived it. In the end, all I can say is the Savants, they was one magnificently biddy-bip-bip clan. I loved them, and damn, I miss them, even crazy Salome, and Alchemy most of all.

THE SONGS OF SALOME

Almost No Memory

Babydeath. Bodydeath.
    Breaking apart.
    Into the dark matter.
    Goodbye, my sons,
    goodbye.
    I sing my songs no more.

THE MOSES CHRONICLES

Infinite Rest

The future that died that night is reborn each day in Alchemy's eternal music—the man becoming the myth and the myth becoming the vision, singing through time.

Moses will travel to Orient Point. Alone.

He will pass the house where he was born but will not enter. He will walk along the shore where he was conceived. By the grave site of his brother and what was once his, and one day will be again.

He will fall.

His lips will close in a wry smile that turns suddenly sublime.

Above him are no stars. The moon not yet down. The sun not yet risen. The pink-blue-black dust swirls and becomes his sky. No ascent to heaven. No descent to hell. No more questions without answers. No more howls for meaning.

At last, and forever, peace.

APPENDICES

ALL THE CHARACTERS FIT TO PRINT

PRIMARY CHARACTERS *in order of appearance*

SALOME SAVANT (b. 1943) Artist.

MOSES TEUMER (b. 1958) History professor.

ALCHEMY SAVANT (b. 1971) Rock star.

AMBITIOUS MINDSWALLOW (b. Ricky McFinn, 1974)
Founding member of the Insatiables.

LALUNA (MARIA APPELIAN) (b. 1990)
Musician, muse, and mother.

PERSEPHONE SAVANT (b. 2013) Child of the Moon.

SECONDARY CHARACTERS *alphabetically by first name*

A (b. 1960) Czech exile living in Berlin. Friend of Salome.

ABSURDA NIGHTINGALE (b. Amanda Akin, 1968)
Founding member of the Insatiables.

AKINS FAMILY Absurda's family in Fond du Lac, Wisconsin.
Sister: Heather, mother: Ginny, father: Jimmy, Sr.

CHARACTERS

ALEXANDER HOLENCRAFT (b. 1952) Founder of *I, Me, Mine* magazine. Coolhunter. Paramour of Salome's.

AMY LOO (b. 1990) Cofounder of riteplay.com, which was funded by Alchemy.

ANDREW PULLHAM-LARGE (b. 1964) Oxford-educated Englishman. Cofounder of Surface-to-Air group that manages the Insatiables.

ART LEMCZEK (b. 1925) Alcoholic friend of Salome's from Orient Point.

BEN BUTTERWORTH (b. 1935) Originator of RANT therapy. Moses and Alchemy's therapist.

BERNARD RUGGLES (b. 1938) Salome's doctor for more than thirty years at Collier Layne.

BLIND LEMON SOCRATES (b. 1914) Novelist, avant-garde filmmaker, friend of Nathaniel.

BOHEMIAN SCOFFLAW (b. circa 1964) Fictional 1960s radical.

BRYN SMITHSON (b. 1989) Pharmaceuticals saleswoman. Girlfriend of Mindswallow.

CAMILLE JAVAL (b. 1980) Actress in Paris by Night. Girlfriend of Mindswallow.

CARLOTTA SOLANO (b. 1985) Party planner. Wife of Mindswallow.

DEWEY WINSLOW (b. 1973) Partner with Elizabeth Borden in political management firm.

ELIZABETH BORDEN (b. 1980) Partner with Dewey Winslow in political management firm.

EVIE-ANNE BAXTER (b. 1982) Student at SCCAM. Musician.

FALSTAFFA (b. 1963) Bodyguard and roadie for the Insatiables.

FRANK PETERS (b. 1950) Art critic. Catalyst in securing Salome's Hammer Museum exhibition.

CHARACTERS

FRANKY NOVALINO (b. 1974) Childhood friend of Mindswallow's from Flushing.

GODFREY BARKER (b. 1979) High priest of the Church of Cosmological Kinetics.

GRETA GARBO (b. 1905) Actress.

GUS SAVANT (b. 1915) Farmer on Orient Point, Long Island. Salome's father.

HANK FIELDING (b. 1938) Moses's oncologist. BA in eighteenth-century English literature from Johns Hopkins.

HANNAH TEUMER (b. 1937) Lawyer with Bickley & Schuster. Mother of Moses. Wife of Malcolm.

HEINRICHA VON PRIEST (b. 1966) Lead singer of the Wannaseeyas in Berlin. Friend of Salome.

HILDA SAVANT (b. 1920) Salome's mother.

HUGO BOLLATANSKI (b. 1965) Lawyer and boyfriend of Absurda.

JACK CROUSE (b. Date uncertain) Movie actor. Friend of Laluna. Member of the Church of Cosmological Kinetics.

JAY BERNES (b. 1967) Art consultant. Moses's wife. Gifter of the Book of J.

KIM DOOLEY (b. 1973) Paralegal. Law school education was funded by the Insatiables. Later their legal council.

KYLE (b. 1941) Childhood friend of Salome's who died in a car accident.

LABAN LIVELY (b. 1920) Friend of Malcolm Teumer and William Bickley, Sr. Worked for OSS and CIA.

LESLIE TALLENT (b. 1940) Art critic and Salome's first champion.

LEVI FURSTENBLUM (b. 1917) Author of *Chambers of Commerce* and *Mystical Mistakes*. Holocaust survivor.

LILY FAIRMONT (b. 1928) Salome's Los Angeles gallerist.

CHARACTERS

LOUISE URBAN VULTER (b. 1968) Radio talk-show host. Senator from Arizona.

LUX DELUXE (b. Lionel Bradshaw, 1969) Founding member of the Insatiables.

MALCOLM TEUMER (b. 1921) Father of Moses. Husband of Hannah.

MARCEL DUCHAMP (b. 1887) Artist and chess player.

MARLENE PASSANT (b. 1956) French writer, gallerist, and supporter of Salome.

MARTY (b. 1970) Bodyguard and roadie for the Insatiables.

McFINN FAMILY from Flushing, Queens. Sister: Bonnie, brother: Lenny.

MURRAY GIBBON (b. 1935) Gallerist. Salome's longtime art dealer.

MYRON HORRWICH (b. 1932) Conceptual artist and early lover of Salome's.

NATHANIEL BROCKTON (b. 1937) Political activist. Salome's longtime companion.

PARNELL PALMER (b. 1980) Government investigator with the Committee on Anti-American Activities.

PHILIP BENT (b. 1947) Lead singer of British band The Baddists. Alchemy's father.

RAPHAEL URSO (b. 1930) Poet and friend of Nathaniel and Salome.

ROBERT SLOCUM (b. 1960) Dean of Moses's department at SCCAM.

SHEIK FAMILY (b. Sheikstein) Founders of Kasbah Records, the Insatiables' first record company. Buddy (b. 1945), Randy (b. 1948), and Walter (b. 1953)

CHARACTERS

SIDONNA CHERRY (b. Date unknown—and likes it that way)
L.A.-based detective.

SILKY TRESPASS (b. 1976) Member of Come Queens. Lead
guitarist of the Insatiables 2004–08. Played with Absurda
in the Mendietas.

SOMERSBY (b. 1953) Friend of Salome's when she lived
in Virginia.

SPENCER FRIEBERG (b. 1988) Cofounder of riteplay.com,
which was funded by Alchemy.

STEPHAN SONTAG (aka Shockula, b. 1921) Salome's first therapist
at Collier Layne.

SUE WARFIELD (b. 1960) Beverly Hills native. Cofounder of
Surface-to-Air group that managed the Insatiables.

TRUDY CHAMOUN (b. 1963) Former photographer. Yoga instructor
who lives in Jerome, Arizona.

TRYX (b. 1960) Dutch curator and late-life lover of Salome.

WILLIAM (BICKS) BICKELY, SR. (b. 1893) Founding partner
of Bickley & Schuster. Conservator of Salome's estate.

WILLIAM (BILLY) BICKELY, JR. (b. 1926) Partner in Bickley &
Schuster. Second conservator of Salome's estate.

WILLIAM BICKLEY III (b. 1956) Partner in Bickley & Schuster.

XTINE BLACK (b. 1940) Photographer. Lover/friend of Salome.
Lives in Chelsea Hotel.

Z (b. 1959) Czech exile living in Berlin. Friend of Salome.

ZOOEY BELLOWS (b. 1982) Salome's last doctor at Collier Layne.

THE INSATIABLES DISCOGRAPHY

1993-1994 (single in '93; CD in '94)
More (Is Never Enough) (CD and song)
- "Chicks and Money" ('93)
- "Face Time Is the Right Time"
- "Licentious to Kill"
- "I Wanna Be Seen (at the Scene)"
- "Futurific"

1996
The Insatiables Get Large (CD)
- "Get Large"
- "Papa's Gun"
- "Eight Is Just Enuf" (sung by Absurda Nightingale & Alchemy)
- "Saturnalia on My Lap"
- "Black Holes and Bum Fucks"
- "Loverrs"

1998

Blues for the Common Man (CD and song)

- "No Destiny"
- "Invisible Party"
- "The Ruling Class"
- "E Pluribus Unum Wampum/(Money, That's What I Want)"
- "The Sleep of Faith"

2000

Multiple Coming (CD and song)

- "Six Times Tonight"
- "No Master, No Messiah"
- "Adam and Lilith"
- "Zim Zum Blues"
- "Eve of Deconstruction"

Recorded in 2000, 2001; released in 2003

The Noncommittal Nihilists for Nuthin' (CD)

- "La Pantera Rosa (Falstaffa Nights/Martian Days)"
- "Friendsy for You"
- "Fuck Like a Woman" (sung by Absurda Nightingale)
- "You Coulda Been but You Ain't"
- "The Nihilist's Prayer"
- "Outrage...Big Deal"
- "Mystic Fool" (added after Absurda's death)

U.S. Tour 2003–2004
Euro Tour 2005–2006

DISCOGRAPHY

2006

Dieseasee (Alchemy, Silky, and Lux;
  Mindswallow on about half the tracks)
- "Dieseasee"
- "Knot My Neck"
- "The Meth House Around the Corner"
- "Viagral Newmoanya"
- "Mysteries and Enemies"

2008

The Great Awakening (their last studio record)
- "Saturnalia Gone Down"
- "Exile's Revenge"
- "Shake, Shimmy, and Shibboleth"
- "Hungrier, Harder, Sadder"
- "Too Free to Be Free"
- "A Theist Falls"

2012, recorded in 2010

More or Less, Alive (Mindswallow rejoins; Laluna joins)
- "Live at the Grand Canyon"
- "Beat Attitudines"

2016

Oeuvre and Out (boxed set)
Two new songs:
- "The Harmony of Doing Nothing"
- "Savant Sensation Bluz"

OTHER PROJECTS

1970

Fast Enough (the Baddists)

1975

Chain Saw Disco Massacre (the Baddists)

1989

The Slo Learners (Absurda and Alchemy's first band)

1991

I'm Your Black Doorman (cowritten by Alchemy; recorded by the
   Hip Replacements)

1997

Puttin' the PFunk in FPunk (Lux Deluxe solo album)
Down on Me (the Come Queens, guerrilla-girl band with
   Absurda, Silky Trespass, Dress Shields)

1999

Mah Dude Was a Slut from Tulsa (and He Made a Slut Outta Me)
   (recorded by Tammy "No Win" Flynn aka Absurda, and
   Jimmy "Bad Breath" Davis aka Alchemy; written by Alchemy)

2007

Songs for Pedestrian Tastes (CD of cover songs done by
   Mindswallow)
Alchemy, American Style (Alchemy solo; ltd. edition vinyl EP)

"Goin' Down with George" (single released in '04;
    backed with "Between Iraq" and "My Heart Place")

"Dyin' to Be Your Hero"

"Zombie" (cover of Fela)

"I Ain't a Marchin' Anymore" (cover of Phil Ochs)

"Fixin' to Die Blues" (cover/mashup of Bukka White
    and Country Joe tunes)

"Whitey on the Moon" (cover of Gil Scott-Heron)

"Once I Was a Soldier" (cover of Tim Buckley)

"American Ruse" (cover of MC5)

2009, 2013-2015

Ferricide (Mindswallow's heavy metal band)

Smeltdown (2009, CD)

Pedd-o-file (Performance-Enhanced Death Drugs) (2013, CD)

Ferricoshus (2015, CD) (with Alchemy uncredited on "Irony's
    Maiden")

2015-2016

Chansons (Alchemy and Laluna) (only as download;
    no vinyl or CD)

• "Liquid Love"

• "Mirror Me"

• "Dreaming Double/Nightmaring Alone"

• "The Harmony of Being One as Two"

2009-2018

33 Visitations (recorded but never released by Alchemy)

SALOME SAVANT CV

REBIRTHDAY
September 21, 1966

EDUCATION
Ph.D. in Mystagogy
Advanced degrees in Sanity—Collier Layne Institute
    of Mental Depravation, various dates

SELECTED SOLO EXHIBITIONS

1965   *ARTillery*. Street Side Gallery, New York
1966   *Art Is Dead*. Central Park/Murray Gibbon Gallery,
         New York
1969   *Do Not Disturb*. Murray Gibbon Gallery, New York
1971   *This Is Not a Pipedream. Dream and Listen*. Video;
         Gibbon/Documenta
1976   *Flowers, Feminism, and Fornication*.
         Murray Gibbon Gallery, New York
1982   *Women of the Scourge (and One Day Myth of Fine Arts)*.
         Murray Gibbon Gallery, New York

1985   *The Berlin Wall Burning.* Performance/sculpture; West Berlin

1995   *My Head IS Different.* Lily Fairmont, Los Angeles

1998   *The Beauty of My Weapons.* Gibbon-Passant, New York; Lily Fairmont, Los Angeles

2008   *Pillzapoppin'* and *Electroshock Ladyland* installations *Baddist Boy* collages. Hammer Museum, Los Angeles

2011   *Electronic Fire.* Special installation; Art Basel Miami

2013   *Remembrance of Things Past and Future.* Stedelijk Museum, Amsterdam

2020   *Myths and Mystagogues.* Whitney Museum, New York (she does not attend)

CREDITS

58: *that week I was dying too.*
Grace Paley, "Living" (1974)

90: *a man got to have a code.*
Omar Little, *The Wire* (2006)

93: *The sleeper is the proprietor of an unknown land.*
Djuna Barnes, *Nightwood* (1937)

153: *foul dust*
"Gatsby turned out all right at the end; it was what preyed on Gatsby, what foul dust floated in the wake of his dreams that temporarily closed out my interest in the abortive sorrows and short-winded elations of men."
F. Scott Fitzgerald, *The Great Gatsby* (1925)

153: *a new screaming comes across the sky.*
Thomas Pynchon, *Gravity's Rainbow* (1973), first sentence

299: *the little pleasures of life*
Wassily Kandinsky (1913)

315: *Don't mess with the Wongs*
Richard Price, *The Wanderers* (1974)

317: *have mercy on the man who doubts what he's sure of*
Bruce Springsteen, "Brilliant Disguise," *Tunnel of Love* (1987)

373: *his bloodless aged lips*
He suddenly approached the old man in silence and softly kissed him on his bloodless aged lips. That was all his answer.
Fyodor Dostoyevsky, *The Brothers Karamazov* (1880)

385: *Someday you will ache like I ache*
Courtney Love, "Doll Parts," *Live Through This* (1994)

401: *the ceremony of innocence is drowned*
William Butler Yeats, "The Second Coming" (1919)

468: *You don't own me*
John Madara and David White, "You Don't Own Me," recorded by Lesley Gore (1963)

503: *to the time with you to keep me awake and alive*
I get so tired of working so hard for our survival
I look to the time with you to keep me awake and alive
Peter Gabriel, "In Your Eyes," *So* (1986)

527: *The impossible is the least that one can demand.*

But in our time, as in every time, the impossible is the least one can demand—and one is, after all, emboldened by the spectacle of human history in general and American Negro history in particular, for it testifies to nothing less than the perpetual achievement of the impossible.

James Baldwin, *The Fire Next Time* (1963)

537: *imminent peril threatening you and all the faithful*

It is the imminent peril threatening you and all the faithful which has brought us hither. From the confines of Jerusalem and the city of Constantinople a horrible tale has gone forth.

Pope Urban II, speech at Council of Clermont on the capture of the Holy Lands by the Seljuk Turks (1095)

541: *One can look back a thousand years easier than forward fifty.*
Edward Bellamy, *Looking Backward* (1888)

563: *And don't be late. Don't be late.*
If I don't meet you no more in this world then
I'll meet you in the next one
And don't be late
Don't be late
Jimi Hendrix, "Voodoo Child," *Electric Ladyland* (1968)

ACKNOWLEDGMENTS

Over the many years that this book came to life, I depended upon the critical insight and support of so many friends. I am grateful to them all. There are many more—and they know who they are—who have my unending gratitude.

Raj Bahadur, Corinna Barsan, Michelle Berne, Mike Brander, Peter Bricken, Christine Byers, Mike Cahill, Christine Cassidy, Edward Cohn, Nathan Currier, Heather Dadamo, Dennis Danziger, Ken Deifek, Samantha Dunn, Hope Edelman, Leslie Fiedler, Peter Frank, Amy Friedman, Seth Greenland, John Harlow, Hal Hinson, the late Dr. Al Hudder, Tony Jacobs, Mickey Kiernan, Michael Korie, the late Paul Kozlowski, David Martino, George Melrod, Heather Miles, Dr. Jeffrey Miller, Tom Martinelli, Dwayne Moser, Stephen O'Connor, the Oliva Family, Allen Peacock, Craig Pleasants, Sheila Pleasants, Marie-Pierre Poulain, Steve Rand, Dr. A.J. Rellim, Rachel Resnick, Steve Rockwell, Alison Rowe, Britt Salvesen, the late Imogene Sanders, David Schulps, Kathy Seale, Michael Small, Jon Wagner, Dr. Kathleen Walker, and Nancy Wender.

My agent, Jennifer Lyons, for her sanity-saving phone calls.

ACKNOWLEDGMENTS

The 18th Street Arts Center, The Virginia Center for the Creative Arts, The Durfee Foundation, and The Los Angeles Department of Cultural Affairs (COLA division).

Everyone on the great staff at Other Press. Especially Judith Gurewich and Anjali Singh, for their ceaseless efforts to make this book better. And an extra special thanks to the remarkable Terrie Akers.

To all of my cousins, who often think I've descended from another planet, but who always support and love me.

Most importantly, my mom, who passed away this past spring, my dad and my wife, Suzan.

⊞ OTHER PRESS

You might also enjoy these titles from our list:

AND THE WORD WAS
by Bruce Bauman

When the tragic death of his son compels Dr. Neil Downs to flee New York City for India, he is introduced to the paradoxes of Indian social and political life.

"Bauman's first novel is a magnificent debut, smart and intense, but accessible and riveting… Simply a great novel." —*Booklist*

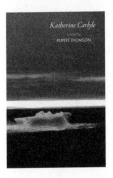

KATHERINE CARLYLE
by Rupert Thomson

Unmoored by her mother's death, Katherine Carlyle abandons the set course of her life and starts out on a mysterious journey to the ends of the world.

"The strongest and most original novel I have read in a very long time… It's a masterpiece."
—PHILIP PULLMAN, author of the best-selling His Dark Materials trilogy

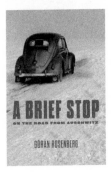

A BRIEF STOP ON THE ROAD
FROM AUSCHWITZ by Göran Rosenberg
WINNER OF THE AUGUST PRIZE

A shattering memoir about a father's attempt to survive the aftermath of Auschwitz

"A towering and wondrous work about memory and experience, exquisitely crafted, humane, generous, devastating, yet somehow also hopeful."
—*Financial Times*

Also recommended:

OUT OF SIGHT: THE LOS ANGELES ART SCENE OF THE SIXTIES
by **William Hackman**

A social and cultural history of Los Angeles and its emerging art scene in the 1950s, 60s, and 70s

"A deeply absorbing account of the midcentury years during which Los Angeles's once-marginal art scene transformed into a prominent locus of the avant-garde." —*Library Journal*

DIARY OF THE FALL by **Michel Laub**

A powerful novel centered on guilt and the complicated legacy of history that asks provocative questions about what it means to be Jewish in the twenty-first century.

"A spare and meditative story that captures the long aftereffects of tragedy." —*Kirkus Reviews*